"Terror Wea ... '
"The Red ... and
"Return from Cormoral"

THREE CLASSIC ADVENTURES OF

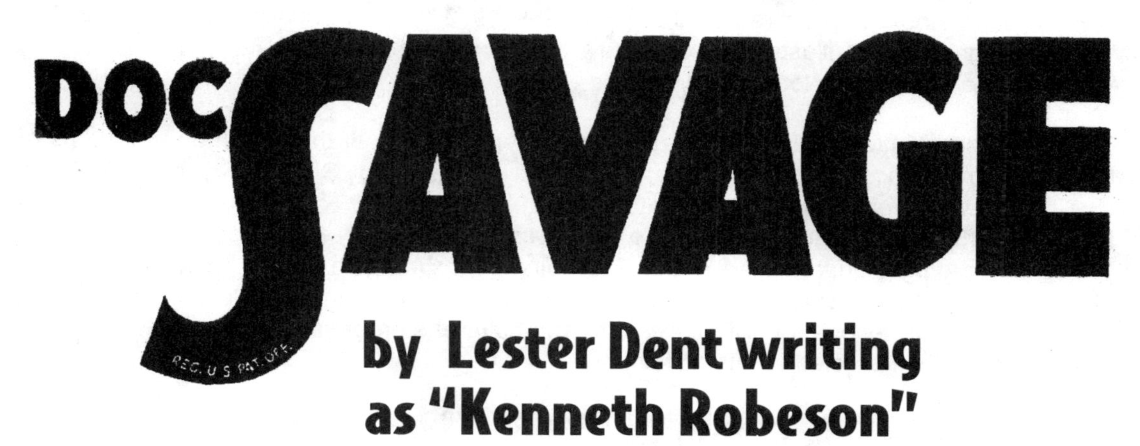

by Lester Dent writing
as "Kenneth Robeson"

plus "DOC SAVAGE, SUPREME ADVENTURER"
by John L. Nanovic

with new historical essays by
Will Murray and Anthony Tollin

Published by Sanctum Productions for
NOSTALGIA VENTURES, INC.
P.O. Box 231183; Encinitas, CA 92023-1183

This Nostalgia Ventures edition is an unabridged republication of the text and illustrations of two stories from *Doc Savage Magazine,* as originally published by Street & Smith Publications, Inc., N.Y.: *Terror Wears No Shoes* from the May 1948 issue, and *Return from Cormoral* from the Spring 1949 issue, plus *The Red Spider* which was originally published in paperback in 1979. "Doc Savage, Supreme Adventurer" was first published as a limited edition pamphet in 1980. This is a work of its time. Consequently, the text is reprinted intact in its original historical form, including occasional out-of-date ethnic and cultural stereotyping. Typographical errors have been tacitly corrected in this edition.

ISBN: 1-932806-91-1   13 Digit: 978-1-932806-91-5

First printing: March 2008

Series editor/publisher: Anthony Tollin
P.O. Box 761474
San Antonio, TX 78245-1474
sanctumotr@earthlink.net

Consulting editor: Will Murray

Copy editor: Joseph Wrzos

Proofreader: Carl Gafford

Cover restoration: Michael Piper

The editors gratefully acknowledge the contributions of Tom Stephens, Cathy and Robert Nanovic, Jack Juka, Albert Tonik, Dean Cartier, Jay Ryan and Bob Larkin in the preparation of this volume, and William T. Stolz of the Western Historical Manuscript Collection of the University of Missouri at Columbia for research assistance with the Lester Dent Collection.

Nostalgia Ventures, Inc.
P.O. Box 231183; Encinitas, CA 92023-1183

Visit Doc Savage at www.shadowsanctum.com and www.nostalgiatown.com.

Thrilling Tales and Features

Front cover painting by Bob Larkin
Back cover by Bob Larkin, George Rozen and Walter Swensen
Interior illustrations by Edd Cartier and Paul Orban

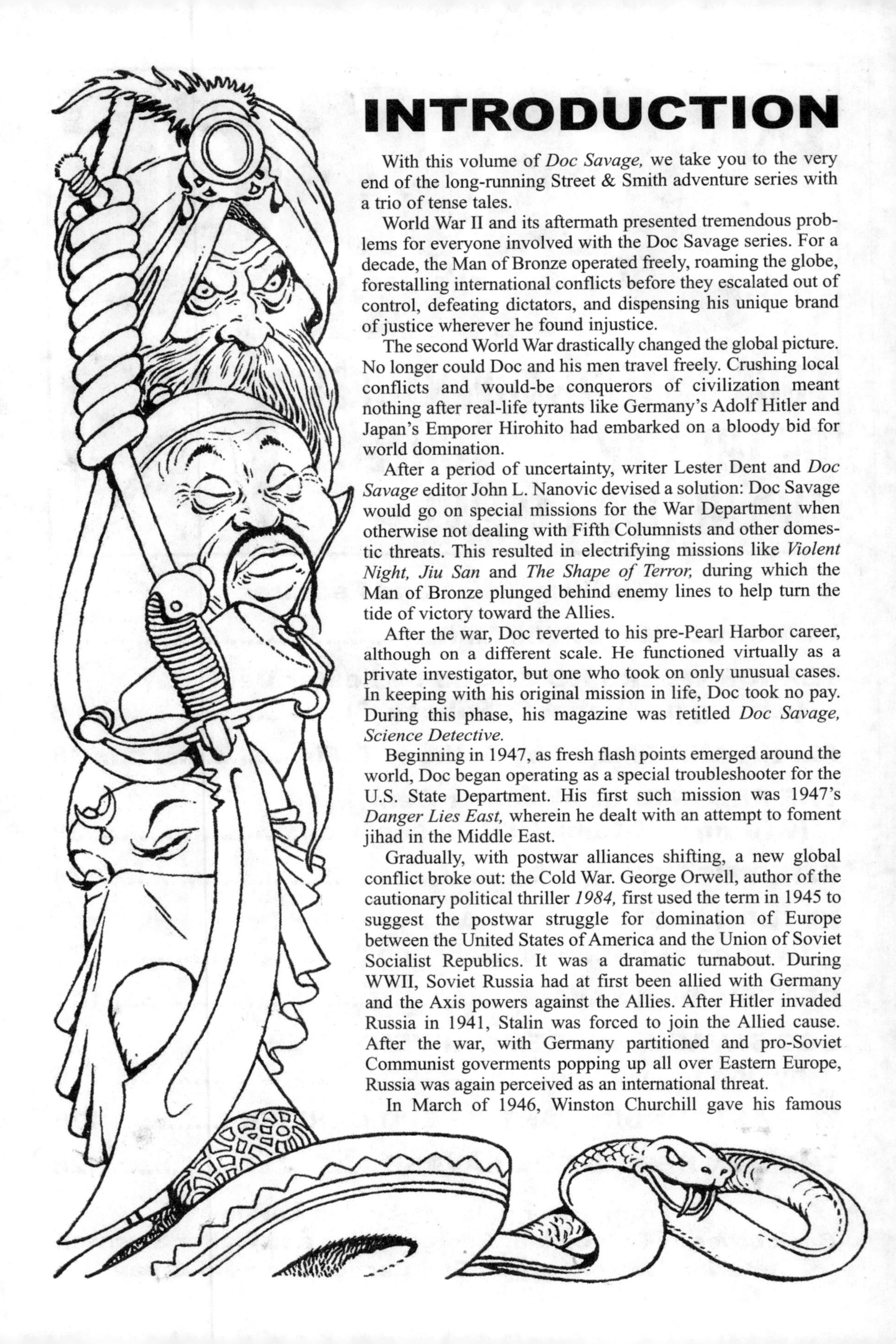

INTRODUCTION

With this volume of *Doc Savage,* we take you to the very end of the long-running Street & Smith adventure series with a trio of tense tales.

World War II and its aftermath presented tremendous problems for everyone involved with the Doc Savage series. For a decade, the Man of Bronze operated freely, roaming the globe, forestalling international conflicts before they escalated out of control, defeating dictators, and dispensing his unique brand of justice wherever he found injustice.

The second World War drastically changed the global picture. No longer could Doc and his men travel freely. Crushing local conflicts and would-be conquerors of civilization meant nothing after real-life tyrants like Germany's Adolf Hitler and Japan's Emporer Hirohito had embarked on a bloody bid for world domination.

After a period of uncertainty, writer Lester Dent and *Doc Savage* editor John L. Nanovic devised a solution: Doc Savage would go on special missions for the War Department when otherwise not dealing with Fifth Columnists and other domestic threats. This resulted in electrifying missions like *Violent Night, Jiu San* and *The Shape of Terror,* during which the Man of Bronze plunged behind enemy lines to help turn the tide of victory toward the Allies.

After the war, Doc reverted to his pre-Pearl Harbor career, although on a different scale. He functioned virtually as a private investigator, but one who took on only unusual cases. In keeping with his original mission in life, Doc took no pay. During this phase, his magazine was retitled *Doc Savage, Science Detective.*

Beginning in 1947, as fresh flash points emerged around the world, Doc began operating as a special troubleshooter for the U.S. State Department. His first such mission was 1947's *Danger Lies East,* wherein he dealt with an attempt to foment jihad in the Middle East.

Gradually, with postwar alliances shifting, a new global conflict broke out: the Cold War. George Orwell, author of the cautionary political thriller *1984,* first used the term in 1945 to suggest the postwar struggle for domination of Europe between the United States of America and the Union of Soviet Socialist Republics. It was a dramatic turnabout. During WWII, Soviet Russia had at first been allied with Germany and the Axis powers against the Allies. After Hitler invaded Russia in 1941, Stalin was forced to join the Allied cause. After the war, with Germany partitioned and pro-Soviet Communist goverments popping up all over Eastern Europe, Russia was again perceived as an international threat.

In March of 1946, Winston Churchill gave his famous

by Will Murray

"Sinews of Peace" speech at Westminster College in Dent's home state of Missouri. In it, the former British prime minister spoke of an "Iron Curtain" having descended over Eastern Europe. It was a phrase that had been coming into common use before Churchill popularized it. In fact, Nazi Propaganda Minister Joseph Goebbels had employed the term only months before Germany collapsed under a two-pronged U.S.-U.S.S.R. attack in 1945. There, he warned of postwar Soviet intentions to control Eastern Europe. But Churchill's speech crystalized the image in the popular imagination.

By 1948, the Cold War was settling in like a long winter snow. The Berlin Blockade by Russia had begun in June. Swiftly, the U.S., England and France responded with the round-the-clock Berlin Airlift, designed to keep the city supplied with food and other essentials. This was just the first of many powder keg events of the Cold War era, which lasted for 45 years and redefined the last half of the 20th century.

Lester Dent saw in the reemergence of a belligerent Russia a new challenge for his indomitable bronze hero. Ironically, the leader of Russia, Marshal Joseph Vissarionovich Jugashvili had taken the last name of Stalin early in his pre-revolutionary career. It meant "made of steel." The Man of Bronze was going to take on the self-styled Man of Steel. Out of this burgeoning conflict came two of the top Doc Savage novels of the series' final years.

Terror Wears No Shoes focuses on a threat that still hangs over the United States even today, sixty years after it was first published. Although Russia is only hinted at, no 1948 reader could have failed to deduce the national origin of the menace to America Lester Dent depicted.

The Red Spider has been hailed as one of the best Doc Savage novels Lester Dent ever penned. Taut and tightly-written, it harkens back to Doc's riveting wartime behind-enemy-lines missions. Written in 1948 as "In Hell, Madonna," *The Red Spider* ran afoul of swift changes in the editorial regime at Street & Smith, and was shelved until Bantam Books printed it for the first time in 1979. For this edition, we take pride in restoring two pieces of unpublished art by legendary illustrator Edd Cartier originally done for the issue of *Doc Savage, Science Detective* that would have carried the novel.

Return from Cormoral was originally planned by Dent as a Cold War story, but the same editorial shift that killed "In Hell, Madonna" back in those paranoid postwar days mandated that Dent change the story while it was still in the outline stage.

There is much more to say about all three novels, but first, return to 1948 and learn why... *Terror Wears No Shoes.* •

TERROR WEARS NO SHOES

A Doc Savage Adventure by Kenneth Robeson

"Our job is to find Long Tom Roberts"—and that's the beginning of a weird, wonderful adventure that involved characters like The Honest Pole and a glamour-puss named Canta, who was a legend before she was twenty-five.

Here it is—Doc Savage and his aides at their best!

Chapter I

HE met her finally. He arranged it through the aid of a man called but obviously not named the Honest Pole. The Honest Pole was short, near-sighted, and he over-filled a Ceylon silk suit. He was only half Polish, and the other half was anybody's guess as long as the guess was amber skin and slant eyes. He was called the Honest Pole for the same reason that fat men are called Slim.

He paid the Honest Pole some money—half the price of the job, but it looked like a lot in Chungking dollars—and he explained to the Honest Pole what he wished. Where, when and how.

"Four men," he said. "Don't you think four men will be enough? I don't want it to look fishy."

"Four men. Excellent," said the Honest Pole in his English that would have been superb if he hadn't spoken it through his nose.

"It will be done, then?"

The Honest Pole examined him thoughtfully. "More than four men, if you wish. You are very big. Very powerful, obviously."

"But I walk with a cane."

"True also. Maybe four will be enough."

"My leg is not reliable. If it should collapse during the proceedings, it would be embarrassing."

"I will warn the four men about your leg. Not to kick or strike it. But I would like more than this as a down payment."

"It's enough. I'm no fool."

"She is quite a woman. Such a one as few have ever known. To tinker with her is worth more money in advance."

"That's the bottom cent now."

"I would like more advance money."

"You won't get it."

"All right, you are plainly a fine man, and I will trust you more than my custom," said the Honest Pole, at the same time wondering in the back of his head who this big man had killed, robbed or swindled in the past and how profitable it had been.

She was called Canta. If she had another name it was not public property.

The Honest Pole went to her at once. He told her about it.

"A great bumbling fool," he said. "He paid me ten times what was needed, and half that in advance."

"He sounds like a fool."

"He is."

"And you are going to take what he paid you, deliver no services, and be seen by him no more?"

"That will be as you say," said the Honest Pole, grinning.

He'd had some trouble getting to see her. He was surprised he had. She was rather legendary, and he'd wanted to meet her for a long time, and better still, do her a service. He'd like to be one of those who worked for her. She was generous. She was always finding the means that enabled her to be generous. She was clever. Not yet twenty-five, certainly, the Honest Pole thought, looking at her but not staring, and already a legend.

She had sat at a teak desk while listening to him. The desk was a masterpiece of femininity, inlaid with ivory and tufted with pastel silk. Some of the stuff on the desk was gold and her cigarette holder was platinum.

She arose now and went to the window, the great expanse of window, a whole wall of glass, that overlooked the packed matted thickness of the city. From this height and magnificence, the city seemed colorful and beautiful and the sampans on the river and the steamers lying in the stream or at the docks made an intriguing combination of the stuff that looks well on travel folders. It was the height and the magnificence that did it.

The Honest Pole thought: I wish I had for income what she pays for this hotel penthouse. That I do wish.

She said, "Do what he wishes."

The Honest Pole jumped a little, not having expected this.

"Indeed?" he gasped.

She nodded. "Things are a little dull with me. This is simple-minded diversion, and if it isn't entertaining, I can do something about that."

"You wish me to proceed as agreed with him?"

"Yes. With slight alterations."

"Alterations?"

"Yes. Have the four men you hired rough him up a little."

The Honest Pole hesitated. He thought of the things he had heard of this unusual woman. He preferred to do his murdering with a little more discretion. "How much do you wish him roughed?" he asked.

"Enough so he'll earn it."

"That would be very rough indeed, to pay for the privilege of meeting you," said the Pole gallantly.

"Don't overdo it. Not a hospital case. Just teach him a little lesson."

"I see. A payment for folly?"

"A payment," she said, "for thinking up an asinine, childish, soft-headed gag like the one he's trying to pull."

So he was roughed. It took place that evening, while she walked alone in the Crown Regal garden, one of the few places in the city where it was ten percent safe for a woman to walk alone at that time of night. Not, however, that she wasn't an exception and could have gone alone and untouched, unspoken to, in any part of the city at any hour, excepting the rare chance that she might meet some dunce who hadn't heard of her. Somebody who wouldn't have heard of Stalin, or Chiang, or Truman or Clark Gable.

The four men came at her. He was soon to the rescue. He bounded from the spot where he had been waiting, a great figure of a man who hop-skipped favoring his right leg and who waved his cane. That was the idea.

Not a new idea. Just about as new with mankind as the act of breathing. He had hired them to molest her, and he was going to save her from them. Be a hero. Lady in distress; gallantry to the rescue. Whiskers down to here.

He didn't know, of course, that the four men had orders to whale the tar out of him. But his ignorance didn't long persist. They tied into him. The Honest Pole had been choosy, and he had hired men who knew how to hurt a man. Scum who had been strained through the sieves of Hongkong, Canton, Shanghai, men whom the Shanghai Municipal Police, said to be the toughest in the world, would have gone at with care. They had orders to take him apart, but leave the pieces hanging together, and that was also soon evident.

She watched. She instantly saw how bad they were going to be. She was shocked. She knew violence, and she could see, and she didn't want it that nasty. Not nasty enough that she would be bothered with anything like pity.

She spoke shrilly, angrily, in Kwangtungese. A branch of the Chinese language full of snake-tongues. A small automatic pistol, gold and jewels where it didn't need to be on excellent steel, was in her hand.

They didn't hear her. They didn't see the gun. They were busy. The air, about eighty cubic feet of it, was full of manpower. The general effect was that of a dark ball out of which came barks, yelps, grunts, hisses, and in the course of a few moments, men in various degrees of injury. Those who could, ran. The other two crawled away into the bushes.

He picked up his cane. His hat. He didn't have any shirt and his trousers had one leg more or less intact. He leaned on the cane and looked at her.

"How long did it take?" he asked.

She wanted to giggle. She had an overwhelming impulse to do so. She had wondered what speech he planned to make when he had established himself as Galahad, the hero, the savior. She wondered if it was this one. If so, he might be somewhat original after all.

His next statement was a bit more in form: he said, "You shouldn't walk alone around here at night."

She gave him a bromide herself. “You saved my life!” she said. She got proper drama into it.

He grinned slightly. “I didn’t know it was going to be that rough.”

You probably didn’t, she thought. But you did all right. In fact, you did about as good as I’ve seen done.

“You were wonderful!” she exclaimed.

“You think so?” he said. “I do best with odd numbers, really. Fives, sevens, nines.”

“You needn’t joke.”

“I’m not.”

She said, a little more thoughtfully than she intended, “I can almost believe that.”

He was indeed a big man, and his features were not bad, not bad at all, and his eyes had a cast of copper in them that caught the small lights from the lanterns on the *hsiao lu.* She detested handsome men, and they always reminded her of two things, either throat-slitting weasels or knives with brown bone handles. This one wasn’t too handsome. And he was remarkably big for one without any fat at all.

He said, “If you will care to walk to the safety of the *fan-dien,* I will walk well behind you to see that you get there.”

“Why well behind?”

“Obvious reasons. No shirt, for one thing.”

She said, “Don’t be silly. I’ll get you a shirt. I owe you that much, surely.” She was thinking that he’d taken a big chance, offering to step out of the picture that way. Or maybe he hadn’t—because wasn’t she inviting him along?

She was equally uncertain about him an hour later, when he left her. It had taken that long to have him brought a shirt, a finer one than he’d had torn off him, undoubtedly. Because he wasn’t expensively dressed. Not at all.

He’d used the interval waiting for the shirt to show her his obvious traits, which he seemed to think, or gave the impression that he thought, were good ones. He was a braggart. He made bum jokes. Not dirty ones; just naïve and not clever. He boasted incessantly without bragging of specific deeds, but giving the impression that he was a killer-diller.

It didn’t soak into her until later, but the only specific things she learned about him was that he was using the name of Jonas and he lived at the Shan Loo Hotel.

Adding it up, watching him hitch-step his way down the hotel corridor, she didn’t get it. He hadn’t made a pass. He hadn’t asked for a job. He hadn’t offered to let her in on any big deal. Why, then, all this finagling?

Maybe he was a slow and cunning worker.

He walked a few hundred feet through the grimy winding and slightly dangerous tunnels of the native streets, then hailed a *mache* pulled by a knock-kneed horse, giving the address of his hotel, the Shan Loo.

The Shan Loo was no dump. The Nip officers had favored it with their patronage during the occupation, but it had been refurbished, was back under old management, and full of the better-heeled foreigners and more successful local black-marketeers. There were a few Generals of the type that used to be called War Lords, a scattering of diplomats, and quite a foundation of American businessmen out to squeeze a dollar.

He was well into the lobby when he met one of these businessmen, a Mr. Wesley T. Goltinger. Mr. Goltinger traveled on an expense account of a hundred dollars a day. Oil.

The meeting with Goltinger was a loud encounter.

“Doc Savage!” Goltinger yelped. “Good God! Imagine meeting you here!”

He stopped—he had to; Goltinger was in front of him like an autograph hound that had just discovered Jimmy Stewart—and looked through and beyond Goltinger.

“Some mistake,” he said.

“Mistake nothing!” howled Goltinger. “I’d know Doc Savage anywhere. Why, I met you at an oil chemists meeting, remember? You gave a technical talk for thirty minutes, and I didn’t understand one word.”

“Mistaken,” he said.

He stepped around Goltinger and went on and vanished somewhere.

“That’s a hell of a way to treat a fellow American citizen!” Goltinger complained.

Chapter II

THE thing that now occurred to Goltinger shouldn’t have happened to a dog. He said so himself just before he received a punch in the stomach.

Goltinger headed for the bar. He felt that he’d been insulted, and that the condition would be abetted by a drink, which would also be company for several he’d had already.

A strange voice at his elbow suggested, “Let’s have a little detour, pal.”

Goltinger looked down at a short, wide, homely man who wore a considerable crop of shingle-nail hair of rusted color. The stranger was so homely that he seemed a little ridiculous.

“Go away, beautiful,” said Goltinger.

“Never mind my looks,” said the other. “You and me are going into conference.”

“Go find a baby to frighten,” suggested Goltinger.

He didn't know ... that the four men had orders to whale the tar out of him.

The short one laid a hand on Goltinger's arm and said, "Let's not debate it here in public."

"Debate hell!" said Goltinger. "I been insulted. I been ignored by Doc Savage, a fellow American. By God, the first good New York face I've seen in days, and he snotted me. It shouldn't happen to a dog, the way he—"

The fist made some sound, but not much. Not enough for anyone to notice. Goltinger's mouth opened, stayed open, and his knees buckled as his legs turned to spaghetti. But he stayed on his feet, held there by the stocky man who was wearing the same amiable grin he'd worn all along. Goltinger was in fact walked outdoors with his feet skating along the floor, and he was heaved into a waiting car. The homely man got in also, forced Goltinger's mouth open, and popped a capsule into his mouth. Then he whacked Goltinger's Adam's apple smartly so that Goltinger had to swallow.

Twelve hours and an odd number of minutes later, when Goltinger awakened, he made the difficult-to-explain discovery that he was on a plane. A clipper. He looked out of a window. He saw more water than he liked.

"Where the hell am I?" he blurted at his seat-mate.

The seat-mate, a slender young man with the air of a professional diplomat—dignity, a ready smile that wasn't to be too much believed—touched Goltinger's arm and suggested, "Sit down and take it easy, Mr. Goltinger. I'm your escort."

"Escort! What the hell is this?" Goltinger gasped.

"A quick voyage home for you, Mr. Goltinger."

"By God, nobody can do this to me!" said Goltinger feelingly. "I'll talk to our diplomats about this!"

"Then you can spill it to me," said the seat-mate. "I'm one of your diplomats."

Two hotel servants had been near enough to hear Goltinger hail the big man as Doc Savage. One of these was from Yu San, and by now he was home in Yu San, not a little confused. He'd received a month's vacation with pay, something that had never before happened to a servant in that hotel. The other lackey was in jail in Canton, which was also quite a few miles from the hotel lobby where Goltinger had hailed the big man. He could have had a paid vacation as well, except that it happened he was wanted by the Canton police for a little matter of skull-thumping an Englishman a few months previously.

Having made these arrangements, the short homely man who had all the rusty hair got around to tapping on the door of the big man who had given the woman Canta the name of Jonas.

"Who is it?"

"It's me."

The man using the name of Jonas opened the door, and said clearly in a pleasant voice, "Thank you for returning the suit so well-mended, Mr. Wang. Thank you very much. I shall call at your shop and take care of the bill."

The homely man, who hadn't brought a suit, and couldn't have mended one either, said, "Thank you, Sir." He winked elaborately. "It is a pleasure to have your business." Then he went away.

He went to a rather expensive room in a hotel patronized by many foreigners, Americans plentiful among them, and which had the not inconsiderable virtue of exits opening on four different streets.

There was another man in the room, a slender and very dapper one who wore afternoon clothes because it was afternoon, and who carried a slim cane of dark wood. The homely one addressed the overly-dressed one as Ham, and was in turn addressed as Monk. That was the extent of their civility. They began quarrelling, not as men who really had a deep-seated grudge, but more as a matter of habit. They spent the next forty minutes thinking up insults, and the dapper one unjointed his cane, which proved to be a sword cane, and while continuing the squabble, freshened an application of some sticky drug which was applied to the tip of the sword blade. He made no comment about the cane, and Monk did not seem to think it was extraordinary, hardly noted the operation.

Jonas came finally.

Monk looked at him. "Doc, you think your place may be wired?"

"No point in taking a chance," Doc Savage said. "How about Goltinger and the two hotel employees?"

Monk, rather pleased with himself, explained about that. "No fuss. No feathers. They're gone with the wind and won't be missed."

"The two servants—they have a chance to spill anything where it might not be good?"

"Nope. And I don't think they even overheard Goltinger call you Doc Savage."

"We can't take a chance."

"We didn't."

Doc Savage swung to the window. The hot morning sunlight came through the panes in long pale blades and out before him the city was coated with groundfog that the sun would soon burn away. He stood straight, with no suggestion of stoop nor limp, and the absence of either gave him a completely different appearance.

Presently he moved a little, shaping up his

reflection in the windowglass, and frowned at it, comparing it with his normal appearance, which was quite a bit different yet. He ended that by shaking his head.

"Disguises," he said, "are always uncertain. But not that uncertain." He swung around suddenly. "Take a look at me! What's wrong?"

Ham Brooks jointed the cane together with a soft whisper and flash of steel. "Nothing is wrong, Doc. You don't look anymore like yourself than Pike's Peak looks like the Empire State. Less."

"But Goltinger, half-drunk, recognized me at a glance."

"He was eleven-twelfths drunk," Monk said.

"Shut up, dopey," Ham told Monk. Then he told Doc Savage, "That puzzled me, and I did some checking on this Goltinger. The guy is a face-remembering freak. You've heard of those mental oddities who can glance at a newspaper page and a year later tell you everything that was on the page? Well, Goltinger does it with people. I got on the trans-Pacific telephone and dug up that information. So it's nothing to worry about. It was just one of those unfortunate things that happen."

"It's covered up now?" Doc asked.

"Thoroughly."

"Good enough."

Monk scratched an ear. "How did your pick-up with the tiger lady come out?"

Doc Savage frowned. "That rascal, the Honest Pole, doublecrossed me. He told the four men to beat me up. To stop it, I'm almost afraid I had to appear a little too good in a brawl."

Monk grinned. "I'd like to have seen that."

"See if you can't arrange for something mildly unpleasant to happen to the Honest Pole," Doc directed.

Monk nodded. "Can do."

Doc eyed him doubtfully. "Better let Ham handle it. The last time you arranged a mild unpleasantness for me, the victim came near never leaving the hospital."

Monk wasn't hurt. He said, "But you and the tiger lady got along all right?"

"It went as planned."

"I'd like to make some plans with that babe," Monk said longingly. "Couldn't we arrange that? After all, I might be a handy gadget to have around."

Ham Brooks snorted.

Doc Savage frowned at Monk, and said quietly, "Our job here is to find Long Tom Roberts, if he is alive, or learn what happened to him if he is dead."

Chapter III

"I HADN'T intended to," said Canta when he called her about four. "But I will."

They went to the Chung Restaurant—the proprietor was not named Chung; the place was called after the Chinese word *chung,* which meant any insect—and had a private dining room with a little stage all of its own on which a succession of performers appeared with their acts. She ordered an exquisite *seng-tsai,* and *gao-yang ruh* specially killed for them and served with a *gidi-moh* sauce, topped by a particular rose petal coffee and a *nui-nai bing* of rare species from Szechwan province.

"I can see this is going to cost me," he said.

"I hope so," she said.

"Why did you change your mind?" he asked.

"When was that?"

"About not going out with me."

"Oh, that was before you called," she said.

"Really?"

She nodded. "It was when I heard that our friend the Honest Pole had met with an accident."

"Accident?" His face was as enigmatic as hers, but he was wondering what Ham Brooks had done to the Honest Pole, and whether it wouldn't have been just as pleasant for the Pole to have let Monk do it.

"Accident," she said, "spelled b-l-a-c-k-j-a-c-k. According to my information, the Pole will not look the same again."

"Let's hope not."

She frowned sharply. "You're cold-blooded."

"Me?" He feigned astonishment. "Matter of fact, I don't even know the gentleman, do I?"

She smiled at that. Deliberately, and with intent to stir him, one way or another. He had no intention of really being stirred, but he wanted to act as if he was, and he put on a show of being so. Such a good show that it was too good, and he wondered which was acting and which was actuality.

She was lovely. No question about that. Her smile was an electric light or a warm bath, whichever you wished. And just looking at her was about the same thing. He made the latter discovery, and promptly unhooked from the business at hand, stared into space, and gave himself six or seven warnings in quick succession.

A waiter brought rare Burmese wine in which the candied eyes of larks floated and glistened, together with an array of early dynasty crockery that made him have visions of what it would cost him if she dropped a cup. Museum stuff, strictly.

"Do you like hamburgers?" he asked.

"You've been to the States?"

"On and off."

"What do you mean?"

"On the lam, and off again when it got warmish."

She laughed a sound of bells tinkling, and he began telling her a whale of a lie about an episode in San Francisco of which he was the hero. He followed that with another adventure in Cairo of which he was an even greater hero. She was not impressed.

"I don't understand you," she said.

"That's what I'm taking care of now. I'm explaining myself. I'm quite a guy, in case you're missing the point."

She shook her head. "I had a check run on you by some friends of mine," she said. "You're a cheap crook."

He blinked at her. "Is that nice?"

"You're not even a good crook, either," she continued. "You smuggled in two Java political refugees, and they both got caught by the police, so you won't get any more business from that source. You hijacked a shipment of opium from a ring, and the police got it away from you and nearly got you, and you're in bad all around. The hijack victims love you not, and neither do the police, who strongly suspect you. You've been rushing around organizing a gang of crooks. If you're going to organize, that's no way to do it—by rushing around. You're a big sap with tinhorn ideas."

"By God!" he said. "Is that any way to talk to the savior of your life?"

"That's a point," she agreed, "that I intend to mention."

He tasted the *gao-yang ruh.* "So you know about it?" he asked ruefully.

"Did you think for a minute I wouldn't?"

"Well, they shoot people for hoping, I hear. But I thought I'd take the chance."

She looked at him disagreeably. "I think it was dumb. I think it was typical of a stumblebum, and quite in character."

"I figured the dumbness made it good," he said. "You used to read about that gag in books years ago so it must have had something."

"The Honest Pole told me about your little trick."

He grinned at his plate. "He who serves two masters is bound to get a leg caught."

"Is that why you had him hospitalized?"

"Frankly," he said, "it was because he let you talk him into having his four hired boys give me a walloping. That shows a weakness of character."

"So you had his character reenforced with a blackjack?"

"That sometimes helps."

She put down her fork and told him again that he was a cheap crook, a scamp, a small-time chiseler and not half smart. She had more than that, and the words to deliver it with, and she did so. He listened approvingly.

"That's exactly the opinion a young lady should have of a guy like me," he said. "Very commendable. Why are you sitting here delivering it, though?"

"I don't know," she said angrily.

WHEN he stepped out of the elevator in his hotel later, Monk Mayfair detached himself from the shadows and remarked, "I see your research is keeping you up late."

"Come in and have a good cry," Doc suggested amiably. "I should have let you attend to the Honest Pole. I hear Ham neglected to take off his gloves there."

"You do any good?"

"I've got her puzzled."

"Will that buy?"

"I'm also magnetizing her," Doc said. "When she has the proper charge, I think it might get us what we want."

Monk moved around the room, lifting a few pictures and looking behind them. He unscrewed a couple of light bulbs and inspected them closely to see whether they were microphones in disguise—he knew that trick could be done, and the light bulbs would still give the proper amount of light and everything. He looked at Doc, and Doc shook his head warningly, so Monk spoke in Mayan, the ancient dialect of Mayan which they had learned long ago at considerable pains, and which as far as they knew no one but themselves in so-called civilization was likely to be able to speak.

Monk said, in Mayan, "We exhausted the last possible clue as to the identity of Washington Smith today."

Doc frowned. "No results?" He spoke Mayan also.

"Absolutely none. Whoever Washington Smith is, was, or where, is a complete blank mystery. And believe me, we've done some pretty subtle combing on the matter."

"The name's pretty obviously a pseudonym."

"Just a name somebody used for that one act of tipping you off to this business, you mean?"

"Yes."

"That doesn't help much."

"No, it doesn't. But I can understand the use of an assumed name, and the extreme care to conceal identity."

"Sure, Washington Smith's life wouldn't be worth two bits," Monk agreed, still in Mayan. "But I'll lay you a little bet that when we find Washington Smith, if we do, the party turns out to be somebody with a knowing way in dark places. No amateur could cut off a trail so completely."

Doc Savage dropped the Mayan and said in English, "Well, we've got to find some trace of Long Tom Roberts somehow." He said this as if it was the matter they had been discussing.

Monk had sprawled in a chair. He got up. "I think we've about got that one drilled out," he said.

Doc Savage looked at Monk sharply, and made a soft sound that meant considerable excitement. "You don't mean Makaroff?"

"That's right."

"What about him?"

"He got in from the north," Monk said. "He's at her hotel. Suite seven-zero-nine."

"Alone?"

Monk snorted. "Practically—for him. Three bodyguards who never seem to sleep. Maybe their non-slumber ability is why he felt able to cut it down to three."

Doc Savage said with a kind of violent pleasure, "This *is* a break!"

"You going to talk to Makaroff?" Monk asked thoughtfully.

"I doubt if it would be feasible to just walk in and have a chat with him."

"I doubt it too," Monk said. "Unless we took along a company of marines."

"Has he contacted her yet?"

"Who knows." Monk shrugged. "That babe seems to have more secret life around here than a ghost. Nobody knows when she goest and whither she comest, half the time."

"But she works with Makaroff."

Monk hesitated, said, "That word work is susceptible to various meanings. She does business with him, I hear. Profitable chunks of it."

"Shady business?"

Monk shrugged. "She has been go-betweening for Moslems who are anxious to ease out of Hindu territory with their property intact, so it would depend on whether you were a Hindu or not, how shady it looked."

Doc Savage dismissed the character of the woman Canta with a wry grin, and said more grimly, "This fellow Makaroff is our last link to Long Tom Roberts. In his final report, Long Tom indicated he was going to contact Makaroff."

"I don't like the way you say *final,*" Monk muttered. And there was a silence for a time, during which neither man looked at the other, nor looked at any other object with any pleasure. Then Monk blurted, "By God! I wish we knew what Long Tom was working on!"

"That would be a help," Doc admitted grimly. "Perhaps we can pry it out of Makaroff."

"He'll deny anything."

"Possibly not."

"No, the guy was born with his head in the sand, like an ostrich. He hears nothing, sees nothing, says nothing. It's chronic with him."

"We might cure him of that ailment."

"You'd better have a spare along when you try that," Monk said dryly.

Monk left then, and Doc Savage watched him go uneasily, and was not relaxed at all until, some twenty minutes later, the electric clock buzzed twice. Then he went over and, leaning above the clock, said, "Well, we might as well get some sleep." And the clock buzzed again, briefly in acknowledgment.

He stood for a while looking absently at the clock, wondering if anyone who had searched his room had been clever enough to discover that the clock was a wired-radio transceiver—capable of communication with any similar gadget plugged into the lighting system anywhere in the city. It might not, he reflected, make much difference whether the gadget was solved. They wouldn't be able to tap the circuit, because eavesdropping on it was no mere matter of hooking on a wire or tuning another set to a given frequency. The circuit had a scrambler arrangement, and it was a technician's research job to set up data for a duplication.

The buzzings meant Monk had gotten to his hotel safely.

Doc Savage changed to pajamas and lay on the bed. He did not sleep—did not try, because he had sufficient control of his nerves to sleep when he wished.

He thought of Long Tom Roberts. His associate. One of the small group of five specialists who had worked with him for a long time. Long Tom Roberts was an electrical engineer—and that was merely a statement of Long Tom's profession, not his ability. The man was an electrical wizard. So fantastic as to ability in fact, that he had been one of those few dozen men who had vanished mysteriously early in 1942, been heard of not at all during the whole course of the war, and only reappeared a few weeks ago. In short, he had been top secret like the big bomb and a few other things.

The war had been tough on Long Tom Roberts. Spending more than five years in assorted laboratories tinkering with cathodes and making electrons say Uncle must have been hard on the skinny electrical wizard. Because Long Tom liked excitement, the pursuit of high physical adventure, and it was this yen that had associated him with Doc Savage and the other four. They all had it. They were all thrill-chasers. They didn't admit it, but their avocation of going about the far corners of the earth righting wrongs and punishing evildoers outside the effective clutch of the law had no credible excuse other than the pursuit of excitement.

Doc's work during the war had been much the same as usual; in Washington they thwarted his efforts to get into uniform and mollified him, not fully, by handing him devilish jobs that they professed to feel were impossible of solution. He solved them. Not prettily, always. But they seemed to think it was stupendous in Washington, and put out a lot of pap about his contribution to history with which he didn't agree.

But Long Tom Roberts had missed even that. Long Tom had gone into top-drawer seclusion looking his normal anemic, thin, sickly, probably-fall-over-in-the-next-breeze appearance. He had come to the light of day again twenty pounds heavier, tanned, looking as if he might whip a fourteen-year-old kid—quite robust for Long Tom—and declaring he'd never felt worse in his life. Which was probably true, because he'd developed a stomach ulcer. His anemic system wouldn't have supported an ulcer before.

Doc prized Long Tom highly. He hoped the rail-thin electrical expert was doing all right. The possibilities to the contrary had, Doc discovered, turned him damp with perspiration. And he had no mood for sleep.

What was that old cliché about the tide of human resistance being lowest about four o'clock in the morning? Well, why not? He couldn't sleep anyway.

Chapter IV

HE had an argument with her three-hundred-pound Mongolian houseman, and in the course of it he learned that there is a defense for the judo grip known variously as the *kami-yui,* the Hairdresser's Delight, and the *kenson.* Then he laid the Mongolian respectfully on the saffron yellow rug and went to a chair and used a leverage on it to get his wrist back in joint. When he turned, she was standing just inside another door giving him a completely grim three-eyed inspection with the aid of the little jeweled gun.

"You made some noise," she said.

"I know it," he admitted. "But it's all right. I intended to announce myself."

"I can imagine. At four o'clock in the morning?"

He looked at her, feeling he shouldn't show appreciation, but suspecting he was. He was supposed to be the strong silent man of few words, impervious to temptation, the fellow who succeeded where others failed.

"You should wear more than that," he said finally. "Or less. I don't know which."

She indicated the Mongolian. "Is Tham hurt?"

He shook his head. "Not now. But he will be when he wakes up, if he tries what he tried again. I know how he does it now."

She whistled softly. Surprise, the way a man shows surprise. It was the first thing deviating even slightly from the softly feminine that he had seen her do, in spite of the fact that she was as completely a casual hard-boiled case as he had ever met. She said, "Tham was almost judo champion of Japan at one time. The only thing that kept him from being so was the fact that he isn't Japanese, and their national pride couldn't stand that a few years ago."

"I'm glad to know I was partly disjointed by an expert."

"You look all together."

"When my wrist gets done swelling, I can probably use it for a balloon and float around."

"I trust you're not depending on waiting for that means of transportation out of here?"

"No. We'll leave as soon as you can get decently dressed."

She frowned. "What's the idea?"

He walked past her and the gun—not with too much confidence, because the only thing of which he was certain about women was that they were uncertain—and dropped into a chair. Casually, he hoped. He waved vaguely at another chair.

"I had hoped to continue my subtle winning of your confidence, Miss Canta," he explained. "But the schemes of mice and men—you know how it is." He spread his hands eloquently, added, "I got hurried."

She approached, took the chair he had indicated, and advised, "If you think you've been building up my confidence, you're haywire."

"Oh, you suspected me of motives?"

"That's a very small word for it."

He nodded amiably. "Almost as good. Let me tell you about a certain man I know. Chotwilder is his name. An Australian. A very stout lad, except for a certain weakness of character where a bit of pound sterling is concerned. It so happened that a few weeks ago, Chotwilder came to your city on a spot of business concerning a matter which we will pass over lightly here—"

"Incoherence," she said sharply, "is all right in its place. But does it belong here?"

He looked injured. "Chotwilder was never incoherent without justification. I never said he was."

She examined him speculatively, and presently asked, "Is this going to make sense?" When he nodded, she leaned back. "Since you broke up a sound sleep, I might as well listen."

"Chotwilder," said Doc, "was collared by a man named Long Tom Roberts, who is the representative of another man named Doc Savage. Is that better?"

She was staring at him fixedly. She didn't say anything.

"Why did you jump?" he asked.

"Did I?"

"Just partly out of your skin. But so did some others, evidently. To continue with my story: Long Tom Roberts grabbed Chotwilder and asked him questions using first a lie detector and then truth serum. Do you know how truth serums operate? They induce a drugged mental state in which the victim is unable to remember lies to tell. Unfortunately, afterward the victim is apt as not to be uncertain about what he said while under the effects of the stuff."

She was sitting rigidly. He could tell nothing from her expression, except that she was profoundly shocked, and not in the least disinterested in his recital.

He continued: "Let us say that Chotwilder could be connected with a certain business organization with which I am also affiliated, and that we were no little concerned about Chotwilder's experience. This man Long Tom Roberts is an associate of Doc Savage, an advance agent for Savage."

He paused and pretended to examine his wrist, but actually trying to see how his tissue of falsehood was getting across. He had been listening to himself, and didn't believe he sounded like a liar. She wouldn't know there was nobody named Chotwilder, and no organization for him to be affiliated with. The Orient these days was smallpoxed with thieving groups, and even the phenomenal adventuress Canta could not be expected to know about all of them. He hoped she didn't, anyway.

He toyed with his cane, wondering additionally if she'd noticed that he hadn't felt so much need of it while distracted by what the Mongolian had done to his wrist.

She asked suddenly, "You were sent here to get Long Tom Roberts out of the way before he learns something that might be troublesome?"

"Exactly."

She shook her head. "I doubt that. You've been going around the city making like a cheap crook. If you're a man of sufficient skill to be trusted with dealing with one of Doc Savage's associates, I don't believe you would practice petty stuff."

"I was making duck-calls."

"What?"

"Each petty criminal activity in which I engaged was connected in some way—we won't go into the ways either—with a bit of greater activity in which we have reason to think Long Tom Roberts would be interested. In other words, I was quacking like a duck and he was duck-hunting."

She put the gun away. She said angrily, "I wish you would stop being funny! This is serious! Doc Savage is phenomenally dangerous."

"Oh, I wouldn't say that," he said modestly.

"Then you're a fool!"

"An unsuccessful one, too," he agreed blandly. "I didn't draw the duck-hunter."

"And lucky for you that you didn't!" she snapped. "You wouldn't have lasted ten seconds!"

"Is that the voice of experience?"

Shaking her head, frowning at clenched hands, she said, "I don't know Savage except by reputation—and I feel myself very fortunate to be able to say that." She lifted her eyes suddenly. "What are you doing here? Why are you yanking me into this?"

"I need help."

"Against Savage? You must think I'm crazy."

"Savage probably has his ordinary points," he suggested hopefully.

"If he has, I haven't heard of anyone noticing them. You haven't answered my question. Why are you trying to hang me, too?" She stared angrily at the ceiling. "Oh God, why was I dope enough to fall for that phony rescue when I knew it was phony! That's what curiosity gets me!"

"Oh, curiosity was the one?"

"Exactly, I was curious to see a fellow dumb enough to pull an oldie like that. I should have known that guy doesn't live here anymore—not in a city like this." She glared at him. "You made a fool out of me!"

"It was about fifty-fifty, wasn't it?"

"What do you want?"

He leaned forward, suddenly serious, and said, "we have reason to know Long Tom Roberts was in touch with a man named Makaroff. I want a word with Makaroff. I want to know from Makaroff where to lay my hands on Long Tom Roberts, and quick, before the kettle boils."

She threw up her hands a little too desperately. "If you wish to talk to what's-his-name—Makaroff—then why on earth bother me?"

He shook his head wonderingly at her.

"Didst expect better in the way of deceit, fair lady."

She jumped up, stamped a foot, and cried, "Now I know I've been suckered! You're no fool!"

"Thank you. But don't jump to any hasty conclusions."

"I suppose you know Makaroff got back into the city tonight?"

"I hear so."

"How? How, for crying out loud?"

"Oh, I have a good ear for the ground."

"You must have. Makaroff moves from place to place more quietly than diphtheria. It'll be interesting to see how he reacts to hearing he might as well have arrived with a brass band."

"Good. I knew you'd wish to see it."

"See it? Me!"

He bent his head firmly and advised, "Yes, you're going to introduce me to Makaroff and be my character reference. At least I hope you are."

He didn't go for the kind of a smile she gave him. "And what," she inquired, "leads you to feel I will sponsor you?"

He grinned what he hoped was a pixyish grin and said, "To tell the truth, I've begun to wonder. Oh well, you can pass along to Makaroff the job of making chowder out of me, and be around to watch it. Isn't that any inducement?"

She stamped the foot again. "I'll say it is." She threw an angry glance at the clock. "You be here at nine o'clock sharp, and I'll take you to him."

"Why not now?"

"He's not in the hotel. He'll be back at nine, though."

Chapter V

HAM BROOKS broke a lump of sugar precisely in half, added one half to his coffee, stirred, drank, put the cup down, tapped his lips foppishly with the napkin, and said, "She told the truth about Makaroff being away from the hotel. He is."

Doc did not show too much confidence. "I wish somebody would build me a contraption that would show a red light when a woman is lying to me."

"I could use one of those, too," Ham agreed.

"What is Makaroff up to?"

"Business. Diamonds, I think it is. Anyway, he came in from Madras, and there have been several big jewel lootings around there lately, and the people he's visiting are dealers in that sort of thing."

"It wouldn't hurt to turn the police loose on him for that, after we're through with him," Doc suggested.

"We'll have pictures and a full set of notes of his itinerary tonight."

"That'll help."

"But the thing—the only thing that is important—is to find out what has happened to Long Tom Roberts," Doc stated flatly.

"We'll get up to that eventually."

"We may crack that mystery when we get hold of Makaroff."

"Either that, or crack Makaroff," Ham agreed.

They fell silent as the waiter arrived, scuffling about, filling the water glasses, snapping some crumbs from the tablecloth. He was an old man with a seamed face, a waiter grown old at his trade, and he presented the bill for payment with just the right deference, face-down on a tray which he placed unobtrusively beside the large bowl that contained several varieties of large-sized tropical fruit.

Doc placed a banknote in Hongkong dollars on the bill, and the waiter began making change. Ham sighed, examined the fruit in the bowl, selected one. It was an enormous citrus fruit that he chose, and it had quite a rotten spot on the bottom. He grimaced and, irritated, pointed out the unsound spot to the waiter. The latter started to replace it in the bowl, cackling apologies. But Ham said angrily, "Take that rotten thing away! You want to ruin my breakfast!"

The waiter gabbled some more apologies, left with the questionable piece of fruit. He carried it into the kitchen, on through the kitchen and out a side door, and told a man waiting there, speaking Mandarin of a better class with the Kwangtung accent, "He forced me to take it away."

The man he addressed was young, smoothed-faced and possibly an eighth part Oriental. He was also cold-eyed, short-worded and as subtle as a hammer.

"What?" he said. "What are you telling me, you fool?"

"The one who wears the clothing of a peacock, Ham Brooks, forced me to take it away from the table."

"Why?"

"The rotten spot. The rotten spot turned his stomach."

"Oh, it was just the decayed spot in the fruit?"

"Yes."

"His stomach would have been more turned if he had known the truth."

"No doubt. The rotten spot was there so he would not make the embarrassing move of selecting the fruit for consumption and begin peeling it. I could think of no way other than a spot of rot to discourage them from selecting this particular fruit."

"It was all right. It was a good idea."

"But he sent the fruit away. It is useless now."

"Maybe not. Did they discuss anything of importance?"

"I do not know. They are dry of words when I am near."

"Then they were talking business."

"It may be."

The young smooth-faced man now took the piece of fruit, held it a few inches from his chin, and addressed it in a somewhat embarrassed fashion. "The project seems to be at an end," he said. "I am sorry. It is not the fault of our man Loff, the waiter. It is the fault of an accident."

He handed the fruit to the waiter. "Take the radio set out carefully when you have time," he said. "There will be other uses for it."

The little transmitter, which operated at a frequency of better than three hundred megacycles, was good for only line-of-sight transmission, and hardly that since it was of extremely modest power. But it was sufficient to reach a hotel room several blocks away, where the man Makaroff was listening to a receiver tuned to the frequency of the trick transmitter.

Makaroff sat very still, scowling at the radio receiver. The latter now gave nothing but the hard-breathing sound of very high frequency receivers, with, occasionally, a terrific clattering as the distant transmitter in the piece of fruit was jiggled in being carried. A violent thump ended this. The fruit had been placed aside somewhere for attention—removal of the transmitter—later. Makaroff deliberately took a sip of a brandy-coffee mixture. The coffee was terrific black stuff; the cup would be half-full of grounds when he put it aside.

Another man, thin-bodied with clipped blond hair and the bleached blue eyes of a snake that had spent its life in overbright sunlight, arose and turned off the radio receiver.

"Too bad," he said. "But we heard enough."

Makaroff swallowed his coffee a quarter-spoonful at a time.

"So that is the voice of Doc Savage," he remarked. "I can't say I'm glad I heard it. It is a remarkable voice, one of the very few I've ever heard which bespeaks the strong character of its author." He lifted his eyes. "Didn't it frighten you, Karl?"

"I don't frighten," Karl said, but not boasting about it.

"Yes, I have heard that of you. I don't consider it quite healthy, but we will not go into that. The point is that you should have felt some emotion."

Karl smiled and struck a slight attitude. "I recognized the voice of an enemy of the people. I shall remember it."

"You could easily find an argument on that, Karl."

"On what?"

"That enemy of the people stuff. Savage is hailed in many quarters as something quite the contrary. In fact, the man has a worldwide influence. I know that. His power touches very high places. He is not to be underestimated."

Karl held his attitude, which was that of man before a firing-squad—the fellow who was going to give the order to shoot, not the one being executed.

"He is an enemy. We are not underestimating him."

Makaroff indicated the radio receiver. "According to that, he is coming to see me."

"To question you. Yes, sir."

"About Long Tom Roberts, his associate."

"Exactly."

"You sound as if you considered it simple."

"Isn't it?"

"Long Tom Roberts is dead."

Karl nodded curtly. "But Savage will visit you. He will be convinced Long Tom Roberts went suddenly to India and is there now. Once sold on that idea, Savage will go to India." Karl shrugged elaborately. "This is not a bad situation. There is a Chinese saying for it: *Sheeah sheeow yeu.* 'It is raining a little.'"

Makaroff looked at his henchman unpleasantly. "You think that is so?"

"Yes."

"I don't."

Blankness came to Karl's face, did not leave it, and he did not say anything.

Makaroff said, "I will feed Savage the false stew we have prepared concerning Long Tom Roberts being in India. But I shall watch him closely, and if I am convinced he is not deceived—and mind you, deceiving such a man is asking for a miracle—the instant I believe he doubts, I shall end everything."

Karl started. "End! But you cannot! Too much is at stake! The whole success of our purpose, the future trend of political and social thought—"

"You misunderstand, Karl. I meant finish it for Savage."

"Oh!"

"And his henchmen, Monk Mayfair and Ham Brooks."

Karl brightened. "That isn't a bad idea either." Then he examined Makaroff speculatively. "So it is soon to come?" he asked. "You have heard? It is soon to take place?"

Makaroff nodded. "Sooner than that. Tomorrow night."

"What!"

"The liner *Crosby Square.*"

Karl's face got a blankness and this increased, and he mumbled, "Then the material is aboard the ship already?" He sounded downcast. "I did not know."

"It's aboard."

Karl's stoicism had broken completely. He lost color and his right hand, when he lifted it and pointed it at Makaroff, shook a little. "Then this Savage is an incredible menace."

"Since when wasn't he?" Makaroff asked dryly.

"But now! This very instant! He is a ghastly danger to our whole purpose."

"Take it easy, Karl."

"But I didn't know the plan was this far along," Karl wailed. "I thought there was time for adeptness, for conniving to get rid of Savage in our good time and with safety."

Makaroff put down the coffee cup and stood. He was upset himself now.

"I imagine we'll have to kill Savage and his two men without delay," he said.

Chapter VI

HAM BROOKS was doing the character of an Englishman, a traveling gentleman from Birmingham—country home in Warwick, and all that—who was huckstering cotton-mill machinery. Doc had already regretted the choice of camouflage, because Ham was silly-awssing the English accent all over the place. Ham had opened a temporary office in *Poo Tow Shoo* Street, and Doc rode there with him in Ham's rented limousine.

Ham spent most of the ride holding his jaw with a hand, then said suddenly, "You know what I think? That fruit with the decayed place—a snitzy restaurant like that wouldn't have a decayed fruit in the bowl."

"It was there," Doc said.

"Uh-huh. So we wouldn't peel it and find something inside. You reckon?"

Doc nodded. "They did a pretty clever job replacing the part of the peeling they had to remove."

"Oh my God! Then I'm right! And you noticed it?"

"It had a trinket in it, all right," Doc said.

Ham had become a little pale. He leaned back. "My nerves must be going bad, the way little discoveries like that scare the spats off me." He looked down at his feet. "My feet are even cold! What do you know about that! Do a man's feet really get cold when he's frightened?"

"To tell the truth, I never stopped to notice," Doc confessed.

"They heard what we said at the table, then?"

"I wouldn't bet they didn't."

"Whoosh! Holy cow, as the fellow would say! Did we bandy any words we shouldn't have?"

"I think not."

Ham got out a handkerchief and gave his face and the nape of his neck a quick go-over. "Kind of startling to find they're looking us right in the eye. Kind of like discovering you're bewitched."

"I think we're doing all right," Doc said. "I hope so." Doc reached for the door handle. "Her hotel is a block over. I think I'll get out here."

Ham stopped the car. "You think this who's-got-the-button will go on much longer before it all breaks out in the open?"

Doc got out. "Hard to say. But this go-around with Makaroff should tell the story. Either we fool him, or else we'll have our hands full."

"For God's sake, be careful!" Ham gasped. "This thing is international. There was nothing as dirty as this took place before the other war. I wish we had the army and navy with us."

Doc said dryly, "Settle down in your office and have a good shake. You'll feel better. I'll call you later on the pocket radio."

"Keep us posted as you go to Makaroff."

"Right. I'll have to use code, though."

"Right. We'll be tuned in."

Doc watched Ham Brooks drive on. Ham, he reflected, was probably scared. If so, it was one of the rare occasions when this had happened. For that matter, Doc reflected, he was far from easy of mind himself. It was all pretty complex scheming, and would be wonderful if it all worked out, though.

He walked to Canta's hotel, and the Mongolian greeted him with a marvelously polite bow and a statement in the native tongue. The statement was to the effect that he, the Mongolian, hoped to see Doc in four well-scattered fragments in the not distant future. Doc pretended not to comprehend the Mongol's language, and took Canta's extended hand.

"You are like sunlight on a mountain of lotus blossoms," he told her.

That was about the general effect, too, although she wore European slacks and blouse. Paris tailored probably, and in one of the Paix shops not too far from the Place Vendome. Many women could be well-dressed for a year on what they had cost. But she couldn't do without a garish touch, and this time it was a dragon brooch of enamels and jewels that was about as inconspicuous as a screaming parrot.

"I have trapped Makaroff for you," she said.

"Good."

"You want me to go along?"

"Without your company, the sun would set this instant," he told her.

She seemed a little angry about that. "Judging by the lie-percentage you've been running, that means you'd rather bury me," she said. "Well, I'm going along anyway."

"You needn't, if you'd rather not."

"Oh, I like to watch Makaroff work."

"You like the way he pulls the wings off flies?"

"Don't be ugly when you're specific," she said. "Too much truth can be in bad taste."

Makaroff was in the same hotel, so they walked down two flights. Doc was surprised, but not relieved, when they were not looked over by anyone with guns. He kept his hand in his coat pocket, not because he had a gun there himself, but because he had a portable radio there and was tapping out Continental code on it, giving his location. The radio, he imagined, was vaguely similar to the one that had been in the fruit. Except that this one was disguised as a folding camera, tourist variety.

Makaroff proved to be a man who should have been fat and wasn't. All his lines were round bulging ones, but the surface of him had a plane hard shine so that all of him, all of his body that they could see, and probably the rest of it as well, was like the surface of a wrestler's bald head. He had a wire-brush moustache and black mice for eyebrows.

Makaroff greeted Canta enthusiastically enough for Doc to envy him his gift of flowery flattery.

"This is Jonas," she told Makaroff. "He finagled me into meeting you."

Makaroff popped his heels and looked at Doc, but didn't do anything else, except ask, "Jonas is your name?"

"For the time being," Doc said.

"I see. You think you have business with me?" Makaroff asked.

Here, Doc thought, is a man with the mind of a snake and the power of an old-time Hitler henchman. He tried to keep the notion off his face.

"I have questions," Doc said.

"I don't answer questions."

"I don't either," Doc told him. "So that's fine. But I'm interested in a man named Long Tom Roberts."

Makaroff's face gave no more expression than scraped bone, but he showed he was interested by suddenly switching from hardness and becoming the affable host. He poured them vodka, with beer chaser. Doc didn't touch his. He waited until they were settled in comfortable chairs, then began talking.

"This story will be shorter than you may think at first," he opened.

Canta listened, a slight paleness mixed with her casual loveliness, and she seemed rather surprised that he told Makaroff much the same tale that he had told her earlier when explaining why he desired to meet Makaroff.

For Doc, the telling was different this time. He was more careful. He was as painstaking as if doing a delicate brain operation. The whole thing was a tissue of lies and imagination, and he knew he was dealing with a man who was an expert liar himself and accustomed to being lied to. It was so vitally important to get this across. He began to feel perspiration along his backbone.

In giving the story of representing a syndicate which feared that Long Tom Roberts was investigating it, he dropped in some touches that he had omitted with Canta earlier. These bits were names of people and places and incidents with which he surmised that Makaroff was familiar, or might familiarize himself if he checked the story.

"So," Doc ended, "I've come to you because we heard Long Tom Roberts was going to contact you."

Makaroff shook the beer glass to make foam rise. "And you wish?"

"Long Tom Roberts."

"For what purpose?"

Doc snorted. "You guess."

"I want nothing to do with a thing of that sort," Makaroff said.

"Who said anything about you having something to do with it? You just tell me where I can find Long Tom Roberts."

"Why did you come to me?"

"Need we be naïve?"

"What do you mean by that?"

Doc said nothing. Makaroff drank all of the vodka, all of the beer, and lighted a brown cigarette that presently made the room smell as if a fire had been started in the fireplace with old shoes.

"You think you have something there, do you?" Makaroff asked finally.

"Haven't I?"

"I answer no questions. But this Doc Savage—you have stated that Long Tom Roberts is his hunting dog, one of five of them rather, and I'll admit you have something there. It doesn't concern me, though. I am a peaceable, home-loving, honest man with nothing to hide."

"Oh, I understand that," Doc said. "And it's not you who is bothered about the possible appearance of Doc Savage. It's me and my associates. So how about a bit of help, for the good of the cause?"

Makaroff thought. Whether he was thinking about the advisability of giving aid was questionable. Doc wished he knew, and found himself reviewing some of the things they knew about Makaroff in Washington, and some of the things Doc had personally learned that weren't in the Washington files. Nothing came to Doc's mind that would ease anybody's anxiety.

"Your cause," Makaroff said, "is hardly mine."

Doc, still reviewing Makaroff, said nothing. Makaroff had been twice a murderer before he was sixteen years old, but they were political murders and he had done well by himself as a result of them. They had established him as true Party material. That was rather ghastly, but true; ghastly to think that the leaders of a nation regarded a thing like that as proof of ability. But they did. They were slave-masters, not leaders, in Makaroff's land, and the altars at which they worshipped were built of dishonesty, strife, deceit, conniving and bloody-handed force. It was too bad that the last war had not smashed them, as it had smashed so many tyrants, and the rest of the world was beginning to realize this rather sickly. It hadn't seemed important during the last war. But now it was.

Makaroff grunted explosively. "I'll have to go with you."

Doc came forward in the chair, showing excitement. "Then you know where Long Tom Roberts is?"

Scowling, Makaroff replied, "The man never contacted me. He intended to. You can imagine how I felt when I learned of that—the man a representative of Doc Savage. So I took some measures."

"You had him killed?"

"Why, you silly fool. Do you think I would in any remote way connect myself with the death of a Doc Savage man? I would as soon assassinate the president of their country."

"Then what did you do?"

"Nothing. But certain friends thought of misdirecting his attention to India. And he went there."

Doc Savage sat very still for a ten-count. Then he sprang to his feet, roaring. He made nothing but rage sounds for a while, then for a bit longer vilified Makaroff, his character, his ancestors, all men who might remotely resemble Makaroff.

"You dirty whelp!" he yelled. "It was you who put Long Tom Roberts on our trail—to get him off yours! Our operations are in India! You put him on our backs!"

There were no operations in India—the whole thing was imaginary—but Makaroff grinned as if it was a fact, and as if he was pleased with himself. "An accident, purely, that he got on your backs," he said.

"Well, by God, he wouldn't have, if you hadn't put him there!"

"Oh, shut up!" Makaroff was tired of the discussion. "I'll take you to a man who knows where Long Tom Roberts went."

"You do that, damn you!"

Canta was frowning and shaking her head, half frightened, and half in admiration, the latter reluctant. She tried, with her expressive eyes, to give Doc warning: Makaroff was not a safe man to curse. Doc swore at him anyway. He called Makaroff a particularly nasty variety of jackal. He was on his feet, and waving fisted hands. He was acting, wondering if he was overdoing it.

Makaroff was on his feet, and Makaroff's face was a little blue but still shiny.

"We'll go," Makaroff said. "But drink your drink."

"I don't drink."

Makaroff stood very still. He was about ten feet distant. "Drink your drink," he repeated.

"Why? Did you poison it?"

"Yes," Makaroff said.

Doc went silent. He didn't get this. He wasn't sure that Makaroff meant it. If Makaroff did mean it.

"You think I didn't poison it?" Makaroff demanded.

"I don't know."

"Well, you know now. It was one way at you. One of about twenty ways that are all set for you. You haven't a chance."

"I haven't?"

Makaroff showed teeth that were long and spade-shaped and looked as if they had been honed to a geometrical pattern of evenness.

"I could have made you think he went to India," Makaroff said. "I really could have. Hell, the trail was perfect and would have fooled anyone."

"Who?"

"Long Tom Roberts, your henchman."

"He isn't in India?"

"He's dead."

Doc didn't move, although a few sinews in his neck did, barring out rigidly. He seemed completely stunned, thwarted, at a loss for a move.

Canta, confused, began taking slow steps backward. Her eyes were wide, her mouth also, with genuine surprise. She was puzzled. Confused. She looked at Doc Savage and made, considering the circumstances, an excellent job of arriving at a fact.

"You're Doc Savage!" she said.

Doc and Makaroff stared at each other. She might as well not have been there.

Makaroff said, his voice different now, higher: "You want to know why I didn't go through with my little plan to send you off unharmed to India? I'll tell you this much: it's your fault! You scared me into not doing it. You were too damned good. Your acting was too perfect. You frightened the hell out of me, and I just couldn't pass up this chance to take you in."

"Let's be at it," Doc said.

"You haven't a chance."

"No?"

"No," Makaroff said, and swung up a hand, bringing odd gun-sounds into the rooms. It was a silenced gun, small calibre and Doc, already moving—he had changed the position of his head first because sudden attacks nearly always go for the head—felt a bullet, or perhaps only knew that a bullet passed close above his head. Then his head was down; he knew the source of the fire. Behind him. Behind him, where there was only a blank wall, a few pictures on the wall. He was wondering what picture as he went forward and down.

Makaroff hadn't fired. Doc even had a little

trouble straightening that out. The way the man had moved his hand, he had for an instant suspected legerdemain, a flesh-colored freak gun of some sort. He'd never heard of a flesh-colored gun, but he thought of it now.

Then small-calibre bullets were hitting his body. He could feel the hammering of them through the chain mesh undergarment that he wore. It was not bad. They did not break any ribs. And the marksman was very good, carefully placing each bullet on the body, where naturally the armor mesh was thickest.

Doc was making for Makaroff. He had taken two steps already and was taking a third, and things had the illusion of being in slow motion. Every movement, noise, bit of business was clearly etched and seemed to register its significance. Desperation was like that to Doc. A couple of seconds seemed to stretch into a couple of careful minutes.

Makaroff had a little of it also. All men who know and actually like violence probably have a little of it. Most pugilists have it. A three-minute round is hardly three minutes for a pugilist; it's more like three hours in the ring.

Makaroff was going away. Head back, mouth gaping with strain; his feet whetted at the rug, and tore the rug getting traction. Then he was off, and Doc, groping for him, missed. It wasn't as slow now. Makaroff was bothered too; he'd depended more than he should have on the gun.

Makaroff went across the room in straightaway flight, going—crazily, it seemed to Doc—direct at a wall. But the man knew what he was doing. He came against the wall with hands and then shoulder, and used it to turn his course. He was away, going, and Doc came against the wall himself and used the same device, although it seemed silly and he decided he wouldn't again, decided he could turn quicker on foot.

He was gaining on Makaroff. He wanted his hands on the man. Once he had them there, he wasn't going to fool around. He came closer, cutting the space between himself and Makaroff. Makaroff was making straight for another wall.

Now Canta had gotten to the door. She was trying to open the door, jerking, her hands slipping off the knob helplessly. Without turning her head, she began to scream that the door was locked. It was the door into the hallway.

Doc watched Makaroff go for the wall as he had before, hands out and shoulder muscle-lumped for the shock. Doc thought: I'll get him on the rebound. Any man can move more accurately on his feet than bouncing off a wall like a billiard ball, logic said.

He was probably right, but never knew, because there was a panel in the wall. Makaroff went through it. The panel slammed shut an instant before Doc, having changed course, hit it himself. He felt it give a little, but not enough to be encouraging.

He wasted no time, came around—he was keeping his head low as much as possible, because there was where they could shoot him effectively—and got a table. It was a large table, heavier than he had thought, not as heavy as he had hoped. He lifted it, got it between his head and the spot the bullets had been coming from, and lumbered for the hall door.

"Get clear," he told Canta. And then, catching the odor of bitter almonds, he added, "And don't breathe. They're putting cyanic in here."

She stepped back, and he came against the door with the table. He gave it all he could. If he didn't break the door down, he would probably die in here. It was that important.

The door was steel. But the table was an incredible thing; it must have weighted close to four hundred pounds. He ached all over from carrying it fifteen feet. And the door came open. The lock didn't give. The hinges did, which was as good, and he pushed Canta through and followed.

He saw no one in the hall. Monk and Ham should have been there. He had directed them there on the pocket radio, tapping it out in code. He could hear the small-calibre rifle whacking foolishly in the room he had left.

He yelled, "Monk!"

No answer, and a door down the hall opened and a baseball of iron came sailing at him, hit the floor, skittered and bounced and he was on it like a soccer player, kicking. He sent it on down the hall, lifting into the air; it hit a window, the glass broke; there was presently a blast outdoors as the grenade let loose, and the glass, every vestige of it, vanished from the window.

He said, "Stairway!" But Canta was already going in that direction. She knew where it was, which was a help. The steps were hard mouse-color concrete, not too clean. Their feet going down made the sounds of dice in a twenty-one girl's cup.

Monk and Ham were not on the stairs either.

He called, "Monk! Ham! Be careful! They've gone rough and open on us!"

No more answer than there had been before. It gave him a cold ugly feeling, heavy with shock, and he clamped a hand to the pocket that held the radio, wondering if the thing had gone on the fritz.

Three floors down, he said, "You want to go to your apartment?"

"If you think I'd be safe there, you're crazy," she said. Woman-like, she was angry at him and blaming him for everything. Which wasn't out of line, at that.

CARTIER 47

"You didn't know who I was," he said. "Makaroff probably understands that."

"And I understand Makaroff," she said. "He will kill me. He's been thinking about it, anyway."

He let that go for later—he'd supposed she and Makaroff were fairly amiable. He was worried about Monk and Ham. He got out the trick radio, and when he pressed the keying gadget, the little window where the film exposure number was supposed to show glowed a faint red. It was a neon test light to show antennae radiation. So the thing was putting out. Then why no Monk and Ham?

"I've got a notion to go back up there," he said grimly. "I think maybe they've got two friends of mine."

She told him, "Makaroff hasn't got anything but a white rage. I know the man. If he had two friends of yours, he would have used them to force you to do what he wanted."

"They may be dead."

"He would use them anyway. Why, even Makaroff's government practices that kind of terrorism. Haven't you heard? And why go back if they're dead?"

Doc said, "We'll see what the police can do, then."

"They won't try."

"In this case, they will."

She was not convinced and said, "Don't you know who Makaroff is? He's the second in line to head his government, that's all. The lists the newspaper correspondents make up place him sixth or seventh down. They're crazy. He's next in line. Do you think the police of this poor impoverished revolution-torn nation are going to jail a man like that?"

"They will if they get him."

"Well, they won't get him either."

Doc made a telephone call, but not to the city police. He phoned the United States consulate, asked for a specific individual, and was even more specific about what he wanted. "Get the police on Makaroff, and get our own agents on him too," Doc said grimly. "And see that everybody sweats a little."

The man he was talking to was named Gilpatrick, a quick-voiced, harried man of many anxieties, most of the latter justified. He said, "So you dropped the egg?"

"It was dropped, but I didn't drop it," Doc told him. "And it isn't scrambled—yet. So strike some sparks around there."

Canta had overheard and she was looking at Doc thoughtfully. "You weren't out here for your health," she said.

"Something like that."

Chapter VII

THE small ugly cyclone that had gone through Ham Brooks' cotton-mill machinery office on *Poo Tow Shoo* Street had left a narrow path. One smashed chair, an upset inkwell, a crushed bag of native candied *bo lo mee* of the type which Ham liked to nibble between meals, and one dead body. The latter wasn't Ham.

The deceased was a thin wiry man with a mop of wavy yellow hair, and his demise was due to a bullet put into him after he had been made unconscious by the stuff that Ham Brooks used on the tip of his sword cane. Doc made a deduction that he trusted was logical: they hadn't wanted to bother with hauling an unconscious man around with them. That made it seem that they had wanted to walk somewhere in a normal-looking fashion, which meant walking with Ham Brooks. Because Ham hadn't escaped. They had him. Ham would have been at Makaroff's hotel if otherwise.

Feeling that his face must be quite white, he said to Canta, "You say that Makaroff likes to use a victim to force someone to come to terms?"

"You should know." She was still angry. "You're Doc Savage. You're supposed to know everything."

"I just wanted to be reassured. Do you know this fellow they didn't want to carry along?"

She said gloomily, "I should apologize for being nasty, I suppose. Makaroff has your friend, if you had a friend using the office."

"Yes, it was Ham Brooks, one of my associates."

"That isn't good, but I don't need to tell you so. Yes, I've seen that fellow on the floor. With Makaroff. He was a General or something like that in the intelligence division of their army."

"Rather an important one to just shoot because excess baggage would be inconvenient."

"Not when you consider the importance of what they're doing."

"What do you mean by that?"

"I don't know," she said without changing expression. "But this is a business with a lion and not a mouse. I hope I've got eyes enough to see that."

Doc made some inquiries, and managed to set the time of Ham's misfortune exactly. A clerk in a silk firm had heard the shot, and knew the exact minute: nineteen and one half minutes past nine. He'd been looking at the clock, and he had the kind of a mind—he was a bookkeeper—that retained such items. Doc checked it carefully. He looked at his watch and did some figuring.

"This happened while I was chasing Makaroff through walls and breaking down doors," he said thoughtfully.

Canta nodded. "He had it all set up, in case he decided to do it."

"That was awfully fast work, getting word to his men to grab Ham."

"From Makaroff, that's nothing. You haven't got a corner on that kind of magic, I think you'll find out."

"You're mad at me again, aren't you?"

She didn't say anything.

They used Doc's car to where Monk had been stationed. His hotel. The cyclone there had left a somewhat broader path and no bodies. Nearly all of the furniture that would break in the kind of a fight that Monk would make had been broken. It was hard to tell how much blood had been scattered on the premises, but it looked like a gallon or two.

The matter of timing here was simpler to ascertain, although not as exact. A fight like this one couldn't escape notice, and the hotel people were in the room, sputtering with indignation. Nine-twenty-five. A little later than Ham's downfall. And they had walked out with Monk, although Monk wasn't walking, being tied and gagged. They had been seen doing that.

The police were there, too, and being anxious for an arrest were short-sighted enough to take Doc into custody. That lasted about four minutes. Long enough for a telephone call to Central Station on *Beh Tow Park.* Apologies followed.

"What will you do now?" Canta asked. "Makaroff is all set for you. If you make a move, he'll kill your two men. He was rigged for you going and coming. In case you got away from him in his hotel, which you did, he still had you hooked."

"True. But he's had experience, so that may help."

"What do you mean?"

"Makaroff doubtless knows that no cat is really skinned until its hide is tanned and on the market as Tibetan Mink."

"I still don't get it."

"I don't think Makaroff will kill either one of my friends until his back is against the last wall. He's not against any wall at all now. In fact, he is doing quite well."

She said, "You talk a cold-blooded morning's work."

"I'm not cold-blooded at all," he said. "We'll go somewhere where we can talk—you'd better pick the place; you should know of one—and I'll talk you into a rough idea of just how scared I am."

She frowned. "You want me to pick a hideout for us?"

"Yes."

"You're sort of trusting, aren't you?"

"No. I'll explain that, too."

She took him deviously, very deviously, to a *geoow-lee'en-dee* on Fung Street, and he was a little embarrassed. It was a hairdresser's place that catered to wealthy native and Eurasian ladies, and he didn't feel at ease there. The parlor where they were closeted was too effeminate in the cloying Oriental fashion for his taste, and he said so.

"We're perfectly safe here," Canta assured him. "For a couple of hours, possibly."

He nodded and, distrusting any of the delicate furniture, sat crosslegged on the floor. He looked up at her thoughtfully. "Don't let this seeming delay get on your nerves," he said. "We have a little time to lose, and it has to be lost. Later, things will be looking up."

"I'm sorry you don't like it here," she said, but didn't sound as if she was sorry.

"You know a lot of unusual places, don't you?" he commented.

"Some."

"And unusual people, too," he added.

"Makaroff?"

He shook his head slowly, "Not him especially. You lead an unusual life for a woman, and a very pretty woman at that. You don't make your living with your looks, although you could, and they probably help. You're a legend through this neck of the woods, but you know that."

She was silent.

He asked, "Mind telling me how you happened to become the Orient's mystery lady?"

"Is it necessary?"

"Well, our friendship isn't getting along too well, and I think it needs a foundation. That might be one. If I knew your background, it would at least be one less mystery on my mind."

Canta shrugged, looked away, and finally said, "Oh, well, if you're going to keep prying at it. Where do you think I was born?"

"Centerville, Iowa."

She jumped, brought her eyes to him sharply. "You've dug deeper than I thought."

"Pretty deep," he admitted. "You were a missionary's daughter, weren't you? And your parents lost their lives when the Japanese came. Is that what set you off on this rather brazen career?"

She nodded freely enough. "If you have to have a reason, I imagine that one will do. I kept out of the hands of the Japs, but didn't leave the city. In the beginning, I suppose I stayed because I couldn't get away, then I became involved with the Chinese underground—became sort of a leader. I had lived in Japan several years. My parents were on mission service there. So I knew how the Jap mind worked, and knew the people here, too, and I became sort of a leader. Not deliberately.

I don't think I had any ideas of destiny, but I did have a grudge at the Japs, and so I just gravitated into heading an underground cell."

"And that is how you built your organization?"

"Yes. After the war, I found I had a first-rate set of confederates who could be trusted. And I suppose the war dulled certain ideas of right and wrong, or at least changed them somewhat." She lifted her eyes abruptly, frowning, and added, "But get this: I haven't dealt in drugs, women, or a few other things. Since you know as much as you do about me, you probably know some of my business angles. Some black market. Some racketeering. Mostly arranging property transfers that the local politicians, and the politicians elsewhere, don't like to see arranged. The whole Orient has been a mess since the war. There's plenty of money to be made if you use some nerve and cunning."

"Yes, I knew that about you," he admitted.

She gestured impatiently. "Well why are we talking about me? Haven't you anything more important to do?"

"I told you I wanted a foundation."

"For what?"

He settled himself. "For this: Makaroff's country is planning an aggressive war. They've tried by propaganda and cells of political agents all over the world, but that is being pretty well thwarted and even stamped out. So the only thing that remains is war—or that's the way they look at it. They're worse than the Hitler clique in many respects."

She was watching him intently. "You've understated it, probably."

"Probably."

"You make it sound like nothing."

Doc Savage, his face somewhat wooden, said, "It doesn't sound anything of the sort, and you know it. Plunging the world into another bloody world war is ghastly madness, because the next one won't be fought like any before. The last one hit the civilian populations worse than the armed forces—and the next one will be more so. Armies won't be wiped out. Civilians will be. And the ugliest part of it is that Makaroff's government is a dictatorship, regardless of what it calls itself, and the whole thing is merely the hunger of a few beastly minds to be the first rulers of the entire world."

"Why bother telling me that? I know it. Is there anyone who doesn't?" she asked grimly.

"Quite a few don't seem to, although they're coming around to seeing the light."

"Well, why repeat it anyway?"

"Four or five weeks ago," Doc said, "my associate Long Tom Roberts was in Shanghai on an electrical project. He's an electrical engineer. He received a tip from someone using the name of Washington Smith. Washington Smith was anonymous."

Canta, looking fixedly at the wall now, said coldly, "Tips from people who give no names are usually worthless."

"This one wasn't."

"No?"

"Washington Smith," Doc Savage said quietly, "is very likely to go down in history as an unsung hero or heroine—we received no indication of whether Washington Smith was man or woman."

"There are no unsung heroes. Only heroes—being one is not a state of mind."

"It might be a state of mind, and if it is, Washington Smith should be very proud."

"Why?"

"Because the tip to Long Tom Roberts might—more than just possibly might—be the instrument that saved millions of lives, and stopped cold as ghastly a horror as has been contemplated by any of the would-be world-kings."

She did not say anything. He had returned from taking a look through the window, and she was there now. He sat crosslegged on the floor again. He watched her light a cigarette, and shook his head when she extended the package.

"Are you trying to scare me?" she asked.

"Not particularly. Only that being scared goes with this story I'm telling you."

She looked down at her cigarette, watched the thin blue yarns of smoke curl. She shuddered. "Well, it's taking effect."

"You don't think I'm overstating?"

She shook her head. "You're Doc Savage. . . . They don't understate anything you're involved in, I've heard."

"That's not as good reason as the truth," he said. "The truth is so bad that when you put the words to it, it sounds silly and overdone. I'm not a carnival barker standing in front of a tent of wonders and extolling each as the onliest, greatest, stupendous that there is or will be."

"You don't need to draw it out in big letters," she said. Her voice wasn't quite right. "I get the point—you don't like what you're up against."

She came away from the window. He got up and went there instead. He did not look nor act particularly nervous; but in going to the window, he had shown he was. Very nervous.

He said: "Well, here it is: it's their answer to the atom bomb—they hope. It's bacteriological warfare. It's a germ. They developed it. We developed the atom bomb, along with some help. And they fixed up this germ, all by themselves. It's a germ that will kill anyone, kill him or her in a week, and there's no cure for it, no immunization, no treatment, no refuge, no hope."

He had spoken softly, bitterly, to the window. She did not say anything.

He added, "They're ready. They're going to try it out. They're ready for a Pearl Harbor. They're shipping it to their agents in the United States, and the agents are going to give it a try. They'll hit our key cities first, just a few—Long Island and Tennessee and Washington where the atom bomb plants are, and Detroit and Wichita and the other plane manufacturing cities. And a few key seaport cities, of course."

He still spoke softly and like a minister at a funeral, earnestly trying to preach a deceased sinner out of hell, and not quite confident that it could be done.

He continued: "You see how cunning they are? At the worst, for them, the Americans will find a cure or preventative for the stuff after a few hundred thousands or a few millions have died. If we find the cure, they may not attack with their army and navy—or may, depending on how much damage their bacteriological attack has done. But in any event, they've done the deed secretly and it can't be pinned on them. They can deny."

"But you know what they're doing!" she said sharply.

He shrugged. "You'd be astonished how little proof I have. The word of a nonentity named Washington Smith. A person who doesn't exist, except as a fake name, and the memory of a tip."

She asked, "You sent Long Tom Roberts to investigate?"

He nodded. "And you can see the results of that. I came here as soon as possible. I have plenty of backing—the whole resource of the American government—if I can find a place to use it."

"What is this germ?" she asked.

"I don't know. It's a form of virus, so Washington Smith said."

"You're depending a lot on this Washington Smith."

He nodded. "But I believe the tip was straight. So do our diplomats and agents. And we're grateful. I'll tell you something—there's nothing we wouldn't do for Washington Smith to repay this favor."

"But you'll find a cure for the virus, won't you?"

"How do I know? We can't cure a common cold. We can't cure cancer. You'd be astonished how many man-killers we can't deal with at all. Yes, we might find a cure—in ten, fifteen, twenty years. Research is slow. There isn't any fast way to do it. It's just slow."

"Do you think they're taking the virus into the United States?"

"Yes."

"When?"

"I think darn quick now. I've had agents all over the place. Not just Monk and Ham, my two friends—we've used all the secret agencies our government can command, and what we've dug up amounts to very little—except that we think they're about to do it. Just about. I think the shipment is here in this city now."

"Then if you could find it—?"

"Fine. Find it how?"

She frowned. "Is it going to be hard?"

"I don't know whether you've thought of this, but you will," he said. "The virus can be in many forms. It can be a batch of mail destined for various cities in America. It can be a shipment of almost any product that is distributed in the States. It can be almost anything. A virus is something you don't see with the naked eye, and not always with a microscope."

She stubbed out the cigarette. She was remarkably pale.

"I don't see why you contacted me," she said.

"You're angry about that, you mean?"

"No. No, I mean—why the specific interest in me?"

"To get you to lead me to Makaroff, or rather to present me to Makaroff as an acquaintance and more or less an adventurer of your own—well, your own profession."

"Ilk. You almost said ilk," she said. "So you think I'm pretty bad, don't you?"

"You haven't exactly been qualifying for a halo the last few years."

"All right. But that's not why you contacted me," she said.

"No?"

"There must be another reason."

He shrugged, said, "If you are hunting something to guess at, that will serve as well as anything. Hop to it."

He consulted his watch, pocketed his hands, turned from the window and moved about the room. His manner was tight with restraint, waiting, poorly subdued impatience.

"What are you waiting for now?" she asked.

"A break that just possibly might come."

"For instance?"

"Makaroff is going to keep Ham Brooks and Monk Mayfair in the very safest place. Isn't that reasonable?"

"Yes. To keep you from rescuing them."

"All right. The very safest place would be where the shipment of virus is also stored, wouldn't you imagine?"

"It could be."

"Well, there are various scientific methods of locating a man, or two men, when you have carefully prepared for it in advance. There are radiant substances that leave clear trails for a Geiger counter, or for the several radiant-detecting gadgets that are so sensitive they make the Geiger look like a blind man feeling his way."

"Oh!"

He took a chair. "So we'll wait."

She frowned at him. "You might tell me why you did contact me."

"I have."

"One tenth of it, I think."

He stretched out his legs very carefully, placed his hands with as much care on the chair armrests. He was taking pains to relax, to force himself to ease off, and the fight was so strong that it was clearly apparent what he was doing. Looking at the ceiling, not seeing anything there, he verged off again to a relevant point, but one they had not been developing.

"Washington Smith," he said, "should be very proud. I said that before, didn't I?"

"Yes."

He nodded soberly several times. "Yes, I can't imagine anything short of being an angel fully accredited in Heaven that would make anyone feel better than Washington Smith should feel."

"That would depend on the kind of a person Washington Smith is. Whether just a cheap tipster, or someone who did this as a result of sober thought and the urgings of character."

"Yes, we wondered about that. We wanted to know. You see, we—and the whole world—owe this Washington Smith a great deal."

"There's no pay-off for something like that, is there?"

"Of course there is. Eulogy. In the history books, name and picture. Savior of humanity."

"If Washington Smith values that, it might do."

"Well, there are other things, too. For instance, Washington Smith might be a criminal of sorts, and I'm sure a full pardon could be arranged without trouble for past rashness in dealing with the law."

"That might not be interesting."

"I think it would be."

She came up straight, more than a little rigid, and eyed him. "So that's what you're leading up to?"

He nodded.

"Well," she said, "you took an indirect way."

"Yes," he agreed, "but you didn't make it too obvious that you were Washington Smith. But you are, of course."

Chapter VIII

THE liner *Crosby Square* was no war child. She would not be with that name, because the name Crosby Square to those who know what Crosby Square was had a fine old dignity that went with ships by fine old individualists with the care and pains that came of knowledge they were sinking their own money and not the taxpayers' and would have to get a profit back. She had been built to compete with the *Queen Mary* and the *Normandie* and the *Rex* when those governments were subsidizing their shipping concerns. She'd been built for stiff competition. She was a fine passenger liner. She had been when she was built; she was still.

Doc Savage moved carefully in the night and found the place he wanted.

"This is supposed to be it," he whispered to Canta.

She was silent. The moonlight did not cross their faces, because they were in shadows, but out before them was spread the river and the harbor with its sampans like waterbugs. The moon made the noisome harbor look almost sanitary; it cleaned up the flotsam by subduing it, and the wind had a god-given direction, not from river nor from city, so that it too was clean, and came with the fragrance of flowers and the pear trees and the peach that were in bloom in the country. It was the hour of *ban ye,* and the city was nice.

"How did you know you were to come here?" she asked.

He said, "Don't worry about it. I think it was the thing to do."

She was silent again. Not because he wouldn't tell her anything she believed—he'd told her he had received a message, and she knew better. At least he hadn't received any message in the hairdresser's place. Maybe before. But not there.

She was silent because of another thing he'd told her that she didn't believe. He'd said he'd known she was Washington Smith after taking a look at her character. She hadn't liked that.

"Is it that ship?" she asked. She pointed at the *Crosby Square.*

The liner was an easy thing to point at. It was a giant beside them—they were at a spot in the wilderness of trucks, wagons, bales, boxes that always seems to litter an Oriental waterfront.

"I hope so," he said. "Yes, I hope so."

"All right," she said. "Now tell me how you learned I gave that tip—how you know I was Washington Smith."

"It's sort of a professional secret."

"I don't care," she said grimly. "I want to know. If you found it out, Makaroff can. And if he knows, can learn, I want to be warned."

He was watching the ship, listening to the darkness, frowning at the moonlight that might reach them if they had to wait here too much longer. "I didn't think of that," he admitted. "All right, here is how it led to you: we felt the tip was too detailed to have come from a chance eavesdropper. An eavesdropper wouldn't be permitted to hear information of that sort anyway. No money was demanded. That meant Washington Smith was operating out of patriotic or humanitarian reasons, and that Washington Smith didn't need money, or wouldn't take money for a thing like that, which adds up to the same thing—someone important in his own right. One of Makaroff's countrymen would have asked for money—they're built that way. So that narrowed it down to a wealthy humanitarian or patriot not of Makaroff's nationality, and someone important enough to have been told the secret and not overheard it. We looked over the list of people Makaroff dealt with, and about a dozen names came up. Yours, believe it or not, was one of the dozen, and no more than that, in the beginning—until, in fact, you admitted it back there in the hairdresser's."

"You mean that if I'd have denied it then, you still wouldn't have known?"

"Probably."

"I was taken," she said. She sounded relieved. "Well, Makaroff won't figure that one out. I'd better tell you how I learned of the infernal thing myself."

"Yes. I wish you would."

"He tried to hire me to get it into the States and distribute it."

"What!"

She gave Doc Savage a look that must have been glassy in the darkness. "I had never wanted to kill anyone before—not personally, with my own hands, to watch their blood flow or their brains splatter in the dirt. But I did then, and would have if it would have been practical."

"Makaroff wanted to employ an outside agency to test their new weapon?"

"Yes. He phrased it something like that, too."

"That wasn't too dumb. Makaroff is known, and his best agents are known. He was trying to get rid of that risk percentage."

"Well, that's how I learned."

"He told you that much?"

"Not at first. I've never bought pigs in pokes. He finally came around to telling me about what you've just told me—or told me back there in the hairdresser's. But not any more than that."

"Did Long Tom Roberts ever interview you?"

"No."

"I don't think he ever had the least idea who Washington Smith was."

"I wonder what Makaroff did to Long Tom—" She went suddenly silent, not quite gasping, but sounding as if she wished to do so. She sent out a hand and fastened it on Doc's arm. "Oh my God!" she breathed, and pointed. "Do you see that man?"

"The thin and very brown one with no hair?"

"Yes."

The man had walked through the splatter of light from an automobile's headlamps, and had stopped where the forward cargo gangway lights outlined him. He stood there, a thin dour figure who contemplated the activity without expression.

"That's Karl Sundwi," she breathed. "He works with Makaroff. I think he's a special observer of their security police who was sent to watch how Makaroff handled this. And he isn't bald. He has blonde hair, clipped very close so that he looks bald."

"Makaroff is too big a man to be watched."

She shook her head. "No. Their security police watch everybody, and the head of it is not a friend of Makaroff's. No, this Karl Sundwi came ostensibly to be of service to Makaroff. His credentials show him under Makaroff's orders. But Makaroff thinks he is secret police. And Makaroff is afraid of him."

"That would make this Karl a bad one."

"Very bad."

They watched the man. He lit a long dark cigarette, hardly smoked it, kept changing it from lips to hands to lips again, one side of his mouth and then the other, the red coal of its lighted end moving endlessly.

Doc said, "He seems nervous."

"He's like that all the time. A cat on a hot stove."

Presently the man Karl Sundwi shot his cigarette at the cobblestones, stepped on it, shrugged and went toward the passenger gangplanks. They watched him board the liner.

Canta whispered excitedly, "I don't know what brought you here, but it was a good idea."

Doc asked, "How'd you like to sail for San Francisco on that ship?"

"What?"

He hesitated, then said, "I have an extra ticket, bought with that in mind."

She said sharply, "You're damned confident! No, wait! Do you think the shipment is on the *Crosby Square?"*

"Yes. I'm fairly sure."

She seemed to be looking up at him in the murk. He supposed she was frowning. "Would I be any help?"

"Yes, I think so."

"Name one way," she asked suspiciously.

"That's easy. You know Makaroff's men better than I do. You can point them out to me."

"Don't tell me you're going at this alone?"

"Yes."

She gasped audibly now. Her voice was a little odd as she said, "That I suppose I should see. All right, but I'm going to get darned tired of these clothes I'm wearing. They'll be watching all the places where I could pick up things."

"The *Crosby Square* isn't a tanker. You can get what you need in the shops aboard."

He said, "Come on, then," and led the way—not very far, a few yards—and stopped beside a large wicker hamper. He raised the lid. "You won't find this too uncomfortable. There's a kind of safety belt inside. Better fasten it in case you get turned upside down."

She touched the basket wonderingly. "This is pat. It's almost too pat planning."

"Wait until you see the awakening, the big finale."

She was silent for a moment. "Yes, I'm beginning to think it might be something to see." She got into the hamper quickly and easily, like a boy.

He fastened the lid, received her assurance that she had found the safety belt, and secured it. Then he went to a ship's officer and arranged for the hamper to be taken aboard. "It's labeled for the stateroom," he said. "I want it there."

It was not his stateroom. It was the one he had reserved in the name of Mme. Coltene Florai, which he hadn't thought, when he made the reservation, sounded at all like Canta's personality. Now he wasn't so sure about her personality, though, and he wondered about that idly while checking with the passport people and the purser, and while a steward was showing him to his own cabin, where he remained until the ship sailed, at four o'clock in the morning with the ebb tide, noisy little tugs huffing and churning to keep the sea giant in the stream.

He left his cabin then. It was still dark, and the ship had quieted considerably. It started to rain just as he came on deck, and he walked what seemed hundreds of yards in the rain, which came down listlessly in large drops.

The *Crosby Square* was nearly nine hundred feet at the waterline, a hundred and thirty-five feet from keel to boat-deck. She was a floating city. She was so big that probably no passenger on an ocean crossing had ever seen the entire vessel. Searching her would be an impossible task, when he didn't know for what he would be hunting. The virus shipment might be in any of hundreds of disguises; he hadn't told Canta anything amiss when he said the stuff could be a shipment of mail, or any other product for distribution. That was in his mind, and heavy there, as he went to the stateroom he'd reserved nearly a week ago in the name of Mme. Coltene Florai.

The hamper was there. He tapped on it, after closing the stateroom door. "All right," he said. "You can come out."

"I already have," she said, appearing from the dressing-room. She had the small jeweled gun in her hand, dangling. "You didn't think I was going to stay in there all night."

He frowned. "You took a chance. Makaroff may have paid the stewards to make a check of the staterooms."

She shook her head. "Nobody has been in there but a stewardess."

"Well, it's too late anyway."

She wasn't contrite. "Don't think you're going to order me around."

He looked at her speculatively. "Beginning to regret your move, are you?"

"What do you think? The last thing I expected this time yesterday was that I would be starting an ocean voyage I had no intention of taking, and no desire to take, and starting it in a basket. It's silly."

He went to the door. "Maybe sleep will improve your temper. I'll see you about noon."

"Now who's mad?" she asked.

He said, "I wouldn't know," dryly, and backed out, pulling the door shut.

She was motionless after he left, looking a little startled. Twice she made gestures, angry surprised ones, with a hand. Then she said, "Who does he think he is?" and went to the berth and flung herself upon it. She was wearing a slacks and shirt combination she'd had the stateroom stewardess purchase for her in the shop just after sailing-time, and she thought now: maybe I shouldn't have had the stewardess buy those things. I guess I shouldn't have. I've been having one of my dumb nights. Even my being on this ship is dumb—it wouldn't be dumb at all if I knew Makaroff was taking his country's planting of virus on the vessel. But I don't know that. Doc Savage said so. But he could be mistaken. I think even he could make a mistake.

"If he wanted me to stay parked in that silly basket, why didn't he say so two or three times!" she complained. And looked up, for there was a knock on her stateroom door. She hesitated, not violently alarmed, but not easy of mind either, and then changed her voice somewhat, to ask, "What is it?"

"Breakfast. Madam." It was a male voice. Nothing unusual about it.

"I didn't order breakfast."

"I'm sorry, Madam. A gentleman, a very large gentleman with a cane, ordered it for you. Do you wish me to return the tray?"

Peace offering, she thought. And was relieved."

Once a man made a peace offering, he had as much as admitted he was in the wrong, and therefore she could browbeat him some more if she wished.

Happy about it, she jumped up, opened the stateroom door, and looked into the scowling face of Karl Sundwi, the Makaroff henchman—the man of whom Makaroff was deathly afraid. Karl Sundwi held no tray of breakfast, but held instead about what she would have expected him to be holding. She had seen them a few times. The underground had used them sometimes because, once you knew what they were, the menace of them was more terrible than a knife or gun.

The thing was a water pistol. There was a tiny blob of soft wax over the spray tube to keep it sealed until the triggering mechanism was given a hard pull. That was to prevent leakage of the contents, which could vary. Liquefied varieties of cyanic were quick, and there were other preparations. Sometimes the victim managed to scream once. Sometimes not.

"The stewardess deserves a little bonus," Karl Sundwi said dryly in excellent English. "Wouldn't you say so?"

Canta was wordless. She came out of the stateroom when he beckoned with the gun. He closed the door, and they moved silently along the deck, faces against the bloody sunlight that was trying to get through the soft rain.

Chapter IX

KARL SUNDWI was traveling well. He had a suite, and they waited there twenty minutes, Canta suspended on the edge of a chair, Karl Sundwi draped alertly on the edge of a bed-lounge, and a block-bodied man who was faceless as to expression and whom Canta had never seen before guarding the door in military fashion, spread-legged like an old-time Nazi. Then Makaroff came.

Makaroff carried his jaw prominently. There was rainwater on his hat and he snapped it off angrily.

He said, "What do you mean, sending for me? Who do you think you are?"

That was before he saw Canta, and then his jaw went down and he put the hat back on his head, forgetting to set it straight.

Karl Sundwi showed his teeth, not pleasantly. "What were you saying?"

Makaroff swallowed vaguely. "It doesn't matter."

"Yes, it does," Karl Sundwi said, shaking his head gravely. "It is a point we had better straighten out, a dog we should kill now. You came in here raving about your dignity being injured by my sending for you, didn't you?"

"It's not important."

"I think so."

Makaroff swung slowly on the man, and already he was getting a glazed look that meant fears and rages and doubts were crawling together in him. "I didn't know that it was the girl you had here," he said. "But since you're making a point of it, suppose we clear it up. Suppose we do that."

Karl Sundwi smiled thinly. "That's what I mean. Suppose we do that. And here's what I mean: from now on, you work closely with me. You do nothing, make no move, without discussing it fully with me. And I may, it is needless to add, have certain advice which you will heed."

Makaroff stood stiffly, raised his eyes to the ceiling, and called a curse on himself. "I will be damned," he added, "if I am going to tolerate talk like that, even from a fellow who did catch this girl—"

Karl Sundwi's hand was up. "Just a minute, Makaroff. You have bungled this. You have boobed it thoroughly. And so you won't start howling at me, I'll tell you how and why—Doc Savage is aboard."

Makaroff stood winded. His eyes became twice as large, and then half as small, as they had been a moment before. "On this ship?"

"The girl came aboard with him."

"How do you know?"

"Let's go back a bit, Makaroff. You were advised by the central cell that I was being assigned to help you some ten days ago. I don't think you liked it, did you?"

Makaroff managed to scowl. "Have I made a secret of that?"

"No. You figured I was from security police, didn't you?"

"Aren't you?"

"That's right," Karl Sundwi said. "Assigned to keep an eye on this deal, Makaroff. You're a good man, Makaroff, but you're more of a politician and throat-cutter than you are a mechanical planner. I imagine someday you'll be my superior. You are now, technically, but you can't give me an order I do not wish to perform. Let's get that straight."

"Have you credentials to that effect?"

"Certainly not, and you know it, and you know how to check up on the matter," Karl Sundwi said. "Let's not be juvenile. But let me finish what I was saying: you will doubtless someday be my superior, and it will be due in part to me. To Karl Sundwi, who watched over you, had my personal agents keep track of Doc Savage and this girl and learn they had boarded the ship."

Makaroff's jaw was down again. "You have agents of your own?"

"Certainly. And don't ask about them. No one knows them. No one will."

That seemed to make sense to Makaroff, and he had weighed the situation sufficiently in his cunning mind to see that nothing was to be lost, and perhaps a lot gained, by being coöp erative. He made a mental note, though, to see that Karl Sundwi was purged at some future time.

"I take it," he said coldly, "that you have some advice to offer."

"Exactly. First, the girl is not to be killed."

"That needs a reason."

"She's going to lead us to Doc Savage."

"If she does, that won't be bad."

"Secondly," said Karl Sundwi, "you're not going to get excited and kill the two Savage aides, Monk Mayfair and Ham Brooks."

"For the same reason?"

"Not exactly. For the reason you've been holding them—to insure Savage's coöperation."

"If he's aboard the ship," Makaroff said angrily. "I call that coöperation! Yes, I do! They've been of no use to us and getting them aboard the liner secretly was the devil's own job and furthermore—"

"Wait." Karl Sundwi had a thin hand up. "We're going to use Savage in this, since he has involved himself. Savage is a doctor and research scientist, and has done bacteriological work of outstanding character. He is a national figure in America, at least in informed quarters. Suppose like this: suppose it got around that Savage developed this virus, and then let it escape and is responsible. How is that for a smoke screen? We want a smoke screen, don't we, to last until we see how effective the stuff is going to be? And by effective, I mean eight or ten millions dying from it. Until we know it will make their atom bomb look futile. How would Savage do for the smoke screen?"

"My God! Is that a plan that came from over my head, or did you just think it up?"

Karl Sundwi looked at the guard speculatively. He said, "Well, it is your idea, developed a little."

Makaroff glanced at the guard also. The man wasn't important enough to matter, and could be taken care of it he did begin talking. "So it's my idea," he said thoughtfully.

"I'm not in a position to have ideas," Karl Sundwi said dryly.

Now Makaroff's face became foxy with approval, and he said, "You may be all right, Sundwi. But have you thought of a way to arrange this thing?"

The other shook his thin-skulled cropped blond head. "First, catch our bird."

"You've got something there." Makaroff looked at Canta. "What do you think of the idea of putting Savage in our hands?" he asked her.

Canta told him how little she thought of it. She left no doubts.

"What about that?" Makaroff asked Karl Sundwi.

Sundwi told the guard, "I don't like her answers. Gag her." And when that was done, Sundwi took off his coat, tossed it on a chair, and asked, "Are you touchy about seeing unpleasantness happen to a woman?"

Makaroff smiled uncertainly. "No."

"I didn't think you would be," Sundwi said.

Makaroff was not unfamiliar with secret police methods, and there had been a time when he had made a study of them himself, when thinking of organizing a security police, so-called, of his own, actually as a spying force for his own information and for the liquidation of an occasional rival. He had abandoned that project, finding it simpler to control the man who controlled the security police, and he had managed to do that most of the time, except on special occasions when the Leader gave specific orders. No one double-crossed the Leader. He was not a safe man to irritate. The Leader had, in the course of his long dark career, assassinated two of his own brothers for political reasons.

But Makaroff, watching Sundwi's technique, found that he was seeing something new in the psychological. Makaroff didn't think much of it at first. *Why, the man is being silly,* he thought. Because Karl Sundwi was merely talking, rather convincingly it was true, giving a general talk on the background of torture, its history and origin and general evolution. Not particularly dry stuff Makaroff would have admitted. But not terrifying. Or was it? Makaroff, listening, began to feel a little sick around the diaphragm. He presently had an overpowering desire to get up and leave the room to stop hearing Sundwi talk.

Makaroff stood up abruptly. "I'll be back later," he said, and went out on deck and used a handkerchief on the back of his bone-colored neck. He had changed his mind about Sundwi. The man was a genius. The man could administer terror hypnotically.

Why haven't I heard more of this Sundwi? Makaroff wondered. The man, as far as he knew, was rated a minor figure who had been assigned continually to the hinterlands, to handling certain unpleasant features of administration in the territories that had fallen under the "protection" of their government during the other war. Makaroff had never met Sundwi before. That, he reflected, had been an oversight.

He grew bitterly philosophical about men like Sundwi. They came up, unnoticed, and suddenly they were terrible fellows and you had difficulty coping with them, and one day you might meet one who had developed too far to be handled, and in that case you were a dead duck. Makaroff had no illusions about politics in his country. The thing to do about men like Sundwi was use them if they could be kept down, and if they couldn't be kept down, take no chance and get rid of them. Makaroff grinned thinly, with no humor at all, and gave Sundwi three months to live. Then he went back into the stateroom.

Canta, white-faced, looking as if she had been terribly beaten, although there was not a mark on her, crouched on a chair. Her eyes were sick, her face colorless, and she wouldn't take her eyes from the floor.

Sundwi was back on the edge of the bed, casually draped there. He told Makaroff, "She wants a little money. Enough to get her clear of Doc Savage's friends."

"Cheap enough," Makaroff said.

"Not too cheap, though," Sundwi said dryly. "Ten thousand dollars. Cash. Now. She thinks that might get her away from Savage's friends."

"It's too much."

"She'll have to go pretty far."

The nape of Makaroff's neck became a little more bone-colored. He didn't like taking suggestions from Sundwi when they were given that way. He already knew that Sundwi hated him intensely. But he shrugged, said, "I have it available. I'll get it."

"I was wondering about that much. Good. Get it," Sundwi said.

Makaroff left the stateroom. Sundwi sat silently, no expression on his long and rather unhealthy looking face. He had a deeply tanned skin, apparently a deliberately tanned skin, but otherwise he had an almost tubercular gauntness and fragility that was belied by his cold actions.

Canta was neither rigid nor relaxed. She seemed loose, defeated. She did not look up.

When Makaroff returned in five minutes, he carried a raincoat and from the pocket of this he produced a sheaf of U.S. currency about half an inch thick and wrapped in a pliable transparent substance resembling cellophane. He handed the money to Canta.

"You will not need to count it," he said. "I will guarantee the sum to be exact."

She took the money listlessly.

"How will she give Savage to us?" Makaroff demanded.

"Simply done. She will come to us again and show us where he is."

"Good enough."

Sundwi stood up, took Canta to the door, said, "I trust your memory isn't too short, my dear." He bowed her out and closed the door.

Sundwi and Makaroff now looked at each other, and both seemed self-satisfied in a cold-blooded calculating fashion.

"She is not a weak character, that one," Sundwi said.

"No one has ever said she was. Suppose she doesn't go through with it?"

"She will. If not, we've lost nothing much. Savage knew we were aboard anyway, and that is all she can tell him. And if she does cross us, I will personally make restitution of the money, and see that she doesn't enjoy her future."

Makaroff couldn't keep a triumphant grin away. "I already took care of that."

Sundwi's too-blond eyebrows went up. "Yes? I take it you've acted without consulting me. Wasn't something said about that?"

Makaroff kept his grin. "She won't enjoy that money long in any case."

"No?" Sundwi stared woodenly. And then he said, "I think I see. So that's the method of distributing the virus?"

"Exactly."

Sundwi whistled softly. "I did not know—it's one I hadn't thought of."

Makaroff struck, just a little, the attitude he used when he made his browbeating speeches before the U.N. and the Preparations Commission. "An entirely appropriate weapon for war on certain interests."

"True."

"I have," said Makaroff, "a little over four hundred thousand dollars in U.S. currency. It will be brought in under diplomatic immunity when we reach San Francisco. That is all arranged. As a diplomatic official, I can do that, and the Ambassador is also aboard."

Sundwi was clearly awed. "How will the distribution be arranged?"

"The money," said Makaroff easily, "will be paid through the usual channels to our cells of workers and fellow-travelers in the States. Such payments have been regularly made in the past. The American F.B.I. is aware of this, knows most of the agents to whom it is distributed, and will happily watch them as it has before, believing that a full check is being kept on our American operations."

"Our workers in the States will distribute the money—"

"They won't know. They'll just spend it. They spend it like water anyway."

"Then they'll die also!"

"Why not! Of what real use are they? They've failed in their work of converting the United States to our way of government and our philosophy of human economy. Why shouldn't they be punished."

Sundwi, except for his amazement, did not seem particularly affected. "This might hook in very well with my thought of laying the blame for spreading the virus on Doc Savage."

"Yes, I thought of that. If the word that Savage launched a private war on our agents, and it got out of control and began wiping out the nation itself—that is the sort of thing you mean?"

"That is the sort of thing."

Chapter X

CANTA faced Doc Savage. She stood with both hands gripping a chair, and speaking in a low voice that was without rise or fall, told him what had happened to her. She said that Sundwi had terrified her. "I have never met anything like him," she said. "He has twice the brains that Makaroff has, and I couldn't tell you with words how he built terror. It's something you'd have to experience."

Doc Savage had listened patiently. "So you agreed to turn me over to them?"

"To tell them where they could get at you. And I didn't agree not to tell you I had sold out. They didn't ask anything about that."

He said absently, "Well, that keeps your honesty intact, anyway."

"It means something to me, whether you think it does or not."

"Maybe we can arrange for you to go all the way."

"Show them where you are, you mean?" She looked shocked.

"Maybe. We'll have to see. The point is that this hasn't gotten us far. We've got to find that virus shipment. We could have grabbed Makaroff and his men at any time, but unless we get their poison, we've done no good. Makaroff, as important as he is back home, would be a small sacrifice in their opinion for the success of this thing."

She shook her head. "I didn't learn a thing."

"Nothing? No intimation whatever as to how the virus is being taken into the States?"

"None."

"Well, that's not good."

"I didn't accomplish anything." She was getting angry again. She took out the sheaf of money, still with the transparent film covering around it, and eyed it. "I don't see how they found me so quick. When they don't know where you were."

"The stewardess, didn't you say? You should have stayed in the basket."

"Oh, don't start telling me how right you are!" she snapped. She hurled the money at the table and it hit and bounced and went across the floor hopping over and over.

"What's that?"

"My bribe."

He said, "There's no reason to treat ten thousand dollars so disrespectfully." He went over and picked up the money. He looked at it for a while. His bronze features seemed to become more metallic than usual. He said, "Who gave you this?"

"Sundwi made the deal."

"Sundwi gave you the money?"

"No. Makaroff did that." She came forward. "I might as well count it. Makaroff probably shortchanged me, or the bills are counterfeit or something. It's against his principles to make an honest move when a crooked one could be managed."

He did not hand her the money. In fact, he held it out of her reach.

"Now what?" she asked coldly. "You going to hold out on me?"

"I don't think you want it."

"Not want ten thousand dollars? Don't be silly."

"The packaging is too unusual."

"You mean the cellophane or whatever it's wrapped in?"

"Not cellophane. I don't think ordinary cellophane would filter out the virus."

"What?"

"I think," Doc Savage said, "that this wrapping is on the money because the virus is on the money, and they don't want it released until the packages of money are distributed and opened."

"Good God!"

"Mind you, I'm not sure."

"How will you check it?"

Doc frowned at the currency packet. "If the ship hospital has rabbits or guinea pigs, and I don't know of any reason why they should have, the check might be simpler. As it is, and if the virus is outside the range of a microscope—frankly, I'm not sure how we can check it in a hurry."

"This is pretty wild." Canta stared fixedly at the money. "No, no, it isn't either. Makaroff would like something of that sort. And money would be easy to scatter widely, wouldn't it?"

"Money," Doc agreed, "probably distributes itself faster and without attracting undue attention, than any medium they could have chosen."

"And Makaroff would want to kill me!" Canta gasped. "That is the kind of a trick he would—" She did not finish and her eyes went wide and round, glassy with shock in a moment, and she tried to speak, but only made a series of sounds like hard-driven breathing.

Doc had his back to the door, and the direction

of the door had produced the glazed effect on her. He asked, "Is it safe to turn around?"

Karl Sundwi, stepping into the cabin quickly, said, "Probably the only completely safe move you'll make for some little time."

Doc swung. Sundwi closed the door, leaned against it, and his eyes went over the room like hunting animals until they located the bundle of greenbacks, where they became fixed.

"You opened that money yet?" he demanded.

"No."

"Don't."

Doc blew out breath quickly. "So that is how they're taking the virus into the States."

"That's right," Karl Sundwi said. "God knows, I was long enough finding it out. But Makaroff just told me. He got cute with himself, and told me. I think I sort of led him to wanting to exhibit his mental superiority. I should have thought of that approach before—I didn't know it would work with Makaroff."

Doc said, "Then we're ready to crack this."

"We're ready to try, you mean."

Chapter XI

DOC SAVAGE told Canta, "His real name is Long Tom Roberts."

Canta still looked at Long Tom with glassy terror; she was unable to accept, so suddenly, the concept that he was a Doc Savage associate. Surprise had piled against surprise, and the impact was nothing coherent.

Long Tom looked at her—his face was pleasant enough now, although she couldn't register that either—and explained, "I guess I was pretty realistic with you. But there didn't seem to be any other choice."

She said something then, probably thought she spoke more than she did, but the first was just lip movements and the last pretty much incohesive until two or three words began to hang together at a time. There was something about, "—was murdered by Makaroff several days ago—"

"Oh, that," said Long Tom Roberts. "Well, that would worry Makaroff also, if he knew about it. You see, they did murder a man. They went to a very great deal of trouble to do it, and they were sure it was me. But it wasn't. I did a little switcheroo on them, and it was Karl Sundwi they knifed and put in an acid bath. Sundwi had come down alone to watch Makaroff, and he had a briefcase full of the most wonderful credentials. It happened I'd known Sundwi from the past, and he was a man of about my build. All I had to do was dye my hair and eyebrows, give myself a coat of suntan lotion, and be a little reckless."

Doc Savage was looking at Long Tom Roberts, and he shuddered. Not too perceptibly but a shudder anyway. He could imagine how simple it had been. And he knew one thing that Long Tom hadn't mentioned; the death of Sundwi hadn't been deliberate on Long Tom's part; it had been an accident of sorts, and Long Tom felt oddly about it.

Doc asked, "Know where the money is?"

"I've got a good idea. In Makaroff's baggage, no doubt. In the diplomatic pouches that are marked official business—those things that go through without a customs inspection."

"What about Monk and Ham?"

"They're alive but not very happy," Long Tom explained. "They have been all set a couple of times to make a break. But I managed to get to them and warn them to hold off until we had some idea where the virus was located."

"Where are they?"

Long Tom named a stateroom suite. "They're there, but they may be drugged. I'm not sure. They were drugged when they were brought aboard, and hauled on as invalids."

"How'd they get them past the health officials with that?"

"Papers they already had fixed up. This Makaroff seems to be able to do about anything he wishes to do."

Doc Savage had seemed to be giving full attention to Long Tom's story, but now he moved abruptly, went to the door in silence, yanked it open. In an instant, the panel of the door opening was a pantomime of shadow and sick rain-filtered sunlight as Doc Savage struggled with the man who had been there.

The fracas did not last long, but during it they could hear another man's feet going away frantically along the deck. Long Tom, lunging forward, tried to get at the runner, but came against Doc and the other, and the tangle was more involved for a few moments. Then they were down, the three of them, but only the one, the eavesdropper, unconscious.

Doc asked grimly, "One of Makaroff's?"

"That's right. One of his bodyguards." Long Tom dived through the cabin door and looked after the one who had run away. "That's another one of them."

"We've got to start operating."

"I'll say."

"Let's get Monk and Ham out of it first."

They ran then, heads back and already breathing hard, along the deck. And Canta, shaking the shock out of her muscles, followed them wildly. She tried to scream at them, twice, that she wanted a gun. Where was there a gun for her? But they did not understand—she hardly understood the words herself—and they went on.

They knew where they were going, or Long Tom did. But they didn't seem to know what to do when they got there. They reached a cabin door. It was in the second-class section, in a long cream-colored corridor of innumerable other doors identical except for the gold-leaf numerals.

"How many will be in there?" Doc asked.

"Four, probably," Long Tom said.

"That's enough to make it active, but let's go in."

"Very active," Long Tom agreed. "I'll try my Sundwi personality on them."

He whanged on the door with a fist and got from inside a growled order not to disturb, which he answered with a password. The door lock clattered. He followed the opening door inside, pushing hard. He saw something then that Doc could not see, and doubled down, diving forward, and in a moment two men were on him, one with a clubbed gun, the other with a knife.

Doc Savage lunged at the door, and met it as one of the men tried to kick it shut. He forced his way in, and Canta, trying to follow, was struck by the door as it again came shut. This time it closed, and spring-locked.

Canta, wildly alarmed, wrenched at the door until a bullet came through, making a hole, a tuft of splintered steel, a few inches from her eyes. She shrank back then, appalled by violence, the proximity of death.

Sounds that came from inside were neither subdued nor reassuring. There was only one more shot, then a succession of mixed cries, thumps, blows, the bone-breaking noise of things being smashed, of men in violent physical contact. Finally it ended, and the door came open again.

Long Tom put his head out, looked both ways along the corridor, and said casually enough, "We were expected. You'd better get in here. They'll be coming back in a hurry."

She entered, and saw the two guards—only two—in shapes of violent unconsciousness on the floor.

She saw also a wide-bodied, hairy, remarkably homely man who presumably was Monk Mayfair. He had been bound with bandages from the shoulders down, and Doc Savage was slitting the bindings.

Long Tom told Canta additionally, "They were faster than we thought. They—two of the guards and a fellow who came giving the alarm—took Ham Brooks away. They were coming back for Monk."

Doc now freed Monk. And Monk, trying to spring to his feet, rolled helplessly on the floor. His legs, the circulation hampered for hours by the bandage bindings, wouldn't take orders.

Doc said, "Rub some circulation back, Monk. Then try to get to the bridge. The Captain has orders to supply help."

Monk wailed, "Dammit, they've got Ham! I'm not going to be any messenger boy while they're probably slitting Ham's throat!"

But Doc was not listening. He was back at the door, and, probably knowing Monk, said, "Do you know where they'd take Ham, Long Tom?"

"I've no idea. Probably not Makaroff's suite, though. They've got half a dozen suites aboard. One is as good a bet as another." Long Tom's voice had a wild sound, as if his throat was unable to do anything with the words.

Canta had backed into the corridor, and now she shrieked, pointing. A man had come into the passage at the far end; whether it was one of Makaroff's men she didn't know; she merely shrieked on the principle that the way that things were going, nothing that happened could be good.

The man turned, ran. He was out of view in an instant, but Doc had seen him. Doc went down the passage with sprinting haste that was as fast, Canta thought, as she had ever seen a man travel on two feet. Long Tom was back of him, losing ground.

At the end of the corridor, Long Tom whirled, screamed, "What color coat was he wearing?"

"Brown!" Canta screamed back. Presumably Doc had not seen the man after all, and had come in sight of two or more men and was confused.

Now Monk Mayfair came out of the cabin. He was moving as if he had wooden legs with the joints rusted, and making ghastly grimaces. He yelled, "Where'd they go?"

"You're supposed to go to the bridge and get help—"

"Where did they go?" Monk screeched at her. "Goddam it, they were going to kill Ham Brooks!"

She was upset herself, and she put her face against Monk's homely one, almost, and yelled, "Don't tell me stuff I already know! Let me have your arm. I'll help you."

The helping was not too successful and they had two falls, Monk going down alone the first time, then both of them getting tangled together, before they reached the end of the corridor. But they made it in good time in spite of that, and Monk was working the stiffness out of his legs.

They could hear a man screaming somewhere ahead. Monk said of the sound, "That's one of them! I've heard them sound like that before when Doc got them."

Canta hadn't noticed the quality of the scream

particularly, but now she gave it attention. It had a stark all-out intensity and the emotion in it was as raw as a small skinned animal.

They passed cross-ship and into another corridor, and she saw why the man was screaming like that. Doc Savage had him—it was the man she'd seen take flight in the passage, the brown-coated one—and Doc was doing something to the man's body with his hands. Between convulsive kicks and screeches, the man presently began to try to point to another section of the ship. Doc struck him and dropped him then, and went on, Long Tom Roberts with him.

Canta and Monk reached the dropped man. The latter was still conscious. Monk leaned down and took care of that with a fist blow that shaped the man's jaw differently. "That guy," Monk said with satisfaction, "had been trying to elect himself as my executioner when the time came. After he wakes up I'll be back and give him another treatment."

I hope you're not optimistic, Canta thought wildly.

She said, "You're supposed to get help from the ship's officers."

"That would take too long to organize," Monk gasped. He was taking great frog-like hops on his stiff legs now, and didn't need propping up.

They went on. Doc and Long Tom were far ahead now. Out of the Second Class section. There was an ornate rail with a politely worded request for Second Class passengers to keep out of Cabin First domains. They vaulted that gate, and a moment later, Monk tried to vault it the same way and took another fall. He didn't mind, apparently. The falls seemed to be loosening him up. At least he was on his feet again without apparently pausing.

It will be Makaroff's suite, Canta thought. Makaroff was hard-pressed, or he wouldn't have let it happen there. Even the great Makaroff, No. 2 ruffian of the poor world's bad-boy nation, would have difficulty smoothing out the murder of Ham Brooks in his suite. Makaroff must be a little hysterical. She had wondered if he wouldn't become that way if pushed really hard.

She screamed, "It will be Makaroff's suite! Watch out!"

But they didn't look back, so they already knew it. Long Tom would know, of course. Long Tom was Sundwi, or rather had pretended to be Sundwi, after Sundwi had died. She felt foolish, and did not cry out any more.

They came to a door, and it seemed to be locked. She saw from a distance down the corridor Doc Savage lay a hand against the door and the panel came out, and Doc went in, Long Tom after him.

The sounds that came out of the room were like those that had come from the other cabin a bit ago, but there were more of them. And their quality was touched up somewhat.

Monk Mayfair began to swear. He swore terribly. He said, "For a month I been sweating on this! And by God, I lose out on the windup! I'm a lame duck when the cork gets pulled!"

This time the door was not closed. The suite was large. First a main cabin, sixteen by twenty feet; there were bedrooms, solarium, private dining room, a solid glass bath opening off that. Ample room for the festivities.

Canta found trouble picking exact facts out of the mêlée, but she guessed at approximately seven men in the suite at the beginning, not including Ham Brooks, whom they had been engaged in sewing in a stout bedspread, including a typewriter at his feet for ballast. Ham was still alive, but bandaged and taped until he could only participate in the affair with glares.

One man was down and out already. He must have been in the way of the door. Another was crawling across the floor in a dazed fashion when Canta saw him.

The other five, with Doc Savage and Long Tom Roberts, were making all the noise. There was less shooting than in the preliminary scrap. One shot only this time. A lean moustached patriot endeavored to shoot Long Tom Roberts in the stomach, and somehow the bullet got into Makaroff's leg, high up and in the fleshy part. The things Makaroff then said stopped anymore shooting. They used fists, teeth, knives, feet and the furniture on each other.

Monk, passing Canta into the cabin, remarked, "What do you know! I made it after all." He was then knocked down with a chair and, as unaffected by that as by his falls, took the chair away from the wielder and threw it aside, and broke the man's nose and caved in half his teeth with an unaided fist.

Canta, coming inside herself, ducked a large glass vase which was thrown at her. When the vase bounced back at her feet, she picked it up, broke it over a table, and used the jagged end to menace a man who came at her. He backed away.

It didn't last long. It couldn't. It was too violent. Canta thought wildly: *They should watch Makaroff. He'll try to keep the money from them. It must be in his suite.*

That notion sent her skirting the fracas, running intently, making for the bedroom, which seemed a logical place for the virus-laden currency to be concealed. How right the notion was became plain when Makaroff broke away from the fight.

She wished then that she hadn't acted on the idea, because Makaroff came at her, head back, short legs plunging. She tried to slam the bedroom door in his face, screaming as she did so. She failed, and Makaroff was upon her, struck her, went past her. She had, for an instant, the impression of foul breath and more foul words. He was gibbering in his frenzy.

After striking her once, dropping her, he slammed the door and went on and dived on hands and knees for the underside of the bed. The treated money seemed to be in the most homely place of all, under Makaroff's bed. A suitcase. He snatched it out.

Dazed, Canta tried to get at Makaroff. She shoved a chair at him. He only cursed. His swearing was quite coherent—he was going to scatter the virus-laden money; he was going to throw it in their faces. If they wanted it, they'd get it.

But he had trouble with the suitcase. It was locked. He couldn't seem to remember where he had put the key, in which pocket. He got a hand stuck in a pocket in hunting, and tore that pocket out, and then tore out another pocket, fell on the contents that scattered on the floor, and got his key. He unlocked the suitcase.

Canta pushed the chair at him again. He kicked it away. He had the suitcase open. He scooped out currency, a dozen of the membrane-wrapped packets, and hurled them in Canta's face. She screamed then again, the most genuine scream she would ever give.

But it seemed that the membrane was a protective wrapping. Because Makaroff began trying to open the packages. He picked at it ineffectively with his fingernails. He started to try his teeth, changed his mind about that, and again fell on the floor, pawing in the litter from his pocket, seeking his pocket-knife.

He was doing that when Savage came in and took him by the throat.

Chapter XII

HAM BROOKS had been laughing for ten minutes. Not continually—the mirth would come from him in spurts of two or three seconds, spaced variously from a minute to two or three minutes apart. He used the time in between to rub his legs—he was in worse shape than Monk had been from being bound tightly in bandages for several hours, and they had beaten him some also—and to make pain shapes with his mouth.

Monk Mayfair, having decided finally that Ham was going to survive, was displaying a studied lack of sympathy.

"What's so funny?" Monk asked.

After he had asked that three times, Ham Brooks looked up and said, "All of the preparations we made, all of the gadgets we used, all of the schemes that were planted—and it ended in an old-fashioned run-after-'em-and-knock-'em-on-the-head!"

"Is that funny?"

"I think so," Ham said. "Maybe I'm a little dizzy."

"It was pretty satisfactory, too," Monk told him. "And you're no more dizzy than usual."

Long Tom Roberts finished lining up the prisoners, tying those who seemed to need it, and prolonging the unconsciousness of those who showed signs of reviving, using for the latter purpose the leg of a chair. There was no fully intact chair in the cabin, and no other piece of furniture that was quite like it had been before.

The Captain of the ship had come in, received the story, whistled at the damage, and was outside assuring passengers that it was just a brawl and that he regretted it greatly. Canta listened to him, and thought he did an excellent job of lying.

Canta went back into the bedroom.

Doc Savage had replaced the virus charged money packets in the suitcase, and was inspecting them carefully with a magnifying glass.

He turned his head, said, "You'd better tell them to quarantine this suite and all the prisoners. Have them shut off the air conditioning so air from this place won't be circulated through the ship."

Canta, shocked by how pale his face was, asked, "Do you think any of the packets broke open?"

"I don't think so. But we'll take no chances."

"You mean we have to remain in here for the rest of the voyage?"

"That's right. And then we'll have to be segregated for several weeks afterward. That won't be so bad—we'll be in the mountains somewhere, at a laboratory that we'll set up to find out what this virus is and dig up a vaccine or treatment."

"Can that be done?"

"It can be tried," he said. "Go on, tell them to keep everyone out of here, and keep the prisoners in the suite."

She frowned at him. He seemed detached, absorbed in the matter of solving the virus that lay ahead. There was no visible elation about him, and certainly no noticeable interest in her as a woman, and a very pretty one.

Canta felt an odd, helpless sort of rage.

She turned and went out and stood by the suite door, listening to the Captain of the *Crosby Square* tell expert lies to his curious passengers.

THE END

ALPHA AND OMEGA by Anthony Tollin

For everything there is a beginning and an ending. This fifteenth volume of our Doc Savage reprints continues our celebration of the Man of Bronze's diamond anniversary as we reprint the first Doc Savage story ever written, along with the last Lester Dent Doc Savage novel ever published.

Readers first encountered the pulp era's greatest superhero 75 years ago when the first issue of *Doc Savage Magazine* debuted on February 17, 1933. Writer Lester Dent's premiere Doc Savage novel, *The Man of Bronze,* introduced readers to Clark Savage, Jr., and his amazing aides, launching a publishing phenomenon.

However, Lester Dent had himself been introduced to Doc Savage the previous December during an editorial conference. For while Dent breathed literary life into the series, Doc Savage had originated months earlier in the fertile imagination of Street & Smith's general manager Henry W. Ralston.

"The beginning of Doc Savage was in the mind of Mr. Ralston," John Nanovic recalled in 1974. "When he brought this up to me, one lunch, he had ALL the characters in mind, with names and descriptions, He also had the purpose of Doc Savage strongly in his mind, and passed all this on to me, and then to Lester Dent.

"After one of the discussions with Les, I wrote a condensed version of what Ralston and I thought the first story should be. And Les worked from that."

"Doc Savage, Supreme Adventurer," written by Nanovic in 1932 from Ralston's plot and concepts, became the prototype for Dent's first novel. "However, this does not mean that Les Dent did not have a major part in the development and 'creation' of Doc Savage. Les put the life and the action into these characters. He made them real, and he made the plots—whether from joint ideas or his own—really zing."

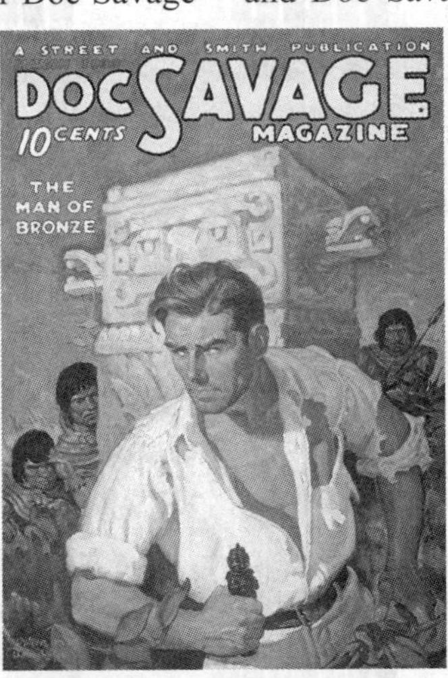

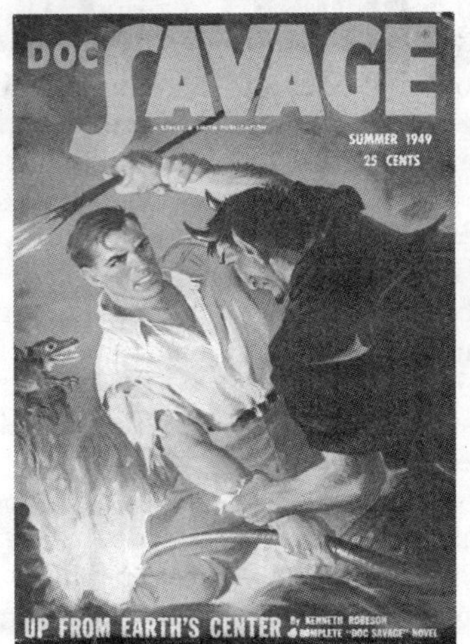

The runaway success of *The Shadow Magazine* and *Doc Savage* led to an explosion of single-character hero pulps. "The success of these trail-blazing magazines kept the pulp magazines alive for an extra decade," Nanovic believed.

After a sixteen-year run, *Doc Savage Magazine* was finally canceled in 1949, along with the rest of Street & Smith's pulp magazine and comic book line. The final issue sent the Man of Bronze to the underworld in *Up from Earth's Center,* the last Doc Savage adventure Dent ever wrote.

However, in 1964, the Man of Bronze staged an unprecedented return to the printed page. Bantam's paperback revival of Doc Savage resulted in a publishing phenomenon that was chronicled in major news stories in *Newsweek, Publishers Weekly* and *Time.* Bantam's Doc Savage reprints launched the numbered paperback adventure format later imitated by *The Executioner*, *The Destroyer* and even *The Shadow.* In 1971, *Time* reported that Doc's "10.5 million copies now in print have realized about $4.5 million in sales." The publisher eventually reprinted all 181 *Doc Savage* pulp novels, along with a lost treasure.

A single Doc Savage thriller had remained unpublished with the 1949 cancellation of the pulp magazine. After a manuscript carbon was unearthed by Norma Dent and Will Murray, the story finally saw print in 1979 as *The Red Spider,* to the delight of Doc Savage's army of fans.

Sanctum Productions and Nostalgia Ventures are proud to commemorate Doc Savage's 75th anniversary with the alpha and omega of the pulp's ultimate superhero: the Man of Bronze's prototype adventure and the final Lester Dent Doc Savage novel to see print, published for the first time with the never-before-seen illustrations created for the story in 1948 by Edd Cartier. •

THE RED SPIDER

A Doc Savage Adventure by Kenneth Robeson

FESTE: Good madonna, why mournest thou?

OLIVIA: Good fool, for my brother's death.

FESTE: I think his soul is in hell, madonna.

OLIVIA: I know his soul is in heaven, fool.

—*Shakespeare*

Chapter I

AT fifteen minutes past six, a Colonel Renwick reached a village named Tyrolstadt, in the American zone. Lunging out of the staff car, he glanced at his wristwatch for the time—it was eighteen-fifteen the way he read it—and he blurted, "Holy cow!" He began to run.

The ramp had been built on the *familen abfahrt,* an easy ski trail at the east edge of the village, and the Colonel reached the spot red-faced and panting. A radar technician named Roberts grinned at the Colonel and said, "Made it!"

"Yeah," gasped Colonel Renwick. "I had a flat tire this side of Salzburg. After that, I had visions of the top brass snatching these chickens off my shoulders."

"There's more than your chickens at stake."

"That's right, too."

"Well, you got here," said Roberts. "Eighteen-forty is Z hour."

The early darkness had a lacing of moonlight, and there was no snow here in the valley, but enough snow smeared the adjacent mountains to make them look like great soiled goats. The ramp was not a terrific thing as rocket-launching ramps came, but it was impressive standing there alone in the alien mountain beauty, like a river bridge out of its element, somewhat. About thirty men were around, either looking or working, more in uniform than not.

"The Russians pushed their hard noses into it, I see," remarked the Colonel.

"Yes. Half a dozen of them," said Roberts.

"Are they full of bliss?"

"Ignorance being bliss, you mean?"

"Exactly."

"I believe they're bliss up to here," said Roberts. "I hope they stay that way."

Roberts said warningly, "Let's change the subject. No telling where you run into a lip-reader these days." He pointed and added, "They're getting ready to ramp the rocket now."

The service party whipped the tarpaulin off the cart on which the rocket was resting, and a loading crane arched up with gears whining. Floodlights came on and covered the scene with an unnecessary amount of blinding light. The radar-tracker keyman in Position Zero jumped out of his nest of apparatus and cursed the floodlight operators for a bunch of Kentucky baboons. They ignored him. The loaders began cursing; the Russians had rushed in and started taking pictures and measurements.

The Russian move was obviously planned, concerted, and surely intended to be as much obstructionist and irritating as fact-getting. As anyone knew, photographs of the outside of the rocket and the tape-measurements they insisted on taking wouldn't tell anybody much about the complicated guts of the thing. The Ivans went right ahead. Camera flashbulbs popped. Steel-tape rulers and notebooks waved. Russians shoved Yankees, and the favor was returned. Colonel Renwick waved his arms and screamed for order. He had a considerable voice, the Colonel had; peasant dogs began barking in alarm as far as two miles away.

With some order restored, Colonel Renwick made them a little speech in which he said he was clarifying the situation.

Radar, the Colonel said, wasn't a new thing, so he wouldn't bother to tell anybody what it was. He presumed everyone knew it was a process of bouncing very short radio waves off an object and catching the reflections and showing them on a screen similar to that in a television tube.

Jamming a radar set so it wouldn't function reliably, the Colonel said, was not a new endeavor either. It had been done with varying success with several methods, beginning with releasing numerous ribbons of metalized paper in the sky, during the last war.

But a method of really messing up the atmosphere over a considerable area so that radar was really jammed, continued the Colonel, was another matter. It was theoretically possible, though, if one ionized the atmospheric layers, preferably those below the tropospheric zone, so that radar microwave lengths were refracted the same way that shortwave radio frequencies are affected by the ionization mystery of the Heaviside layer.

This was the purpose of the experiment tonight. Thanks to the electronic genius of Thomas J. "Long Tom" Roberts, eminent New York electrical engineer in his own right, and associate of the supereminent scientist and adventurer Doc Savage, they were going to show that Yankee ingenuity had triumphed again, and war-minded nations might as well discard their radar for all the good it would do them. There was a slight implication here that the Russians weren't too far from the Colonel's mind.

The eminent Long Tom Roberts listened to the oration, mentally noting a few flaws in it. Except that the mention of Doc Savage wasn't exaggerated—in Long Tom's opinion, it was hard to exaggerate Doc Savage—the speech was a bunch of mush. The facts that were there were all true, so it wasn't mush because of that. It just happened that the Russians were understood to have a radar-jamming rocket similar to the one being shot off tonight. It also happened that the Americans had a considerably better one under wraps. The omissions, rather than the insertions, flawed the Colonel's oratory.

The rocket was to go north to the North Sea.

It didn't. It climbed to twenty thousand feet, threw a whing-ding, and headed for Moscow.

This, as far as the Americans were concerned, seemed to be a calamity. The radar-check network was excellent; the course of the rocket was graphed, charted, and annotated straight to the Iron Curtain. Presumably it passed through and beyond Moscow somewhere and struck the earth or disintegrated in midair when its push-charge was exhausted, depending on whether or not the self-demolition head worked.

The American ambassador sent a note of apology to Moscow. The American commanding general in the zone sent Moscow a note demanding return of the rocket remnants uninspected. The Russians ignored both notes. A writer for Izvestia called the Americans imperialistic toads, boors, thieves, bloated monkeys, said that two thousand people starved to death in New York City that day, and Florida had declared war on California. Molotov vetoed.

In the privacy of the staff car, Colonel Renwick and Long Tom Roberts shook hands ceremoniously.

"I would say," remarked the Colonel, "that we suckered them."

"A perfect scald at this end," Long Tom Roberts agreed. "Or it looked like it, anyway."

"You sure they won't be able to spot an aircraft following the path that rocket took?"

"For about three hours," said Roberts, "Ivan's radar will be blind as a bat."

"How was the timing?"

"On the nose."

"Then the rest is up to Doc."

"The rest," said Long Tom Roberts, suddenly sober, "is really going to be something."

Colonel Renwick looked at him thoughtfully. "You like excitement. Don't you kind of hate missing it?"

Roberts shuddered. "I don't like it when it's tied up with sudden death the way this is going to be."

Chapter II

THE pilot's voice had a faraway, cut-in-glass quality in the ear-plug receivers. He said, "Altitude thirty-four thousand, two hundred and fifteen seconds from Check Nine. Airspeed Mach one-point-sixteen. All green."

Doc Savage said, "All green. Right. All green here, too."

It was already hot in the ship. At slightly under a speed of one thousand miles per hour, there was considerable friction-generated heat, and the refrigeration mechanism was performing as usual—which meant that it either kept things too hot or too cold.

Doc Savage was not riding in the most advantageous spot, either. He was in the pop-off blister, and they needed to do some more design work on it, because the streamlining which had looked well enough in the wind tunnels was not perfect at this speed. Or perhaps it was the altitude; thirty-four thousand feet was pretty close to the earth for speeds over sound. The trouble, though, was that if they went higher, above fifty thousand, where the conditions were better, there was a chance the Soviet radar might top the blackout path made by the runaway rocket—the runaway so carefully computed—and so they were keeping at a comparatively low level. The speed was being kept down, not much over breakthrough, but it was still uncomfortably hot.

Doc Savage waited without much visible suspense on his rather pleasant bronze face. The moonlight that came in through the transparent stress plastic of the blister had a bluish quality that added to the metallic impression that his face gave, and enhanced the slightly darker bronze of his hair, and the remarkable flake-gold aspect of his eyes, which were probably his most striking characteristic.

He wasn't particularly comfortable in the pop-off blister. Each time he tried to shift position to let a little circulation move to another part of his body, he was reminded that the space had been made for a man of average size. He didn't qualify as average. This was not the first time that it had not been an asset to be, as a newspaper had called it, a muscular marvel.

"Cloud floor?" Doc asked, laying a fingertip against the throat microphone.

"Cloud floor twenty-one thousand below," the pilot responded instantly. "Position now forty seconds past. Check Ten. Airspeed Mach one-point-fourteen. Reducing."

"Thanks."

"Heat bothering you, sir?" asked the pilot.

"Not much. I'm wringing wet, is all."

There was a moment of silence. The silence, considering everything, was really remarkable, because at that speed they were flouting sound. The silence of beyond-sound flight, Doc Savage reflected, was one thing that he would probably never become quite accustomed to; it was too much of a contrast to the thousands of hours he had flown before the jet was developed.

He heard the pilot's voice saying, "I hope it doesn't give you cold, sir. There will be what you might call quite a draft when you take to the parachute. And drafts are hell for colds."

In a moment the pilot added, "What are you laughing at, sir?"

"The idea of thinking about catching cold in a situation like this just struck me as funny," Doc told him. "Sorry. No offense. Where are we?"

"Position eight seconds past Check Eleven—two hundred and fourteen miles from Moscow. Altitude still thirty-four thousand feet."

"Break through at Check Twelve."

"I understand, sir."

The pilot's voice had a sudden high edge of tension in it. He was experienced with rocket ships, so going through the wild and still unpredictable zone of compressibility surrounding the speed of sound was not new to him; but doing it had evidently given him nothing but respect. The low altitude wasn't any asset, either.

"Deceleration."

"Right," Doc said.

"Barrel four off."

"Okay here."

"Speed now Mach one-point-zero-nine. Cutting Barrel three."

"All green."

There was no sign that the ship was losing speed; she was pinned in that weird silence, and only if one looked down and saw that the clouds were seemingly moving, was there much impression of existence at all.

"Time zero minus fourteen. Error minus two. Airspeed Mach one-zero-zero-two—I mean, one-point-zero-two." The pilot sounded flustered. "Hell, we're going through, sir. Cross your fingers and pray," he added.

Cracking the sonic wall from the topside was not the hair-raising adventure it had been to the pioneers, but like knowledge about which end of a gun the bullets come from, it could be unnerving when faced. Doc started to take a deep breath; the breath was half indrawn when he knew already they were into it. There wasn't much doubt. It was like going into the jaws of a gigantic machine operating at crazy speed. Like falling into such a machine if you were a tiny object and as fragile as a penny matchbox. It lasted—well—it was hard to know how long it lasted, because terror was timeless, as it always is, and then they were through and the controls were hard again and the rocket ship all in one piece.

"You all right, Savage?" the pilot asked in a shaken voice.

Doc touched his nose and discovered it was bleeding a little. "All green here," he said. "I think the next time I do that, I'd prefer it be at a high altitude."

"Oh, brother!" the pilot said. "You and me both. I'll go up to forty thousand before I try it on the return trip."

"Check point?" Doc asked.

"One minus Check Fourteen, sir. Altitude thirty-one thousand. Airspeed five hundred and eighty."

"Cut to three hundred gradually."

"Right!"

"Scan for signal," Doc directed.

"Scanner on. Signal spotted. Bearing two-seven-three. Error two-point-five."

"Set blow-sight," Doc said.

"Blow-sight set. All green. Error two-point-five dialed." The pilot apparently swallowed. "Good luck, sir. It's been a privilege, if I may say so."

"Thanks, and good luck," Doc said.

He steeled himself and waited. Three-point-eight-one seconds later, the blow-off sight, which was similar to an automatic bomb sight, functioned and the blister in which he was riding was hurled clear of the ship by an explosive charge.

When the blister had decelerated to the proper point, the automatic toss-out sent the parachutes aloft, and the shock that followed was not bad. After that, there was quite a lot of swinging during a long monotonous fall into the cloud floor.

In the cloud floor, there was anything but monotony. He went in at eighteen thousand, the altimeter in the blister told him, and his eyes told him what he was going into—cumulonimbus. The great nodular stacks of clouds like the intestines out of a monster, with the shipped-away anvil tops meant cumulonimbus, thunderheads, wind, lightning, hail, rain, and trouble. Even big planes avoided such things.

He began to feel the darting and jolting of the nachelle; he watched the rate-of-climb uneasily; in this case the instrument might properly be called a rate-of-fall. As he watched it, it stopped and actually began to climb again; the up-currents inside a thunderhead were frequently terrific. He began to tighten all his muscles, then caught himself showing this nervousness and relaxed.

The thunderstorm was not entirely unexpected; even the weather was supposed to be secret behind the Iron Curtain, but the meteorologists were no fools, and they had computed a cold front lying across Moscow. A cold front meant thunderstorms. He had hoped, though, that he wouldn't have to come down through the center of one.

The rate-of-climb needle showed descent again. He watched it, deciding both chutes were still intact and pulling. Losing a chute wouldn't be too bad; there was a reserve for the nachelle, and he wore a pack-chute himself. Every precaution had been taken along that line.

The real danger, the thing that bothered him most, was that the storm might ruin the spot-drop. He was being pinpointed; he had been dropped like a precision-aimed bomb.

Down below on the earth somewhere there was a microwave-beam projector, and the blow-off blister was self-directed automatically and would land somewhere near that. Or would it? The thunderstorm might ruin that.

Rain smeared the plastic blister shell. It made the world a void of grease. Lightning stood out intermittently about him in rods and shaking forks. He could hear the thunder as cannonading. Once there was the ugly clatter of hail against the transparent plastic.

A warning horn began twittering. It was set to operate at three thousand feet above terrain. He consulted gauges quickly; rate of fall was normal, all strain lights were green. He decided not to use the back-pack chute.

He touched the guide-path check-control button. Green. But the orange beside it flickered also. He was, then, not exactly on scheduled descent path, but not too far off it.

He had now a short burst of seconds in which to be tormented by whatever was at hand in his mind to torment him. In other words, he was waiting to hit the ground.

His thoughts went, automatically, to the project as a whole, its magnitude and its significance. These still seemed impressive; they seemed worth the risk he was taking. It was not a nice business, quite likely he was now engaged in the most placid part of it, and he was quite sure this would be the least dangerous portion. But he saw no regrets, and that was important.

He hit.

GOOD GOD, I've landed in a river of some sort, he thought. But then, when there was no rolling and tumbling, and after the first wild bouncing and splash a comparative stillness except for the thunder of the rain, he changed the conviction. He had merely hit the edge of a gully or ditch and bounced into it. There was a sensation in his feet and he looked down and saw the faces of the instruments—luminous by radiance—disappear one by one. When he explored with a hand, the hand went into water.

He came out of his inactivity, startled to realize he'd just been sitting there enjoying the novelty of being earthbound again.

His hand located the black-light projector and he pointed it outward and pressed the control. At the same time, he put on the scanner that went with the arrangement for seeing in the dark.

He was sitting like a rather elongated glass egg

in a ditch about ten feet deep and not much wider, and the coursing water was about two feet deep. It was raining pitchforks, and the rain didn't help operation of the black-light scanner.

He remained where he was, perfectly attentive to a certain light. It was supposed to flash, controlled by the man who was to meet him here. Presently it did glow. Green.

Throwing open the safety belts, he touched the exit trigger; with a jolt the blister opened almost in two halves. When he stood up, the naturalness of the rain was against his face.

A voice on the ditch edge above addressed him in very good Russian. *"Kak vahse zdarovye, tovarich?"*

Although it was the equivalent of a "How are you doing, pal?" he jumped violently, then said, "That's a fine greeting. Where is your sense of drama?"

It was Ham Brooks on the ditch edge; he knew that in spite of the darkness. Ham Brooks was one of his group of five aides who had been associated with him almost from the beginning of his career.

"I take it you're all right," Ham said. "Well, I'm not. It's this damn mud. I never knew mud could be so thoroughly mud. Whenever I take a step, I keep expecting it to squirt out of my ears."

Ham's handling of the English language was completely Harvard; it was an oddity about Ham that he spoke a number of foreign languages with completely native accenting, but his English was so affected as to be almost irritating. He was a lawyer by trade. A superior lawyer. But he rarely took time out from the pursuit of excitement to do any court work.

"Coast clear?" Doc Savage asked.

"As far as I can tell," said Ham Brooks. "You missed the zero spot about a hundred and fifty yards. I guess it was that thunderstorm. How was the trip in?"

"Fine," Doc said. "Here, catch this line. I want you to haul up two equipment packs."

The apparatus was in two aluminum cases enclosed in sponge rubber and waterproof plastic film. Ham drew them out of the gully. "Grab the end of the line." Then, when Doc stood beside him, Ham asked, "What about the chariot you arrived in?"

"The dropping blister, you mean? It is autotimed for demolition in two hours."

"Won't the explosion leave pieces and get attention?"

"No explosion," Doc said. "A Thermit compound. Everything will simply burn up."

"In this rain?"

"All materials entering the structural composition of the blister were impregnated during manufacture. They'll burn, all right, rain or no rain."

Ham suddenly laughed. "Doc, you've no idea how good it is to hear you casually tossing off the incredible. I've been in this dopey country just long enough to forget that your kind of efficiency exists."

"What is the general picture?" Doc asked, interested.

"Not good," Ham said. "There's more bestiality than efficiency. But don't get me wrong—on the side of bestiality, there is plenty of efficiency."

"You're not just speaking as a capitalist?"

"No," Ham said. "I'm speaking as a guy who wishes the human race would come to its senses and stop letting cold-blooded tyrants cut its throat."

"What's your transportation?"

"I have a car," Ham explained. "It's parked in the brush down the way a bit."

"Car? How did you manage that?"

"Monk."

"Oh."

"That part's a long and painful story which I will skip at this point," Ham Brooks explained. "But I think I should break the news to you—hold your hat—that our Lieutenant Colonel Andrew Blodgett "Monk" Mayfair is now a commissar in the Russian Textile Workers' Union. I don't understand exactly what that is, but it can't be as important as he claims it is."

"Monk's status rates him a personal car, eh?"

"And a chauffeur."

"Oh. Where is the chauffeur?"

"It galls my soul to tell any man this," Ham said bitterly. "But the chauffeur stands right in front of you. Me."

"You!"

"Pray to God it may never happen to a dog—yes."

Doc had trouble with a grin. "Hard for you to take, eh?"

"Frankly," said Ham, "rather than put up with the indignity, I have seriously considered letting civilization go right ahead to hell."

Chapter III

THE car was a Russakoff, and seemed to be a very earnest imitation of one of the best-known American makes, even to body line and radiator grilling. It ran quite well, too—that was because it was a commissar's car, Ham Brooks explained.

They loaded in and drove through squirm-drifting sheets of cold rain over a road that was bumpy and full of abrupt twists and turns. It had also been paved with cobblestones of the general size of washtubs, probably during the reign of Ivan the Terrible.

"About thirty miles to Moscow," Ham said. "We will enter by the Nikos Kaja a Ulitza, Ulitza Dsershinskoge Spelenka—that's all one street, to give you an idea of how simple things are around here."

"Do I need any briefing?" Doc asked.

"You'll have more need for the luck of a saint," Ham said. He hesitated, then added, "No, you'll just need to operate in your usual fashion. I tell you, this place runs people nuts, and I'm forgetting just how efficient you can be."

"Let's have some details," Doc said. "Less the around-the-bush technique."

"Nobody takes a straight line in Russia," Ham said. "It gets you to tomorrow too quick. Seriously, though, we've had some good luck and some bad."

"How bad?"

"The worst snag," Ham said, "is picking our apple, now that we've found him. I'll skip a lot of the details, some of which have been in your hands for some time, and some of which we felt too vital to chance interception. But the general picture is that there is one official, a central coordinator or whatever you want to call him—one spider who has hold of one end of all the threads that make up the web—who is our answer. If we can grab him, get truth serum and drugs into him, get the facts out of him, get them recorded, and get them back to the part of the world where they know what daylight is, well, we've done our job. His name is Frunzoff."

Doc Savage watched the spongy blobs of pale milk light that the headlamps were pushing over the road. He was impressed.

"Ham, that's a remarkable piece of work in itself," he said. "Nobody, as far as I know, and I've had access to the most confidential reports of several nations, has been able to learn the identity or even the existence of such a spider, as you call him."

Ham Brooks was surprised. "But, hell, you told us that was what we were to look for when we started the job."

"I didn't have a single fact," Doc said. "But it is only logical that Stalin, in view of his phobia about assassination, and its not remote likelihood, would have established a master control responsible only to him, and completely unknown even to his associates in the Kremlin."

"He has. Frunzoff is it."

"Who is Frunzoff? What is his background?"

"That," said Ham, "is what I could be trite and call the sixty-four-dollar question. Frunzoff can be male, female, bird, beast, or catfish, and we would be none the wiser. And not surprised, incidentally."

"You haven't put your finger on Frunzoff, then?"

"No."

"Any leads?"

"Monk claims he has some," Ham said. "I'm not too sure. You know how the big ape is."

Doc said fervently, "I hope his leads aren't female, the way they've been known to be."

"So do I!" Ham said explosively.

"How about that?"

"Well, for Monk, he's been remarkably nonpartial so far," Ham admitted. "I think that this commissar job has let him see enough of the way they do things here to keep him thoroughly scared. He has warned me a dozen times that if there's one slip, we'll all disappear like drops of water on a hot stove."

"That doesn't sound too much like Monk."

"Wait until you see Commissar Michevitch—that's Monk," Ham said, chuckling. "When you've seen that, you've seen something."

WIND struck the car, repeated rushing roaring blows, and the rain made great washings overhead and a sound of a continuous small waterfall under the wheels. There were no streetlights yet. Doc palmed some of the condensation from inside the window, looked out, and decided with astonishment that the number of ramshackle frame huts, typical Russian village *izba,* meant they were in the outskirts of Moscow.

"Any chance of roadblocks and an inspection?" Doc asked.

"I was hoping you wouldn't think of that," Ham told him uneasily. "Sure there is. If it wasn't raining cats and dogs, I would guarantee it. How are you fixed for identification?"

"That's taken care of. I'm Ivar Golat, a messenger for the GPU, the State Political Administration. You don't know me, so in case we're stopped, I'm just a *tovarich* you gave a lift. Where are you quartered?"

"With Monk. On Ulitza Ogarewa."

"That's near the Kremlin."

"A few blocks away."

"Monk will be there?"

"Supposed to be." Ham suddenly slammed on the brakes, changed his mind, blew the horn angrily, and stamped on the accelerator. The performance had no effect on the bedraggled raincoated soldier who stood in their path; he simply pointed his rifle at them. Ham said, "Damn!" and slid the wheels to a stop. "Road check," he told Doc. "Means nothing, probably."

The soldier, a gaunt rough-looking specimen, took his time and worked on their nerves a little; he aimed his rifle with great deliberation, first at Ham, then at Doc, after ostensibly cocking the piece. Then he strolled around to the side of the car and kicked the door.

"Predooprezhdeneeye?" he said.

"How in tophet do you expect us to see any warning signs in this rain?" Ham demanded in Russian, thrusting out his head. "And why don't you stay in shelter, you fool?"

The soldier sneered, jerked open the car door, and popped a flashlight beam inside. He noted the labels on Doc's equipment cases, and the official seals—they were good counterfeits—and he jumped back hastily. *"Mne zhahl!"* he said uneasily. He waved them on.

Ham put the car in motion, and when they had rolled a ways, said, "Decking you out as a messenger for the State Political Administration was a good idea. When he saw the phony seals, he figured you were working, and it scared him into some courtesy."

"Is that a good sample of courtesy?"

"It's the general idea," Ham said. "That guy was probably a security agent. You can generally spot the small-timers like him by their insolence."

There were streetlights now, and a little automobile traffic. Doc could distinguish houses of the czarist era with their pillared porticoes, and here and there a church, usually abutted in close proximity by some large and ugly barrackslike structure which had been built during the anti-religious era prior to the German invasion. They were following Ulitza Dsershinskoge, one of the main thoroughfares which wheel-spoked from the Kremlin area on the Moskwareka. The street had a tramway and a busline, and both types of conveyances were incredibly crowded.

Ham made a turn, got on Nikos Kaja a Ulitza, and presently he said, "This is a little out of the way, but everybody drives past here once."

They were in Red Square, the area along the Kremlin's somber wall, between the Nikolski and Spaski gates, where was located the Bratskiye Mogili, the Brothers' Graves, where were buried the five hundred revolutionists killed in the October Revolution, and others added later, including the victims of the explosion of August 25, 1919.

Here was the shrine of Soviet. They could see presently the Lenin Mausoleum, which stood out from the other graves, a somber red structure, designed by an architect named Schuseff in 1924, built first of wood, then made over in stone. At the entrance, spotlighted, were the guards always to be seen there, and the area on the roof where Stalin and high Soviet associates are so often newsreeled while reviewing displays of Soviet pageantry.

Ham saluted the Kremlin wall with a wry, "Behind there, presumably, good old Joe is hard at work. They tell me he functions at night, like an owl."

"Let's hope he has no crystal ball in which he sees a couple of Americans with bad intentions in the neighborhood."

Ham chuckled. "I second that with bowed head."

THEY turned on Red Square, which was approximately a kilometer long, and Ham drove west and across Bewojuzli Place. They began to leave the neighborhood; the old city which had been residential at one time, but was now taken over by the offices of Soviet bureaucrats.

Ham Brooks saw Doc Savage's hand at the open window, frowned, and said, "You toss something out?"

"Yes."

"What?"

"Just some stuff. A powder."

Ham grimed uneasily. "You've done it three or four times, haven't you? Think we're being followed?"

"It would be worth knowing if we were," Doc said.

"If you want to see a man jump squarely out of a perfectly good skin, just let me find out we're being followed," Ham said.

The street where Ham and Monk were living had a tired grimy age about it, as if the dead years had been stacked there to wait out eternity. Ham turned the car into what had once been a coach entrance, first alighting to unlock large iron-strapped doors, and Doc waited until the lights were off and the engine dead. Then he removed his equipment cases and followed Ham up a succession of worn steps.

"Monk will sure be glad to see you," Ham said. "He has been putting up a big front about not worrying." Ham came to a door, winked at Doc, then gave the door a kicking and said in a vicious guttural voice completely unlike his own, "Security police! Come out with your hands up, son of a capitalist!"

Ham wore a considerable grin during the first thirty seconds of waiting; then he lost the pleased expression slowly.

Doc said dryly, "You fellows are still pulling practical jokes on each other, I take it."

Ham grimaced. "I wonder if I scared the big lug so bad he jumped out of a window?" He inserted a key in the lock, turned it, and called prudently, "Take it easy, you missing link. Our visitor's here," before he pushed into the room. Then he looked around, said, "Hey, where are you, Monk?" He ran into the kitchen and bedroom. "He doesn't seem to be here," Ham said, and alarm made his voice a little higher.

"Would that be serious?" Doc asked sharply.

"If he's not getting back at me for that gag, it's serious," Ham said. "He was going to be here." Ham began a second tour of the apartment, which was furnished with almost painful sparseness. "I don't know what to do about this," he said.

"Let's check to see whether we were followed," Doc said. He opened one of the equipment cases, took out a small vial, glanced at Ham, and asked, "One of us will have to saunter out into the street. You belong in the neighborhood, so maybe you'd better do it."

"What in blazes do I look for?"

"Got a cold?"

"No."

"All right. Take a sniff of this." Doc uncorked the small glass vial and passed it to Ham.

"Quite a perfume," Ham said, puzzled. "A little different from anything I ever smelled before."

Doc told him, "Just go out in the street and cross it a couple of times. See if you detect the identical odor. It's distinctive enough that you won't make an error. But it will not be very strong."

Ham was gone from the apartment not quite five minutes, and he came back wearing alarm.

"It's in the street, faintly," he said. "What in the devil is it?"

Doc named the chemicals. "You're not a chemist, so that may not mean much. But several times during the trip in from where I landed, I tossed small quantities of two different chemical concoctions out on the road. One type at one point, and the other a couple of hundred feet farther on. The wheels of any machine following us would pick up one, then the other—the two when combined cause that odor."

"Good God!" Ham blurted. "Then we were followed!"

"It isn't positive," Doc warned. "It could have been another car accidentally following our course part of the way."

"Maybe, but the way I buy it, it scares me." Ham yanked a suitcase out and began dumping clothing into it. "Let's get out of here."

Chapter IV

DOC SAVAGE slid over the edge of the windowsill and poised there a moment, supported by the grip of his bronze fingers, while he told Ham, "I'll leave the cord in place, in case you want to come out in a hurry by the same route. If it's an ambush, both front and back doors will be watched, and they might watch this route, too. So be careful."

Ham shuddered and said, "I remember climbing down that cord one time. I'd about as soon jump. Be careful yourself."

The cord was silk and there were knots at eighteen-inch intervals, and at every third knot there was a small attached loop which could be of use. To one end of the cord was affixed a small folding grapple hook. The whole thing was a somewhat childish gimmick, and certainly primitive except for the excellence of the workmanship, but Doc Savage was convinced that the thing had saved his life more than once in the past, so he always carried it. He descended to an alley court below, and although he did not seem to expend much effort, climbing or descending the cord was, as Ham had indicated, not an easy feat.

He had made no perceptible noise, and now he moved quietly along a wall, beginning to feel a little silly about the precautions, and shoved his head around a corner, almost against the back of a man who was standing against the wall, doing his best to make himself part of it. A nice quick dividend for caution, Doc thought, wondering if he could ever start breathing again.

Considering that the man was all of twelve inches from Doc's eyes, he seemed a remarkably vague figure. Doc withdrew around the corner with all of the reckless haste of a snail in heavy going. Then he tried to decide whether the man was really nine feet tall and bristling with machine guns. Probably not. Thank God for the thickness of the night, though.

The important thing was that the fellow had been looking in the other direction. Doc waited. He could hear the other taking the long halting breaths of a man doing a nerve-racking job that was going too slowly.

That lasted two or three minutes, then Doc heard footsteps. The watcher heard them, too; he promptly stepped back around the corner, which put him where Doc had been standing an instant before.

It was very dark. The rain had stopped falling, but water still dripped from eaves. Everyone and everything seemed to be listening and straining.

"Seryi!"

The footsteps stopped.

"Psssst! Seryi!" This from the watcher who had all but backed into Doc bodily.

"F chom d'la?" asked a woman's pleasant voice. "What is the matter, Mahli?"

"It is you, Seryi?"

"Of course."

"Ah, good. No one has left by this route. How long do I have to stand here in the infernal rain?"

"It has stopped raining, Mahli."

"It will start again. How long do I have to stay here?"

"No longer. You may go now, Mahli."

The word *mahli* was Russian for "little" or "small," and the girl Seryi was using it in a

... Doc put out a hand all cupped to go over the girl's mouth.

manner that indicated a dry humor, Doc concluded. The fellow Mahli was only slightly smaller than a tank, Doc reflected, watching him stalk off without another word.

He waited for some sign from the woman. There was none. Apparently she was standing perfectly still. Then a long ruffianly gobble of thunder came from the dark bowels of the sky, and a sudden spotting of rain fell. Feet clicked lightly, and Doc recoiled. The woman Seryi had chosen the same shelter as the man: she stood almost against Doc.

Having weighed everything, Doc put out a hand all cupped to go over the girl's mouth.

SERYI was somewhat taller than he thought, and so he got hold of her throat at first; finally he had to tighten down on the columnar softness of her neck to preserve some silence. A few things—the smoothness of her skin, her activity, the swiftness of her reactions—indicated a young woman. He was also kicked, scratched, and had some hair loosened. He said, in Russian fortunately, *"Teekha!"* He said it twice. Then she stopped kicking, scratching, and hair-yanking. She was very still in his grip.

He repeated the word for quietly again. *"Teekha!"* Then he asked, "Will you scream if I release you?"

She shook her head vigorously no.

"Will you give sensible answers?" he asked.

Her head moved to indicate yes.

He removed his hands warily. "All right. Who are you?"

"Seryi," she said.

"I don't mean your name," he said

She turned around and gave him the jackpot. "Mr. Savage, you and Mr. Brooks must get out of here in a hurry," she said. "It's very important. You are in definite danger here."

Doc took a moment to recover. "Who do you think I am?" he asked cautiously.

"Stand here and play guessing games!" She stamped a foot. "Let the secret police show up! Then have guessing games!" She reached out and gripped his arm. "Oh, I'm doing this all wrong. Monk Mayfair sent me."

"Who?"

"I was in a car waiting near the Minin and Pozharski monument on Red Square," she said. "I was supposed to spot your car, but I didn't. I missed it. I drove into this street and turned and drove back again, and waited at the corner awhile. I didn't see your car, concluded you had arrived, and came around to tell Mahli I would take over—"

"Who is Mahli?" Doc asked. "Besides being the human tank who just left here."

"Mahli? My cousin. I asked him to help me." She was speaking in a low, excited voice. Suddenly Doc turned his flashlight beam on her face for a moment. It was a very sweet face and surprisingly composed. She gasped at the light, said, "I hope you're satisfied."

"I'm satisfied you're very good-looking," Doc said. "Unfortunately, that's about the size of it. Who is this Monk Mayfair?"

"Your caginess is a little childish," she said bitterly. "Mr. Savage, Monk Mayfair discovered the secret police suspected something. Monk couldn't come here. He would be seized. He sent me to intercept you and take you to him. What could be simpler than that?"

"Almost anything would be simpler," Doc said. "Come inside."

They reëntered the house via the back door, and Ham listened with astonishment to the pretty Russian girl's story. "You can take us to Monk?" he asked suspiciously.

"Not tomorrow or next month," Seryi said angrily. "I might if you accompany me at once."

Ham looked at Doc unhappily. "You know Monk and his reaction to a pretty face. I thought he was cured, but maybe he wasn't."

"I think," said Seryi, "I should resent that very bitterly."

Doc asked Seryi, "You actually saw Monk recently? Is that your story?"

"Yes," she said. "Of course."

"When?"

"Tonight."

"By any chance, did Monk shake hands with you?" Doc asked speculatively.

"I don't recall Monk shaking my hand," Seryi said. And then she flushed. "But I do think he held both of them for awhile."

Ham laughed bitterly. "I believe she knows Monk, all right."

"Let's see your hands," Doc said. He did nothing but hold the girl's hands for a moment, then release them. But Ham Brooks broke out a relieved expression.

Puzzled, Seryi asked, "What is that perfume? It's quite distinctive, isn't it? We don't have much contact with perfume here in Russia, but I like it."

THE car to which Seryi led them was quite old, and parked some distance down the street. Doc, eyeing the machine, doubted very much that it would run; they did have trouble starting it, the battery being down. Doc used the crank that Seryi pushed into his hands. He gathered, from the way she gave instructions, that she was quite familiar with the wreck.

"To rate a car, even a clunker like this one, you

must be someone rather important," Ham said suspiciously.

"I am a secretary in the Supreme Council of National Economy," Seryi said curtly. "And it is a very dependable car. It is much superior to walking."

The machine began to shake all of its loose parts. Doc tossed the crank in the back and got in. "What has happened to Monk?"

"I told you, Mr. Savage. He suspects they have become suspicious of him."

"What I probably meant," Doc said, "is how did he happen to send a girl, a strange girl at that, with such an important message?"

"I would say it was very logical. He had to send a messenger who would not be suspected."

"And you wouldn't be suspected."

She nodded. "Not by the secret police." She glanced wryly at Doc. "But by you, I think I am very suspect."

"You blame me?"

Seryi drove the old car at a sedate pace. It held together, although it seemed to gather itself and leap with a great clatter over some of the rougher places in the street.

"I think I'd better tell you two things," she said. "First is about my brother, Ancil—he is supposed to have left his life when a Soviet plane crashed in the Nazi territory near the end of the war, but actually he walked away from the crash quite alive and made his way by means of a great effort to New York City, where he is now married, at peace with the U.S. Immigration Bureau, and very happy in his work as a dance instructor in the theater. That is the first thing. The second thing is that my brother Ancil met Mr. Monk Mayfair in New York in the course of some interest which Mr. Mayfair showed in the theater—"

"In the chorus girls, probably," Doc said.

"Well, I would say so, too," Seryi said, smiling slightly. "Anyway, my brother Ancil asked Mr. Mayfair to look me up if he ever traveled through Moscow, and Mr. Mayfair did so. That is how I met Mr. Mayfair."

"Is that why you're doing this?"

"It is one reason," she said. "I am most grateful to know my brother is alive and well—and quite glad, also, that the secret police don't know about it. If they did—poof. Off to Siberia I would go."

"The other reason?"

"I will be frank about that, too," Seryi said. "I would like to make a friend who could whisk me away to America."

"That would interest Monk, too," Ham said sourly.

"There is one more thing," Seryi explained.

"What's that?"

"I am to tell you that Frunzoff has one gold tooth and lives at Seven Botsch Bronnaja Ulitza," Seryi said. "That means nothing to me. But Monk asked me to tell you."

DOC SAVAGE had the impression that he had been hit squarely between the eyes with a hammer; he was so surprised that his head began aching. He heard Ham, beside him, resume breathing with an effort. "My God!" Ham gasped. "Monk must have been busier than a clamdigger!"

"The name means something to you?" Seryi asked.

"What name was that?" Ham asked warily.

"Frunzoff."

Ham hesitated only a moment, then lied glibly, "Not a thing, I'm sorry to say. And I'm surprised Monk would ask you to pass along something like that. Let's see—could it be code? But I can't imagine what kind of code."

"Mr. Mayfair was very excited," Seryi said. "So it could be some kind of code, perhaps."

"What excited Monk?"

"Danger, I imagine. As a matter of fact, Mr. Mayfair was dreadfully upset."

On a rising alarm, Ham said, "That doesn't sound good. Normally Monk wouldn't be upset with a wildcat in each hip pocket."

"He was particularly emphatic that I should tell you of Frunzoff," the girl said.

"What address was that again?" Doc inquired.

"On the Botsch Bronnaja Ulitza, number seven."

"I see."

"Do you know where that is?"

"It's a little beyond Twerskoj Boulevard," Doc said. "That right?"

"Yes."

Doc became silent. He was inclined to mentally damn Monk for giving this girl the Frunzoff name. Frunzoff, the way Ham had explained it, was the key to the whole elaborate plot. Frunzoff was the man they wanted—therefore it was vitally important that nobody know that they wanted Frunzoff. Their scheme was intricate, and included getting the information they wished out of Frunzoff without even Frunzoff knowing it had happened. Doc glanced at Ham when they passed a streetlight, and Ham's face was a mask of alarm. Monk was in desperate straits, Ham believed.

Doc leaned forward and tapped the girl's shoulder. "Where are you taking us?"

"To Mr. Mayfair," she said.

"Be more specific."

She hesitated. Her shoulders rose and fell. "It's my apartment, as a matter of fact."

Ham whistled softly—and got his face slapped. The girl's hand flew out; the whack of her palm against Ham's cheek was a sharp sound. "Hey!" Ham blurted. "You little tramp—" The girl began to sob, and the car swerved.

Doc reached over and grasped the wheel. "Easy on the temperament," he said.

"Damn you, I'm not what do you call it?—a tramp," Seryi sobbed angrily. Then she looked up, her face became much more distorted, and she screamed, "Watch out! The secret police!"

DOC had already seen the car, an old-fashioned job with a squarish body, a sedan. It had come up beside and moved out to pass them; now it made a lunge at their front wheels, and Doc had a moment when he felt sure that the old car was beefed up with armor plate around the fenders. It was too late for the notion to be of any help, because the police car promptly hit them.

There was no siren, no shouting. The machine just hit them. Their front wheels held together, but a tie rod snapped. The car went out of control, took a crazy lunge to the left, then to the right, and smashed into the rear of the assailant machine. The latter car, knocked crosswise of the road, skidded a few yards and rolled over on its side. Men spilled out as their own car came to a crazy stop.

Doc gripped Seryi's shoulder, asked, "Know which way is south?"

"Yes! But they're armed! We haven't a chance—"

"Run south," Doc said. "Don't argue. Two blocks, then turn on Glinischt Street. We'll overtake you there." To Ham he said, "I'm going to use smoke on them."

The street winked redly twice with flame from a gun muzzle. Doc fumbled for a moment in his clothing, seeking the gadget he wanted, then found it and let fly. It was a smoke grenade, cylindrical, not much more than an oversized Fourth of July firecracker in size. It landed in the street and made very little sound letting go, hardly any sound at all, but produced a great deal of astonishingly black smoke. The stuff started as a dark melon, became progressively a sheep, a calf, a horse, a small house in size.

There was another shot in what was now complete blackness. *"Net! Net! Net!"* an excited Russian voice said. *"Smatreete!"* There was no more shooting after the warning.

Doc, very loudly in Russian also, said, "There is a fire!" There was no fire in the sense he hoped they would think, but they might believe for a moment the smoke was coming from a burning car.

He began retreating, and came out of the smoke. In a moment, another figure stumbled out of the blackness. Ham. They ran away from the spot as quietly as possible.

Doc looked ahead, saw no sign of Seryi, and Ham was evidently doing the same thing, because Ham whispered, "Good Lord, she's fast on her feet to get out of sight."

They lengthened their stride now. They came to Glinischt Street, turned into it. They stopped.

"She isn't here. She didn't run for it," Doc said grimly. "She wasn't harmed. I told her exactly what to do."

"I heard you," Ham said. "I can't understand what could have gone wrong." He turned and stepped back into the street where the smoke was. His dive for cover was phenomenal, accompanied by a crashing of pistol fire.

"Don't be a fool," Doc said.

Ham shuddered. "Now you tell me! I think they're running away themselves, though."

"What?"

"Take a look. I don't mean stick your head into the street; for God's sake, don't do that. But you've got that mirror gimmick, haven't you?"

The mirror gimmick was more or less conventional, a mirror attached with a swivel to a telescoping rod affair. Not the best sort of periscope, but compact. Doc, examining the street by thrusting the thing around the corner, felt that it left a great deal to be desired. But it showed him a great deal to be puzzled with.

"They've got the girl?" Ham asked, carefully getting nowhere near the corner.

"Yes, I think so. You're right about their flight, too. They're leaving. In a hurry. And not coming this direction."

"That's odd," Ham muttered. "For secret police, that's a mighty odd move."

Doc asked dryly, "You think they are secret police?"

"No more than you do," Ham said bitterly. "Doc, we're being foxed. This was arranged. That girl didn't flee because she didn't want to."

"It wasn't an assassination attempt," Doc said. "It went through the motions of one, but there was no steam behind it."

"Could the whole object have been to give the girl a chance to leave us?"

"Maybe. A trifle elaborate, though, wouldn't you say?"

"It has me stumped."

"No, I think you got the essential point," Doc said thoughtfully. "The girl made contact with us, gave us Frunzoff's address, and with her job done, she was removed from our clutches, so to speak, in a way that might let her be useful to them again later."

"In other words, we're supposed to think she's what she said she was, a girl very grateful because she has a brother happily in New York?"

"I'm guessing about that," Doc confessed. "I don't like the guess too well. She seemed a decent sort."

"They always do. What about Frunzoff?"

"Did you bring one of the equipment cases?"

Ham said, "Yes." He went to a niche and produced the case. "You've got the other, I see. Does this mean we go to that address and try for Frunzoff?"

"We've got to," Doc said. "There's too much at stake to be cautious."

Chapter V

NUMBER seven on Botsch Bronnaja Ulitza was one of those low aristocratic mansion houses with pillar-porticoes against a background of church cupolas and a few modernistic boxes of buildings turned shockingly ugly by city grime. They reached it to the accompaniment of an appropriate display by the weather—thunder ran thumping through the narrow street and rain began falling in bucketfuls.

"What the devil do we do now?" Ham asked gloomily. "Walk in? That's crazy, isn't it? I wish we knew what happened to Monk."

Doc found a niche which afforded some shelter from the downpour. "Let's use our heads a little before we get in any deeper," he said. "First, about Monk: either they've got him, or he's alarmed and hiding out. The girl said he was hiding out in her apartment."

Ham blew rainwater off his lips. "I don't believe a word she said."

"Does Monk have two-way radio?"

"Yes, but that's not going to help. We found out one thing—the Communists have electronic monitors that scan every wavelength automatically, and the moment an unauthorized signal goes on, a receiver is thrown on that frequency. We haven't dared use radio."

"What about alternate hideouts?" Doc asked.

"We have two. But Monk wouldn't be—or would he?" Ham swore gently. "Damn! Do you suppose I've overlooked the obvious answer to his whereabouts?"

"How far are these hideouts?"

"Not so very far. We bunched them, figuring we might want to get from one to another in a hurry. One is on Nastass, the other farther out."

"Go check them," Doc said.

"Now?" Ham gasped.

"Yes."

Ham hesitated, then said gloomily, "Who do you think you're fooling? You're trying to get me out of here in case it's a trap."

"I'm not trying to fool you," Doc said quickly. "I do want you away from here in case it's an ambush. And why not? If they get all of us, the whole project is shot. And I'm also worried about Monk, and want to locate him if he's free."

"Is that an order?" Ham asked bitterly. "If it's not, the devil with it."

"It's an order, Ham."

"You can guess what I think of it," Ham said. "But all right. Where will you meet me?" Ham gave the address on Nastass Ulitza, and another farther out in the suburbs on a street called Corski. "They're just rooms we rented. Will you try them?"

Doc indicated the house where Seryi had said the man known as Frunzoff lived. "My work in there will take at least two hours."

Ham shivered. "You think you can do it single-handed?"

"I can try."

Ham said, "I've argued with you before. I'll be back here, then, provided I have a potful of luck."

WHEN Ham had sidled warily away and was lost in the blinding rain, Doc Savage unscrewed the mirror from the small telescoping rod which had held it, and now he had about eighteen inches of hollow tubing. The diameter of this, at the small end, was not much more than a darning needle. To the large end, he attached a small rubber bulb which he first filled with colorless liquid from a small flask which he kept unsealed no longer than was absolutely necessary. During this operation, and particularly while the flask was open, he held his breath, and after that he was careful to carry the tube with the filled bulb attached well to the lee so that the lunging wind would whip the fumes away from him.

Now he moved brazenly on the sidewalk, walking openly and directly to the house. Three stone steps led up to the garish portico, and he mounted them quickly.

He stood beside the door, felt for the lock, located the keyhole, inserted the end of his hollow-tube gadget, and gave the bulb a long slow squeeze. He held his breath during this operation, and not until he stepped away from the vicinity of the door did he resume normal breathing.

A passageway, carriage-width, separated this house from the adjacent one, and he walked into that, reloading the syringe affair as he went. There was a door at the back, but it had no lock or keyhole that he could find; evidently it was secured by a bar inside. He knelt down and tried the point of the tube under the door, and it would pass. He emptied the bulb again.

If there had been a sound in the house, the whooping of thunder and the beating rush of the rain had blanketed it.

Back at the front door again, he used a lock pick for a few moments. That got the door open about six inches—as far as a chain inside would let it swing. He tinkered with the chain for awhile and got nowhere.

He used a Thermitlike compound on the chain; a bead of it which he quickly embedded in a sticky pellet that would ignite it presently by chemical reaction, and which also served as an adhesive to hold the Thermit to the steel chain. He closed the door and waited.

The stuff burned through the chain briefly. He could see traces of the glare around the edge of the closed door, and inside the house the display must have been blinding. But it was quicker than fooling around with a hacksaw. The stuff was, in effect, a chemical substitute for a cutting torch.

He opened the door and stepped inside. In chairs on each side of the door sat men with thick bodies and heavy faces, uniformed, with submachine guns on their laps.

Doc Savage looked thoughtfully at the two guards. Presently he said in a voice of normal loudness, *"Slyshyte lee vy menyah?"* When they did not stir, he repeated the same thing amiably in English, "Do you hear me?" No response.

He reached out and put a finger against one of the heavy narrow foreheads and shoved lightly. The guard toppled and would have fallen had Doc not caught him quickly and righted him. "Nice nap, boys," he said cheerfully, and went quickly to the rear of the house.

There were two more guards at a back door. There was one at a window. All were in chairs, and all slept from the effects of the anaesthetic gas he had introduced with the syringe gadget.

The house had three floors, and the downstairs area had been severely plain. He found a staircase and began climbing; at the top he found another guard, this one lying on the floor and breathing heavily through his nose.

Now the furnishings changed suddenly from drab to utter luxury; he was walking on a carpet that seemed to brush his ankles, passing mirrors in great gilt frames and oil paintings which were museum pieces. The paintings startled him. He saw a Veronese, two Van der Weydens, a Michelangelo, a Rubens, a Gainsborough which he suspected was a copy but which might not be.

He began to wear a frown, and back of it was an excitement rising and tightening. At a rough guess there was around two million dollars' worth of paintings here in the hall, and that did not seem the stuff that a trap would be made of.

Frunzoff, as they understood it, was the faceless nonentity who, if anything happened to Stalin, would suddenly become number-one man. Frunzoff, then, would be the one man Stalin had decided to trust; he was the receptacle for all the centralized knowledge to which Stalin and no one else had access. Such a man would be important. He would be likely to have a couple of million in old masters hanging in his hall.

He began using the syringe gadget on doors. There were three doors opening off the hall, all closed. He went to each in turn, working rapidly. The anaesthetic gas, colorless and odorless, was one that he had developed a long time ago. It produced quick unconsciousness, and the period of stupor could be varied by changing the ingredients. The formula he was using now ensured about three hours of coma. The effect occurred entirely within the first minute of release; after that it went through an oxidizing process with the oxygen in the air and became harmless. That was why he was holding his breath.

He tried the doors. Two were unlocked. The first of these let him into a conference room, the second into an office. He leaped to a desk here and noticed that his hands were made a little unsteady by excitement as he searched. The name was Frunzoff, all right. But Frunzoff was the first name. The second was Nosh. Frunzoff Nosh. "Nosh" meant "knife" in the Russian language, which might be significant.

He used his lock pick on the third door, and stepped inside. The sitting room was enormous. There was a Gobelin on the wall; the rug was a priceless Oriental that dated back to Crusade days. He passed through a door.

For a moment he looked down at the man who slept on a great silly bed that was all of twelve feet square and placed in the center of the room on a raised dais. The man wore silk. Everything in the room that could be silk was silk, and it was all one shade of bird's-egg blue.

The man himself would have fitted better in monk's cloth, but not in a monastery. He was a frame of great bones with dark leathery hide that good living had softened and diseases had pocked and stained slightly. The one homely touch was his false teeth; they rested in a glass of water beside the bed, like anybody's false teeth.

Doc placed his equipment cases on a table. In a moment, he went to the bed and gave the man—if there was a Frunzoff Nosh here, this was he—the first administration of truth serum.

THIS part of the plan was direct enough. Frunzoff was unconscious from the anaesthetic, but the bridge-over into twilight coma could be secured with a stimulant administered simultaneously with the sodium-amytal formula he intended to use. It should not take too long.

Waiting for the medicinal reaction, he set up the small portable wire recorder, gave it a test run, and adjusted the audio gain.

He said into the microphone, "This is Clark Savage, speaking from number seven Botsch Bronnaja Ulitza, in Moscow." He consulted his watch, gave the hour, minute, and the date. He added, "I have gained admission to the house, which I have reason to believe is occupied by a Russian official named Frunzoff Nosh, for the purpose of questioning the man while he is under the effects of truth serum." He gave a brief description of the house and means of gaining entrance, not because the information was of much record value, but because he was waiting for Frunzoff to respond to the chemicals, and the recording might add authenticity.

He shut off the recorder suddenly. There had been a sound downstairs. He whipped to the door, listened, heard nothing, and then made for a moment a low trilling sound that had once been a rather peculiar habit, a thing he did in moments of intense excitement, but which he had broken himself of making. It was done deliberately now, as a means of identification.

"Doc!" Ham Brooks' voice came sharply from below.

"Yes?" Doc said. "What is it? What about Monk?"

Monk's own voice, a small raspy affair, answered that. "What the devil kind of a joint is this?" Monk demanded.

"Monk, are you all right?"

"I'm more confused than I've been in some time," Monk said. He and Ham came leaping up the stairs. They saw the paintings, and Monk said, "For crying out loud! Are those daubings *real?"*

Doc asked, "What happened to you?"

"I got a telephone call earlier tonight," Monk explained wryly. "I was advised to get the heck out of the place where I was waiting for you and Ham. I figured it was good advice, particularly since it scared the devil out of me. The voice on the telephone seemed to know too much."

"Who called?" Doc demanded.

"Search me."

"A woman?"

"No. Man's voice. I never heard it before, that I recall."

Doc Savage concentrated for a moment, recalling the man named Mahli who had waited for the girl Seryi in the rear of the house where they had first gone. Doc then spoke a few words, imitating Mahli's voice with remarkable fidelity. "That sound anything like it?"

"That's the guy," Monk said, amazed. "Who is he?"

"A girl named Seryi said he was her cousin."

"Who is this Seryi?"

"Don't you know?"

"Never heard of her," Monk said. He added with the air of a man misunderstood, "I haven't made a pass at a babe since I've been here. I've turned over a new leaf."

Ham snorted. "I'd call that a whole book."

"I went to the other hideout, and Ham showed up," Monk explained. "Now, what goes on? I thought this whole thing was supposed to be the biggest secret since Pearl Harbor."

Ham laughed. Monk was not built to register confusion in any but a comical way. His height was a little over five feet, his width not much less, and his homeliness was almost preposterous. His forehead was about a single finger width, and he bore in no respect any resemblance to an eminent chemist, which he was.

"Fan out your ears, and I'll tell you what happened," Ham advised him. "Then you're really going to be bewildered."

DOC SAVAGE did not use hypodermics for the drug, but a mechanical means of administration which resembled in a dwarf form the setup for delivering intravenous saline dosage. His equipment had been prepared in advance; the whole theme had been aimed at what was happening now—to get hold of the man who would know what they wanted to know, drug him, and extract the information.

Frunzoff suddenly heaved, moaned, then gave an explosion of Russian words. He was cursing. Delirium, and he was reliving some particularly tight moment in his past.

"Hold him down," Doc said. "He's in the middle stage now, and we'll be ready to work on him in a few seconds."

Monk and Ham listened to the man's babbling. Ham said in amazement, "You hear that? He has killed someone, and he's reporting to a superior that he did it. Someone named Uritsky. I seem to have heard that name."

Doc frowned. "Uritsky was a terrorist leader killed during the early days of the Soviet. He was supposedly murdered by the opposition—but the opposition didn't win, and if this fellow killed Uritsky, it was part of a plot to stir up trouble and to get Uritsky out of the way. That sort of thing has been done before."

"Nice guys," Monk said.

"The recorder on?" Ham asked.

"Yes. Ham, you've got the general picture, and you have some experience at cross-examination. Suppose you start the ball rolling."

Ham nodded. "Fine by me." He leaned over

Frunzoff and began the casual questioning that they had found it was best to employ to lead into more important matters. Even the drug was not completely effective on a mind suddenly jabbed with a vital question. "What is your name?" Ham asked.

The man mumbled that it was Frunzoff Nosh. He gave his age when Ham asked for it. Fifty-seven. Was he a party member? He was. For how long? Since 1916. Had he known Lenin? Yes. Did he know Stalin? Yes. How well? Quite well. What was his present connection with Stalin? He was Stalin's coordinator.

Doc Savage said, "Develop that coordinator thing a bit farther with questions. It will help background what we are after."

Ham asked half a dozen questions, then added a comment which summed up Frunzoff's general job.

"Hatchet boy for the head guy," Ham said.

"I'll take it now," Doc said. He replaced Ham beside Frunzoff, and asked quietly, "Frunzoff, you have general information concerning all Soviet preparations for war?"

"Da," the man mumbled.

Because the word "truth serum" as applied to the chemical they were using was a misnomer—there was no chemical magic which would make anyone speak the truth and nothing but the truth—it was necessary to keep a continuous barrage of questions going. The man was literally without consciousness; he could not reason, would not remember what had happened afterward in any coherent fashion, but since he was without the capacity to reason, skillful guiding through the drug-induced delirium would produce remarkable results.

"Have you the atom bomb?" Doc asked.

FORTY-FIVE minutes later, Doc Savage turned to the microphone and gave the chemical composition of the drugs that had been used, and finished, "This concludes the interview with Frunzoff. All that remains now is to get back to Washington with it."

He switched off the recorder, removed the spool of wire, and put it in a chamois-lined case. Then he looked up at Monk's and Ham's pale, drawn faces.

"Rather shocking to find it out, wasn't it?" Doc suggested grimly.

"Blazes!" Monk moistened dry lips. "I don't think I ever spent forty-five minutes that scared me worse."

Ham cleared his throat. "That plant near Kazan, where they're processing the Polish uranium—I wish we'd gotten a better description of its location and the method they're using."

"I don't think the man has the technical knowledge to help much there," Doc explained. "As for the location, that's definite. General Staff in Washington knows about that plant—but, I'm quite alarmed to say, they don't have any notion at all that about three-quarters of the others exist."

Monk stared. "The hell! I always suspected the top brass in our army of having the same stuff in their heads that's on their shoulders. But you'd think with all the espionage they've been doing, they'd have more than a child's portion of information."

Doc shook his head. "It has been too well covered. I'll make you a bet that no one outside of Stalin and this fellow here has the information on the Soviet's atomic-warfare status that we just recorded."

Ham looked at the unconscious Frunzoff, scowling. "You know, it's too bad we're partly civilized. A little overdose of the drug would stop that devil's heart and close the lid on a lot of scheming."

"It's an idea," Monk said.

Doc had finished recasing his equipment. "I imagine that will take care of itself, once this recording unwinds through a loudspeaker at a United Nations session. Which is what I hope will ultimately happen. And I believe it will."

"First," Ham said dryly, "we've got to get out of Russia with that thing."

Chapter VI

DOC SAVAGE produced half a dozen small glass ampuls and divided them among Monk and Ham, keeping one for himself. "Break one of these in your handkerchief and hold it to the nostrils of each guard," he instructed. "In other words, give it about the same way you would chloroform. A minute and a half to two minutes of administration should be sufficient."

"They're knocked out already," Ham said. "Why give them an extra shot of this stuff, whatever it is? Incidentally, what is it?"

"Merely another type of anaesthetic," Doc explained. "One that can be counteracted quickly by a stimulant in vapor form."

"Oh, so they'll all wake up about the same time?"

"That's it," Doc agreed. "The information is important, but covering up the fact that we have it is just about as essential. Because of the way the anaesthetic sneaks up on you, and the complete lack of aftereffects, nobody here is going to realize what happened. If we're lucky, of course. The anaesthetic gas is almost unknown. I'm sure no one here in the house realizes the stuff exists. The guards and Frunzoff will simply wake up, perhaps feel a little puzzled, then think no more of it. Frunzoff, of course, was asleep and will never know what happened. The guards will conclude they dropped off to sleep, and the penalty a Russian guard gets for sleeping on duty is going to keep them quiet."

Ham Brooks indicated Frunzoff. "Yeah, but you used a needle on his arm three times. You can see the bumps that were raised. A guy who took all the precautions he took is going to ask a doctor what the devil happened to his arm."

Doc shook his head. "I've prepared for that, I hope."

"How?"

Doc got a small container, ventilated, from the equipment case. "I'm a little self-conscious about the childishness of this one," he said.

He opened the container and released about three dozen ordinary fleas on Frunzoff's person.

Ham laughed heartily. Monk looked startled and asked, "What did you do? Take a vacuum cleaner to a dog?"

"To that pet pig, Habeas Corpus, that you keep in New York, if you must know," Doc said.

"If they're fleas off that ghastly hog," Ham Brooks said, "they'll have Frunzoff half-eaten by morning. He'll never notice a few little things like hypodermic-needle punctures."

"Check over everything to make sure there is no sign that we were here," Doc directed.

"When are you going to release the stuff that will revive them?" Monk asked.

"On the way out. Which will be in a couple of minutes, I guess."

DOC SAVAGE looked up and down the street, then stepped through the door and moved aside to let Monk and Ham pass. He closed the door and made sure the spring lock clicked. He stood there a moment, mentally checking to be sure things inside were as they had found them—no furniture displaced, the same lights on that had been on; there was a multitude of small things that could go amiss, and any one was important if it aroused suspicion.

He moved down the steps. The rain had changed suddenly to sleet, and it was a great deal colder than it had been. The cold front had passed, but before morning there was likely to be quite a lot of sleet and perhaps some snow, according to the predictions of the meteorologists in the American zone.

Monk and Ham had gone to a small sedan of a make popular in Germany prior to the war.

"Stolen car?" Doc asked dubiously.

"No, it's one I chiseled off Trans-Caucasian Soviet Federation, and cached for an emergency," Monk explained. "I figured this was an emergency."

"It's not one the police will be looking for, then?"

Monk hesitated. "I don't see why they would be. I hate to run my neck out too far, though. This Seryi babe and her pal Mahli bobbing up in the picture sort of makes an unbeliever out of me."

"Has anyone the least idea who Seryi and Mahli are?" Doc asked.

No one did have. Monk put the little car into motion, and immediately began to have trouble with the icy street.

Doc Savage was silent, thinking about the situation. The first leg of the project—getting into Moscow and extracting the atomic-warfare-status information from the one man in Russia who probably came nearest to having it all—had gone off, everything considered, not too badly. Doc felt some satisfaction about that. Back of tonight's operation lay several months of careful preparation; Monk had been in Russia since early last summer, and Ham almost as long. The fact that all the facilities of the United States government, and those of most of the other nations allied against world chaos, had been available did not mean it had been easily done. Monk could probably attest to that, and Ham as well.

The information on the record wire was fabulously important. It was, Doc imagined, as vital to the future of world security as anything could be; certainly it was data that would definitely weigh the balance of peace or war. That made it a matter affecting many lives. Not a few hundred or a few thousand lives, but millions—all of the millions who would be drafted into the next conflict.

Specifically, the wire held—he could feel its slight weight in his pocket, a presence almost intangible for such weird importance—the full facts of Soviet atomic work. The locations of all plants, the parts being manufactured in specific places, the whereabouts of the storage depots, and the master plan of Communist operations—all of that was on the wire.

There wasn't the slightest doubt in Doc's mind but that within a week or ten days after the wire was unspooled through a reproducer before the United Nations security organization, the whole disease of totalitarian aggression, which the previous world conflict had failed so piteously to end, would be a dead duck.

Viewed from another point, he had the life and future of every Communist dictator and satellite in his pocket. The minute he got out of Russia with the recording, life and future for totalitarianism would have its throat cut. But quick. There would be no dallying. As everyone now realized, there had been too much patience already.

"Monk," Doc said.

Monk jumped nervously. "Yeah?"

"You're working according to plan, aren't you?" Doc asked. "In other words, you're headed for a spot where you have a shortwave radio transmitter concealed?"

"That's right."

"I'm uneasy about that," Doc said frankly. "There has been a leak somewhere. The way that girl Seryi stepped into the picture. Mahli's phone call to get you away from the meeting place so the girl could contact us—and the way she was taken out of our hands later—all that had a quality about it of being rigged."

"I don't see where the hell the leak could have been," Monk muttered. "God knows, Ham and I have been so careful we fooled ourselves."

"How do you explain this Seryi?"

"The same way you do—a counterplot of some kind." Monk squirmed uncomfortably. "But what kind? What's the rig?"

"Apparently we aren't being followed. We weren't molested at Frunzoff's place, although the girl herself gave us the address."

"Blazes! You think they may know about the radio station and be laying for us there?"

"Why not? If they knew as much as they did, they could know about the radio."

"Doc, we've *got* to get to a radio transmitter. Otherwise we're behind the eight ball. Touching off the rest of our plan depends on that."

"Turn north at the next corner," Doc said abruptly. "We're going to raid a Soviet shortwave station and use that."

ON the Kashira road, a few miles south of the Moscow city environs, they turned off the main thoroughfare and parked at the foot of a hill on which stood a group of radio towers.

"We've got to do this quick and clean," Doc warned. "We'll try it the way we got to Frunzoff."

"Wonder how many engineers will be on duty," Ham said uneasily.

"Two, according to the information I have."

Ham glanced at the big bronze man in surprise. "You mean you dug up information like that ahead of time?"

Doc shrugged. "It wasn't hard to get. The consulate obtained it—remember the fuss that was kicked up recently about Soviet radio jamming our own propaganda broadcasts? The Communists denied it, of course, and made a big show of naming and identifying all their radio stations—actually revealing about half of them, probably. Anyway, we got enough information from that."

They worked through the darkness, sleet making walking difficult. The steepness of the path did not help. They came presently to a drab block of a concrete building with lighted windows with a big Octo*pozho!* warning sign about high voltages.

Doc wheeled suddenly, said, "Listen!"

Startled, Monk stiffened so abruptly that his feet slipped on the ice and he fell. He did not fall heavily, and remained as he landed, supported on his braced hands.

In the night there was nothing that seemed abnormal. Only the humming of a transformer inside the building, the glassy creaking of sleet on tree twigs.

"I believe I heard a car stop down there on the road," Doc said uneasily. "I'm not sure. We can't take a chance, though. Monk, you'd better check on it. And be careful."

"Nobody could have followed us," Monk muttered. "And nobody knew we were coming here. We didn't know it ourselves an hour ago."

"Be careful anyway," Doc warned.

Monk grunted. "You want me to wait at our car, if it's a false alarm?" He turned and began retracing the route downhill. He went with care, keeping in the very darkest places, and listening frequently. He had barked the knuckles of his left hand when he fell a moment ago, and he twisted bits of ice off a branch that whacked him in the face, and held the ice against the raw areas.

Having heard nothing and seen nothing alarming, Monk reached the vicinity of their car. Now he went with great care, a step at a time, although he was convinced that Doc Savage had made one of his rare errors. A car had stopped on the road? Hell, what if it had? Anybody driving a night like this would be stopping often to whittle ice off his windshield. It was inconceivable that anyone had trailed them.

Monk suddenly grew colder than even the chilly night warranted. His mouth felt very dry. Still, he had heard and seen nothing. But he didn't like the idea that had just hit him.

He moved forward a step at a time, now with a gun in his hand. The car had become something to be feared and avoided—but he had to learn whether he was right. He found the right-hand door, opened it warily, felt inside, and located the tiny portable two-way radio which he had kept in his possession on the chance that its necessity would outweigh the almost certain fact that the fancy Soviet monitoring system would spot any bootleg transmitter a couple of moments after it went on the air.

Monk turned on the receiver. He could check what he wanted to check with the receiver alone. He advanced the gain only enough to register the tube hiss, then began running the tuning mechanism through all the frequencies it would tune. When he got into the very-high-frequency end of the spectrum, it began to "block."

His blood chilled. Receivers would "block" in this fashion only when a transmitter was so very close that its immediate field paralyzed the vacuum tubes.

He tried to swallow. *Monk, you fool, you've been suckered with a trick you've used yourself a dozen times!* There was a shortwave transmitter attached somewhere to the car. It needn't be large; a case the size of a couple of cigarette packages might contain it. And it could be traced easily with almost any sort of loop or beam directional antennae.

Doc had been right, then. There had been a car on the road, and it had been following them through the medium of radio. *My God, where can that transmitter be hidden? How long has it been there? Who put it there?*

That line of thought iced up completely when he felt metal against the back of his neck.

"Khto tam?" a voice said unpleasantly, and reworded the inquiry in English. "Who is this?"

"Use that gun on him," another voice said sharply, and Monk had the absurd and ghastly feeling that he had gone far out somewhere in a black endless space that was flecked faintly with crimson; there was no impression of falling or even of motion, but everything was perfectly static and as restful as death. There was the added disagreeable fact that he didn't seem to have his head with him.

Chapter VII

INSIDE the radio-transmitter room, Doc Savage stood frowning down at a turntable on which a record was being broadcast. It was a propaganda piece, optimistically beamed at the United States in English, and so unbelievable that it wouldn't be convincing. The same thing had happened to the Nazis when they started believing the sound of their own voices.

Ham Brooks said, "We won't have to change the beam setting for direction. The indicator says approximately due north, and there's enough spread to hit the monitors which will be listening for us."

Doc crossed over and swung out the transmitter rack cover and examined the oscillator section where the frequency was first created which would later go out on the ether in the form of radio transmission. It was here that he would have to change the wavelength of the transmitted signal so that the monitor stations in America would get it immediately.

The transmitter, he knew, was a copy of an American rig, even to the shape of the crystal holder. The crystal controlled the wavelength.

"You mean you came prepared with a spare crystal cut to our American monitoring frequency?" Ham exploded.

"It seemed like a good idea," Doc said. "Here we go. That telephone is going to ring the minute we go off the air. Answer and tell them it's transmitter trouble."

He pulled switches, got the outfit off the air, yanked the crystal, substituted his own, did a quick job of retuning, picked up a microphone, and adjusted the gain on it.

Ham's jaw fell when he heard the coded message Doc spoke into the mike. It was spoken in Russian, cleverly done, consisting of a berating tirade directed against the engineer in the station. It was something that would pass as a row which two engineers were having over an electrical difficulty with the equipment. Something that a live microphone might have happened to pick up.

Doc finished, jerked the station off the air, changed the crystals back the way they were, and began retuning again. The telephone rang. Ham picked up the instrument, listened, said angrily in Russian, *"Eta ochen groosna!"* He was evidently shouted at, because he shouted back, this time without an apology. He ended with a tirade, tore the phone loose from its wires, and said, "I hope these engineers had a reputation for bad tempers."

"The station is back on the air," Doc said. He went over and broke a restorative ampul under the nostrils of each of the two Russian station engineers, ensuring their awakening within a few moments. "Let's get out of here."

"How long have we got to wait?" Ham asked.

"Four or five hours," Doc guessed. "That is based on the weather, though. If everything is grounded, it might be more difficult."

"These sleet storms usually break up a little after daylight, don't they?"

"Let's hope this one does."

THE girl Seryi stood in the darkness, a tall cold figure in a sheath of a black raincoat on which the ice clung.

She spoke two English words and one Russian one: "You understand *roozhyo?"* She also moved her hand a little to make sure they saw the dark gun there.

Doc Savage stared at her blankly, thinking how silly it was that she would ask them if they understood a gun, phrasing it that way. Then he realized she was probably very terrified, even if more determined than terrified, and to be dealt with cautiously.

"I waited here in your car," she said. "It will hold three, will it not? I wish to ride back to the city with you."

Ham Brooks said, "Oh, brother!" softly, and then on a wild note demanded, "Where's Monk—?"

He changed that hurriedly to, "Where's that monkey-faced commissar?"

"That is why I wish to ride with you." Seryi's voice was as loose as a leaf in the darkness.

"Huh?"

"I am instructed to tell you," Seryi said, "that the commissar—shouldn't we call him Mr. Monk Mayfair, eminent chemist, adventurer, and Doc Savage associate—has exactly two hours to live unless you rescue him."

"How come?"

"Hold it a minute," Doc Savage said. He had been trying to figure out how they had been trailed here, and he'd gotten the same thought Monk had investigated. Doc switched on the shortwave radio, tuned the higher frequencies, and got the telltale receiver blocking. He investigated.

The transmitter was in a cardboard box that was properly marked *Vnootrennyaya troopka.* Inner tube. Doc tore it open and stopped transmission. He went back and confronted the girl.

"All right," he said. "We have been outsmarted. Your outfit trailed us here, and grabbed Monk. Now what?"

"Two hours isn't much," Seryi said nervously. "You'd better get moving."

Without a word, Doc put the car in motion. He backed and turned carefully, and on the ice-glazed highway he headed toward Moscow. The wheel chains made a monotonous whining, but the sleet did not seem to be falling as heavily. The girl's voice began to come, a thin sound of fright driven through defiance, from the darkness within the rear seat.

"Here it is," she said. "Wherever there is an organization with people in it, and some have power and some haven't, there is continual scheming and maneuvering by those who are not at the top and want to climb there."

Doc said, "Is she holding that gun on you, Ham?"

"She's holding it on you," Ham said. "She's keeping it pointed at the middle of your back."

"All right. I wanted to know. Go ahead, Miss Seryi. If that's your name."

"It's Seryi Mitroff," she said bitterly. "As I started to say, where there is power, there is invariably hunger for that power—"

"Skip that part about human greed," Doc said. "What you're saying is that in politics there are two groups. Those in. And the outs. Which are you?"

She hesitated, then said curtly, "I'm an out."

"And you're working with a group of outs?"

"Yes."

"And you want in?"

"Naturally," she said.

DOC SAVAGE swung the car abruptly, turning into a side road which, according to the maps he had memorized before starting the project, circled through a village named Tormas, then entered Moscow by a route that would put them on Twerskaja Street when they approached Red Square, which was the heart of the city.

"You aren't being followed!" Seryi said.

"Not if we can help it," Doc agreed. "You don't mind our taking a less obvious route into the city? After all, we've made one fool move tonight."

"You weren't so foolish." Seryi hesitated, and then added with a little pride, "We have in our group about ten men who are as skilled espionage agents as any in the Soviet, which I imagine makes them the best in the world. Those ten have been working on this with all their wiles, and they haven't found out too much."

"They certainly learned too much to suit us," Doc told her wryly.

"No. We're quite puzzled."

"You learned Monk and Ham were my associates."

"Not until tonight. All we had been able to ascertain was that they were up to something—and they were looking for the mystery man of the Soviet. Frunzoff."

"How did you know it was Frunzoff?"

"Who else could it be? Or was it Frunzoff? That's what we want to find out, for one thing."

Her voice had become sharply eager in the back seat, and Doc noted the excitement, speculated about it a moment, and then said, "It was a clever idea, Miss Mitroff. You didn't exaggerate when you said your associates were experts at espionage."

Ham demanded explosively, "Doc! Doc, I don't think they *knew* that Frunzoff was the spider who held all the webs!"

"That's what I mean. They're trying to use us to confirm that fact. That's why they furnished us with Frunzoff's address."

"Damn! We haven't been half-smart."

Seryi Mitroff remarked wryly, "You think not? You might ask Mahli. Mahli is one of the greatest undercover agents who ever lived. Just to show you how great he is, I'll tell you this: he has been personally decorated by Stalin five times." She hesitated when Ham Brooks laughed, then demanded angrily, "What is funny?"

Ham told her, "You sound like the people with the swastikas on their arms sounded a few years ago when they spoke of the paperhanger. Remember Adolf? He handed out a few decorations in his time, but looking back now, they didn't mean much, did they?"

"Go ahead and insult me," Seryi snapped.

"I was paying you a compliment—Mahli knows skill, and he was vastly impressed by your performance. Of course, he didn't know that you were associates of the fabulous Doc Savage. He only knew you were clever espionage men on a job, and that you were seeking Frunzoff."

You mean," Ham asked in astonishment, "you didn't know Frunzoff was the all-important one until you saw we were trying to find him?"

"That's about it," she confessed. "You can see why we were impressed. You had come into Russia, two foreigners, and you dug up something we had only suspected was true, and moreover, you learned the man's identity."

"You're impressed?" Ham asked dryly.

"Certainly."

"I'm not," Ham said. "Right now, I can't think of a job where Monk and I made more fool moves and got in a worse mess."

Doc asked, "What is your proposition, young lady?"

"Tell us what you found out from Frunzoff, and give us the proof you took—the kind of information you got from Frunzoff would be so startling that you would have to prove its authenticity—and that is all we want."

"And the price you offer?"

"The return of your man Monk Mayfair, alive."

"And an unhindered escape from Russia, I presume?"

"Naturally. We could help you escape, if you wish. But presumably you have a better plan for flight than we could concoct."

"Just what," Doc asked, "do you intend to do with this information which you seem to imagine we got from Frunzoff?"

"You got it, all right," she said.

"How do you know?"

"You went to his house, didn't you? And then headed for a radio station. Oh, you got what you came after, all right."

"What," said Doc, "do you think you would do with this plum you feel we picked?"

She laughed grimly.

"How long," she asked, "do you think Frunzoff would last if the Central Committee knew three foreign agents had calmly walked in and milked him of all they wanted to know?"

"My impression," Doc said, "is that the Central Committee doesn't know Frunzoff exists as anyone of importance."

The girl started to say something, stammered, and fell silent.

"To put it more correctly," Doc suggested, "if the Central Committee can be shown Stalin has prepared such a secret ace as Frunzoff, Stalin's hold will be weakened. The idea is to tear down Stalin. Right?"

"I don't see why you should object to that," she snapped.

Doc said in a conversational tone, "I can't think of a very sound reason, either. Ham, is she still holding the gun on me?"

"She keeps the gun pointed right at your back," Ham said.

"At the middle of my back?"

"Yes. The bullets would go through the seat, of course."

"Take the gun away from her," Doc said.

HAM must have worked very fast. Doc was set for the shock of the bullet—not that he quite lacked confidence in the bulletproof chain-mesh undergarment he was wearing, but the idea of stopping a bullet wasn't reassuring. When the gun exploded, which it did twice, the slugs drove through the side of the car. He heard the gun fall to the floor. But that didn't settle it; a series of sounds of violent motion followed, then a long, painful yodellike expression of pain from Ham Brooks.

Doc stopped the car, which was not moving fast. He turned in the seat, and as nearly as he could determine in the darkness, Ham was getting the worst of it. Doc, amazed, joined the struggle with some caution. The caution was justified, because the forefinger of his right hand got a quick disjointing, he narrowly missed losing an eye, and his neck got a painful wrench. All of that in about two and a half seconds, before he subdued the girl.

There was a period of silence in the little car.

"Whew!" Ham said weakly. "Don't ever, whatever you do, let Monk hear that a slip of a girl practically took me apart and threw the pieces away."

"Are you badly hurt?" Doc demanded.

"Of course I'm hurt!" Ham yelled. "I'm hurt all over. My God, this babe knows judo tricks I never heard of."

"If you'll hold her," Doc said, "I'll get the truth serum ready."

"Do I have to?" Ham asked gingerly. "All right. I'll try to hold her. But be ready to rescue me if she as much as gets one finger loose."

Doc found the gun and tossed it out of the car. Then he gripped his disjointed finger, wrenched it back into normalcy, and felt gingerly of his aching neck. He got out the equipment case that held the truth serum and its necessary apparatus.

"Let me have her wrist," he said.

Seryi Mitroff made a completely cold-blooded comment. "So that is how you got to Frunzoff," she said.

Chapter VIII

MAHLI, the great oaf of a man, finished explaining the situation to Monk Mayfair, speaking English so naturally that Monk could have imagined, had he not been too frightened to imagine anything, that he was listening to a salesman try to sell him an insurance policy in New York. Mahli was clearly one of the very few men whom Monk had met whose looks were more deceiving than his own. Mahli had the build and appearance of a hooligan of the most stupid type. By now, though, there wasn't any doubt in Monk's mind about the man being educated, clever, and probably as warmhearted as a blackjack.

"You understand?" Mahli asked.

"I guess so," Monk muttered. "I'm your down payment on the information you imagine we got from Frunzoff."

"Exactly."

"It's all right if I don't feel happy about it, isn't it?" Monk asked bitterly.

"You're physically intact. You should feel somewhat fortunate about that."

"And about this knot on my head, I suppose? Presumably this lightning that keeps striking me is coming from some sort of protuberance? Do you mind if I feel and find out?"

"Sit still."

"Okay."

"Sit very still," Mahli warned. "It has finally dawned on us that you are a Doc Savage associate. That, if you don't mind my saying so, will persuade us to shoot you instantly if you as much as sneeze."

"Okay. I had gathered that."

"Good."

"Where are we?" Monk asked.

"No answer to that," Mahli said.

Monk glanced around, being careful not even to move his eyes too abruptly because he didn't doubt in the least that he would be shot if his captors became alarmed. Not that they weren't alarmed already; they just weren't at the point of disposing of him. Monk felt they wished to do so. He had never seen a group of men who were more convinced they had caught a Tartar. Doc Savage's reputation, Monk reflected, could be quite a liability.

He saw a grimy cavern of a room furnished with three iron cots, some bedclothing, a coal stove, a table, two chairs, and not much else, if one omitted the odor of too much unwashed occupancy. Someone's living quarters, presumably.

"There are seven men guarding you," Mahli warned suddenly and hoarsely. "You haven't a chance to escape."

"Take it easy," Monk said. "You're so nervous you're getting me upset."

"No chance for you in flight, understand! There is myself and seven very good men. There is the Russian Security Police, the OGPU, the NKVD, the VSNK—"

"We have a little of that alphabet soup back home," Monk said. "Is here where it started?"

"You mustn't try to escape."

"Oh, mustn't I?"

Mahli scowled, then muttered, "It would be a relief if you would promise not to try. Would you give your word?"

Monk laughed in his face. "Sure. I'll promise—that it won't be a try. It'll be a success, brother. You won't know what's happened until its *sleeshkam pozna,* comrade. Too late." Monk hesitated, eyed the big man, and added, "Why the outsized tizzy, large *tovarich?* I don't make you as a guy who gets that scared of me."

"Much is at stake," Mahli said frankly.

"Yeah?"

"I will speak straight words, ugly one. It has long been suspected that Stalin has groomed a faceless one to step into his shoes. It would be a relief to many if that one were eliminated."

"A relief to the other candidates," Monk said. "I see what you mean."

"If Stalin has prepared this faceless one, it will make him no friends."

Monk nodded. "Among the other candidates. I can see that, too."

"Is Frunzoff such a faceless one? And did you get proof tonight?"

Monk grinned. "What was it you said awhile ago? 'No answer to that'? That's me all over, *tovarich.* You're speaking to a fencepost."

Beside the grimy window a man cursed impatiently. They listened, and there was the sound of a man singing in the distance, loudly and happily. The aria was a Tchaikovsky bit, and the singer applied Russian words, then switched over into another tongue that was certainly not Russian. There were but a few words of this, then he swung back into Russian. "A noisy fool for so early in the morning," muttered the man who had sworn.

Monk leaned back, trying to look relaxed. It was Doc Savage out there, and the language that was not Russian was ancient Mayan, understood by very few in the so-called civilized world outside of Doc Savage and his aides.

The information Doc had inserted in the song was a little upsetting. They were out of anaesthetic gas, Doc said. Any help Monk got would be the hard way.

MONK placed his feet on the floor so that he could get a quick start, made a mental notation that he would like very much to be safe in New

York, then waited. That was about all he could do. That, and hope it wouldn't be too long, which it wasn't.

The fire began in an alleylike court at the rear. Monk, because he was expecting something, saw the smoke first, and had difficulty keeping from pointing it out. Then a man yelled, pointed. There was, as might be expected, a rush for the window. What was burning down in the alley, they never found out, and it was the least of what happened anyway.

The window went first. Sash, glass, everything, it came to pieces, letting in a sheet of bluish flame, a gulp of driven air, and an incredible amount of noise. Monk understood fully that it was a small explosive grenade, applied to the window for a distraction. He was surprised, though, when Doc Savage came in through the window after it.

Monk was on his feet and after the guard at the door by now. The guard, the only man at the door, had been bounced back against the panel by the explosion—by the surprise of it rather than the force—and had half-turned and was fending off with one arm and fumbling for a gun with the other. Monk did his best to put his right fist entirely through the man's middle, and when the fellow doubled, used his right fist to change the shape of the man's jaw considerably.

He knew by now that Doc must be in the room. There was quite a bit of smoke, but enough was added to the activity to indicate Doc. The building was an old-fashioned stone affair with ledges outside the window, so he imagined Doc had stepped in from next door.

Monk turned, picked up a chair, and made for Mahli. The latter was on his knees, fumbling for a gun that he must have dropped in the excitement.

Doc said in Mayan, "Get going, Monk. Never mind cracking heads."

Monk hesitated, thought of the beating he'd taken in the night near the radio station, and threw the chair at Mahli. It didn't damage Mahli much. Monk started for the big Russian, but Doc said more sharply, "Cut it out! Get going."

Ham Brooks was outside the door. He said, "You took long enough getting out of there," to Monk, and they ran down a passage, then downstairs. The night outside was turning into a shiny ugly dawn that made their faces look a little more red and harried than they were.

"Where is this good-looking Seryi babe I've been hearing about?" Monk asked. He was not puffing noticeably.

"Tied up in the back of the car," Ham said.

They came to the little Russian copy of a German motorcar. Monk piled into the rear, then asked, "In the back of what car?"

Doc, on an impressive note of disgust, said, "She's gone, you mean?"

"Then so will the car keys be, and probably the ignition wiring too," Ham predicted.

He was wrong, though.

THEY drove hard and deviously for about one *verst,* the Russian equivalent of two-thirds of a mile, then traveled decorously. Reaching the wide Twerskoj Boulevard, Doc reached down to tinker with the radio receiver and get it on the Moscow police frequency. Mostly he tuned in electrical interference from the tramway cars which, even at this ungodly hour, were packed with work-bound people.

"How about briefing me on what happened?" Monk asked. Ham did so, finishing, "That Seryi turned out to be about the poorest example of truth-serum efficiency we ever saw. But we did get it out of her that you were being held at that address."

"And you left her tied up in the backseat?" Monk inquired.

"Why not? By all normal standards, she would have been woozy from the truth serum for an hour longer."

"Who tied her up?" Monk asked.

"I did," Doc said uncomfortably. "And let's not go into that."

Monk noted the swollen finger which Seryi had unjointed for Doc earlier. "That's a bad-looking finger you've got. What happened to it?" Monk remarked.

Doc drove intently and said nothing.

Monk turned to Ham and asked, "You blacked your eye, shyster? Or did you know you've got a very outstanding shiner?"

Ham winced. "There was a little fight a minute ago. Or didn't you happen to notice?"

"I thought it took half an hour or so for an eye to get black after the punch," Monk said dryly. "What have you developed? A quick color change?"

Ham hastily changed his explanation to, "I guess I got an eye bruised when I slipped on the ice back at the radio station. Sure, I recall it now."

Monk expressed his disbelief with a snort.

"You boys are tearing down my yen to meet this Seryi," he said.

"I do hope you meet her," Ham snapped.

"Yeah?"

"Nothing would give me quite as much satisfaction," Ham assured him disagreeably.

Chapter IX

BEYOND the picturesque iron bridge over the Moskwa River near the southeast Kremlin wall, they turned into a side street, parked, left the car, and walked four blocks over the glazed pavement to a small private garage where Monk and Ham had a change of cars waiting. This one was a light U.S. Army command car which had been converted with a coat of paint and a brand plate giving the false impression that it was Soviet-made.

"The airport now?" Ham asked.

Doc Savage consulted his watch, then nodded. "Yes. About the right amount of time has elapsed."

"Provided," Ham said, "the American monitors picked up our radio message."

Monk shuddered. "Don't be pessimistic. Smile at fate and keep her happy."

Ham was tuning the radio to the Soviet police wavelength again. "You been listening to the local cops?" he demanded. "If not, just fan out your ears. They're not passing up that mess we just made of Mahli and his friends." Ham pointed at the radio. "Go ahead. Listen. Then be an optimist."

What they were hearing was the Moscow police spreading a dragnet. There was a grim efficiency about it. And to complicate matters, the police had a general description of them—they were pictured as three men, one a giant, one an apish fellow, and one *kraseevyi.* Monk grimaced when he heard the Russian word describing Ham. Ham chuckled. "That's me. Handsome," he said.

The radio was an all-wave model, and Doc indicated it impatiently, saying, "Never mind amusing yourselves listening to the police uproar. Tune in on the Soviet Air Traffic Control frequency, and let's see if we're going to stand a chance of getting out of this."

The SATC wavelength was disturbingly quiet when they got the radio set up on it. They drove in silence, listening. Doc's face began to get a metallic angularity that meant strain. Ham and Monk stared at their watches uneasily.

They had driven about ten *verstahs.* Outside, the sleet no longer fell, the windshield being clear except for the condensation on the inner surface, which Doc kept scrubbing away with a palm. There was a cold wind that blew hard and tumbled dark sheeplike clouds and occasionally nudged the car insolently.

Suddenly the Soviet Air Traffic Control came to life, spluttering and astonished. An American transport plane was scheduled for early arrival at the Moscow airport. There was some confusion about clearance for the ship. Soviet Army Air Force Interceptor broke into the communications channel with the pointed information that the plane was going to be shot down. That added quite a lot to the uproar. Air Force Interception was informed the plane had special diplomatic clearance.

Interception wished to know—in about those words—how the blue hell that had happened. They were informed that the answer was simple enough for even Interception to get through its thick head—a very important American was on the plane. An American that had enough weight internationally that instantaneous clearance had been arranged. Who would that imperialistic so-and-so be? Interception wished to know.

Doc Savage. Doc Savage was aboard the plane. It seemed that last night a demonstration of radar-blocking by rocket in the American zone of Germany had gone wrong, and the rocket had mistracked and probably landed somewhere in Soviet territory. The experiment had been conducted by two of Doc Savage's aides, Renny Renwick and electrical wizard Long Tom Roberts. They were testing a device on which Doc Savage had assisted in development.

Doc Savage was flying to Moscow to personally demand the return of his radar-blocking gadget that had strayed. With him were two of his aides, Monk Mayfair and Ham Brooks.

Monk grinned at Ham.

"So you're twins," he remarked. "As the fellow says, 'What a revoltin' development that is.'"

WITH the Moscow airport hangars bulking on their left, Doc Savage swung the car around to the rear of the Comrade Soldiers' Club, a large drab wooden building with the single word *Eentendahnstva* across the front. There were other cars there, and a couple of trucks.

"You fellows are familiar with the procedure we hope to follow?" Doc asked.

Monk nodded. "I should be. I've repeated it to myself every night since I've been in Russia. Sort of a part of my nightly prayer." He glanced at Ham. "Cripes, have you gone back to carrying that cane?"

Ham Brooks, for as long as Monk had known him, had invariably carried a slender black sword-cane. The cane had rarely been out of Ham's hand, and it was almost a part of him, and certainly a part of his character. During the time they had been in Soviet territory, Ham had naturally forsaken his trademark.

Monk pointed at the cane Ham had extracted from the car trunk. "That's not yours. It's not even the type you would carry. Where'd you swipe it?"

"Come on, stupid," Ham said.

The cane was a heavy knurled article of ironwood with inlaid bands of gold and silver—platinum, Monk decided, taking a closer look and revising his opinion—and it bore no resemblance whatever to Ham's neat dark sword cane. It looked valuable, though. And useful in a skull-breaking contest.

They crossed a cobbled road, passed between two buildings, and Doc stopped at a narrow door. He tapped on the door. Three raps, a pause, two, a pause, then three more rappings. They waited. The building eaves were heavy with icicles, and one of these broke loose and fell, causing Monk to jump, literally, out of one shoe. He bent over, grumbling and embarrassed, and was stamping his foot into the shoe when the door opened.

A man came out of the door. A sullen-faced man in workman's clothing. He muttered the Russian good morning, *"Dobraye ootra,"* without any visible pleasure whatever, and stalked past them. If they meant anything to him, it certainly wasn't evident.

"I remember that chap," Ham said with pleasure. "The last time I saw him, he was a prince of the Imperial Japanese family in Tokyo, about a year after Pearl Harbor."

Doc said, "We're to wait inside. It seems to be going according to schedule."

The room which they entered was a naked place without furniture, but with three nails driven into one wall. From the three nails were suspended clothes hangers with three suits, shirts, neckties, to fit them. Socks and shoes were ready on the floor.

Monk's necktie was a terrific yellow. He eyed it with pleasure.

MOSCOW Zone Traffic Control kept the American transport plane circling the airport for half an hour by claiming there was a stack of air traffic in the overcast, which was a lie. The object of the discourtesy, uniquely enough, was not characteristic nastiness, but an effort to delay the ship's arrival until a Russian dignitary named Zardnov reached the field.

Zardnov—his full name was Oldenny Zardnov—was currently an acting delegate to the United Nations. This meant that he functioned at Lake Success when Molotov and Gromyko were absent, and it also indicated that Zardnov was currently in favor. That made him an important man. Regardless of the Russian obstruction attitude in the U.N., they had certainly assigned their top men to the sessions. So Zardnov was prominent. He was currently in Moscow for instructions.

Zardnov reached the airport with his face still puffed from sleep, and his temper bad. He was a stocky man of about Molotov's build, but with thicker lips and large damp eyes. Indicative of his status, he was accompanied by four bodyguards and two secretaries in two other cars.

It was inevitable that Zardnov would be called to deal with Doc Savage's descent on Moscow. Zardnov stared upward angrily, although the plane was too high in the overcast to be heard. He had made a violent speech at Lake Success concerning Doc Savage, branding the bronze man a charlatan and a troublemaker, and had been laughed off the floor for his pains.

"Let the ship land," Zardnov said grimly. "I will make this Doc Savage a speech before we send him back without his silly rocket. It will be a satisfaction." He turned to a secretary. "Has the rocket been found?"

"There is a great search, and it will be found," said the lackey cautiously.

THE plane broke through the overcast at fourteen hundred, and it made an impressive sight approaching the field. It was a six-jet ship with V-wings and a probable airspeed top of well beyond five hundred. It came in hot, gear down, touched the runway, and presently taxied along the strip to a tired brick building that was a former administration building, now unused since the construction of the new terminal in which Zardnov waited.

"Tell them to come here! Here!" Zardnov yelled.

The control tower conveyed the information to the Yank pilot, who informed the tower that an American embassy attaché was waiting at the old terminal to greet Doc Savage, and that was where they were going. The hell with Mr. Zardnov.

Zardnov got the point. He raised his cane on high and shook it. The cane was quite a hefty one of ironwood with gold and platinum inlay, and carrying it was not an affectation with Zardnov. He needed it. During the early days of red terror, two days following August 30, 1918, when a girl named Kaplan shot Lenin as he left a workers' meeting in Moscow, Zardnov had himself received a bullet in the knee, which had left a permanent disablement. The knee was inclined at the most unexpected moments to fold and deposit Zardnov on the floor if he didn't have the cane for quick support. Consequently he was never without it.

The car whisked Zardnov to the old terminal, and he saw with some satisfaction that political police had surrounded Doc Savage, Monk Mayfair, and Ham Brooks the instant they stepped from the plane.

Zardnov saw with a touch of disgust that American embassy attaché Clyde Warper had forced his way through and joined the plane arrivals. The disgust wasn't for Clyde Warper personally. It was just that diplomats had an understanding, a gentleman's agreement, that each fellow's country wouldn't abuse the other's diplomats. The diplomatic gentlemen might plot wars and casually arrange the slaughter of a few million civilians, but they mustn't have their hair mussed. That was the deal from time immemorial, and Zardnov certainly wasn't going to break up the play, being a fellow who needed diplomatic immunity more than anyone else.

Clyde Warper had whisked the arrivals into a room in the old terminal before Zardnov could join them. That was all right; the political police were on the job.

Warper and Zardnov were as polite as two cats climbing out of a cream jar. Clyde Warper introduced Doc Savage, Monk Mayfair, and Ham Brooks.

Zardnov leaned on his cane and scowled. He had not personally met Doc Savage or his aides previously. He was interested in the group.

The big bronze man was carrying a metal equipment case, and as he began telling Zardnov the purpose of his visit to Moscow—it concerned the incident of the runaway rocket last night, the way he told it—he gestured with emphasis with the hand holding the case. The case lid flew open, apparently by accident, and a number of objects fell out. One of these burst with about the commotion of a ripe egg, and an incredible quantity of black smoke exuded from it.

In a couple of seconds the inside of the room was as black as the interior of a goat.

"It's harmless! It's harmless!" Doc Savage was shouting. "It's merely a smoke grenade. Quite harmless. Stand where you are, everyone. Somebody open the window."

Nobody seemed to be doing much standing still. Feet were whetting the floor excitedly.

The cane which was supporting Zardnov was jerked from under him, and he sat down heavily on the floor. The cane left his fingers somehow.

The room rang with Russian profanity.

Someone opened the window. Smoke came out.

In the American plane, the crew members saw the smoke, heard the excitement, and they left the ship and bolted in a body for the administration building to learn what was happening and offer whatever aid seemed appropriate.

The smoke exuded from the window rapidly, the air in the room cleared, and so did the excitement.

Zardnov discovered a uniformed Russian policeman standing beside him holding his, Zardnov's, prized cane. "Did you jerk that from under me, you fool?" Zardnov snarled.

The Soviet cop became as white as a Siberian winter, probably not without reason. "Oh, no, sir! It was pushed into my hand. Someone thrust it upon me in the blackness!" he blurted.

The crewmen of the American ship returned to their craft, at the pointed suggestion of the police. It seemed they didn't have clearance to leave their ship, a technicality newly devised for the embarrassment of individuals the Communists wished to embarrass.

Not unnaturally, considering the excitement, no one happened to notice that three more men returned to the plane than had left it to investigate the uproar. Three. A large man, a short wide one, and a slender one. Other than this physical similarity, however, they bore no great resemblance to Doc Savage and his two aides.

In the old terminal, Doc Savage was apologizing for his carelessness.

FROM apologies, Doc shifted to a stiff demand that he be given custody of the remains of the radar-blocking rocket which had strayed. He intimated there was great likelihood that the Soviets had found the lost rocket by now. Hadn't they had representatives at the scene of the rocket firing in the American zone last night? There was an intimation that Doc thought the Soviets weren't above tampering with the rocket to cause the accident.

Zardnov's argument took the line that this was a petty matter, and under the jurisdiction of another department anyway. He, Zardnov, was powerless, as a matter of fact. This, of course, was a colossal lie, but Zardnov enjoyed telling it.

The argument grew heated. This didn't mean the language was profane, although the meanings inherent in the words were more blistering than a mule skinner's vocabulary.

Zardnov said he would do Doc Savage a great favor and telephone the Central Executive in Charge of Finding Lost Rockets. He did go to a telephone, and called his wife to learn whether she was still being unreasonable about the Kronstadt girl with whom Zardnov was living part-time. She was. Not bothered much, Zardnov returned to Doc Savage.

"I am informed there will be a full investigation concerning the rocket, and a decision reached. That will take about ten days. You will be informed," Zardnov said without batting an eye. "I am very sorry."

Doc protested vociferously. He noted Monk and Ham watching him impatiently. The switch with the three ringers from the plane had been managed deftly during the experience with the smoke grenade. Through the window, Doc had seen the ringers board the ship. They were safe. The ship's documents numbered them among the crew, in case there was any doubt in Russian minds. Nothing remained, then, but to wait to be ordered out of Russia, which Doc imagined would not be long coming.

The switch at the airport, quite an elaborate bit of chicanery, had two objectives—to make it seem that Doc, Monk, and Ham had been on the plane and could not have been in Moscow that night, and to draw attention to the matter so that when it was publicized later, it would be believable. The first was a temporary blindfold for the Russians; the second would be a headache for them later, if things went well.

Zardnov was grinning.

"I have also other news for you," he said in his poor English. "Your permission to visit Russia has been canceled. You will, unfortunately, have to leave immediately."

That was what Doc had been awaiting, but he made a loud objection.

"You will have to leave," Zardnov insisted.

Doc glanced at Monk and Ham, and to their relief, shrugged. "There'll be plenty of hell raised about this," he assured Zardnov.

They prepared to leave. The man from the consulate, Clyde Warper, registered his formal opinion. Outside, the plane skipper signaled, and the crew began getting into position.

A Russian arrived with a wild look and grabbed Zardnov's shoulder. Zardnov, the man said, was wanted on the telephone. Looking surprised and uneasy, Zardnov turned and hurried toward a booth.

"I don't like the looks of this," Doc said grimly. "Let's get out of here."

They had almost reached the door when Zardnov screamed; the high piping sound of the man's voice went running through the building like raw little animals.

"Seize them!" he shrieked. "They mustn't escape! They have—" He apparently realized he didn't know what they had done. "That was the Kremlin itself on the telephone!" he croaked.

Doc Savage, lunging through the door, found himself looking down the muzzles of half a dozen guns, and more weapons were joining the battery.

"Hold them!" Zardnov was bellowing excitedly. "The Kremlin wants them."

Chapter X

THEY could see, beyond the window with its lacing of steel bars, the pale pink brick wall of the Kremlin with its battlements and citadellike towers. It was very cold; the sleet gave the outer world a shiny effect, and a few thin hard snow pellets were traveling in the air like frightened gnats.

The room where they waited was of stone and bare, hard, ancient *doop* wood and as naked as they were. Their clothing had been taken. They were still dripping from the violent shower bath they had been forced to take.

Somewhere in the ineffectual daylight outside, a peal of bells began. The sound came from the tower above the Spasskiye Vorota, the Gate of Salvation, that an Englishman had built in the fifteenth century. The bells pealed the "Internationale," which meant that it was noon. The "Internationale" was played at twelve and six o'clock, and at three and nine o'clock the Russian Revolutionary Funeral March was on the repertoire.

"Twelve o'clock," Doc remarked.

"Damn, I'm cold," Monk complained.

"Think about the firing squad," Ham advised him. "That should warm you up."

"You believe they'll do that to us?" Monk asked in alarm.

"Why not?" Ham said bitterly. "After all, we—"

"—are perfectly innocent," Doc interjected warningly. He added in Mayan, "There seems to be no hidden microphone, which probably means there is one." In English he continued, "This is an outrage. Our diplomatic immunity as military emissaries has been violated. Such a thing is unheard of, even here."

The door opened, armed guards entered, and they were told harshly, *"Syoodah!"* The march carried them down a corridor past an almost continuous array of armed men who eyed their nakedness with ugly pleasure.

The destination proved to be the X-ray room of the Kremlin hospital, where they were X-rayed in rapid succession from head to toe.

"What's the idea of this shenanigan?" Monk pondered angrily. "They trying to identify us by our dental work or by my flat feet?"

"A further search for secret weapons, probably," Doc guessed.

Ham contributed, "Or maybe they think we swallowed the keys to the city."

The X-raying completed, their skin was subjected to inspection with infrared and ultraviolet light, clearly a search for secret writing. Their fingernails were examined, scraped; their hair was combed and the combings passed on to a laboratory. "This is getting preposterous," Monk muttered.

THEIR next session was held in a larger room that had a few leather chairs and an enormous mahogany table at which were seated five men, two of whom—Frunzoff and Zardnov—were not strangers. Doc and his two aides pretended not to know Frunzoff. The other three men at the table, it was not hard to guess, were security-police executives.

"Silence!" bellowed an SP man when Doc began a vociferous objection. "You will answer questions. That is all."

Doc Savage frowned.

The security-police officer whipped open a briefcase at his elbow, extracted a spool of recording wire—it resembled the tin spools on which adhesive tape is sold in the States—and slapped it on the table.

"This was found in your plane," the man said angrily. "It is an odd thing to be in a plane. How do you account for it?"

Doc pretended a slight surprise, said, "I shall account for nothing, naturally. This whole thing is an outrage perpetrated against an American scientist who came to Moscow to recover a strayed rocket."

"This spool was found in the plane."

"Was it?"

"It is recording wire."

"Indeed?"

The interrogator glared, shouted, and a nervous-looking Russian was pushed inside. In response to bellowed questions, he explained that in searching the plane he had found this spool of recording wire on the ship's radio-transmitter box, where it had evidently been placed for concealment.

The security-police officer swung on Doc Savage, pointed at the spool, and demanded, "How does it happen there is nothing on it?"

"Isn't there?"

A Russian electronics engineer brought in a recorder, obviously an American machine, the spool was placed, and the apparatus set in operation. The result that came from the loudspeaker was not encouraging. It consisted of garbled and indecipherable quackings and whisperings.

"Merely cross-talk," Doc remarked. "The same sort of stuff is found on most recording wire when it has not been too efficiently wiped of the previous recording."

The engineer leaned over and whispered. The police official swore, turned to the man who had found the spool, and demanded, "You say this was lying on the radio-transmitter case in the plane?"

"Da."

"Was the radio transmitter turned on?"

"Yes."

"Around the radio transmitter," explained the electronics expert, "there might be enough of a high-frequency field to demagnetize the wire. Since the sound is planted on the wire magnetically, the demagnetizing would naturally wipe off the wire to a greater or lesser extent, depending on how strong the field was—"

Zardnov interrupted. "Never mind the lesson in electricity. Someone in the American crew saw the ship was going to be searched, placed that spool of wire on the radio, where it would be demagnetized, and wiped out the information on the wire. Is that it?"

"That could be it."

Frunzoff looked relieved.

Zardnov waved a hand triumphantly. "At least we stopped the information they had gotten."

Frunzoff said, "There was no information. There couldn't have been. I would know it if they had questioned me, wouldn't I?"

Zardnov shrugged. "What happens to you when you are dealing with Doc Savage, who can say?" He gave the guards an order. "Take them away."

THIS time they were given clothes—coverall suits of coarse cloth and unlovely cut—and then taken across Communist Street, the one street inside the Kremlin, to a building beyond the tall green building called the Poteshny Dvortez, the Pleasure Palace. They were passed through a steel door, entered officially in a record book, and then urged forward again. The place was a prison. There wasn't the slightest doubt of that.

To their surprise, they were shoved into an enormous room in which there were at least a dozen other prisoners, and the door was locked behind them.

Abruptly, in Mayan, Doc said, "Pretend you do not recognize anyone here, and stick to it."

"Don't worry," Monk said. "We've been tossed in with Mahli and his bruisers." Monk spoke Mayan. He added, "Is that babe yonder the inimitable Seryi?"

"You don't know her!" Doc warned.

"Who said I did? That's the truth, too!" Monk eyed Seryi admiringly and added in English, "You know, that's a real dishy female. I wonder if she would like to talk to a gentleman and a scholar?" He sauntered toward Seryi.

The huge Mahli—he showed considerable battering at the hands of the police—came over to Doc Savage and said bitterly, "So they got you?"

"I don't believe I understand," Doc said blankly.

"Don't give me that I-don't-know-you look," Mahli growled.

"Am I supposed to knew you?"

Mahli considered the answer, rubbing his bruised jaw, and finally shrugged. "I don't know who is the fool. Me, probably." He grinned with no humor and fell in with Doc's pretense, explaining, "You see, three gentlemen who I had reasons for presuming were Doc Savage and two associates extracted information of value from a man named Frunzoff. I tried to recover that information. I failed, and in a rage, I informed the police of the truth. They threw me and my friends in jail."

"That is interesting," Doc admitted.

Mahli, in a louder voice and for effect, added, "I had the interests of the party at heart. The party has made a mistake, but I am sure they will find it out and release me. There is no man in Russia stronger for the party than I."

Ham Brooks grinned. "Do you think that little speech, coming in over the microphones, will boost your stock?"

Wryly, with his lips only, Mahli said, "It doesn't hurt to try."

"What will happen to us next?" Doc asked curiously.

Mahli shrugged. "Usually men in this room at noon are shot at sundown," he said.

IT was cold in the room. They had been given no shoes, and the stone floor was a numbing chill against their bare feet. They sat, as some of the other prisoners were doing, cross-legged for warmth. There was not much conversation.

Monk Mayfair had managed some sort of conversation with Seryi, and seemed to get some satisfaction from the scowls Ham sent in his direction. Presently Monk rejoined them.

"She seems to be a very sweet girl," Monk said.

In English Ham said, "I'm sure she is." In Mayan, with his face as straight, he added, "I want to be around when you make your first pass at her. Five will get you twenty that they'll have to hunt for the parts."

Monk grinned. "Sour grapes."

About three o'clock, their friend from the U.S. consulate, Clyde Warper, came to see them. He was upset and harried. "Are you all right?" he asked anxiously.

"I wouldn't call it all right," Doc said. "We are still physically intact."

"I had a hell of a time getting in to see you," Warper explained. "Things are in a mess. I'm having trouble getting word of this affair out to Washington so pressure can be put on. I've been informed the sleet storm destroyed all c ommunication. A likely excuse."

"It's a hornet's nest," Doc agreed. "But don't get to feeling you are responsible. It was our doing, and except for an accident, we would have left Russia safely."

Clyde Warper hesitated, then said, "You've got good nerves, I hear."

"What do you mean?"

"I would hate to pass this information to a weak sister," Warper said, "but you can take it. Here it is: you are scheduled to be shot. The word has come straight from Stalin himself."

"That seems rather definite," Doc said.

"It's more than that. It's final." Warper moistened his lips. "There'll be plenty of hell to pay later, but I guess they're willing to risk that."

"They're not noted for being afraid to take risks."

"They're not noted for a lot of things," Clyde Warper said. "I'm going to leave you, and see how many fires I can build under swivel chairs. I don't think the fools realize the international consequences that will come from shooting you fellows."

"Do what you can," Doc said.

"I will."

When Clyde Warper had gone, Ham Brooks said, shivering, "That was an openhanded way of discussing the end of our trail. My God, I'm just beginning to realize they will shoot us. I think I knew it all along, but somehow it didn't register."

Monk shuddered and sat down. "Find a more cheerful subject, won't you!"

With a startling clanging, the steel door slammed open again, and blank-faced soldiers, rifles in hand, marched inside. Orders were shouted and the prisoners lined up.

Doc Savage found himself beside Mahli in the lineup, and the big Russian looked up at him wryly.

"The visit of your friend from the embassy was unfortunate," Mahli remarked.

"In what way?"

"In the most direct way," Mahli said. "They're going to shoot us now. Immediately."

Chapter XI

DOC SAVAGE'S flake-gold eyes whipped over the faces of the prisoners, and it came to him that he was probably the only one who hadn't realized what the influx of armed soldiers meant.

Not that there was quailing before death. Most of the men had Mahli's erect cold acceptance of fate. Two or three were very pale. No face in the big stone room was wearing its natural color, probably.

Seryi stood straight, without trembling. Her face had a restraint that was complete, Madonnalike, lovely and distant. Doc looked at her wonderingly. For a fullness of steel-wrapped nerve without outward strain, he had never seen better, man or woman. Madonnalike was the description. A young woman of extreme and unusual capabilities, facing with acceptance and resignation the hell that this room would become when the rifles began smashing.

"Monk," Doc said, using the Mayan tongue, "this is going to be rough, even with all the breaks. We'll need what numbers we can get. So I'm going to team up with the other prisoners."

"All right by me."

"Get the information to Mahli. Have him pass it to the others."

"How the hell will I do that?" Monk blurted.

"I don't know. But try."

Doc Savage stepped out of the line, held up a hand, and approached the execution-squad leader.

He told the man, “Get Zardnov here. Or Frunzoff. One or the other. You understand?”

The Russian had been expecting something like that, Doc surmised, although the man took his time, scowling, demanding, “For what purpose?”

“Tell them I have something to offer,” Doc said. “Tell them the bargain will not be repeated. It is now or never.”

The Russian laughed. “Now or never—I would say so, too.” However, he swung, snapped a command at a junior to take over, and left the execution room, the door being carefully unlocked, then locked behind him again.

Zardnov had been waiting nearby, obviously. He appeared in brisk order, but said coldly, “I happened to be passing. They were lucky to catch me. What is this nonsense?”

“There was a spool containing wire,” Doc said.

“You admit that, then?”

Doc shrugged. “I wish to make a deal.”

“What deal?”

“The obvious one—for my life and those of my friends.”

“And so?”

“Don’t be coy with me, Zardnov,” Doc said coldly. “This is of quite an importance to you. Stalin is involved, and a great deal of ill feeling throughout the Council. I imagine the gossip is already around, and it isn’t going to do the regime any good.” Doc eyed the man intently, and added, “You, I imagine, are not uninterested in the existence of Frunzoff as a prepared successor to—”

“Shut up!” Zardnov blurted. He came close to Doc Savage, adding, “Lower your voice, you fool. If you knew the bitter feeling among the Central Committee members—”

Doc reached out, seized the man, jerked him close, and slapped a hand against the anaesthetic-gas grenade which he had planted in the show handkerchief in Zardnov’s breast coat pocket during the mysterious goings-on at the airport when the smoke grenade had been “accidentally” detonated by Doc’s double.

Doc held his breath.

HE turned his head, saw Mahli wheel wildly and whisper to the man next to him in the line of prisoners. An order, Doc knew, to hold his breath for as long as possible, and to pass the instruction down the line.

The trained reaction was wonderful to watch. Doc recalled how Seryi, earlier in the night, had said that Mahli was a top agent and that his men were superior. She had not exaggerated. No questions were asked. Obedience was instant and complete. The word to hold breaths went down the line faster than a gossip rumor.

It held, even when a guard shot two prisoners in cold blood with his rifle. That happened after the guards and execution squad began to fold down on the floor.

Zardnov was already loose in Doc’s arms. Doc frisked him hurriedly, taking what documents he could find, and particularly Zardnov’s diplomatic papers and local police passes. They might be handy.

Counting seconds mentally until they reached a minute, Doc released his breath, said in Russian, “Let’s go. Get into Communist Street, turn left, and there will be two cars parked near the Poteshny Dvortez. The keys will be in them. Leave no one behind. The cars are armored. Make for the Tanitzkiye Gate.”

Mahli blurted, “This was arranged?”

“Come on,” Doc said curtly. “This was planned for months. There are escapes prepared from every predicament we could visualize.”

Mahli grinned an ugly grin. “You are not disappointing me after all, Mr. Savage.” He wheeled and bellowed at his men to be sure to grab ammunition for the rifles they were taking off the gassed guards.

Going down a hall, Seryi ranged alongside Doc Savage and asked wonderingly, “How did you plant the gas grenade on Zardnov? It was a gas grenade, was it not?”

“Yes. It was put there earlier. At the airport.”

“But you asked the executioner for Frunzoff. Suppose he had come instead of Zardnov?”

“There was a plant in every suit of clothes Frunzoff had,” Doc said. “We arranged that last night while we were working on him.”

“I’m beginning to think you are infallible.”

“Only every other hour,” Doc said. “Or I wouldn’t be here. We’re not out of it, you know.”

IN the ancient thoroughfare that was the only street in the Kremlin, they ran in a compact group. Doc noted that Mahli snapped an order, and his men moved to positions which ringed Doc, Monk, Ham, and Seryi. Mahli said wryly, “We’re not ungrateful. This is a protective measure, not a device to surround you.”

“Never mind the gratitude,” Doc said rapidly. “Before we get out of this—yonder are the cars. I hope they hold everybody.”

“They will, under the circumstances,” Mahli said.

The shooting began now. Sporadic at first, three or four spaced reports, then a flurry or two. Then it stopped.

They jammed into the cars. Doc, Monk, Ham, Seryi, and some others took one machine. Mahli and the rest wedged into the other touring car. Mahli shouted, “After we are past the gate, let me lead. You may know Moscow, but not the way I know it, I assure you.”

The shooting started anew. Two bullets came into their car, smashing windows, and a man threw his body back in an arching bend and made ghastly mewing sounds.

"Keep down," Doc said. "The car bodies are armor steel. Or were supposed to be."

He slid down himself. He was driving. The plan—originally it had envisaged nothing as elaborate as this break—was for them to leave through the Tanitzkiye Gate, where only one guard was stationed. There was even an arrangement for an American secret agent who had operated a fruit concession nearby for several weeks to shoot down the guard if necessary. It didn't prove needed. One of Mahli's men shot him expertly long before they reached the gate.

The cars piled ahead wildly, reeling through the small landscaped park, swinging in sharp turns. Mahli led, and he, as he had said, knew the streets. He chose with an uncanny facility those which were least slotted with traffic, not a mean accomplishment at this hour of the day.

In the western business area, Mahli's car swerved to the right and dived into an arched areaway. Men were leaning out, beckoning Doc's party to follow. They did so.

Unloading from the cars in haste, they sprinted through doors and hallways, Mahli finally turning through a door which proved to be the rear entrance to a tailor shop presided over by a very fat and very startled tailor. The proprietor barked anxiously at Mahli.

Mahli told Doc, "There are security-police uniforms here to fit everyone. In a tailor shop? Why not?" He slapped the fat tailor on the back. "Ivan is a resourceful fellow."

Doc said, "You keep a few aces in your sleeve too, I see."

Mahli nodded. "In Russia today, who can tell when it will be very convenient to look like a soldier? You will find credentials in each, incidentally."

The tailor seized Doc's arm excitedly. He was not, he yelled, certain that he had a uniform large enough for Doc. A uniform for a large man, yes. But a large man with a great belly, if he did possibly have one.

He had one uniform long enough, and as the tailor said, it had an excess of midriff.

Mahli came over to Doc.

"There is another car near here which you can use," he said. "It is an army vehicle. It will fit well with the uniforms."

"Fine."

"I would like to suggest," Mahli added, "in view of the hell all of Russia is going to be for you in an hour or two, that you try the bold way."

"The airport?"

Mahli nodded. "The crew of your plane are being held there." Mahli described the spot, explaining the information had come from his tailor friend. "I'm confident, having seen you function, that you can free them, get to your plane, and take off."

"Thanks."

"It is a favor," Mahli said. "You could return it, you know."

"How?"

"I am an ambitious man," Mahli said. "The present regime will not last forever, and after that, who can say? Maybe an ambitious young fellow like myself, no? It would be a help to me if I knew whether Frunzoff is the man prepared for the number-one spot."

"He is," Doc said.

"Thank you." Mahli was deeply grateful. "The information makes Frunzoff a very poor insurance risk, I can assure you."

Doc frowned. "That sort of violence is never going to establish security for Russia."

There was a thin fierceness behind Mahli's grin. "We shall see. Perhaps I could become a tame man."

"It would be worth considering."

Seryi stood beside Doc Savage. "Mahli is quite a man," she said softly. "He has qualities you have not observed."

Doc looked at her, his admiration suddenly frank. "So have you, if I may say so. A new one, a little more titanic than the predecessors, develops each time I meet you, it seems."

Mahli laughed. "I imagine my lovely cousin has a wish that this thing of meetings and developments continues."

Seryi reddened and said bitingly, "Tact is something you could acquire, you big lout."

Mahli roared. "What is the thing that loses a man a woman quickest? Why, tact!"

The tailor came bustling up. "The army car is ready," he said. "I would not advise a full day of gossip."

Chapter XII

DOC SAVAGE left his headquarters on the eighty-sixth floor of a midtown New York skyscraper, rode a taxi to the rather snobbish club on upper Fifth Avenue where Ham Brooks lived, and found Ham arguing the merits of a recent Supreme Court case with another attorney.

"We'll pick up Monk." Doc consulted his watch. "We've not too much time. The conference at Lake Success is at three o'clock."

"Monk will be at the Corona Theater on Forty-seventh Street," Ham said.

"I'll drive by."

"Monk," said Ham, grinning, "has staged the

damnedest recovery in the ten days since we got out of Moscow. He's convinced some guy he is considering angeling a show, and that lets him hang around rehearsals. Imagine that! Monk couldn't bankroll a decent suit of clothes right now. But you can guess his angle. It's a musical they're rehearsing. Babes."

"Maybe he'd rather miss this."

Ham shook his head quickly. "No. Not this. Monk has great feeling for our old pal Zardnov."

Monk, when they found him, expressed the same sentiment. "I hear our old pal Zardnov hit town last night," he said. "When are we going out to see old pal Zardnov?"

"Right now," Doc explained. "There has been a United Nations committee all set up and waiting."

THE room at Lake Success was small, pleasant except for a reek of cigar smoke that was just a trifle too thin to saw up in blocks.

Zardnov jumped to his feet, glaring, when Doc Savage arrived. The committee had been giving Zardnov a hard time of it, evidently. Zardnov whacked a desk with his cane.

"I demand," Zardnov shouted at Doc, "that you here and now admit as lies all that you have told this committee pertaining—"

"Sit down," Doc said curtly. "You're talking about the incident ten days ago in Moscow, presumably?"

"There was no incident!" Zardnov bellowed.

Monk asked, "What do you guys call an incident over there?"

Doc addressed Zardnov. "I presume you expect me to make a denial that there exists a man named Frunzoff who has been prepared for heading the Russian government in an emergency, and accordingly has more complete knowledge of Russian affairs, particularly the atom-bomb situation, than any other man in Russia other than you-know-who?"

"A lie," said Zardnov. "I categorically and specifically deny—"

"Let's shorten this," Doc said. "We have a wire recording of an interview with Frunzoff, given under the influence of some very fine truth serum. The information in the recording, I can assure you, is going to be very disastrous to Russia."

"That also is untrue—"

"Remember at the airport in Moscow when the smoke grenade went off by accident?" Doc asked.

"Accident!" Zardnov exploded. "The purpose of that was to conceal your silly gas bomb in my clothing!"

Doc shook his head. "It had two purposes. Get his cane, Monk."

Monk walked over, Zardnov raised the cane to strike at the homely chemist, and Monk made a quick feint and got it. Zardnov swore. Monk laughed and retreated with the cane.

"Such hoodlum acts," Zardnov screamed, "are below the dignity of an international body of this type. I demand the arrest of these men."

Monk was inspecting the cane. He gripped it in his powerful hands, twisted, and began to unscrew the top section.

Zardnov's eyes protruded. "That cane is supposed to be solid ironwood—"

"It's not your original cane, Zardnov," Doc told him wearily. "This one, an exact imitation, and I do mean exact, was made several weeks ago when you were in the hospital with a bad cold, and the cane was accessible to us for periods of time."

Zardnov looked sick. Wordless.

"The recorder wire is inside the cane," Doc assured him. "You brought it from Moscow yourself."

Zardnov sat down very slowly and carefully, seeming not to notice that there was no chair.

THE END

INTERMISSION by Will Murray

The Berlin Airlift continued into 1949, when Marshal Stalin, recognizing the determination of the U.N., simply gave up. Later that year, Germany officially split into East and West Germany, with Berlin becoming a divided island in the middle of the Russian sector. Ultimately the Berlin Wall would be erected, turning the concept of an Iron Curtain into a concrete reality.

At Street & Smith, change was sweeping that storied pulp house. Babette Rosmond, editor of *Doc Savage* and *The Shadow* for three years, was preparing to go out on maternity leave in the Fall of 1947. Before exiting, she commissioned a last Doc Savage novel from Lester Dent, *Terror Wears No Shoes*. Dent finished it in September.

The name of the principal villain, Makaroff, suggests no doubt as to Russian complicity, Dent's careful evasions aside. As a matter of fact, the name recalls Dent's Florida sailing days. S. Vadim Makaroff was the captain of the ketch *Vamarie,* which won the sixth annual St. Petersburg-Havana yacht race in 1935. Dent crewed aboard John L. Whitman's *Four Winds,* out of Pittsburgh, during that race.

When Rosmond returned early in 1948, she approved another Doc story ripped from the headlines. *The Angry Canary* focused on the Indo-Pakistan War of 1947-48, out of which emerged the new nation of Pakistan. Then Rosmond quit to pursue a career as a novelist. William J. de Grouchy, under whom Rosmond got her start at Street & Smith, stepped up to resume charge of her titles.

Babette Rosmond

To catch up, he commissioned two new Doc outlines, one of which became *The Red Spider.*

Amid growing international tensions, a worrisome question arose: did the Soviets possess an atomic bomb? At that juncture, the U.S. was the sole nuclear power. Rumors abounded in the press that Russia had—or would soon acquire—one of their own.

Dent outlined a story he first called "From Hell, Madonna" in which Doc Savage tackled the problem. Lester was enjoying a brief resurgence in his writing career. After writing his first successful slick story, "River Crossing," he wrote "In Hell, Madonna," which was his working title. Extracted from a line in Shakespeare's *Twelfth Night* ("I think his soul is in hell, madonna."), it did not go over well with his returning editor.

Dent's telegram tells the tale:

> WILLIAM J. DE GROUCHY
> Editor Doc Savage
> 774 Lidgerwood Ave.
> Elizabeth NEW JERSEY
>
> FOR TITLES WHAT DO YOU THINK OF KILL IN MOSCOW STOP MR CALAMITY STOP ONE MAN SCREAMING STOP MOSCOW MANEUVER STOP
>
> THE RED NIGHT STOP THE PRINCE IN RED STOP WE ARE WEAK ON TITLES BUT HOPE SOME OF THIS HELPS OUT SORRY THE OTHER ONE HAD ODOR BILL
>
> LESTER DENT

Evidently de Grouchy told Dent that "In Hell, Madonna" stank as a title. No record exists of which if any of these alternate titles was chosen.

Further changes swept Street & Smith. De Grouchy abruptly left the company that summer. His replacement was Daisy Bacon, who since 1929 had helmed S&S's best-selling title *Love Story Magazine,* and was in charge of *Detective Story* as well.

Love Story expired in 1948. Now only four pulps remained of the once-formidable chain. After the line was consolidated, three of them fell into Bacon's hands. A decision was made to revert to what was called "pre-war" size. In the fall of 1948, the surviving quartet switched from digest to full pulp size. *Doc Savage, Science Detective* went back to its original title.

Daisy Bacon

Looking over the situation, Bacon saw that despite their quality the fan mail was running against stories like *Terror Wears No Shoes.* An executive decision was made to kill the retitled "In Hell, Madonna" outright.

No correspondence exists between Bacon and Dent covering the matter. But we can surmise much from their exchange regarding *Return from Cormoral,* the story Lester was working on at the time "In Hell, Madonna" would have been going to press.

In September, Dent outlined a story he called "Miracle by Williams," which focused on intrigue surrounding a deposed European dictator hiding in the U.S. under an alias, and a strange man named Macbeth Williams.

"I had planned to use a Florida resort, and one of the Bahama islands," Dent explained in the accompanying letter. "The matter at stake in reality, the future of a small nation, isn't developed too much in the outline, I notice. That should be emphasized, if we're going to keep up Doc's 'saving the world' tendencies..."

Bacon shot the outline back on the 20th of September:

Dear Les:

Thank you for the speed on the Doc Savage outline. I am sorry not to ask you to go ahead with the story as it now stands but I don't think you have given us much to go on and tying it to the European situation is just too easy. The firm wishes to give the European situation a miss and I would rule it out myself anyway because the public is thoroughly fed up with politics and propaganda in fiction. I don't know where the idea of Doc Savage saving the world came from but I suppose it is a hangover from the One World idea. As long as we are dropping the science detective and returning to just Doc Savage, I think that we should return to a real adventure...

It was no doubt a blow to Dent's newfound enthusiasm for Doc Savage. Not only did *The Red Spider* represent an important new direction for the fifteen year old series, but it featured the final appearances of Long Tom Roberts and Renny Renwick, both in wartime military uniform. Doc Savage takes his first recorded supersonic flight. And he encounters one of those rare women who crack his metallic facade, Seryi Mitroff.

The Red Spider contains a cryptic line: "Molotov vetoed." This is a topical reference to Soviet diplomat Vyacheslav Molotov, for whom the Molotov cocktail was named, and who was infamous for his anti-U.S. vetoes at the U.N. He was ousted as Russia's foreign minister in 1949.

A decade in the future, Ian Fleming would make millions writing stories like *The Red Spider.* Here, Lester Dent was on the leading edge of the Cold War spy subgenre—which had yet to flower.

In Daisy Bacon's defense, she was simply being responsive to the general mood at that time.

Lester Dent

With Eastern Europe transforming into the so-called Communist Bloc, and another wartime ally, China, turning to Communism, the reading public was averse to stories focusing on the Red Scare.

In the revived *Doc Savage* letters column, Daisy Bacon printed several letters from readers who begged for a return to more escapist days. One wrote, "During the last two or three years I have not cared for some of the Doc stories; especially those all about spies." Another reader was more blunt: "Please make Kenneth Robeson write some good old-fashioned Doc novels. Tell him to keep his dirty old spies out."

S&S issued the first quarterly pulp-sized issues in the Autumn of 1948. *The Shadow* kicked off the revival with a Fall, 1948 issue. There was no corresponding issue of *Doc Savage,* which returned with the Winter 1949 issue. "In Hell, Madonna" had been scheduled for the October-November 1948 issue of *Doc Savage, Science Detective.* That issue was simply skipped. Most readers probably never noticed that *Doc Savage* was off the stands an extra month.

George Rozen's preliminary cover rough for *Return from Cormoral*

Edd Cartier's surviving artwork, with its curious national flag—half-sickle and half-Swastika—suggests that they were drawn from Dent's outline. As Dent himself wrote in his proposal:

> This one is laid against a background of international trouble that should be even more in the public eye about the time it is published—the question of whether or not the Soviet has the atom bomb.
>
> It isn't a bomb story, because the bomb doesn't appear. And for the sake of a the few specks of international courtesy still floating around, I suppose it would do no harm not to name Soviet Russia as the locale.

Evidently, de Grouchy had either overruled him or Dent experienced a change of heart. The artwork survives today as proof sheets still bearing the working title "In Hell, Madonna" and the date "5/48"—the month it was accepted.

Converting back to the pulp-sized *Doc Savage,* Bacon replaced Cartier with that old warhorse Paul Orban, evidently for his nostalgic appeal. George Rozen, the premier *Shadow* cover artist, was also recalled to duty. He had never before painted *Doc Savage* covers.

Dent dutifully reworked the "Williams" outline, deleting the European aspects. Retitled *Return from Cormoral,* it appeared in the Spring, 1949 issue. But not before Bacon asked for one final change. No doubt adapted from the outline, which mentioned an Arctic mine backstory, George Rozen's cover art depicted a parka-clad Doc Savage crouching before his new personal jet while a Polar bear sniffs the Arctic air. Dent had to reformulate his ending to justify that cover. The story was to originally climax in the Bahamas.

As so often the case, Lester Dent was ahead of his time. The first Russian A-bomb detonation, dubbed "First Lightning," took place on August 29, 1949. The Cold War veered into a profoundly more dangerous direction. But Doc Savage would not participate in that stage. At least, not in print. *Doc Savage* ended with the Summer, 1949 issue.

With Lester Dent's death in 1959, the manuscript for "In Hell, Madonna" was forgotten. But the Street & Smith files contained a reference to it, and that led to Dent's widow Norma discovering the carbon copy among her husband's papers. An arrangement was worked out between Bantam Books and Doc Savage copyright owners Condé Nast, Inc., whereby Mrs. Dent was paid for a copy of the long-forgotten tale—Street & Smith's copy having long since vanished.

First published in July, 1979, *The Red Spider* created a sensation among astonished Doc Savage readers. Now, almost 30 years later, we are proud to represent this exciting tale in a definitive edition, graced by Bob Larkin's stunning Bantam Books cover, and for the first time illustrated with Edd Cartier's hitherto unseen 1948 art. •

RETURN FROM CORMORAL

By Kenneth Robeson

Chapter I

THE docking was scheduled for two o'clock, but at that hour there was no sign of the tramp steamer *Meg Finnegan,* and aboard the tug that had come out to tow the steamer into the harbor they shut off the engines. The tugboat crew lolled about, enjoying the unscheduled leisure, and a couple of the men dropped baited fishhooks over the rail. In the pilot house the tug skipper fretted and called the dispatcher by two-way radio to ask if there had been an error in timing.

Mr. Bradley, the tug's mate, watched the skipper's agitation with some amusement. Bradley, a dark, intense young man, had little patience with the Old Man, or with his own job as second in command of a greasy tug.

"Somebody make a mistake, Sam?" Bradley asked.

"Somebody better not have!" said the skipper, squatting to peer at the little red-green control lights on the two-way radio, which he had always distrusted.

"You wouldn't be put in a tizzy by half a billion bucks, more or less?"

The skipper ignored this. He finished talking

into the radio, cradled the handset and went to the rail and peered into the haze that blanketed the sea. Presently, he complained, "How the devil do I know what kind of a screwball this Macbeth Williams is? How do I know he won't blame me because this old cake of rust he's riding doesn't make port on time?"

Bradley laughed. "How do you know he's a screwball?"

"I've never heard any argument to the contrary," the skipper said. "And what would you say?"

"I've never met the guy."

"Neither have I." The skipper got out a stench-box of a pipe and went through his ceremony of getting it underway. "But I'm looking forward to it. You take a guy with half a billion waiting any time he wants to lay a hand on it, and he never lays a hand on it— that kind of cuckoo I want to see."

Bradley asked seriously, "Is that a fact?"

"Is what a fact?" the skipper snapped.

"That Macbeth Williams could have that many shekels by reaching for them and won't?"

"Hell, yes."

"I see what you mean by cuckoo," Bradley said.

TWO hours later a rust-marred old slattern of the seas hove out of the haze to seaward. Having taken a long time to get from where she had been, the vessel *Meg Finnegan* approached Miami ship channel at a plodding four knots.

As far as anyone aboard would have admitted knowing, the steamer was merely putting into Miami because she was bringing back to civilization four bedraggled scientists who were the victims of a colossal flop entitled the "Cormoral Island Expedition of the Kendall Foundation of St. Louis, Missouri."

Cormoral Island was a scrawny out-jutting of lava in the remote South Atlantic. It was avoided even by goony birds. It was a sure bet to be avoided hereafter by the four scientists of the defunct Kendall Foundation.

The four Kendall men had been stranded on Cormoral Island for some six months. Their parent organization, Kendall Foundation of St. Louis, had gone stony broke shortly after depositing them on the island to do hydrographic and geological research. There'd been no funds to send a boat to take them off and they'd been left to their fate.

At the present moment, having dragged a ship's mattress to the shady side of the deckhouse, the four academicians were engaged in a mild poker game.

All four annotators wore the usual startling explorers' beards, deep sunburns, dirty trousers, and with one exception, that of Professor Macbeth Williams, no shirts.

Dr. Austin Ulm, the expedition's stratigraphist, was dealing from a grimy deck. He endeavored not to toss the cards on the litter of kitchen matches being used for currency.

Professor Williams, smirking, remarked, "I foresee three aces and a couple of jacks in this hand."

Crikeland, the ornithologist, snorted. "Wanna bet?"

"Watch out, Crike," said Swanberg, the archaeologist. "Haven't you learned you're a sucker to bet the prof on one of his predictions?"

"Stop kidding," said Crikeland.

"I'm not kidding," Swanberg replied seriously.

Crikeland picked up his cards. He groaned. "I would like to express an unbiased and fully thought-out opinion of the hands you deal, Ulm," he told the stratigraphist. "My blind Aunt Louise, who has a larcenous and lecherous nature, is far more accommodating."

"Anybody got openers?" Swanberg demanded.

Professor Macbeth Williams, the hydrographer, picked up his hand and examined it. His sandy eyebrows nearly became exclamation points when he saw three aces and two jacks, a full house. First he looked astonished. Then he looked as if he had been struck a dirty blow.

"What's the matter? You pick up something pretty hot?" demanded Crikeland suspiciously.

The professor made an inarticulate sound and sprang to his feet. Without expressing more than the noise, he lunged away.

"Hey! What the devil!" gasped Ulm.

"Come back here with them cards, dammit!" yelled Crikeland testily. "We only have the one deck, and it's no good with a hand missing."

Professor Williams wheeled and came back. His face was pale. "I'm sorry, gentlemen!" he said stiffly, and endeavored to thrust his cards back into the stock part of the deck. But Crikeland, reminding him the deck was still in play, took the cards from Williams' hand and tossed them on the mattress, where everyone saw the three aces and two jacks.

"What do you know, he called the hand before it was dealt!" Crikeland gasped.

"And why not?" Swanberg asked dryly.

MACBETH WILLIAMS moved apart and stood at the ship's rail, where he stared unseeingly and without interest at a small tug standing toward them out of the haze that covered the sea. It did not occur to him that the presence of the small boat meant land nearby; he was too preoccupied. He saw that his hands were trembling, and placed them on the rail where he could watch them misbehave.

Macbeth was an unnecessarily long young man who had the only beard in the collection that was curly and blond. He had a naturally serious manner and the air of being a rather likable young man. The parts of his face not hidden by foliage promised to be modestly handsome.

Macbeth jumped like a Mexican bean when stratigraphist Ulm leaned on the rail at his elbow.

"You out of the game, Williams?" Ulm asked.

"Yes, I think I shall drop out, if you gentlemen don't mind," Macbeth replied uncomfortably.

"How come?"

Macbeth Williams' discomfort increased, and he mumbled, "I suppose I merely don't feel like playing anymore."

"You threw down," said Ulm, "some nice cards."

"Uh-huh," Macbeth muttered.

"Three aces and two rascals."

"Uh-huh."

"An earthquake," Ulm continued, "wouldn't make me lay down a hand like that."

"Earthquake," mumbled Macbeth, "is exactly what it was."

"So the light dawned," said Ulm. He was a stocky man, with a hawk nose and dark eyes nesting rather fiercely in his thicket of whiskers.

Macbeth nodded, shuddering. "Blindingly," he agreed.

"About time," said Ulm.

"I'm frightened stiff," Williams confessed.

"Of what?"

"Of bats in belfrys, of a little canvas jacket with sleeves that buckle in the back," groaned Macbeth Williams. "In short, I'm sure this must be a hallucination."

Ulm grinned. "Hallucinations," he remarked, "are one-man dogs."

"I don't understand that either," Macbeth confessed. "You and Crikeland seemed convinced that I can foresee the immediate future. Even Swanberg is becoming convinced."

"Four of us," Ulm stated, "can hardly be crazy."

Macbeth looked at the other man wryly. "They build insane asylums to hold more than one person."

"Wanta bet you're nuts?" asked Ulm.

"I certainly intend to consult a psychiatrist and find out," said Macbeth Williams. "And at the very first opportunity, too."

The poker game suddenly broke up behind them. Crikeland and Swanberg rushed to the rail. They peered into the haze. "I believe I see land," Crikeland blurted. "My God, I hope it isn't Cormoral Island again!"

WHEN Macbeth Williams walked into his Miami hotel room late that evening, the place seemed incredibly depressing, and he sank into a chair without removing his hat. Even the garish and carnival-like view of the resort city through the window offered no cheer. Macbeth hardly glanced up when Ulm entered. The stratigraphist looked at the younger man in alarm.

"Oh, brother!" said Ulm. "You had us worried. Where the devil have you been?"

Macbeth gazed unhappily at the floor. "You gentlemen shouldn't have worried about me, you really shouldn't."

"I don't see," said Ulm, "how a lad with access to half a billion bucks can look as gloomy as you. Incidentally, that was quite a surprise."

"I don't believe I understand what you mean by surprise—"

"The news that you could have half a billion if you wished."

"Oh," said Macbeth Williams.

"That was quite a bombshell," Ulm went on.

"Uh, was it?"

Ulm grinned. "A little like finding that the old brass bedstead was made of solid gold."

Macbeth Williams held up a distressed hand. "I assure you, Austin, that I'm not made of gold. The whole thing is a great misunderstanding. You see, I don't have a thing to do with the estate. I'm entirely aloof from it."

"That's a lot of dough to be aloof from," Ulm told him.

"True enough," Macbeth muttered. He returned his prominent jaw to cupped hands. "It has, I assure you, bothered me on occasion. Holding aloof, I mean. Frankly, it's not very profitable to be aloof."

Ulm peered at him in amazement. "You mean you don't get an income?"

"A hundred dollars a month."

"Good God! Not even peanuts."

"Oh, I manage to get along," said Macbeth Williams. "I'm careful, you see, not to let anyone know that I'm the only son of the late Roderick Williams, tycoon extraordinary. That makes it simpler to live cheaply."

Ulm examined his fellow scientist thoughtfully. "So that's why none of us knew about it until the skipper of that tug passed the news. How come the tug skipper knew?"

Macbeth shrugged. "The estate management was concerned about my welfare, I suppose. They're very thoughtful that way. If I should die, the estate goes to several charitable institutions, and they might lose their good jobs."

"They've got a point there."

"Possibly. They're fine men, though."

"How did this all come about?" Ulm asked.

"My father left a will," Macbeth Williams explained. Then he added hastily, "It was perfectly agreeable, though. Actually, we talked it over. The will carried out my own suggestions."

"The hell it did," said Ulm. "Who does that make a screwball?"

Macbeth Williams winced. "Almost exactly the words of the psychiatrist," he said.

"What psycho was that?"

"The one I've been consulting this afternoon."

"Oh, oh," said Ulm. "You didn't lose any time."

Macbeth Williams jumped up, went to the window and stood looking out. "I'm afraid the chap didn't help my peace of mind," he went on uneasily.

"What'd the psycho say?" Ulm demanded.

Macbeth hesitated, then decided to make a full confession. "I'm naturally a reticent sort," he explained, "and I find it a little difficult to talk about myself. No man likes to take his own machinery out and display its flaws, even to a psychoanalyst. I understand fully, of course, that an analyst must pry the stuff out, and this one did a good job. He put me on a couch."

"So them guys really use a couch," Ulm remarked. "What'd he do next? Start you to remembering back when you wore diapers?"

Macbeth nodded. "I got the standard routine, I imagine. Yes, he delved into my childhood. I don't think he found it very rewarding. I had a very drab youth, you know. Somewhat on the lonely side. Lots of books and tutors, but not too many playmates. You see, my father was very busy being a tycoon. Quite a remarkable man, though."

Macbeth hesitated, apparently gave something a thorough mental chewing-over, then gave a gesture of resignation. "My father was a man of remarkable foresight. He was a good guesser. All of his guesses proved to be right. The psychiatrist made a good deal of that point, apparently."

"You mean," said Ulm, "that this gift you've got of knowing what is going to happen in the near future is something you inherited from the old man? You know, that could be."

"No, no!" Macbeth held up a hand. "That wasn't the psycho's idea, I'm afraid."

"No?"

"I think he felt my psychosis about the matter is a result of having that kind of a father."

"Psychosis?"

"Neurosis was the word."

"Psychosis, neurosis, little rabbits," said Ulm. "The guy is wrong. You should have proved to him that he was wrong."

Macbeth grinned sheepishly. "I'm afraid I did endeavor to do so."

"Yeah? What'd you predict?"

"That the analyst would have a visitor promptly at three fifteen o'clock," Macbeth explained.

"And did he?"

"Yes."

Ulm chuckled. "Fine. I'll bet that jolted him."

"I believe it did," Macbeth agreed. "But it was an act of a charlatan on my part. You see, I happened to glimpse his appointment book, and there was an appointment down for three fifteen."

"You faked it?" Ulm asked disapprovingly.

"I couldn't resist doing so. The fellow was so smugly convinced I was having neurotic imaginings."

Ulm came over and seriously placed a hand on Macbeth's shoulder. "You mustn't do things like that, old boy," he said solemnly. "This thing you've got is genuine. Don't hoke it. Treat it naturally. When it doesn't want to come don't force it."

"You're being silly!" Macbeth Williams declared. "I haven't any gift. I couldn't have. There isn't such a thing."

"It'll take a lot of unselling to convince me of that," Ulm said earnestly. "I've watched this thing closely. You can't Robinson Crusoe with a man without getting down to his basic mettle. Williams, we spent six months together on that infernal island, and I know what I saw."

"You probably saw a cuckoo," Macbeth told him glumly.

Ulm, with a solemn frown and no hint of levity, said, "I don't think so, son. I wouldn't undersell this thing, if I were you."

Macbeth Williams was making distressed motions indicating there was probably nothing to the whole thing, when the telephone rang. He went to the telephone, where, after a first astonished outcry—it sounded quite alarmed, in a delighted sort of way—his conversation was too low-pitched for Ulm to overhear, although the latter openly endeavored to eavesdrop.

When Macbeth turned, he wore the pain-and-ecstasy expression of a ticklish man being tickled.

"Carlie," he said.

"Is that good?" Ulm asked.

"I'm engaged to her," Macbeth Williams explained.

"That could be good," Ulm said. "Is she pretty?"

"Yes. Oh, yes, indeed," Macbeth Williams replied. "But she's also practical."

"Practical? Is that good?"

Macbeth Williams grinned wryly at Ulm. "What would you say?"

Chapter II

MISS CARLIE McGUIGGAN beamed at Professor Macbeth Williams. "Hello there, hydrographist," she said. She kissed Macbeth, not sparingly, on the lips, thereby causing the hydrographist's eyes to bulge. Carlie McGuiggan was a tall, straw blonde, lovely to look at, but possibly a trifle overdeveloped as to common sense, Macbeth sometimes felt. "Well, what have you to say for yourself?" she asked smilingly.

"I've been away," Macbeth Williams murmured, endeavoring to recover a little composure.

"I believe I noticed," Carlie remarked. "How did it happen?"

Macbeth told her seriously that some months ago he had joined an outfit known as the Kendall Foundation of St. Louis in the capacity of hydrographist, and gone on an expedition to a place called Cormoral Island, a very devil of a spot, where he and his three scientific comrades had been isolated nearly six months when the foundation went bust. They had been rescued only because a tramp steamer had happened to investigate the island for guano. At this point, Macbeth recovered himself and blushed furiously.

"Great Scott, that's no way to talk to a fellow's best girl!" he blurted. "Darling! You look gorgeous! Exquisite!" He flapped his hands to show how words were failing, and gasped, "I'm a darn fool, honey, who doesn't know how to greet the loveliest creature ever!"

"You've got something there," said Carlie. "But you were doing all right. I'm interested in your adventures."

"Oh there weren't any adventures," disclaimed Macbeth. "It was very dull, in fact. The monotony was terrific. It did something to us—me."

"Buy me a cocktail," Carlie suggested. "And explain just how you happened to connect with this go-but-quick foundation or whatever it was."

Macbeth guided her into the bar and ordered Carlie a martini and a lemon coke for himself. "That's about what it was," he said. "Well, I think it was through the well-meant efforts of Dr. Austin Ulm that I got tangled with the Kendall Foundation."

"Dr. Austin Ulm. Who dat?" Carlie asked.

"Friend of mine. Fine chap."

Carlie was unconvinced. "Your friends are always fine chaps. All this one did was get you marooned on a rock for six months."

"He was marooned with me," Macbeth pointed out.

"Which proves what? Except that you must be about equally foresighted?" Carlie said. "But you're back. You look fine. Beard and all. What, incidentally, do you plan to do with that mattress?"

"I plan to cut it off, I suppose," Macbeth replied, fingering the foliage. "My companions in misfortune, Ulm, Crikeland and Swanberg, feel we should retain the beards as a mark of—well, something or other."

"Not a bad idea," Carlie replied. "I can't think why, though. Are you remotely interested in how I happen to be in Miami?"

"Heavens, yes," said Macbeth hastily. "I thought you were in Vermont."

"Oh, you gave it a thought, then?"

Macbeth grinned. "I've got you there, baby. I sent a telegram to Vermont the minute I got ashore."

Carlie patted his hand. "I'm down here on a vacation with Aunt Liz," she said. "There's no adventure about that, either." She looked at Macbeth curiously. "I'll bet you had a heck of a time on that island. You look different, somehow. I don't mean the whiskers, either. You seem different."

Macbeth winced and said hurriedly, "Couldn't we go somewhere tonight? The dog races, perhaps?"

CARLIE'S maiden Aunt Liz was a long bony character with tortoise shell glasses and, Macbeth Williams soon discovered, a terrific yen for gambling. The bright lights, noise and colored pageantry of one of Miami's biggest dog tracks got under Macbeth's skin somewhat after six months on Cormoral Island and three weeks on the tub *Meg Finnegan,* and he glowed. But he didn't glow enough to make any bets.

"It's not that I'm against gambling," he explained uncomfortably. "It's rather that my judgment isn't worth an investment."

Carlie gave him a sharp glance. "Still that way, eh?"

"How is that?"

"Figure you're never right about the future, do you?"

Macbeth swallowed. "I ... ah ... suppose so."

"That," said Carlie, "makes me mad."

"I'm sorry."

"Being sorry," said Carlie, "doesn't repair broken lives."

"I ... I don't believe I understand."

"Never mind."

There was an acute break in the pleasant flow of the evening. Macbeth, suddenly miserable, understood why. The matter they had just mentioned—his confidence in his judgment—was the snag on which he and Carlie had wrecked their romance. At least, that was the way Macbeth saw it. There had been numerous occasions in the past when they had seemed to be progressing happily toward the normal windup of a romance, namely wedding bells, and the matter of Macbeth's attitude toward his own judgment had come up, and things hadn't been the same.

Carlie was a very practical and level-headed girl. The same qualities in a man appealed to her. She considered them important.

They probably were good qualities, Macbeth reflected. The trouble was, he'd always been plagued with a conviction he was a mighty poor man with a plan. He couldn't foresee. He didn't trust his judgment.

He didn't like this in himself, but he didn't see where he could do much about it. It was his psychic rabbit, and he was chained to it.

Macbeth Williams found himself pointing at a lean and ugly looking greyhound in the pre-race parade.

"That one," he announced.

"That one which?" said Carlie.

"The winner," Macbeth said. "That one will be the winner."

He heard an excited intake of breath behind him, and turned and saw Austin Ulm.

"Oh, brother!" said Austin Ulm. "Lemme at the fifty-dollar window! I'll be right back!"

Macbeth Williams gazed after Ulm blankly. He imagined Ulm had chanced to attend the races, had seen him and approached in time to hear the remark about the dog. But that wasn't what gave Macbeth a frightened feeling.

"Who was that fellow?" Carlie asked.

"What? Oh, Ulm? That was Austin Ulm, the stratigraphist of our late expedition," Macbeth explained vaguely, and added, "What if the damn dog should win!"

"Eh?" said Carlie. "What was that?"

Macbeth swallowed. "Nothing. Nothing of importance, darling."

Several minutes later, the hound which Macbeth had indicated came whipping across the finish line an easy winner.

"My God!" mumbled Macbeth.

"What on earth is wrong with you?" Carlie demanded.

"I do wish I knew!" said Macbeth fervently. "The thing frightens the wits out of me."

"Eh?" Carlie eyed him in exasperation. "Just what are you suffering from?"

Macbeth took a deep breath, moistened his lips, and blurted, "I predicted that dog was going to win!"

"So what?" asked Carlie. "So did several hundred others, judging from the odds." She glanced at the odds board, which indicated the win ticket had paid nearly forty dollars on a two-dollar investment, and added, "Well, maybe I had better amend that. But a few others picked the scroot, I'm sure."

Macbeth was about to say that wasn't the point, and try to explain the whole thing, when Dr. Austin Ulm arrived waving a fistful of greenbacks. He buttonholed Macbeth, asking excitedly, "What dog's gonna win the next one? Come on. Quick. Let's have it." He told Carlie, "This is the thing I've dreamed about! Why, we can clean up! We'll need an armored truck to take home our winnings!"

"Shut up!" Macbeth told him angrily.

Crestfallen, Ulm demanded, "You're not going to predict another winner?"

"No."

"Not just one more?"

"No."

"That, my fellow exile, is the dirtiest trick ever perpetrated," said Ulm bitterly. He looked at Macbeth almost tearfully. "I'll split with you," he offered.

"Oh, shut up!" said Macbeth. He introduced Ulm to Carlie and Aunt Liz, and when Ulm started telling them that he, Macbeth Williams, had somehow picked up the uncanny power to foresee fragments of the future, Macbeth lost his temper, seized Ulm by the whiskers and said, "Shut up! Or would you like to have your block knocked off!"

That seemed to settle it. But only for a short time, because at Ulm's suggestion they visited a night club following the last race. It turned out to have a gaming room.

Dr. Ulm did such a suave job of maneuvering Macbeth into the gambling establishment that Macbeth failed to notice the plan at once. They gathered around the roulette table, and Aunt Liz asked idly, "What do you think of the five red, Macbeth?"

"No, play the black nine," Macbeth answered thoughtlessly.

With simultaneous gasps of excitement, Ulm and Aunt Liz stacked what seemed to be their entire capital on the nine black.

"Damn you!" Macbeth said bitterly to Ulm, and seized the surprised Carlie's arm and dragged her out of the room.

"What is wrong with you, Macbeth?" Carlie exclaimed.

Macbeth groaned. He wasn't surprised when Ulm and Aunt Liz came rushing out of the gambling room with almost more money than they were able to carry.

"You tricked me!" Macbeth told Ulm bitterly.

"He sure did!" cackled Aunt Liz. She added excitedly to Carlie, "You've got a gold mine here! All you've got to do is persuade him to work!"

Macbeth Williams, his face pale where it wasn't burning firmly, took Carlie's arm again.

"Carlie and I are going home," he said furiously. "Good night."

THE ride to Carlie's hotel was a quiet one. Carlie was startled and curious.

"Talk, Macbeth," she ordered, drawing the agitated man to a secluded part of the hotel veranda. "Talk is good for the soul. Give."

Macbeth squirmed. "It's silly."

"You're upset."

"It's also impossible."

"Put it in words, Macbeth."

"You'll laugh."

"I don't think so," Carlie said.

"Worse, you'll think I'm a neurotic nut. That's what the analyst thought."

Carlie whistled softly, much as a boy would do to express amazed comprehension. "Macbeth, do you mean you can predict? Is that what's bothering you?"

"I don't mean anything of the sort!" Macbeth snapped. "It's impossible. I'll be damned if I subscribe to any such opinion concerning myself or anyone else!"

Carlie examined him, and said, "If you ask me, you've already taken the subscription. You're upset. You've bought it, or you wouldn't be upset."

"Oh, hell!" Macbeth Williams exclaimed violently. "Excuse me for swearing, Carlie, but what kind of a fool do you take me for?"

"I don't know," Carlie replied. "But I find it very interesting."

Macbeth groaned. He flopped in a veranda chair, nearly knocking over a potted plant in the act. "Dammit, it's bad enough having people thinking I'm screwy for not taking over the management of my father's estate. But I'm not ashamed of that, at least. I'm simply not a man of sound judgment. I can't make plans that work out. To manage a half billion in properties successfully, your plans have to work out. Mine don't. So I'm not ashamed." He looked at the floor and shuddered. "Now, to find myself evolving into a crystal-gazer—well, that's too much. I can't take it."

"How long," asked Carlie, "has this been going on?"

"I'd rather not talk about it."

"How long?"

"Well, it started on the island," said Macbeth reluctantly.

"On Cormoral Island, this place where you were a Robinson Crusoe?"

"Uh-huh. We weren't Robinson Crusoes, though. We had plenty of equipment and supplies, and each other for company."

"But you began noticing you could predict things?"

"Well, yes."

"What kind of things?"

The hydrographist squirmed. "Oh, the sort of thing you could predict on an island that was just a knob of rock. The first instance I really recall was tying my shoes to a stake in the ground, and assuring the others that they should do the same."

Carlie's eyes popped a little. "Tying your shoes to the ground?"

Macbeth grinned faintly. "It wasn't such a silly idea. There is a species of goony bird that packs off loose objects. Like the packrat, you know. Only this is a bird. A sort of a penguin, as a matter-of-fact."

"Oh."

"The others got their shoes carried off."

"I see."

Macbeth flushed. "That isn't a very good illustration."

"There are better ones?"

"Probably. Frankly there's no lack of examples. But, darling, I'd rather not talk about it. The thing frightens me, and makes me doubt my sanity."

There was a silence. Carlie was thoughtful. "Well, it doesn't sound too reasonable," she admitted. "But you did call the turn on the dog race, and you did name the winning number on that wheel."

Macbeth shivered violently. "Don't, darling!"

Carlie frowned. "If it's worrying you so, Macbeth, why don't you do something about it?"

For a few moments, Macbeth pondered. "You know, Carlie, I know a fellow who could solve this, I'm sure. If it's just imagination, a neurosis I've picked up, he's the man who could fix me up. He has one of the greatest scientific minds I ever encountered."

"Who is he?" Carlie asked.

Macbeth became more enthusiastic about his idea. "The fellow is tops as a physician, surgeon and psychiatrist. He's quite an adventurer, too. Worldwide reputation as a troubleshooter, as a matter-of-fact. This might appeal to him. I do believe I'll get in touch with him."

"Why not," said Carlie.

"I can send him a telegram," Macbeth decided. "His name is Doc Savage."

"Oh, brother!" said Carlie.

"You know Doc Savage?"

Carlie shook her head. "No, just heard of him."

"Do you think I should?"

"I'm all for it," Carlie assured him. "I'd like nothing better than a chance to watch that fellow in action. He's a legend, you know."

Macbeth sprang to his feet. "Good! We'll send the telegram now. You can help me write it."

Chapter III

THE telegraph office was a narrow recess in a building on Flagler Street not far from Biscayne Boulevard, and remained open all night, presided over by a round-faced man named Gridley. Gridley was a contradiction to the idea that all fat people are jolly; he had an evil temper, a sharp tongue and bad manners, qualifications which had resulted in his being shunted to this undesirable all-night job. His assets were several years seniority, a willingness to put up with low pay, although there was a qualification to this, and a brother-in-law who was district commercial agent for the company.

Gridley took Macbeth Williams' long telegram with a surly snatch, grumbled about its length, counted the words, and calmly made a dollar overcharge. When Macbeth and Carlie departed, Gridley erased the charge figure, subtracted the dollar, put down the new figure, and pocketed the dollar. This practice accounted for his being willing to work for a low salary.

He tossed the telegram down by the teletype machine. His policy was to delay messages all he could without the company raising too much hell. He sauntered next door to a bar, had a beer, and eventually ambled back into the office, which he had left unlocked.

Gridley sauntered jauntily behind the counter, and found himself looking into the snout of a gun.

No words were exchanged. There was hardly time, and it was Gridley's fault. Gridley was a terrific coward. As a little boy, he had been a fat, soft, insolent brat, and had formed the habit of screaming at the top of his voice whenever threatened by superior force or violence. He was still a screamer.

Gridley found himself looking into the snout of a gun. He began screeching hysterically. Suddenly, he stopped; the sound of a shot filled the office.

Gridley began screeching. He let out one hysterical howl after another, charged with terror and emotional instability.

About halfway into the third squeal, the telegraph office filled briefly with a much louder noise, and Gridley's forehead changed shape very slightly and the back of his head considerably more.

As far as the police could learn, only one man actually saw the killer. A taxi driver observed a man racing from the telegraph office following the shot. But the cab driver was near-sighted, and happened to have removed his glasses and was polishing them at the moment. His description was not of much help.

The police did some futile photographing and fingerprinting. A company clerk took the night's business to the office, where in the bookkeeping department, it was noticed that a lengthy telegram to Doc Savage of New York City, and signed by one Macbeth Williams, did not bear the mark-off of having been sent. A service was dispatched concerning the message. Sure enough, it had not been transmitted. So the wire was despatched, a bit late, and traveled the teletype circuits to New York.

Chapter IV

SEVERAL hours after the time it should have arrived, the telegram penetrated to a private teletype machine on the eighty-sixth floor of one of New York's midtown skyscrapers. Exactly ten dingles from a small bell announced its arrival. It was torn off the machine by Mr. Monk Mayfair, a chemist.

"Another goofer," remarked Monk Mayfair, when he had read the message. He prepared to wad it up and hurl it into the wastebasket, but hesitated, to ask, "You ever hear of a guy named Williams?"

Theodore Marley Brooks, attorney, one-time brigadier general in the U.S. Army, asked sarcastically, "Have I heard of anyone named Williams? Do you want an answer to that? Why not John Smith?"

"O.K., shyster. Start off the day by being wise."

"What Williams?"

Monk consulted the telegram. "Macbeth Williams, it says here."

"From Miami, Florida, eh?" asked Ham.

Monk Mayfair was somewhat more than three feet in width, just a little taller than that, and equipped with bristling rusty hair, a face so homely it was hysterically funny, and one of the finest assortments of wizardry in chemistry in existence.

Monk was an assistant to Doc Savage. So was Ham Brooks.

Having looked blank for a moment, Monk said, "What the hell? You see this telegram before?"

"No."

"Then how'd you know it was from Miami?"

Ham handed Monk the morning newspaper, indicating an item. Monk read it. He rolled his small eyes.

"Half a billion bucks, and the guy won't touch the management of it," Monk remarked. "Now there's a smart boy for you. Just smart enough that this telegram doesn't surprise me."

"What's in the telegram?"

"Mostly that this Macbeth Williams has contracted a new kind of disease."

"Some kind of rare tropical malady, eh?" Ham inquired.

"I would say so. Sure, that describes it."

Ham Brooks took the message, read it, and apparently wished to share Monk's opinion, but disagreed because it was not his custom to agree with anything Monk thought. "Very interesting," he remarked.

"Nutty as a fruitcake," Monk said. "The guy says he can't help predicting things that are going to happen. He wants Doc Savage to come down to Miami and cure him of it. Say, that would prove he was nuts if he wasn't nuts to begin with. Who would want to be cured of a thing like that? Nobody in his right mind."

"You'd better hand that telegram to Doc," Ham advised, "It's probably important."

"What would make it important?" Monk asked. "We get screwball stuff like this every day."

"Half a billion dollars might make it important," Ham suggested.

"You know if it wouldn't swell you up, I might be inclined to agree," Monk said. "A screwball in moderate circumstances is just a screwball, but a screwball with half a billion, even if he won't touch it, is probably some kind of genius."

DOC SAVAGE was one of those rarities among celebrities, a man whose physical appearance was as impressive as his reputation. He was a giant bronze man, quite symmetrical of build, but so cabled with lithe muscle that it was sometimes a little disturbing to be near him. His eyes were striking because they resembled, in the pupils, pools of flake gold that were always in gentle motion. The combination, along with the straight bronze hair not much darker than his skin, made him stand out in the average crowd about like a lion in a basket of kittens. He did not consider this an asset.

His work—surgery and scientific research could hardly be called his main occupations any longer—was a profession for an inconspicuous man. Preferably an invisible man. Certainly a bulletproof one. It also fitted back into history, back when knighthood was in flower and gentlemen wore armor, possibly a little better than it did into the middle of the twentieth century. His work was righting wrongs and punishing evildoers, preferably under unusual and interesting circumstances.

Doc Savage changed hotels frequently as a matter of common-sense precaution, and the current one was located a short distance off Madison in Fifty-eighth Street. It was a quiet place which, unfortunately, hadn't been able to resist the impulse to pass along to a columnist the fact that Doc Savage was a guest there. The squib had been printed by the columnist a couple of days ago. Doc intended to check out at the end of the week as a result.

Doc left the hotel a little after nine o'clock, which was late for him, and because it was a crisp spring morning and he was a demon believer in exercise, he set out to walk to headquarters.

His progress along a New York street was never placid, and this morning he was haunted by surprised stares, hails from would-be pals, and two autograph hounds. It was not particularly irritating, though, and he avoided most of it by striding along rapidly.

He was halfway across Thirty-ninth Street when a taxi, wheeling off Madison, went out of control and headed for a second cab. The resulting crash, which was resounding, sent a cloud of glass flying, and dented the sides of both cabs badly, was not extraordinary as New York traffic smashups go, except for one thing. Had Doc Savage not executed a remarkable leap, practically over the top of one cab, he would have been pinned between the cabs like a fly between swatter and table. However, the driver of the wild cab did scream out a warning.

After the crash, the cab driver continued to shriek. Apparently, he was under the impression he had smashed Doc Savage to a pulp against the other machine.

Doc, safe on the other side of the second taxicab, picked himself up, sidestepped a car coming from the other direction, and called, "It's all right, fellow!"

This didn't reassure the cabby, however. He howled louder, threw his machine into gear, backed clear of the tangle as disengaging metal wailed, and drove away madly.

Approximately halfway down the block, the fleeing cab driver—he wasn't traveling so very fast, and several persons testified as to exactly what happened—seemed to faint at the wheel. The cab, the steering gear knocked out of line by the crackup, faltered to the right, hit the curb, and bruised itself somewhat shapeless against the side of a building.

They hauled the driver out. "Poor devil, he must have had some sort of spell because of the excitement," someone remarked.

Doc Savage hurried up, explained he was a doctor, and assisted in removing the man to a nearby drugstore.

"He's not seriously injured," Doc explained, after an examination. "I think his arm would be better if it were bandaged and in a semi-cast, however. He will regain consciousness presently."

The bandaging and the application of a quick-drying cast was completed by the time the man regained his senses, Doc doing the application.

The cab driver, a slender young fellow with large eyes and a small mouth, immediately became hysterical. He could hardly give his name. "Somethin' went wrong with the steering gear!" he wailed. "God, it was awful! I saw I was gonna hit that cab! I yelled atcha to jump." He peered at Doc. "I yelled atcha. You heard me, didn't you?"

"I heard you," Doc said. "Don't worry about it. Nobody is much damaged."

A cop asked the man belligerently, "Why'd you start to leave the scene of an accident?"

The cabbie—he said his name was Clare Jones—groaned hopelessly. "I don't remember doin' that. I musta been knocked silly."

Doc Savage suggested that the upset driver be allowed to go home and recover his composure. The cop was not enthusiastic about this, but finally agreed.

Doc resumed his walk to headquarters.

THERE was another incident. This one, by an odd coincidence, also involved a man fainting. It was the operator of the elevator in Doc Savage's building, and Doc spoke to him pleasantly on entering the elevator, saying, "Good morning. You're new here aren't you?"

"Yes, sir. My name's David," the operator replied. "I'll give you a quick private trip, Mr. Savage."

"Thank you," Doc said.

The fainting occurred a few seconds after the cage started up. The operator, David, simply folded down, striking his forehead against the control level lightly.

Doc Savage made an examination of the man, then returned the cage to the floor immediately above the lobby, left it there with the door blocked open, and hurried downstairs to the drugstore to get some bandages and more of the quick-drying plaster used for casts.

When David awakened some time later, he found several curious people staring at him. "What happened?" he mumbled.

"You fainted," a man told him.

"I did!"

"Yes. Mr. Savage treated you."

"Where's Savage now?"

"Gone about his business."

David examined his elbow. "What the devil is this?"

"A cast," he was told. "You wrenched your elbow badly when you fell, and Doc Savage thought it advisable to apply a cast. Savage asked me to explain it to you. Leave the cast in place a week or so, and your arm will be all right."

"Is that all that happened to me?" David wanted to know.

"That's all."

"I don't understand it," David muttered, shaking his head. "I think I'll go home."

WHEN Doc Savage entered the headquarters reception room, Monk Mayfair and Ham Brooks were waiting for him, sitting on the edge of an enormous inlaid desk with their legs dangling.

"We got an elfish item for you," Monk explained, and presented Doc with the Macbeth Williams telegram.

Doc read through the message, then went to the telephone. "I want to speak to the Miami telegraph office—" he consulted the telegram—"which uses the code number AU on its telegrams."

Monk and Ham were surprised. "Why the quick action, do you mind saying?" Ham Brooks asked.

Doc indicated the telegram filing-time. "They're stamped with the hour and minute and day when received across the counter. This one was delayed nearly eight hours in transmission. That's unusual for a straight telegram. I just wondered why?"

Monk and Ham exchanged glances. "You could have checked on that, stupid," Ham told Monk.

"Yeah," Monk agreed. "We both started the morning off in a bright way."

Doc Savage finished a conversation with the Miami telegraph office.

"The clerk who received the telegram was killed, murdered, about twenty minutes after he accepted the message," Doc told Monk and Ham. "That accounts for the delay."

"Who killed him?" Monk asked blankly.

"A person yet unidentified. Believed to be a man." Doc picked up the telephone again and asked for Macbeth Williams, in Miami. The address of Williams' hotel was given in the telegram.

"You think the killing and this telegram are hooked up?" Monk demanded.

"I think something is hooked up, or in the process of being hooked," Doc told him. "Two attempts were made to kill me this morning."

Monk asked, when he and Ham had picked themselves up mentally from the floor, "Did I hear that right? Two tries to kill you?"

"One when a cab tried to smash me against another cab," Doc said. "And one in the elevator here in the building, where there was a strange operator who didn't know the code word all new operators in the building are supposed to know, and who had not two guns, but three, secreted in his clothing."

"Holy smoke!" Monk breathed.

"Who are the guys who tried it?"

"That's what I should like you and Ham to find out, if you care for a little exercise of that sort," Doc suggested.

"Where do we start?"

Doc gave them an outline of the fainting episode. "The 'fainting' was due to getting a whiff of our private little anaesthetic gas which I released," he explained. "I don't imagine either scoundrel will quite believe he fainted, but I doubt if they'll have a better explanation."

"But you let them go!" Ham blurted.

Doc nodded. "Each with a plaster cast on his arm."

"Eh?"

"Containing," Doc added, "one of the little radio tracing gadgets we spent so much time developing, one secreted in the thick part of each bandage." The suite consisted of a library and a laboratory containing considerable floor space, and Doc nodded in the direction of the latter. "You might get the receivers and see whether the transmitters are functioning."

The receivers were small directional affairs working on several hundred megacycles, and were not as compact by far as the transmitters. But they were equipped to give a direction fix without the necessity of taking two bearings to learn whether the signal was coming off the back or the front of the loop.

Monk asked what frequency, and Doc told him, adding, "The elevator operator is about five hundred kilocycles lower." Monk got the signal. It was a single "pip" of a note transmitted at two-second intervals. Monk adjusted the receiver for maximum signal. "The guy's north of here," he said. "What do we do about these lugs?"

"Find them. Get your eye on them," Doc told him.

"And then?"

"Follow them and see what you learn as a result," Doc said.

"How long do we follow?"

"That," Doc said, "is where you use your own judgment."

Ham finished checking his own radio and said, "My chap seems to be in the same part of town as Monk's."

"It might," Doc suggested, "be a good idea to lose no time in putting them under observation."

WHEN Monk Mayfair and Ham Brooks departed, Doc Savage settled to wait for his telephone call to Macbeth Williams to go through. While he waited, he used a more conventional type of high frequency radio two-way to check with Monk and Ham, who had equipment in their cars. Satisfied the apparatus was functioning, he settled back.

Monk and Ham were excellent aides, and he was fully aware of it. Both men were eminent in their professions; Monk was widely known in the industrial chemistry field, and Ham Brooks was a noted lawyer. They were not—and Doc was fully aware that this was an important matter—employees in a salary-drawing sense. Their association with Doc was voluntary. They liked excitement and high adventure; they were pushovers for the appeal of the unusual. It was a better bond then any material payment would have created.

Doc's thoughts moved to Macbeth Williams. He knew the young man. Slightly. He recalled Macbeth Williams as a tall young man with considerable geological knowledge, and quite a noticeable lack of confidence in himself. Their only contact, Doc remembered, had been during attendance on a few occasions at a scientific society in which they both held membership.

The telephone rang, and Doc said, "Williams?

Doc Savage. Yes, about your telegram. I received it."

"You probably think I'm touched in the head," Williams said in some embarrassment. "But I'm really quite upset about the thing."

"You actually feel that you can predict the future?" Doc asked.

"I hate to answer. I feel a fool."

"You might," Doc said, "answer it anyway."

"Well, yes, I do feel that I have some power I can't understand. I don't believe it, as a matter-of-fact. I can't. It's too far-fetched."

"But you're convinced against your will?"

"I'm convinced," said Macbeth, "that I need someone like you to straighten me out. You will do that, won't you, Mr. Savage?"

"I'm not," Doc reminded him, "a practicing psychiatrist."

"I know. You're a practicing adventurer."

"You've got it a little wrong, Williams," Doc told him. "I don't hunt excitement for excitement's sake. Someone has to be in trouble, deserving of help, and beyond the assistance of the normal processes of law. And the case has to be unusual and interesting. Those are the qualifications."

Macbeth Williams said uncomfortably, "This should meet one of the qualifications. Unusual."

"It might meet some of the others," Doc told him. "Has anyone tried to kill you?"

"Kill me? Good Lord, no!"

"Have any peculiar things happened to you?"

"Why, no," Macbeth replied. "Not that I've noticed."

"You were marooned on a desert island for six months."

"Well, yes. But there wasn't anything odd about that. The Foundation simply went broke."

"What Foundation was that?"

"The Kendall Foundation of St. Louis, Missouri, which backed the expedition."

"Never heard of them," Doc said.

"Well, they weren't too well-known, I'm afraid."

"What," Doc asked, "had the Foundation contributed to science? With what museums, industrial concerns or institutions were they affiliated?"

"I'm afraid I don't know."

"You didn't investigate?"

"Well, I didn't think it was necessary," Macbeth told him, embarrassed. "You see, my friend, Dr. Austin Ulm, the stratigraphist, sponsored my connection with the Kendall people, and I felt that was sufficient recommendation for them."

"I see. And you have noticed no murders or violence circulating around this matter?"

"Gracious! Of course not."

"Did you know," Doc asked, "about the telegraph office clerk?"

"Who?"

"The one with whom you filed your telegram last night. He was murdered within a half hour."

"Good God!"

"You didn't know about that?"

"No. Certainly not! Did it have some connection with my telegram?"

"I'm not sure yet."

"It couldn't have had. It's impossible."

"Nevertheless," Doc went on, "I think I shall drop down to Miami and find out."

"I certainly wish you would," Macbeth Williams said. "When shall I expect you?"

"This afternoon," Doc told him. "You might, if you wish, meet me at the airport. The one the airlines use."

DOC SAVAGE used the two-way radio to advise Monk and Ham that he was leaving for Miami immediately. "That's the quickest way, probably, to get a close look at this see-into-the-future stuff," he explained. "Have you fellows spotted your quarry yet?"

"They're both in a second-rate hotel on the edge of the Harlem district," Monk said. "Room on the third floor. We've sort of got the idea that more than two of them are staying at the hotel. Not sure yet. It isn't the sort of hotel that puts out information readily."

"Don't draw attention to yourselves."

"We're trying not to. That's why we haven't put the heat on the hotel people."

"Within less than an hour," Doc said, "I'll be out of range of these two-way radios. If you have a report, come to headquarters and use the powerful set here. I'll take a large two-way outfit along in the plane and set it up in the Miami hotel."

"Right."

"And be careful. This affair is odd enough to have something pretty big behind it. I don't like the way it looks."

"You can depend on us to be the souls of caution," Monk assured him.

"Your idea of caution," Doc said dryly, "frequently stands my hair on end. Try to be a little conservative this time."

Chapter V

DOC SAVAGE recognized the lanky young man with the terrific flat of blond whiskers, coming through the afternoon sunlight of Florida, as being Macbeth Williams. Accompanying him were a young woman and a stocky dark saturnine man who also had a beard. Doc flipped a few switches to off-positions, gave the dials of the plane a glance to make sure things were ship-shape, then alighted, extended a hand, and said, "Hello, Williams. You look quite a bit different with that beard."

"I really should part with the foliage, I suppose," Macbeth Williams said. He was obviously excited and awed. "I'm delighted you came." He introduced the others. "This is my … ah … this is Miss McGuiggan and Dr. Ulm."

Carlie McGuiggan took Doc's hand, laughing, and said, "I'm more awed than Macbeth is. I can hardly believe it."

Austin Ulm had a quick hard handclasp. He pointed at the plane. "Some job. I never saw anything quite like it."

The plane, a sleek and unorthodox craft, was already drawing quite a lot of attention. Airport employees were approaching to inspect it.

"It's a jet job of a new type, partly experimental," Doc explained.

"It must have a hell of a performance," Austin Ulm remarked. "Macbeth said he talked to you on the telephone after ten o'clock, and here it's not much after three, and you're in Miami. That's traveling." He climbed up and peered into the cabin without receiving an invitation. "Say, this will carry half a dozen people. You wouldn't think it from the outside. What's the idea of the odd shape to the fuselage?"

"It will function as a seaplane with the gear retracted," Doc told him. "Works very nicely off the water, in fact."

"How about snow?" Ulm asked.

"The same. There's an arrangement in the wings that changes the airfoil, increasing the lift greatly, so that the landing run-out isn't much more than required by some private planes of the reciprocating engine type."

Carlie suggested politely, "Perhaps you'd like to collect your luggage and get out of here. This crowd will be a mob in a minute."

"Thank you, I would," Doc assured her.

Doc Savage removed three rather bulky and heavy equipment cases from the plane, and the two men helped him lug these to Macbeth's rented car. Ulm, who seemed to have a large bump of curiosity, asked, "What's in this case? It's heavy."

"Two-way radio," Doc told him. "I usually carry a set powerful enough to keep in contact with my associates in whatever part of the world they may be."

"You seem to travel well-prepared," Ulm said.

"I try to do so."

When they reached the car, a convertible model with the top down, Macbeth Williams suggested to Carlie, "I wish you'd drive, darling. I … ah … feel rather nervous."

"Relax, Macbeth," Carlie told him. "Doc Savage is here. Your problems are practically solved."

Ulm, already settled in the rear seat, chuckled. "They're just starting, if you ask me."

While Carlie was getting the car in motion, Doc Savage looked thoughtfully at Ulm, asked, "What do you mean, just starting?"

"I mean," Ulm told him, "that a guy with Macbeth's gift is just naturally going to attract excitement. Once news gets out that he can predict the future, things will pop. You can imagine how it'll grab the public imagination. The boy is in for a time."

Macbeth Williams groaned. "I wish you wouldn't treat this thing as if it were a fact."

"Why not?" Ulm demanded.

"It can't be a fact."

"Why not?"

"Predicting," said Macbeth vehemently, "just isn't done. It's unscientific. It's not possible."

Ulm grinned. "Seeing is believing. What do you say, Carlie?"

"I'm inclined to agree," Carlie replied.

Doc Savage noted that Carlie McGuiggan seemed to be a cautious and expert driver. He approved of the way she handled the car in the heavy boulevard traffic.

"Miss McGuiggan, do you actually believe that Mr. Williams has acquired some hitherto unknown power of foresight?" he asked.

"Meaning," asked Carlie, "that you would think I'd be a zany if I believed it?"

"Not necessarily. Naturally, I do not have the details as yet, and so my skepticism hasn't been dispelled. But I'll take your answer with an open mind, you can be sure."

Carlie nodded. "I believe it."

"You've seen it work?"

"Twice last night, and once today."

"Three times today," Ulm corrected. "At breakfast, Macbeth ordered ham and eggs and said he'd bet he would get a kipper. He got a kipper. Later Macbeth said a rental car agency wouldn't have a free car, and sure enough, they didn't have. And driving out here, Macbeth suddenly pulled to the side of the road, and a moment later a car driven by a drunken man careened through the spot where we would have been if he hadn't pulled aside."

Macbeth broke in excitedly, "Wait a minute, now! Those could have been accidents. Coincidences."

"Bosh!" said Ulm.

"All of it," continued Macbeth, with even more animation, "could have been coincidence. A run of luck. It could be that."

Ulm snorted. "I've been watching it grow for

six months, and all I can say is: luck never had a run like that."

"You're a believer?" Doc inquired.

"Damn right!" Ulm declared violently.

"I'll be interested," Doc said, "in observing some of these predictions. Williams, would you care to make one right now?"

Macbeth groaned. "I can't make them consciously. I'm not even aware of making a prediction, until I see it come true."

Ulm chuckled. "Macbeth ought to get the thing under control. Oh, boy! Think what it would mean if he could turn it on when he wanted to! With half a billion capital to work with, there's no limit."

Doc eyed Ulm sharply. "You're suggesting that Mr. Williams take over his father's estate, which I understand he can do if he wishes, and employ his propensity for predicting to speculate?"

"It's a damn good idea!" Ulm said excitedly. "It just occurred to me! Macbeth, you should think about it!"

"Nonsense," Macbeth snapped.

Carlie McGuiggan glanced around. Her eyes were starry with delight. "Macbeth, you really should consider the idea. Why, you could become a greater tycoon than your father."

"What I'll probably become," said Macbeth gloomily, "is a resident in some booby-hatch."

BECAUSE it would be more convenient, Doc Savage took a room at the hotel where Macbeth Williams and Austin Ulm were staying. He was hardly settled when Macbeth Williams knocked on the door.

"I managed to give Carlie and Ulm the slip," Macbeth explained. "I wanted to talk to you privately about—well, the ugly side of this thing."

Doc asked the young man to come in, noting that Williams showed increased signs of nervousness and strain. "So it has an ugly side?" he inquired.

Williams dropped into a chair. "I don't know. I imagine you know what I'm referring to, the murder of the clerk in the telegraph office. After you telephoned me, I got a newspaper and read about it."

"Think there was any connection with yourself?"

"I don't see how there possibly could have been!"

"You've given it close thought?"

"My God, of course!" Macbeth said wildly. "I didn't even know the clerk. The murderer didn't take my telegram to you. Doesn't that prove the killing wasn't connected with the message?"

Doc shook his head. "Not necessarily. The killer might have been seeking the message when the clerk, Gridley, surprised him. He might have shot Gridley because of excitement, or during a struggle. There were reports that Gridley was heard screaming just before the shot was fired. The screams could have frightened the killer into firing the shot."

Macbeth groaned. "It would be awful to think I was somehow the cause of a man getting killed!"

Doc said, "I'm going to describe two men. Listen closely, then tell me if you think you've ever seen them." Doc gave a precise word picture of the taxi driver and the elevator operator who had been after him that morning in New York. He did not explain what they had done, merely described them.

Macbeth shook his head. "I don't believe I know them. Who are they?"

Doc glanced at his watch. "Perhaps we can find out by now." He turned on the powerful two-way radio, opened the window and tossed the weighted end of a fifty-meter antennae across to the roof of a nearby building, and presently was in business with the transmitter.

One-sided business, however. He could not raise Monk or Ham. He checked by contacting a New York station, to make sure he was not in a dead spot.

Finally, somewhat upset, he broadcast instructions. "Monk, or Ham, if you're hearing me, get to a transmitter and give me a call." He repeated the instructions, adding, "I'll stand by here for the next hour."

He spent the following hour quizzing Macbeth Williams about the predictions, but learned nothing very instructive. The predictions, as Macbeth said, were just predictions, given unconsciously and without awareness of particular significance.

At the end of the hour, there was no news from Monk or Ham. Planted in Doc Savage was a small seed of alarm that grew with frightening rapidity.

Chapter VI

DOC SAVAGE joined Macbeth Williams, Carlie McGuiggan and Austin Ulm for dinner, and following that, whatever the evening had to offer.

"In the way of a prediction, is that it?" Carlie asked.

"Something like that," Doc admitted. "Macbeth and I talked it over, and there doesn't seem to be anything for me to do but take the role of observer until one of these predictions turns up."

"Then what will you do?"

"Examine the prediction," Doc replied dryly, "to learn what makes it tick."

"I'll bet," said Austin Ulm, "You get your hat knocked off."

They had an excellent dinner at a place in

Miami Beach. Doc Savage learned quite a bit from Carlie's chatter. She was the daughter of a fairly well-to-do manufacturer of ceramics, had a private pilot's license, liked sail-fishing, and was otherwise a tomboy.

Doc gathered, before the meal had ended, that Carlie was a decisive person herself, and liked decisiveness in others. He also received the impression that Carlie considered Macbeth Williams lacking in confidence in himself, and that this was the obstacle that stood between them. And he saw that Carlie was all for the idea of Macbeth assuming charge of the estate, probably because the manager of such an enormous property loomed in her eyes as a man, of necessity, of courage and firm decisions.

It was also interesting to Doc Savage to note that Macbeth Williams himself wasn't as averse to the idea as he had been that afternoon. Carlie and Ulm apparently had been working on him. Once Macbeth remarked seriously, "You know, even if this gift of mine should turn out to be all imagination, it would be interesting to see what I could do with something really big." He smiled thoughtfully. "I hope it isn't a gift. That would be nice."

"You mean," Doc suggested, "that you would like to have it turn out to be merely good judgment and foresight on your part?"

"Exactly," Macbeth replied. "Frankly, nothing would please me more. I've always been a fellow who didn't trust his own judgment. You've no idea what a burden that can become, when you've carried it all your life."

"A man should discard a burden like that," Doc told him.

"How? I've tried."

Ulm put in, "I'm betting on the predictions. Better turn one out, Macbeth, or Doc Savage will begin to think we're kidding him."

Macbeth winced. "I wish you wouldn't joke about it."

Following dinner, Ulm came up with a suggestion. "You don't," he said, "hunt squirrels anywhere but in the woods. Not if you want squirrels."

"Meaning?" Doc suggested.

"Why don't we take Macbeth to a gambling joint," Ulm said, grinning. "The place to look for a prediction is in surroundings that would stimulate a prediction, it seems to me."

"I see no objections," Doc said.

Macbeth groaned. Carlie laughed. She asked, "What joint will it be?"

"Let's leave it to our waiter," Ulm suggested. "We'll just ask him to name a joint, and that's the one we'll pick. If it's agreeable?"

When the waiter came over, Carlie glanced up at him and asked, "If someone asked you the name of a night club, what name would you think of?"

"The Silver Slipper," the waiter said promptly.

They all laughed at Carlie's thwarted expression, but it was Ulm who suggested, "Perhaps there's a club by that name here. There are always imitations of well-known places scattered around the country. I'll get a phone book and see." He came back presently, triumphant. "There's one. In a pretty good part of town, too."

"Then," said Doc Savage pleasantly, "we'll all go there, if it's satisfactory."

Macbeth muttered, "It's not wholly satisfactory, but I'll go along with the thing. I feel like a guinea pig."

Carlie patted his hand. "Like the goose being watched to lay the golden egg, you should feel, darling."

Doc Savage excused himself, saying, "I'll be with you in a few moments," and went into the lobby. From there, by the side entrance route, he found his way to the kitchen, where he accosted the waiter who'd given them the night club name.

"Would you mind telling me," Doc asked, displaying a five-dollar bill, "how you happened to mention that name?"

The waiter looked astonished. "Why, it just came naturally."

"No one told you that you would be asked for the name of a club?"

"Certainly not."

Doc indicated the greenback. "That's for telling me how you happened to mention the name of that club."

The waiter grinned. "That's an easy five bucks, friend. Me and another guy was arguing about high-class night clubs about half an hour ago, and all the argument got down to the Silver Slipper toward the end. That's why the name was on the tip of my tongue. Does that earn the five?"

"It sure does," Doc said. "Did this other fellow bring the subject around to the Silver Slipper?"

"I don't recall exactly. Maybe he did."

Doc passed over the bill. "The fellow still around?"

"Come here," the waiter said. He led the way to a side door which gave a view of a miniature golf course which occupied a vacant lot beside the restaurant. "See the short guy with the linen suit and red necktie?"

Doc asked, "Is he the one who argued with you?"

"That's right."

"Thanks," Doc said. "You needn't mention that I was interested, unless he's a friend of yours."

"Never saw him before tonight," said the waiter. "And thanks for the five."

MACBETH WILLIAMS was ill at ease, and headed for an uncomfortable evening, Doc could see. By way of breaking the tension, Doc turned the conversation to geology and ocean currents, two subjects on which Macbeth was a master.

The night club was about what Doc had expected. Some fellow had thrown it together out of paint and plywood and mirrors in hopes of making a tourist killing, and had added the usual gambling setup in the back. Access to this was available only to persons known to the management, but a bill in the headwaiter's hand established their credentials in short order.

Ulm nudged Macbeth over to the wheel. "If you get a hunch a number's coming up, for heaven's sake, don't keep it to yourself."

"I don't feel the least bit oracular," Macbeth assured him.

Doc Savage circulated idly through the place, noted the usual number of games were gimmicked in favor of the management, and kept his money in his pocket. Carlie played sparingly, lost more often than she won, and remarked that they needed her Aunt Liz along for moral courage where gambling was concerned.

"Dammit, pal," Austin Ulm told Macbeth when some time had passed. "Come across with a prediction. You're letting us down, to say nothing of the fifteen bucks I've dropped."

"I've told you I can't just pull them out when I wish." Macbeth Williams said stiffly.

Doc murmured dryly, "I understand you didn't know when you were about to produce."

"I don't." Macbeth flushed. "Well, darn it, I don't. What do you want me to do, just start making random suggestions about what number to play?"

"Why don't you try that?" Doc asked.

Macbeth, irritated, said, "All right, play black nine. Play any damned thing,"

Carlie smiled. "That came reluctantly, but I'm going to try it." She put a twenty on black nine.

She won.

"Holy smoke!" Ulm gasped. "And I just stood there! I didn't get any dough down. What's the next one, Macbeth? Give us the next winner quick!"

"Black nine again!" Macbeth snapped. "And I'm sure it was just an accident. I didn't know black nine would win."

The nine black won again.

Macbeth backed away from the table. "No, no, no!" he wailed. "This frightens me. I'm going to get out of here!"

Ulm, who had won more than three hundred dollars, seized his arm frantically. "By God, you can't dry up on me!" he growled. "I'm short of dough. I don't have half a billion bucks lying around loose."

"Take your hands off me!" Macbeth snapped.

"Now, now, don't get upset," Ulm urged. "I'm sorry. I didn't intend to get tough. But just one more bet would mean a lot to me. Please, Macbeth, just one. Try the craps table, if you don't like roulette."

Macbeth, flushed and irritated and frightened at his own inexplicable ability, indicated a gaunt man who was rattling the dice. "He's going to make his point the toss after this one."

Trying to restrain his excitement, Ulm crowded over and got a bet down with the house. The gaunt man's point was ten, a tough one to make. He made it.

Ulm collected, spluttering with greed, and croaked, "The next winner, Macbeth! Quick!"

Macbeth sneered at him, said, "You're just greedy," and took Carlie's arm and walked back into the part of the club where they could see a floor show and have a sandwich. Macbeth told Doc, "I hope you're not impressed by that stuff. It's all a series of coincidences, I'm sure."

"Is that," Doc asked, "the way your predictions usually come?"

"Well, yes," said Macbeth wryly. "Smoke doesn't come out of my ears, and tongues of flame don't accompany the predictions, if that's what you mean."

Doc noted the way Ulm was shaking with excitement. "I wouldn't say it was entirely without effect," he said.

THE next half hour was peaceful and sans predictions. They had fairly good sandwiches, and Ulm an ale to quiet his nerves. The floor show came on.

Macbeth Williams seemed to relax. Then Doc noted that he suddenly became uncomfortable.

"What's wrong?" Doc inquired.

Macbeth flushed, and mopped his face, then the palms of his hands, on a handkerchief. "I've got an odd feeling of apprehension that I don't quite understand," he explained.

"Exactly what sort of a feeling?"

"I hope you don't think I'm silly. But I feel that we're in danger. It's a hard thing to define, just an impression of general danger. It's like an emotion or like the feeling you get when you're a kid and walk through a graveyard at night."

"Could it be," Doc suggested, "a result of worrying about the murder of the telegraph office clerk?"

"I don't know, but it might be," Macbeth replied.

Ulm frowned. "This time, you feel like you know you're making a prediction? Is that it?"

Macbeth said curtly, "I'm not making any forecasts at all, blast it! I'm just explaining that I feel uneasy."

"I'll bet this doesn't amount to anything, if he *knows* he's predicting," Ulm said.

Doc ignored the interruption. "Williams, could it be that you noticed someone who brought on this feeling?"

Macbeth Williams hesitated. "I don't know. That is—well, I don't exactly recall. But, yes, it could be."

"Did you," Doc asked, "notice a short man in a white linen suit and a red necktie?"

"Well, I— You know, that's odd. I do seem to have seen such a man."

Doc Savage made a quick pencil sketch on the back of a menu, caricaturing the man he'd seen on the miniature golf course back at the restaurant. He showed this. "That the fellow?"

"Why, yes!" Macbeth gasped. "Yes, I did notice that chap."

"You noticed him," Doc said, "while you were looking around, just prior to having this feeling of uneasiness?"

"Yes, I believe that's right."

Ulm sneered at them. "This is getting too practical. I'm only interested in predictions. Let's get out of this dump."

Macbeth Williams looked at them, an expression of terror on his fact. "I don't feel we should leave openly and without being cautious."

Chuckling, Ulm patted his arm. "This thing is getting your nerves, pal. But I suppose the joint has a back door, if you would feel better using it."

THE bullet made only one real sound, and that was not at its point of origination; they say a silencer is not too effective, but this one must have done an excellent job. No doubt the gun made some sound off there in the night, but it was lost in the other uglier sound, the solid stopping noise the bullet made against Doc Savage.

Doc Savage, going backward and down, believed he was hit somewhere in the chest region. In fact, there was not much doubt, because in a moment the shock localized in the central chest area, a logical part of him for it, since that was the largest target he presented. When he was down, partly of shock and partly of his own accord, he turned and, reaching and stretching, was able to strike the door with his hand and get it shut. That closed off the light, such of it as did not come from the moon.

"Scatter and stay down," he said. "And stay here. Don't leave."

He got up then, not erect, but lunging forward and to the right, then the left, with one hand exploring in some alarm about the center of his chest. He could feel the bullet, a small thing to have kicked him so hard, lodged and misshapen against the chain mesh of the bulletproof undershirt he was wearing. There was some padding under the chain mail of the best alloy metal that chemist Monk Mayfair had been able to create for such a purpose, but not enough padding, because he had some apprehensions about a rib or a breastbone being broken. But after he had gone a short distance, he decided nothing was cracked.

Somewhere out in the night, a man began running. Doc could hear him. The man's eyes had been accustoming themselves to the moonlight for some time, probably, and he must have seen Doc moving, although it had seemed to Doc that he had moved in only the darkest places.

The man ran away. Doc followed. There were no more bullets for awhile. The running man crossed through moonlight, and he was the short fellow with the white suit and red necktie. And now with a case of near-hysterical fright.

The man's flight took him half a block, to where he had a car parked. He got in the car, and the key must have been in the ignition, because the car was moving, it seemed, as soon as the man was in it, and a thin spike of flame came from the open window. The passage of gases and bullet through the silencer on the end of the gun muzzle was more audible now, perhaps because the two bullets were not close, but chopped off through the neatly clipped shrubbery of someone's yard, and from there could have gone almost anywhere.

The car drew away. The white suit was a faint blur inside it. Doc Savage, with no car available, seemed defeated, but then luck touched him. A car drove into the street from another direction, occupied by someone bound for the club. It slowed and the driver hunted for a place to park where he wouldn't get stuck the tip that was mandatory in the club parking lot. When Doc, running hard, reached the car, the driver looked up, startled. There was a girl with him. Doc said, "I want your car to chase another car. Quick. Don't argue."

The driver had a considerable quantity of jaw and it snapped up and thrust out. The muzzle of a gun followed it. "No, and you better not argue either. I'm Springlatch, Miami police department, detective first grade."

"That's fine," Doc told him. "Now catch the car if you can. Ask all the questions you want to, while you're chasing it. Better put the girl out, because our friend is free with a gun."

"The girl is Policewoman Lorn," Springlatch said. "Get in. Keep an eye on him, Lorn." The car began to move, gathering speed, and Springlatch said, "The way the guy's headed, he's got to veer east when he hits the bayfront drive. We can head him, maybe. Only thing is, you gotta have his license."

Doc gave a number and Springlatch asked, "You sure," and Doc said, "I'm sure." He inferred that they would cut in ahead of the other machine via a shorter route and wait for it to pass.

"All right, who are you and what's the scoop?" Springlatch demanded.

Doc told him. Essentials. His identity. The fact that white-suit had fired on him. "There's a silencer on his gun, a pretty good one," Doc finished. "So don't expect noise. Incidentally, I have a special commission from the Miami police department, if it's not outdated, and if it is, there's a federal commission that should serve."

"I've heard of you," Springlatch told him.

THE rest of it did not take long. Two minutes. Two minutes that passed the longest way, the car they wanted coming around a turn, the driver seeing them turn in on his trail. There were forty seconds of the wildest driving, then another turn, and white-suit didn't make the turn, although there was a moment when it seemed he would miraculously straighten out after vaulting the curb and caroming off the first palm tree. But then the car began to roll, and after three turns, it did one end-for-end swap, as a kind of final flourish.

Office Springlatch said, "He's a tough cookie if he took that." He spoke as their own car was stopping, skidding a little first to one side then the other as it did so. Then a red animal of fire began at the front of the wrecked car and started swallowing.

Doc Savage moved fast. He was at the car far ahead of Springlatch. He got into the heat, groping; he began to pull, and rather to his surprise was able to back out of the worst of the heat with what remained of white-coat. The man was all there, but badly broken, and minus his life.

"Look, harness and all," Springlatch said, for some reason surprised to find that the man had carried his gun in an elaborate underarm holster.

"He was killed instantly," Doc said.

Springlatch was looking at the gun. ".44. For some reason, you don't run onto many of them. Still, somehow, it seems familiar."

Doc said, "It should be."

"Yeah?"

"You probably have a .44 bullet from this gun downtown."

"Have we? How come?"

"Probably because one of your examiners took it out of a dead man last night."

Springlatch was silent. Not from surprise, from self-condemnation of his own stupidity. It was Policewoman Lorn who said, "You're not that dumb, Spring."

"No, but I could have been," Springlatch said. "The clerk in the telegraph office last night. They took a .44 slug out of him. How do you know it was from this gun?"

Doc Savage was going through the dead man's pockets. He found a number of things, money, lighter, a dog-track program, a billfold with some identification that was mostly Canadian. The identification was consistent in indicating the man was named Wilmer Elvin Troy, was a Canadian aged thirty-eight, a member of two associations for mining men, and owned a commercial pilot's license. There were two other items of special interest.

No. 1 special, which Doc showed to Springlatch, was a copy of the telegram which Macbeth Williams had despatched last night. It was made in pencil, and it differed in wording but not in general detail, near the end, from the one Williams had sent. Doc pointed out the difference in wording, Springlatch taking it from there.

"He was interrupted when he had copied down to near the end, took time out to kill telegraph clerk Gridley, some more time out to scram, and finished out the copy from memory later," Springlatch said. "How's that for deducting?"

The second item, which tied the whole thing up in a package, was the address of the Harlem hotel in New York where Monk and Ham had located the taxi driver and elevator operator who'd had bad luck with homicidal intentions.

"What's it all about?" was Springlatch's summary.

"It all ties in, anyway," Doc said. "It's more of a relief than you realize to know that."

Chapter VII

WELL into the early morning, a little after three a.m., the police decided to administer a warning not to leave town to Doc Savage, Macbeth Williams, Carlie McGuiggan and Austin Ulm, and let them go back to their hotels. The beards of Williams and Ulm had helped earn them a bad time.

"This is a devil of a note," said Macbeth Williams, riding back to the hotel. "What if the thing gets in the newspapers? It's going to reflect on the estate."

"I'm glad," said Carlie, "that the subject of Macbeth's predicting didn't enter the official discussions."

Macbeth shuddered. "Yes, that would have been no help. I don't think they considered our stories too credible, anyway."

Ulm stroked his whiskers. "These bushes didn't help. I think I'll invest a little money in a shave."

Doc Savage asked idly, "What estate was that?"

"Eh?" Macbeth asked.

"The one," Doc said, "that newspaper notoriety would reflect upon."

"Oh, you mean my remark a moment ago." Macbeth was silent a moment. "Well, naturally I referred to my father's holdings, the organization that people refer to more commonly as, quote, the half billion the silly fool won't touch, unquote."

"You seem thoughtful about it," Doc said.

"I am," Macbeth replied firmly.

"You're not," Doc suggested, "thinking of changing your mind about taking over its direction?"

"That's exactly it, I am thinking," said Macbeth.

Austin Ulm whistled. "My boy, you're beginning to cook with gas, as they say." Ulm sounded excited and awed. "It's all right to play around with who is going to win at a craps table, but it would be a little more worthwhile if a business deal involving a million or so was the stake. Macbeth, that's what I've been saying. Why waste this thing you've got?" He nudged Carlie McGuiggan. "What do you say, Carlie?"

Carlie shuddered. "I don't like people being shot and shot at."

"Nonsense," said Ulm. "That violence had nothing to do with Macbeth. Anybody who packs that idea is nuts."

IN his room, Doc Savage tried to raise Monk or Ham on the radio. Then he fell back on the long-distance telephone, making half a dozen calls, the last one to the New York police department. Total result: anxiety. What had happened to Monk and Ham? He did not as a usual thing have trouble sleeping, but during the rest of the night, he had plenty. He was unable to recall actually sleeping; what he was able to remember, when the sun burst through the window into his eyes, was an endless recalling of the weaknesses of Monk and Ham that might have caused a foot to slip. Their weaknesses were, except in the wrong places, strengths. Monk, in particular, was a direct fellow who would drop caution and wade in, given part of an excuse. That, in summary, was the thing that worried him. He imagined it was what had happened. They had made a smashing move when a wary one would have been wiser. That something drastic had befallen Monk and Ham, he was sure, or they would have set up a contact.

He rose, drew the blind against the sun, then lay on the bed for a while, drawing back mentally and examining the affair as a whole. He saw it as something like this: Macbeth Williams, who preferred being a mediocre scientist to managing his late father's holdings—Doc was inclined to feel Macbeth's attitude about the estate was sensible—had been signed up by a vague outfit named the Kendall Foundation, through the offices of his friend Ulm. The Kendall setup, Doc felt, should be known to him if it amounted to anything. It wasn't. The six-month isolation on Cormoral Island wasn't too sensible; there were ways open to any organization to get a group of stranded scientists back to civilization. So that the stranding was odd. That made two oddities, the vagueness of the Kendall Foundation, and the pointlessness of the marooning.

Suddenly hot with an idea, Doc Savage dressed and went to the waterfront. The steamer *Meg Finnegan* lay tied in rust-eaten ignominy to a wharf south of the bridge, and Doc saw no one until he had hammered on the grimy door of what obviously was the master's cabin. Then he was confronted by a tired, ugly face, bloodshot eyes, and a scowl.

"Skipper?" Doc asked.

"Yeah, I'm the master," replied the man. "What about it?"

Doc looked at the man as if he were fitting him to a description, then shrugged and displayed his billfold. "I'm here to pay off," he said.

The captain scowled and the thin tip of his tongue made a quick trip across his lips, as if fly-catching. "What the hell! The owners canning me?"

"What gave you that idea? No, this is for handling the little job."

"Yeah?"

"Let's not be coy," Doc suggested. "You got them off the island, making it look as if you just accidentally found them while paying the island a visit to see if there was guano. That was the deal, wasn't it?" He fanned through the banknotes. "Let's see, it was five hundred. Right?"

The master of the *Meg Finnegan* gave Doc an expressive look of greed, knowingness, and puzzled suspicion.

Doc added casually, "The bonus, I'm talking about." He frowned, watching the man, and asked abruptly, "What's this? You didn't expect a bonus for the job?"

The skipper swallowed. "Sure, sure," he said unconvincingly.

Doc made an angry gesture. "What's this! So that polecat intended to chisel the five hundred for himself! He had instructions to promise you a bonus, and deliver it personally. It just happens he was sent to New York, and couldn't make it."

The other man cursed bitterly. "Hell, no, he didn't mention a bonus! Trying to crook me, eh?"

"Maybe he gypped you on the payment, too," Doc said grimly. "How much did you get?"

"Two thousand," the man growled. "How much was it supposed to be?"

Doc Savage pushed the man back into the cabin, followed, showed him, for effect, an old federal commission that he carried for convenience in cases like this one, and said, "Now, let's have the whole story, friend. Or you're going to be in plenty of hot water."

The skipper shuffled back and sat on the bunk. He pondered, and the longer he sat there, the lower his shoulders sank. "The guy came to me in Rio," he said glumly. "It was two thousand to pick these four guys off that island. The guy said his name was Walters, but probably it wasn't. I wouldn't know. I got no information, and no instructions except it was to be an accident, finding them on this Cormoral Island."

"Describe Walters," Doc said.

It didn't take much imagination to fit the description of Walters to the man in the white suit who had died in the crash the night before.

DETECTIVE SPRINGLATCH opened the door sleepily, stared at Carlie McGuiggan in surprise, said, "Oh, you! Hello, there."

"I'm sorry I woke you so early," Carlie said. "You had a long night, didn't you?"

"It was long, all right," Springlatch agreed. "I wouldn't call it productive."

"Well, I wanted to ask you a question, and then I'll leave," Carlie said. "Did you inquire at the night club about that fellow in the white suit who was killed?"

"How'd you know we would do that?" Springlatch asked.

"I just imagined you would be thorough, and think of doing so."

Springlatch eyed her in a friendly fashion. "I'll answer your question if you'll answer one of mine."

"It's a deal."

"We worked that club over, but good," Springlatch told Carlie. "White-coat—Wilmer Elvin Troy, if that's his name—had made himself well-known around there the last few days. Why? The reason will slay you. This Troy wanted all the games rigged so some guy, one particular guy, would win. Troy got his way. It cost him plenty, but he got his way. You interested in the name of the winnah?"

"Macbeth Williams?" Carlie queried.

Springlatch grinned. "Good guess."

"Then the thing was a frame against Macbeth. He didn't play; he only predicted!" Carlie exclaimed.

"What's that about predicting?"

Carlie shook her head. "Never mind. I'll answer your question now, or is that it?"

Springlatch grinned. "My question was: how come you're interested?"

"Macbeth," Carlie replied frankly. "I'm in love with the big dope."

REACHING the hotel where Doc Savage, Macbeth and Ulm were staying, Carlie attempted to telephone Doc. Failing, she wrote a note: "I got to thinking about it all last night and I think it's a plot. The predictions at the gambling place were framed. Ask Springlatch. I'm looking into another idea I have." She left this at the desk for Doc.

Meeting Macbeth for breakfast, she mentioned nothing about her activities. To Macbeth's, "Darling, you're nicer looking than the sunshine this morning!" she smiled happily, and chattered gaily through the meal.

"Honey," she asked later, "where are the other two scientists who were marooned with you? Mr. Crikeland and Mr. Swanberg?"

Macbeth was startled. "Gosh, you haven't met them, have you, sweet? You know, I'd darn near forgot all about them. They're still here in town, I imagine."

"At this hotel?"

"No, they were going in for a little more flash," Macbeth told her. "They moved into a hotel over on Miami Beach. The Flame Arts, on the ocean front. You know, I'll have to call them today. Why don't we have luncheon with them? They're great guys. You'll like them."

"I'm sure I will," Carlie said. "But let's not make it a date until I'm sure I'll be free. I have some shopping to do." She glanced at her watch. "Oh, gosh! I've got to rush now! See you later, dear."

Macbeth jumped up. "Couldn't I go along?"

"No. I won't be long. I'll call you in an hour," Carlie said, hurrying away.

SWANBERG had removed his beard. This had left his face mapped grotesquely in brown and white, and he had attempted to dispel some of the oddity by coating the white with suntan make-up. The effect was slightly bizarre, but he had a lean face that was handsome in a cold way. "Yes, I'm Swanberg," he said.

"I'm Carlie McGuiggan," Carlie told him. "A friend of Macbeth Williams."

Swanberg grinned faintly. "Macbeth is a lucky guy. Won't you come in?" He raised his voice and yelled, "Crike!"

Crikeland came from another room, an older man than Carlie had expected or perhaps about the age she had expected, because she had imagined scientists as older men, with glasses, absent-minded manners, and gruff voices. Crikeland had all of these.

"A great pleasure, Miss McGuiggan," Crikeland said gruffly. "Or is it to be?"

Carlie looked at the two men. She didn't like them much. "I don't know," she said. "It's going to depend."

"Indeed?"

Carlie nodded. "Frankly, I don't see why my cards shouldn't go on the table right now. I've known Macbeth Williams a long time. He's awfully nice. But he can be imposed on. He's a big friendly dope who lacks confidence in himself."

Neither Crikeland nor Swanberg smiled, but Swanberg said pleasantly enough, "You don't need to tell us about Macbeth, Miss McGuiggan. We spent six months on an island with that boy."

"That," said Carlie, "is going to be my subject."

"Eh?"

"I'm in love with Macbeth," Carlie went on. "He's swell. For a long time, I've wanted to make him over. I thought if he had a little more self-confidence, I'd like him better. Now I've changed my mind. I like the guy the way he is."

"Meaning?" suggested Swanberg.

"It's very simple. I don't want him any different."

Crikeland snorted. "Why say a thing like that to us? Who's changing Macbeth?"

Frowning, Carlie said, "I don't know who is, but I believe it's happening. About these predictions, did you fellows notice anything about them?"

"We noticed them," Crikeland told her. "Toward the last, they were about as nerve-soothing as cannons going off."

"Did we notice them!" Swanberg put in. "Lady, there wasn't any other topic of conversation."

"You're not answering my question. I asked if you noticed anything odd," Carlie said.

"Odd?"

"Phony."

"In what way?"

"Staged," Carlie said. "Planted. Rigged. Trickery and thinga-jiggery. Not by Macbeth, either."

A glance Carlie didn't quite understand, and disliked, passed between Swanberg and Crikeland. "We discussed that point," said Crikeland. "And we reached a conclusion. We decided we couldn't see a dang sign of chicanery."

"You feel," asked Carlie, "that the whole thing is genuine?"

"We certainly do."

"Then," said Carlie, "you're pretty dense."

Crikeland eyed her blankly and asked, "What do you mean?"

"There's scheming," said Carlie. "The object seems to be to build up Macbeth's confidence so he will take over the estate management. I don't think that's the ultimate purpose. It's the first step."

"What would the second step be?" Swanberg asked, grinning in ridicule.

"How do I know? And don't smirk."

"It's preposterous," said Swanberg.

"Certainly is," agreed Crikeland. "The idea that Macbeth's string of predictions are the result of careful rigging without his knowledge is utterly unconvincing and without foundation. Why, great grief, I suppose you'll claim next the whole expedition to Cormoral Island was rigged so it could be pulled off."

"Could be," said Carlie grimly.

"Oh, my God!"

Carlie, eyes flashing, said, "Ulm's winning, with Macbeth's predictions, at a gambling house last night was rigged, I can tell you that. And I can tell you the police know about it, and are investigating. Now, what do you think of that?"

Crikeland glanced, speechless, at Swanberg. The latter was equally shocked. Neither spoke.

"I hoped," Carlie continued, "to get some help from you fellows. That's why I'm here. Macbeth looks on you as his friends."

"We are his friends!" Crikeland exclaimed unconvincingly.

"I'm beginning to wonder," Carlie said. "Yes, I'm beginning to wonder."

Crikeland stiffened, muttered, "You're not being very polite, young lady."

"No, I'm not," Carlie agreed. "I think I'll come back later, after I have time to think this out more thoroughly. Good morning, gentlemen."

She turned toward the door, and was reaching for it when Swanberg's heavy fist came against her jaw at the end of a short arc. Carlie collapsed. Swanberg let her fall to the floor, blew on his knuckles, and grinned bleakly at Crikeland's scowl of disapproval.

"That was a fool move," Crikeland growled.

"Was it? She had a good hold on the lid of the box, and she was getting ready to yank it open," Swanberg told him.

"Yes, but now she'll know there's something in the box. Before, she didn't know."

"O.K. So we could have stood by and let her knock the props from under seven months' hard work and conniving. Would that be sense?"

Crikeland shuddered. "No, I guess not. But now what are we going to do with her?"

Swanberg sneered. "You think I haven't got that figured out? You think I just bopped her?"

"Well?"

"We could get in a spot where we gotta make a buy-out. You see that, don't you?"

"I can see a spot."

Swanberg told him, "There's two angles. One, she's bait to get this Doc Savage into a trap. What kind of a trap, we'll figure out, but I think it better be well-figured. Two, to keep Macbeth Williams in line, if it comes to a place where he sees what's happening. Sound all right?"

"No!" Crikeland snapped. "You damn fool, you don't just keep a full-grown girl a prisoner in a city like Miami."

Swanberg sneered. "Not practical, eh?"

"No."

"Well, then, we won't," Swanberg said. He watched Crikeland begin to grow pale, laughed, added, "I don't mean kill her just yet. I mean, let's get her up to the mine."

Crikeland winced. "You are crazy, Swanberg. Six or seven thousand miles! Just move her up there. Like that."

"Ever hear of airplanes?"

"But—"

"We'll be two doctors with a patient," Swanberg went on. "It'll work. If we just use a little brass, it'll work."

Crikeland hesitated, said, "But it's so damned much trouble!"

"Inconvenient, eh?"

"Sure."

"So might an electric chair be."

Swanberg had intended the remark for humor, but it hadn't been, and both were silent. It was Crikeland who leaned over and struck Carlie's jaw a hard blow when she began to show signs of reviving. And Crikeland who said, "Well, if we could get Doc Savage up at the mine, the odds would be a little more in our favor."

"Now you're on the track," Swanberg told him. "Let's get going."

"How do we get her out of the hotel?"

"Where's the whisky bottle? You think a dame who has passed out has never been carried out of a hotel?"

Chapter VIII

DOC SAVAGE, frowning, re-read the note Carlie McGuiggan had left for him at the hotel desk. It did not give him a feeling of assurance, and he called Macbeth Williams' room, got no answer, and a moment later found Macbeth sitting ill-at-ease in the part of the lobby that faced onto the street.

"Hello, there," Macbeth said. "I'm waiting for Carlie. She should be here before long. She's overdue."

Doc took the adjacent chair. "Any developments this morning?"

Macbeth seemed to consider whether he should shake his head or not, and did. "I had a rough night," he told Doc. "I didn't sleep much."

"I don't imagine anyone did."

Macbeth looked at Doc wryly, and asked, "Mind if I confide one of my problems?"

"Go right ahead."

"Thanks. I'm grateful for your help. I appreciate it, particularly because I know you're under no obligation to help me at all." He was silent for a few moments, then asked abruptly, "Mr. Savage, what opinion have you formed of my character? Give it to me without sugar."

"Without sugar, I would say you were a serious-minded young man who is saddled with a feeling of inferiority because he had an outstanding father. I would add that your judgment is probably better than you think it is, but not as good as it would have been if you had given it more of a chance during the last—how old are you? Twenty-eight?—say, twenty-eight years."

Macbeth grinned. "That's not very strong."

"I imagine it's stronger than your candid opinion of yourself."

"Well, you're right," Macbeth admitted. "I'm a dreamer, an introverted sort, and timid. Inclined to be a follower, not a leader. That right?"

"It's not too wrong."

"A guy like that," said Macbeth, "has no business managing a half-billion estate."

Doc made no reply.

"I didn't think you would answer," Macbeth told him wryly. "Well, managing an estate isn't just handling that much money. Very little of the estate is money. It's property, plants, steamships, mines. Quite a lot of mines and mills, really. It's business properties like that, which means people's lives, because a person who molds an enterprise like that molds the lives of the people connected with it."

"Right."

"A mold," said Macbeth, "should be more firm than the material it makes into shape."

"True."

"Which brings me to my question," Macbeth Williams muttered dubiously. "Am I, or am I not, fitted to become the mold? This crazy stuff that has been happening to me lately has given me a feeling of confidence. I don't trust the feeling. A man doesn't become a strong character overnight. Character is built over a period of years, not in a few weeks."

Doc looked at him thoughtfully. "You'll have to answer that for yourself."

"Will I know the right answer when I find it?"

"I suspect you will," Doc told him.

"Thanks."

"Where," Doc Savage asked, "did Miss McGuiggan say she was going, and how long overdue is she?"

"Carlie said she was going shopping, and she's over an hour late," Macbeth Williams told him. "I'm beginning to worry."

"She's not usually late for her appointments? Some women are."

"Not Carlie."

"Then we'd better look into it," Doc said gravely. "She said she was going shopping. Before that, did she ask any leading questions? Questions about persons or places?"

Macbeth shook his head. "Nothing that seemed unusual. She did ask about Crikeland and Swanberg, the two scientists who were with me on the island."

"A casual question?"

"I thought so. She wanted to know where they were. I told her. In a hotel in Miami Beach." Macbeth jumped up quickly, exclaiming, "There's Ulm. Maybe he has seen her."

Austin Ulm's eyes were slightly bloodshot, and there were heavy lines around his mouth. But his manner was quite jovial. "Carlie? No, I haven't seen her this morning. How are the predictions coming, my boy? Any outstanding ones this morning?"

"They seemed to have stopped," Macbeth admitted.

Ulm clapped him on the shoulder. "Just a lull, old chap. They'll resume. And, boy, when you take over the estate, you'll go to town. You'll be known as a tycoon in no time."

Macbeth said uncomfortably, "I'm not as hot about taking over as I was."

"The hell you aren't!" Ulm exclaimed in alarm. "Now that's a foolish feeling to get! If you ask me—"

"I'm worried about Carlie," interrupted Macbeth. "She had a date with me for an hour ago. She usually keeps her appointments."

Doc Savage got to his feet. He said, "I believe I'll look around for Miss McGuiggan. Care to come along?"

"I certainly do!" Macbeth exclaimed. "What about you, Ulm?"

Ulm snorted. "Looking for someone in a city the size of Miami has got a haystack and a needle beat, hasn't it? Oh, I might as well go along."

Doc Savage strode outside, jerked open the door of a taxicab, and told the driver, "The Flame Arts. It's a hotel in Miami Beach."

"That's where Crike and Swanberg are staying!" Macbeth gasped.

THE room clerk at the Flame Arts had a poor memory until Doc Savage told him quietly, "You can give us a better answer than, 'They've checked out,' or you can have this place crawling with impatient policemen asking about a murder. Take your choice."

The clerk gave them a very supercilious stare for possibly thirty seconds, then the look fell apart on his face like snow melting on a hot stove. "Good God, was she dead?" he blurted.

Macbeth Williams made a croaking noise, seized the clerk's arm, and bellowed, "Carlie! You mean somebody hurt Carlie?" He would have shrieked more, probably hysterically, had Doc not drawn him back, and described Carlie McGuiggan to the room clerk.

"That was evidently the girl," the clerk said quickly. "The two men, Crikeland and Swanberg, left about an hour ago, crossing the lobby and half-dragging the girl between them. They put her in a car and drove off."

Macbeth, wrenching away from Doc, cursed the clerk furiously. "How in the hell did they get away with a thing like that?"

"They seemed tight, all of them. They smelled like it, anyway."

"You say they took a car? It wasn't a taxi?" Doc demanded.

"A private car." The clerk was frightened now. "I have an idea," he exclaimed, and hurried to the entrance, where he buttonholed a stocky doorman in a mauve uniform.

The latter produced a notebook, thumbed through it, and showed it to the other man. "I generally jot down the license number of any car where there seems to be something a little odd happening," the doorman explained.

"Give me that number!" Doc said sharply. "I'll get it on the police teletype."

A few minutes later, when Doc rejoined Ulm and Macbeth Williams, Ulm was urging Macbeth to get a drink. "The kid's about to blow his cork," Ulm told Doc angrily. "What the devil have you got stirred up here?"

"It's pretty clear something unpleasant has happened to Miss McGuiggan," Doc told him.

"The hell it has! Crikeland and Swanberg are nice guys, and I resent your suggestion!"

"They certainly seem nice guys, abducting Miss McGuiggan," Doc said.

"I don't give a damn! I was with them six months on that island, and I think they're O.K."

Doc Savage looked at Ulm levelly. "You had better listen to a few facts. Williams, too. You can hear them on the way back to our hotel, where we're going immediately, and start the most complete search possible for Carlie McGuiggan."

Chapter IX

THE midday sunlight lay like a sheet of flame against the window of the hotel room, and Macbeth Williams sat and stared at it bleakly and speechlessly. He seemed to have stopped breathing. Austin Ulm examined his own fingertips, picking at them nervously from time to time. Once he muttered, "I can't really believe all that stuff. I really can't." Williams seemed not to hear. From the bedroom came the spewing of static from a loudspeaker, occasionally a heterodyne squeal or the raucous sound of a voice from the radio, and at intervals, the sound of Doc Savage patiently calling Monk and Ham, but without getting a response.

Doc Savage, appearing in the doorway finally, looked at the two men bleakly. "You've had time to think it over," he said. "The *Meg Finnigan* didn't come across you fellows on Cormoral Island by accident. The skipper was bribed to pick you up and pretend it was a chance visit. He was bribed by the man who was killed in the automobile smash last night, the man named Troy. Troy also bribed the gambling house to let you win any bet Macbeth suggested. The games are all rigged, as you'd have known if you had studied the system. Gimmicked is another word. It was no trick to see that Macbeth predicted winners. The waiter at the restaurant was primed to suggest the name of the club. That was a clever piece of psychology there. The waiter wasn't paid to steer us to the club, but it was done by suggestion through an argument the fellow Troy staged with him. The police dug up that information, and Officer Springlatch told Miss McGuiggan about it. Doubtless that's the information she took to Crikeland and Swanberg, not realizing they were in on it."

Macbeth groaned. "Who the devil was Troy?"

"A Chicago mining engineer who served a prison sentence in Colorado for a mining swindle, who had Canadian citizenship papers. That's about all we know. Except that he was in this with Crikeland and Swanberg and at least two others."

Ulm cursed hoarsely, demanded, "In what? What? That's what I want to know."

"Suppose you guess," Doc said.

"Guess, hell!" Ulm snarled. "You blow up the prettiest dream I ever had, and then say, 'Guess!' Dammit, I could hate you, Savage!"

Macbeth Williams stared at Ulm with dislike. "Ulm, I don't believe you're worried about a thing except discovering my so-called 'predicting' was all goose-feathers!"

"That's plenty to worry about, isn't it!" Ulm yelled. "Man, don't you see what this Savage is doing! Destroying your belief in yourself! Are you going to stand for that?"

"Oh, shut up that greedy yapping!" Macbeth told him bitterly. "God knows what has happened to Carlie, and all you think about is the exploding of a hoax!"

DETECTIVE SPRINGLATCH arrived presently. "You got the dope I sent you on Troy? Colorado mining man with a bad record and Canadian citizenship? We dug that up through fingerprints."

Doc nodded, asked impatiently, "What about the car?"

"The one Crikeland and Swanberg used to take the girl away from the hotel? We found that twenty minutes ago. "

Macbeth Williams jerked stiffly erect. "Was she … did they—"

Springlatch shook his head. "No trace of any of them."

"Where was the car found?" Doc asked.

"On No. 1 Highway, about halfway to Palm Beach. Abandoned. State men found it. But that's no help. They weren't in the car, and nobody saw what they changed to."

"Show me the exact spot," Doc directed, spreading out a road map. Springlatch obligingly drew a circle. "About there."

Doc leaned over, rested a finger on the map for a moment. He straightened suddenly. "Start looking for a plane!" he said sharply. "The beach, half a mile from the road at that point, is hard-packed and lonely. A first-rate landing strip for a plane."

"That's a far-fetched guess," Springlatch muttered.

"Is it? With the whole state alerted for them? With swamp on the inland side of the road? And this whole thing as well-prepared as it is? I don't think so." He swung on Macbeth and Ulm, said, "Come on. We'll check it ourselves."

"What kind of plane?" Springlatch yelled.

"That's why I want to look at the beach," Doc said. "There should be wheel prints."

WITH No. 1 jet shut down and No. 2 loafing, Doc Savage touched the switch control of the airfoil curvature, returned his attention to the airspeed, and when it went below two hundred into the green arc, he dropped the wheels and made certain the green lights showed they were locked. The ship greased into the base leg at a bare ninety, and when the high-pressure dual tires barked against the sand, they were doing sixty-five miles an hour airspeed, against a fifteen-mile wind, and Macbeth Williams was already screaming, "There's some wheel tracks! See them!"

The wheel prints swung out from a spot where wind-beaten jungle overhung the beach, and when they stood there, they could see plenty of signs that the plane had been tied down there, possibly for several days.

Doc ran back to his own plane, changed the oscillator setting on his radio transmitter to get it on police wavelength, and in a few moments was telling Springlatch: "It was a plane, all right. A B-26. That means a converted job. We don't know the NC number, of course. But get men up here asking questions. The plane was tied down on the beach several days, and someone may have remembered the number."

"They'd travel fast, wouldn't they?" Springlatch asked.

"Better than three hundred, possibly," Doc agreed. "It's a B-26, all right. The tread is distinctive enough that we can be pretty sure. Better alert Canadian airports, as well."

"You mean because Troy had Canadian papers?"

"That could be a good reason."

THE airport was three hundred miles west of Montreal, approximately, a rather startling criss-cross of two runways in the otherwise nearly endless stretch of trees that stood in a thin cold carpet of snow. It had been built for the Canadian air force during the war; late years it had seen nothing but an occasional bush flyer who needed no more than a fifth that much runway. The village five miles to the south was a scattering of wooden buildings in a clearing. When Doc Savage arched the jet in over the town, there were suddenly fifty or so people outside the buildings, more than the population of the place seemingly could be.

He swung the ship toward the landing strip, did the necessary cockpit landing-check, dragged the runway once by way of caution, noting the grass that had thrust up through the disused paving in spots. He swung back, landed, taxied to the one lonely wooden shack, and they climbed out into cold astonishingly bitter.

"What a place!" Ulm mumbled, looking about between attacks of shivering. "And on a wild-goose chase, too!"

Macbeth Williams looked at Ulm with no feeling except tiredness and anxiety, and said, "You still haven't given up faith in Crikeland and Swanberg, have you?"

Doc made no comment, but walked, the frozen snow squeaking underfoot, to the shack. It was not locked, and he entered. It seemed thirty degrees colder inside than outdoors.

Soon a man appeared, riding a horse that breathed plumes of vapor. The man slid off the horse, explaining, "I don't stay out here much. Not enough business."

"We came about the plane that refueled here day before yesterday," Doc told him.

"Yeah, I imagined you had," the man said. "Well, it was a B-26, conversion job. Same numbers as on the radio broadcast. Hell of it is, I didn't hear the broadcast until last night."

"You see a girl aboard?" Macbeth Williams demanded shrilly.

"She didn't get out. She stayed in the ship."

"She wasn't hurt?"

"Didn't seem to be."

Doc asked, "How much fuel did they take aboard?"

"All the tanks would hold. Almost cleaned me out of ninety octane."

"Which way did they go?"

"Straight west out of sight. There was some haze. Visibility about three miles. The way they went when they left wouldn't mean anything. They could turn."

"They get anything more than gasoline?"

"Couple of charts, is all."

"How were they dressed?"

"For the country. Parkas, mucks. One guy had bearskin pants. The other wore what looked like a sheepskin flight suit, army issue or surplus."

Macbeth blurted, "Where in the devil did they pick up clothing like that?"

"Probably had it in the plane. They were well-prepared," Doc told him. He turned back to the airport manager. "What charts?"

"North of here. One regional. One planning chart, small scale."

"They didn't mark them or anything?"

The man nodded. "They marked one, but that's no help either. I didn't see what course. You fellows use some coffee? I brought out a thermos. And some moose sandwiches. You like moose?"

"That's fine," Doc told him. "Let's have them in the plane. The cabin is heated."

"You think this is cold?" The man chuckled. "Hell, this is the warmest day this winter." He handed up the thermos and a package of sandwiches. "I'll go build a fire in the shanty, in case you fellows want to stick around. Probably be a Mountie plane or two in soon. This thing has stirred up a hell of a rumpus."

IN almost complete silence, Doc Savage, Williams and Ulm consumed the sandwiches. There seemed nothing to say. It was distressingly apparent that they had reached the end of a trail. Macbeth did not improve the mood when he suddenly groaned and buried his face in his hands. Ulm looked at Doc and mumbled, "Poor kid. I can't stand seeing him beaten down like this. I'm going outside, cold or no cold." Ulm climbed outside, stood beating his arms against his sides, then dashed into the shack, from the stovepipe of which smoke had started climbing.

"Mr. Savage," Macbeth Williams asked brokenly, "what do you think they're doing? Why in

God's name would they take Carlie all the way from Florida to a place like this?"

"The move," Doc told him quietly, "isn't such a dumb one from their standpoint."

"I don't see how you figure that, Mr. Savage."

"There are several of them, obviously. There are now three of us. In Miami, there were the three of us plus all the police facilities."

"Oh!"

Doc Savage went to the radio transmitter, and began another attempt to contact Monk and Ham. His face was grim. He did not give up the fruitless task for several minutes.

"You're terribly upset about your two friends, aren't you?" Macbeth said.

"Very," Doc agreed grimly.

"There has been no word from them?"

"None."

Macbeth closed his eyes tightly and his lips trembled. "I feel terribly guilty for getting you into this. I did, you know. By being stupid enough to let myself be kidded into believing I had some kind of supernatural power. What a ninny!"

"You didn't really believe in it at any time," Doc told him.

"Oh, no!" Macbeth's lips twisted with self-contempt. "You think not? Listen, there were times when I went for it whole-hog."

Through the plexiglass, Doc saw Ulm pop out of the shack. Ulm carried an aëronautical chart which he tucked under an arm as he climbed into the plane. He seemed vaguely excited, but took a seat without saying anything. Presently Doc Savage leaned out of a doorway and shouted to the airport attendant, "We're taking off. You have a radio receiver that will pick up aircraft frequencies?"

The man came over and stared up at him. "Yeah," he said. "But listen, I can't hear a hundred miles out with any radio. It's not the set. It's atmospheric conditions, a sunspot cycle that's supposed to last for maybe another week. Been giving us hell ten days now. That's another reason I didn't hear about this plane with the girl. It's no satisfaction to listen to the radio. Can't hardly hear a thing through the static."

"What about the weather north?"

"Not bad, not good," the man said. "Depends on what you call bad. For us up here, it's not so tough."

"Report into Mounted headquarters that we were here and took off to continue a general search, will you?" Doc asked.

"Oh, sure."

THE jet had not been in the air more than a couple of minutes, and Doc Savage was adjusting an experimental contrivance which, if he ever perfected it, would enable a radar signal to distinguish between certain basic types of metals at a considerable distance. The gadget, for military purposes, would be quite convenient; metallic ingredient in a paint applied to a plane would afford instant identification as enemy or friend at a distance of a hundred miles or more. The only problem was that there were plenty of bugs in the thing; the principal one at the moment being a reflective dispersion of the reflected signal, the bounce-back, which rendered the gimmick highly undependable at a distance of more than fifteen miles. It was marvelous up to about fifteen miles; beyond that, it was a headache.

To divert Macbeth Williams' mind with a less ugly matter, Doc explained generally what the contrivance was.

"You mean," asked the surprised Macbeth, "That you can fly along, and for fifteen miles in any direction, tell what kind of metal you're flying over?"

"Within reason," Doc assured him.

"You could spot a steel automobile body?"

"Yes, we could identify a steel automobile body. But if there were a steel tank, a steel engine, and a steel building of about the same size in the neighborhood, we couldn't tell them apart unless the car moved."

"And you could tell a copper roof?"

"Yes."

"Or a tin roof?"

"Yes."

Macbeth's eyes widened. "Say, what's the matter with using an apparatus like that to prospect for minerals? Could it be done? Is it practical?"

"Only practical," Doc told him, "in that it could identify some—and note I say some, not all, because the gimmick isn't omnipotent by any means—types of minerals on the surface. But not in ledges and veins under the surface."

"Then it's practical!"

"Let us say it's halfway so," Doc told him. "Surface metals and minerals, some types, can be spotted, depending on their atomic structure and reaction upon micro-wavelengths." Doc paused, turned his head, and asked, "What is it, Ulm?" He suddenly saw that Austin Ulm was breathing fast.

"I think I got something," Ulm said. "You know what I did when I was in the shack back there at the airport? I asked that fellow to go through each exact move they made when they were in here and when I got to where they bought those charts, I struck pay dirt."

"You mean you know where they may have taken Carlie?" Macbeth shouted. "Lord, man, spit it out. Let's have it."

Ulm held up a hand patiently. "Easy, boy. I have to explain my method of deduction. They bought a chart. They marked a course on the chart. The airport manager didn't see what course they marked. Now, that much you already knew. But here's what I pried out of the airport man. They didn't have a ruler long enough to serve as a straight-edge when they marked out their course, and they did what pilots do a lot, they folded one chart and used the folded edge as a straight-edge to guide the pencil while they marked the course line on the other chart. Only they didn't use a pencil. They used a fountain pen."

"So what?" Macbeth demanded impatiently. "How would—"

Doc said, "So the pen left a mark along the folded edge of the chart they used for a ruler? That it?"

"That's exactly it," said Ulm triumphantly. "The ink rubbed off the pen nib, showed where they started and made a mark the whole way to where they stopped." He whipped out the chart. "Here, look!"

As Ulm had said, there was a plainly defined inked indication along the fold of the chart, with a very specific starting point and ending, each indicated by a small blot caused by additional ink.

"See!" Macbeth Williams shouted excitedly. "He's right. There's where the pen was set down carefully to start the mark, and where it rested a moment carefully at the destination point! By gosh, we know how far they were going!"

Doc did not share the enthusiasm. "All we really know," he said, "is that there's an ink mark on this chart."

"Hell!" said Ulm contemptuously. "I've got a damn good clue, and you know it. Don't belittle my deducting."

"How do we do this?" Macbeth interrupted anxiously. "We know how far—or think we know—but in what direction?"

"We'll fly straight north the correct distance, and begin a circle, keeping about the same axis," Doc told him. "That's the only thing we can do."

"You'll be able to use the gadget we were just talking about, won't you?" Macbeth asked eagerly.

"What gadget is that?" Ulm demanded.

"Mr. Savage has a contrivance which will identify some types of metal at a distance by use of a new type of polarization of radar transmissions."

"What we need more of," said Ulm, not greatly impressed, "is the kind of luck I had when I learned about that chart."

Chapter X

THE range of the jet plane, because of the restrictions of fuel supply, was limited, and they grew increasingly aware of it. They would be faced, within another hour, with the alternative of turning back, or taking a chance on setting down somewhere when their fuel was nearly exhausted, and possibly contacting the outside by radio to have fuel brought in. The latter, since they were able to hear nothing whatever but static, was not inviting.

Macbeth watched the radar scope with increasing strain. Doc had told him how to make identifications. It was a matter of a difference in the shape and shading of pips on the screen, as a small dial, which Doc referred to as a polarization control, was moved to different settings.

They were depending almost solely upon the trick radar now. There was a high overcast of cirrus clouds, and a layer of ground haze about two thousand feet deep over the snow-blanketed wasteland below. Visibility was possibly two miles, but only large objects, clusters of trees, wind-swept areas of bare stone, or the slick whiteness of a frozen lake, could be identified at that distance.

Macbeth was startled when Doc Savage suddenly pushed his hand away from the radar polarizing dial, and gave it an experimental adjustment or two. Doc stared at the scope. And he made, softly, a strange low trilling sound that evidently meant considerable wonder.

"What is it?" asked Macbeth anxiously. "Not the plane. All I saw was a considerable area of odd-looking pips appear on the scope." He frowned. "Does it mean something?"

"An area of exposed metallic substance," Doc told him.

"You mean a metal building roof?"

"In this waste? No, it was more likely an exposed vein of ore. A large one."

"Oh," said Macbeth disappointedly. "I thought maybe it had something to do with finding Carlie."

"No."

"But you seem excited."

Doc Savage made a notation on the chart. "It's something I'm coming back later to investigate. Unless I'm mistaken about the analysis of the fragmentation on the scope, what we saw was evidences of an extensive deposit of caronite of a high order. I imagine you know that means—"

He broke off his explanation, seized the wheel and whipped the ship sharply to the east. Then he pointed at the scope. "There! Dural metal! A plane!"

"Oh, God!" Macbeth breathed. "I hope it's what we're hunting! Why are you climbing?"

"We'll cross the spot fairly high in the overcast with the engines shut off," Doc told him. "Less chance of being noticed. We'll try that first, and see what luck we have."

Ulm had been pitched half out of his seat when Doc whipped the plane about. Now he came to the cockpit, demanding, "What does that kind of flying mean?"

"Sit down and fasten your safety belt," Doc told him curtly. "We've got something spotted."

A few seconds later, the jet engines became silent, the ship lost a little of its solid headlong feeling, and Doc adjusted the airfoil curvature for maximum glide angle. He followed the object they had spotted on the scope, and they prepared to use binoculars.

The plane, designed for speed, was no glider. It sank rapidly. Doc kept a displeased eye on the altimeter, the scope; abruptly, he swung the binoculars downward.

The terrain underneath was typical of the Arctic, snow-coated monotony studded with starved small trees, ripped open occasionally with a gully, or peaking up in a rocky hill. Suddenly, there was the flat white that meant a lake with its ice carpeted by snow, and immediately thereafter Doc picked up the lines of the plane. It was a B-26, parked on the south edge of the lake.

"See it?" Doc demanded.

"No, I didn't," Macbeth began, and Ulm interrupted, yelling, "I did! On the edge of the lake. Tied down. It's our quarry."

Doc swung the ship lazily to the right, stood it on a wingtip in a nose-high slip that lifted them up in the seats.

"Hell, you're not going to land?" Ulm barked.

"If the lake is long enough, yes."

"Without scouting the vicinity?" Ulm yelled. "That's crazy!"

"We'd be about as inconspicuous as a skyrocket," Doc advised him. "As it is, I think we came in quietly enough not to be noticed. At any rate, we're now low enough that the jets would certainly be heard if we turned them on. So we'll take the north end of the lake and see what happens. We can always get in the air again."

He held the slip, later let the nose swing a little, and at less than five hundred feet, when the expanse of white lake ice suddenly ended, he let the ship drop around, and coasted into the wind. The lake was under them again, not fifty feet below now. He did not lower the gear. The fuselage was designed for water and snow operation, the dual function simplified by the lack of propellers.

So quickly that it did not seem quite real, the east shore of the lake was sliding toward them, the ship rocking slightly. Doc gave hard right rudder; the guide rudder that doubled as snow-and-water helm took hold, and they came slowly about. But not before they had taken a jolting bounce over a low ridge of shore ice, fortunately coated with a mattress of snow.

The ensuing stillness was uncanny.

"We'll sit right here and listen," Doc said. "Incidentally, the cabin is bulletproof, as long as they haven't anything more powerful than hunting rifles."

"By gosh, visibility isn't more than half a mile," Ulm muttered.

Doc dropped out of the plane briefly, dragging a seismographic microphone at the end of a cable. He found a spot twenty feet away where a rock ledge showed bare, set the mike in a crevice, wedging it in place, then he went back to the plane. Ulm stared wonderingly and demanded, "What's that thing?"

Doc explained its purpose. "A microphone developed for making seismographic surveys, sensitive enough to pick up the vibration of a man walking a mile away under normal conditions. If anyone approaches, we should be able to hear them." He plugged the cable into the audio amplifier section of the plane radio and adjusted the gain controls.

The sounds that began coming from the speaker were the noises that bitter cold makes; the creaking of frozen branches in the wind, the shot-like crackle of the lake ice. Ulm started violently when there was a wild and loud clatter from the loudspeaker. "What was that?"

"Some animal running," Doc said. "A wolverine or a small bear. I'd say a bear, but not a large one."

Ulm stared at the contrivance. "I'll be damned!"

"Mr. Savage!" Macbeth Williams blurted.

The strangeness in the man's voice whipped Doc about; he found himself trying to imagine what had caused the look of bleak shock on Williams' features. Williams lifted both hands. They gripped the aëronautical chart by which they had been flying. "Is this where we are?" Williams asked. "This place you marked?"

Doc said, "I've been marking the course right along, yes."

Ulm demanded, "What's the matter with you anyway, Macbeth?"

"It's this location on the map," Williams muttered. "It suddenly clicked with me."

"Clicked how?"

"The estate, my father's estate, owns mining property around here. I think we're on it now."

AN element of surprise settled over the plane. And silence. It was hardly broken by a shuffling clatter from the loudspeaker as the animal, and it sounded like a larger animal this time, moved somewhere out there. Macbeth Williams looked at them in shame, mumbling finally, "I should have noticed it before. But the estate has properties in half a dozen places in northern Canada, most of them undeveloped and so not considered very important. It's only one of many places where there are holdings." He tightened his hands, face distressed, and added, "But I should have thought of it, even if I know very little about the estate. Something tells me it's important."

"I don't see how it can be," Ulm said shortly. "Say, that thing made a noise in the radio again. You sure it's an animal?"

"Bear," Doc said.

"Yeah? That's putting your neck out. If it's some guy with a gun, it won't be so cute."

"I'll go farther," Doc assured him, "and say it's a polar bear. There's a difference in the tread, and particularly in the manner of behavior, that is sightly distinctive."

"Oh, for God's sake!" Ulm exclaimed. "More masterminding!" He climbed out of the plane, adding, "I'm going to look around personally, not that I haven't got faith in your contraption, of course."

"You'd better get Mr. Savage's permission!" Macbeth Williams said sharply.

"Permission, hell!" Ulm stalked off, snow grinding under his feet and filling the seismographic contrivance output with a great roaring and whimpering that was totally unlike footsteps in the snow.

"He's awfully difficult at times," Macbeth said apologetically.

"A trifle obvious, too," Doc added.

Macbeth nodded vaguely, examined his gun—a hunting rifle which he'd picked up, at Doc's suggestion, during their brief stop in New York City—and felt under his parka to make sure that the clip pouch was filled with cartridges. This recapitulation ended abruptly. His voice shook. "I don't want to sound like Ulm, Mr. Savage!" he blurted. "But we can't just sit here, can we?"

"I don't plan to," Doc told him.

"That may not be the plane we're seeking, you know," Macbeth added.

"No, it's the one. The NC number fitted our description."

"Then what are we waiting for?"

Doc glanced at Macbeth, said, "To see how Ulm will make out."

Macbeth winced. He didn't like that too well; he frowned out into the murky waste of snow and scrub pines, evidently feeling the waiting was not like Doc Savage.

The silence that followed was uncomfortable, lasted about twenty minutes, and ended with unexpected—and unpleasant—developments. They had been listening to Austin Ulm's careful prowling. The man had been taking a few steps at a time, pausing often to listen, and otherwise behaving about as seemed reasonable. The sound of grindings, joltings and odd other noises was without warning.

The uproar from the seismographic microphone pickup was very short in duration, but already Doc Savage was on his feet, had snapped back the exit hatch.

"What is it?" Macbeth asked excitedly.

"Someone waylaid him!" Doc replied.

"Yes, but you seem so amazed," Macbeth blurted, piling out of the plane after Doc. "Since he was reconnoitering enemy territory, naturally you knew he was in danger. Why should you be so surprised?"

"Not in some time," Doc said, "have I less expected a thing to happen."

AUSTIN ULM'S progress was not difficult to follow through the snow, because the man had taken no precautions about concealing his footprints. The trail, taking more of a direct line than they had imagined from listening to the amplifier, approached the spot where they had seen the converted bomber tied down on the shore of the lake. Doc Savage stopped, told Macbeth Williams, "Drop back about a hundred yards, and follow me, keeping well to the right, inshore from the lake."

"I understand," Macbeth said, hefting his rifle. "If you get in trouble, I'm to do what I can."

"You're not to shoot anyone," Doc warned, "except as a last resort. And by last resort, I mean under the direst pressure of necessity."

Macbeth shuddered. "I'm not anxious to shoot anybody."

"Remember that."

"I will," Macbeth said, turning off to the right of their route.

Doc Savage remained where he was, then stepped into a thicket of evergreens, shook out the snow cape he had brought from the plane—a coverall-like garment completely of white cloth, similar to those developed for Arctic Troops—and donned the thing.

Now, offering a figure that was as inconspicuous in the dull Arctic waste as it could conveniently be made, he continued tracking Ulm. He kept well clear of the footprints, however, crossing them occasionally to make sure he was on the trail.

All the caution paid a poor dividend when a voice like rocks being powdered said, "All right, choose your medicine!"

Doc became rigid. He did not turn his head.

"Things are froze up kinda tight, and nobody might take the trouble to chop a grave," the ominous voice added. "You might take that into consideration."

"I will," Doc replied.

"Huh?"

"This is the last place I expected to find you, Monk," Doc went on.

"Oh, holy cow! For crying out loud! Doc!"

Doc Savage turned, in time to see Monk Mayfair collapse, half sitting, in the snow. It was not, Doc saw immediately, all surprise that made Monk sit down. Monk was not in good shape. He was haggard, bearded, and bore unmistakable signs of being in the most painful state of starvation, about the third day of it. Anxiety had also taken a hard toll of Monk's normal animal vitality.

"Holy cow!" Monk breathed again. "This guy was telling the truth! He wasn't woofin'!"

Austin Ulm, from a prostrate position in the snow, said bitterly, "Of course I wasn't lying!"

DOC SAVAGE asked Monk, "Are any of them close? Do they have a guard at the plane?" When Monk shook his head, Doc went on, "I'll find Williams, before he gets too worried." Doc then retraced his trail, stripping off the snow cape as he walked along. When he got back, he found an alarmed Macbeth.

"I was sure worried," Macbeth explained. "Gosh, I never saw you a single time after you told me you'd go ahead. I couldn't figure it. Did you find Ulm?"

"Yes. He was captured by one of my aides, Monk Mayfair."

"One of your friends—Oh, no! What a surprise! You don't mean Carlie is safe, too?"

Doc gripped the man's arm, said, "Take it easy," and led him back to the spot where Monk and Ulm were waiting. Glancing about, Doc saw signs that Monk had been concealed there at least several hours. There were no signs of footprints which Monk might have made coming to the ambush spot, which was in a thicket of evergreen shrubs within a score of yards of the converted bomber.

"I been right here nearly two days," Monk explained bitterly. "I'm not proud of it. It was a bum idea. But I thought they would come to have a look at the plane to see if it were safe, and I'd have a chance to start operating."

"What happened?" Doc demanded. "Where's Ham?"

"They got him and took him off to the mine," Monk told him. "That's all I know."

"How?"

Monk grimaced. "Dammit, by one of the oldest devices known. The old broken leg trick the birds use. They faked a forced landing. Ham Brooks and I were trailing them in another plane, about twenty miles back. We made a big circle, came in from the north, pretending to be bush flyers who had just happened along, and saw they had put out distress signals. We landed, all primed when we got out of the plane with our guns, to take everybody in custody. Only two guys got up out of the snow right by us, and cramped our style. Then they brought us here. We made a break, and I got away, but Ham didn't. They chased me. There's a place where the lake empties, down by the mine, a river where it isn't frozen over. I was trying to cross there, slipped and fell in when they sighted me and began shooting, and went under the ice. There was a place where the ice had heaved enough to make breathing space, so I just didn't bother to come out and run any more. They went away finally, and I got out."

Macbeth Williams shuddered. "It must have been terribly cold in the water."

"It made it a little warmer, knowing I was alive," Monk said. "But I lost my gun during the excitement. Also a hunting knife with which I was trying to dig a handhold in the underside of the ice. That was a little handicap when I got out. I haven't been able to find any wild game just sitting around waiting to be picked up."

"How," Doc asked, "did they know you were following them?"

"Blind luck, I guess. Or maybe Ham and I weren't as slick as we thought we were in New York."

"Some of this might have been prevented," Doc told him, "if you had kept in contact with me."

Monk nodded ruefully. "We'll have to take that up with Mr. Sunspots next time. Believe me, Doc, we called our lungs out over the radio. All we heard was static to who laid the chunk." He grimaced and shrugged. "A combination of bad conditions and two overconfident guys."

"Never mind," Doc told him. "This covering I'm wearing isn't exactly glory. What about the mine?"

Monk hesitated. "It could be done. How, I don't know. And I could do with a square meal first."

"We'll look it over," Doc said.

MACBETH WILLIAMS accosted Monk anxiously. "I'm Macbeth Williams, Mr. Mayfair. I'm afraid I'm the cause of all this in one way or another, probably very much to blame, if stupidity is a contributing factor. But tell me this: Is this mine one belonging to my father's estate?"

"Yeah, it is," Monk told him. "Do you want to know the rest?"

"I certainly do!"

"The mine," Monk said, "started out to be a conventional copper test, and they uncovered caronite. The ding-dongedest caronite deposit. Caronite means uranium, and you know what uranium means."

"Oh, I see!"

"Uncovering it meant more than just caronite,

Doc Savage turned in time to see Monk collapse, half sitting, in the snow. Monk stared at him. "For crying out loud! Doc!" he exclaimed.

because of the character of the engineers who made the discovery," Monk added. "They were scoundrels of the first order, and they wanted that caronite. You can't blame them for wanting it. The first thing they did was—" He looked at Macbeth Williams. "You know much of this?"

"Practically none," Macbeth assured him.

"That's funny. It's your property, indirectly, that is."

"I'm the kind of sap," said Macbeth bitterly, "who doesn't pay attention to many things he should, and who lets his friends make a fool out of him."

"Was it your idea," asked Monk, "to ring Doc in on this?"

"Yes."

"That doesn't make you so dumb," Monk told him. "Getting back to my story: the first thing these engineers did was try to buy the mining property from the estate. To lay the groundwork for that, they weaned off production of copper until the property looked sour. They also faked reports, to show the mining property wasn't worth fooling with. Then they made their offer, through intermediaries. I guess they offered all the cash they could rake together, but the estate didn't fall."

Macbeth Williams nodded. "The trustees of the estate are very conservative. They're known for their unwillingness to sell properties. Buy, yes. But sell, never. I don't know that I approve, but they've been right nearly every time, and I've been wrong."

"They were right this time, anyway," Monk said.

"Then what happened?"

"Why, the conspirators began a campaign to persuade you to take over management of the estate, figuring you could be swayed into selling an apparently unprofitable mining property up here in the Arctic," Monk told him.

Macbeth thought this over. Apparently the explanation didn't seem very credible to him, because he began shaking his head slowly. "You don't," he said, "catch a hawk and spend six months training it to catch a chicken, when all you want is a chicken dinner."

"Huh?"

"I mean," said Macbeth, "that there are simpler ways of catching the chicken."

Monk snorted. "They tried 'em."

"But—"

"Don't think they didn't," Monk added. "They tried everything they could, without alarming the estate trustees." Monk examined Macbeth wryly, and added, "I wouldn't say they made such a bad move when they set out to built up your confidence and persuade you to take over. They almost had the job done, from what I hear."

Macbeth winced. "Well—"

"Didn't they?"

"As a matter-of-fact, they almost did," Macbeth muttered. "I can hardly believe I was such a fool."

"Their psychology was all right," Monk told him. "A bit on the bubbly side, but all right. You see, any kind of psychological key is sound if it's made to fit the lock. And this key—convincing you that you were a man of damned near supernatural judgment—was tailored to fit you."

Macbeth's face was red with embarrassment. "Did they think I was fool enough to really believe I had a predicting gift?"

Monk chuckled. "They had that covered. What if you did conclude you had no mysterious gift? So much the better. You'd just naturally be forced to conclude you had damned good foresight and judgment. Wouldn't that have built up your confidence?"

"It sure would have," Macbeth admitted grimly. "It did, as a matter-of-fact."

Doc Savage put in a single question. "How did you come by all this information, Monk?"

"Straight from the horse's mouth," Monk told him. "While they had me prisoner, I kept my ears open. They're a talkative outfit. I think a lot of the talking was to keep their confidence boiling. They were scared stiff of you, Doc. But it also built up the picture for me. I think it's the correct picture."

"I think so, too," Doc said.

Austin Ulm grunted explosively. "All of which," he snapped, "gets us where?"

Monk eyed him disagreeably. "You got any better ideas about spending our breath?"

"I think I have," Ulm said.

"Well, let's hear it. Maybe you're smarter than you look behind that snatch of whiskers," Monk told him.

Ulm scowled. "How's this? Why don't I wander into this mine, pretending to be lost, and let them catch me. Then I give them an elaborate story about Doc Savage preparing to close in on them with the Royal Mounted Police, the Canadian army, and any other forces necessary."

"What," Monk asked him, "would that accomplish?"

"Frighten them into flight."

"You think so?"

"If they've got any sense, they won't want to hang around to be arrested," Ulm snapped.

"Nuts!" Monk told him. "That's the dumbest idea that has come along."

Doc Savage arrested a hot retort from Ulm, and told Monk thoughtfully, "It's possible that Ulm's suggestion may solve everything, Monk."

Monk, jaw sagging, blurted, "It would!" He swallowed, added, "I'd like to know how!"

"Once they're demoralized," Doc said, "we can pick them off one at a time."

"Yeah, but, hell, they're not going to get demoralized that easy—"

"Go ahead, Ulm," Doc broke in. "We'll stand by for developments."

"Thanks," Ulm said. "What do you think of planning it a bit further, though. I'd like to know what your moves will be, and maybe I can help out after they grab me."

For the next fifteen minutes, Doc Savage and Ulm made elaborate plans, agreed on strategy, and repeated code sounds and other arrangements to be employed in the event of certain logical results. Monk maintained a bitterly skeptical silence. So did Macbeth Williams.

"Don't worry, Mr. Savage, I'll see that the demoralization is complete," Ulm said, before he departed in the direction of the mining property.

Chapter XI

MONK was not a man to hide his thoughts. He had an expressive face, and right now it did very well with his feelings. "Demoralization!" he exploded. "So that's our new weapon!"

"Easy," Doc cautioned.

"Doc, I've got the highest opinion of your strategy as a usual thing, but this one—"

"Ulm," said Doc, "figures we're pretty dumb."

Monk swallowed. "Eh?"

"Ulm," Doc added, "fell for it right straight

through. I imagine the map deal is what finally sold him on our gullibility."

In a voice suddenly stricken, Macbeth Williams gasped, "Good God, do you mean that— but there *was* something too pat about the finding of the course-line marked on that chart! I–I had a feeling at the time, but I put it aside."

"You should pay more attention to your hunches," Doc advised him. "They're better than you think."

"Austin Ulm is a crook!" Macbeth exploded.

"Exactly!"

"He's one of them!"

"A kingpin," Doc agreed. "The 'steerer,' is the term in bunco circles. He's the black sheep you followed."

"But you turned him loose!"

"Yeah," Monk said. "Yeah, that I don't savvy. You let him get out of our hands, join his friends. Is there some logic in that somewhere?"

"Let's hope," Doc said, and added, gesturing, "We'd better head for the mine ourselves. How careful should we be approaching it? Will they have guards posted, Monk?"

"They don't need guards, at least not parked around in the brush freezing their ears off," Monk explained. "They used horses to haul stuff in from the outside, and they've put up a fence around the place, ostensibly as a horse corral. Actually, it's woven wire topped by barbed wire, and I think they've got a couple of thousand volts of electricity in the two top wires. It's no horse corral. It was intended from the first to keep anyone from getting too nosey."

"Keep your eyes open for a couple of poles. Dry wood, but stout. Something we can use to jam something against the wires that will short-circuit them." Doc wheeled abruptly, and headed back toward the tied-down B-26.

"They've already removed enough parts so that it won't fly," Monk called. "And I took off some more myself. So you can save your time."

Nevertheless, Doc Savage continued to the plane, poked around inside the cabin, didn't find anything that fitted his needs, and finally climbed atop the cabin and tore loose the fixed radio antennae. He folded this to make a hank about three feet in length, of several strands, and was twisting the strands together when he rejoined Monk and Macbeth Williams.

"Fine! That'll short-circuit the electrified wires on the fence," Monk said.

"But I don't see how we're going to accomplish anything," Macbeth murmured uneasily. "They'll shoot us on sight, won't they?"

"It probably depends on this demoralization," Monk said.

"What demoralizing?"

"Search me," Monk told him. "Around Doc, you wait and learn."

THE mine was not impressive, except in being the only man-made object of any size for possibly a hundred miles in any direction. It stood on an open bleak roll of a hill about a quarter of a mile back from the lake shore, consisted of a log barracks building, a log office building much smaller, two other log structures that were either shops or storage, and a small and scabby shaft structure that had been closed in with rough slabs wherever it was feasible to exclude a little of the bitter weather. Around this was the fence Monk had mentioned, enclosing an area of no more than five square acres. "Not impressive," Macbeth remarked.

"Not," said Monk, "until you think of getting over that fence and crossing all that open space, and a few guys in there potting at you with rifles."

Doc Savage had found a dead tree and wrenched from it a branch several feet long. He twisted the smaller boughs from this, examining the wood for sap or moisture, either of which might serve as conductor for a fatal amount of electric current. Satisfied, he attached his length of antennae wire, now twisted into a short cable, and jiggled his invention about to test its stability.

"That should do the short-circuiting job," Monk said. "It'll either burn the barbed wires apart, or blow the fuse on their generator circuit. In either case, the current will go off."

Doc nodded. "I see no reason to delay this. Now should be a good time. They'll be in a group, those not on look-out duty, listening to Ulm tell how he fooled us."

Monk grinned suddenly.

"You've got a gadget planted," he said.

"In New York," Doc said, "we fixed Ulm up with a parka."

"And?"

"Did you notice," Doc asked, "that the parka seemed conventional as far as the fur hood was concerned, but that the rest of the garment was made of a white cloth which seemed rather shiny?"

"Frankly," Monk muttered, "I didn't notice it closely."

Macbeth said, "I did. I took the cloth to be some sort of plastic product. I remember I thought of remarking about it."

Doc nodded. "The cloth is impregnated with chemicals. I won't go into details, but Monk is familiar with the formula or should be. He helped rig it up a couple of years ago." Doc glanced at the chemist. "You recall it?"

"Uh-huh," Monk said. "You apply another chemical mixture, a reagent, and in about half an hour you've got the nicest production of gas that a man could imagine. Blinding stuff. Worse than tear gas."

"Then all we've got to do," Macbeth said excitedly, "is wait until the gas takes effect, then rush them."

"That's all, to understate it slightly," Monk agreed.

"How long?"

"Ten minutes more should do it, providing Doc applied the reagent when I think he did. Was it when you were helping Ulm get to his feet and brush off the snow after I collared him and had him down?" Monk looked at Doc questioningly.

Doc nodded.

"Then ten minutes is right," Monk said.

They waited. Nothing happened.

It was Doc Savage, circling warily and anxiously in the scrub timber outside the fence, who got the answer. It gave him a sickening shock. He discovered, lying on the snow outside the barracks building, a cluster of garments which he could identify even at that distance as all the clothing Austin Ulm had been wearing. He rejoined Monk and Williams immediately, and the shock was plain on his face, because Monk asked, "It flopped?"

"Completely," Doc replied grimly. "Ulm, or somebody, was less of a dope than I supposed. Ulm stripped off everything he was wearing, on the chance we'd planted something."

"They even," said Monk, "had the foresight to toss the garments on the lee side of the building. The gas won't accomplish a dang thing."

From one of the buildings, a voice, Ulm's, began shouting. "Savage!" Ulm yelled. "Savage, can you hear me? Better answer if you hear me!"

"Might as well answer him," Doc said bitterly. "We haven't too much more to lose."

Ulm gave one loud triumphant laugh when he heard Doc's shouted, "Well, what is it?" Immediately, the door of the hut flew open, and a man was shoved outside. It was Ham Brooks, and he stumbled, fell, got up with difficulty. His arms were bound tightly and he was blindfolded. The door slammed, leaving Ham Brooks outside, thinly clad, a forlorn figure in the biting cold. Then Doc and the others saw that a rope, apparently about fifty feet long, picketed Ham to the building.

Ulm addressed them angrily. "Can you hear me?"

"Yes," Doc said.

"You've got ten minutes to think this over," Ulm bellowed. "Strip off your clothes, all of them, and walk into the gate. We'll shut the current off so you can get inside. Keep your arms up, and remember, not a stick on you. None of those trick gimmicks you're so free at using. The alternative: we shoot down your friend, here."

Doc Savage eyed the scene briefly.

"Monk, they won't understand the Mayan language, and Ham does," he said. "Begin yelling at them. Call them names. Express your feelings."

"That won't be hard," Monk snarled.

"Become inarticulate. Jumble your words. And then put in a few Mayan words. Tell Ham to stumble around blindly and work his way to the west corner of the house. He's to stay there if he can. As long as he's there, against the wall, they'll have to step outside to shoot him. It's up to you and Williams to see they don't step outdoors. You've got rifles."

Monk nodded. "But four or five of them can get on the rope and drag Ham back."

"Not if you shoot the rope in two."

Monk whistled. "At that distance? Oh, brother!"

"Try, anyway. At least, keep Ham alive, and that outfit preoccupied, for three or four minutes."

"I'll try. When does Ham start his act?"

"When he hears our plane," Doc said.

Chapter XII

THE frozen air was flame in Doc Savage's lungs long before he reached their plane. His legs began to get that wooden sickness that meant the ultimate in effort was being spent; he could hear his own agonized breathing; he crashed against the flank of the plane foolishly; for a moment or two he feared he lacked the strength to climb inside the craft. Behind him, from the mine, he heard a rifle cough its magazine empty.

He plunged into the cockpit, the whole universe glazed redly before his eyes because of exertion. He muffed the first attempt to start the jet engines, strangled an impulse to strike the instrument panel senselessly with a fist, and tried again.

Finally, he heard the welcome roar of the jets, looked out and saw the snow flowing back weirdly, melting, becoming steam, under the heat of the exhaust blast.

Doc headed the ship for the lake ice, took the tooth-loosening bounce over the shore ice, and gave the jets full acceleration position. Flaps down. Wing curvature at full lift. Through the Arctic haze, he saw the opposite shore of the lake, the low hill furred with scrub pine, rushing at him.

There was hardly time to comprehend that he should have taken the run the length of the lake, not the short way across, before he had to make the ship airborne. Or crash. He felt it get off. He lifted a wingtip to avoid a cluster of pines, literally vaulted a low ridge, nosed down slightly, then rolled over in a turn toward the mine.

He did not change flaps or lift-settings. Shortest take-off position was also slow-landing. He let everything ride. There was barely time to get the safety belt fastened before he saw the mine buildings with the enclosing fence.

Altitude was not fifty feet, so the perspective with which he saw the place was not changed much. There was only one human figure in sight. Ham. Ham Brooks had reached the corner of the cabin, as directed. He had wedged himself there as best he could without the use of hands or eyes. Monk must be shrieking instructions, and the shack door was open a crack, the rope taut.

Doc let the jet settle. The ship had, he noted, little more than stalling speed. No more than control.

He debated—it seemed that a wailing second or two became an hour—whether or not to take the fence. The electrified wires meant a short-circuit, the snarling arcing of high voltage, a good chance of fire. In the end, he took the chance, picked a spot where the distance between two fence posts was more than the wingspan, and dropped the nose.

The impact was not much. Hardly noticeable. But a moment later, the ship jerked sharply to the left, hit, rocked over, dinging a wingtip. But it did not roll. Behind him, the fence was open.

The plane took two great bounces and a long skid, something impossible on anything but snow or ice. While it was still reeling, he used full left jet to ground-loop and kill more speed. When the wingtip on that side was ready to dig, he alternated with the other engine; now the ship was almost against the log hut.

He could hear the occasional solid sound of a bullet against the armored cabin. The jets were making too much noise to hear much more.

He swung his head, hit the right jet fuel feed again. The ship jerked crazily; abruptly the full heat blast of the engines was pouring against the side of the hut. The door was first to give under the heat. It simply became white, ashlike, and disintegrated. The jet blasts were like unbelievable blowtorches at that close range. The side of the cabin became a sheet of angry flame in which a long thin snake crawled a moment and vanished, the rope with which Ham Brooks had been staked out for execution.

The door of the larger, longer log barracks burst open. Two men came out to stand and deliberately raise their rifles.

Doc fed one of the jets full throttle; the surge threw the plane around, and its blast raked toward the barracks. The steam that instantly arose was like a cloud of smoke, concealing what he accomplished, if anything.

He sent the plane driving toward the barracks, intending to put it in position to fire that one also. The maneuver was not too good; a wing hooked the building, and suddenly he felt the plane crash heavily. The logs gave a little. He could hear them spilling down after he cut the jet fuel supply.

He tore at the hatch, got it partly open, but did not get out immediately when he heard Ulm shrieking commands.

Ulm thought there would be gas equipment in the plane. They were in a bad predicament, Ulm felt. "Get out of here!" Ulm was bellowing. "Stay undercover of the smoke! Run through the smoke. The fence power is off. We'll reorganize outside!"

It hadn't, Doc thought with grim pleasure, occurred to them that the smoke would drift with the wind, and so would the tear gas that should be coming from Ulm's parka in good volume by now.

He settled down in the plane to wait for the sounds they would make when the gas got to their eyes.

It was a satisfying noise when it came.

SPRINGLATCH climbed out of the second Northwest Mounted plane that set down on the lake. He wore, under a parka and bearskin trousers, the linen suit he must have been wearing when he left Florida. He looked over the prisoners, displayed the warrants he had—only two, one for Swanberg, one for Crikeland—and said wryly, "I guess we underestimated. There seems to be a few more than that involved."

Ham Brooks told him, "We counted eleven, all together. We collared nine. Two got away. I imagine they'll be rounded up."

Springlatch nodded. "I guess that's the bag. I don't think we can pin much on the Kendall Foundation."

Doc said, "We didn't have time to look into the Foundation angle. What was it?"

"Jackleg outfit," Detective Springlatch explained. "Ulm approached them to finance this expedition to Cormoral Island, if they would organize it. I don't know whether there was a deliberate arrangement to go broke and strand the expedition on the island, or whether Ulm just calculated so they would run out of money conveniently. I'm afraid we can't hang much on them. Couple of old fools operate the Foundation, anyway."

"Miss McGuiggan is all right," Doc told him.

"They told me. She got a good scare, I take it."

Doc agreed, added, "She stood it well, though. She has a lot of fiber, that girl."

Springlatch grinned. "Enough for her and that Macbeth boob both?"

"Quite enough, probably," Doc said.

"She'll need it. That 'predicting' stuff was about as goofy a hoax as I've ever heard about, and in my business, you hear of plenty. This Macbeth Williams was swallowing it, too."

Doc smiled faintly. "Williams hadn't swallowed

so much that he overlooked calling us into it, remember."

"O.K., maybe he's not all blockhead." Springlatch chuckled. "But for my money, he'll do until a one-hundred percenter comes along."

Doc Savage found Monk and Ham leaning against the charred side of the barracks building. They were just finishing a burst of hysterical mirth, and wiping their eyes.

"Macbeth," said Monk, "is going to take over the estate management. He made the announcement a couple of minutes ago."

"What's funny about that?" Doc asked.

"Nothing," Ham chuckled. "But he made the announcement in front of Ulm, and the expression on Ulm's face—that *was* funny!"

THE END

GENESIS DOC SAVAGE

Doc Savage editor John L. Nanovic once wrote:

> When Doc Savage was born, the only plot that Les Dent had to work on for the first novel was this:
>
> 1. OBJECT.
>
> Clark Savage, Jr., read his father's will in which a double-crossing act of a former partner was revealed so that Clark Savage, Jr., might avenge the act.
>
> 2. OBSTACLES.
>
> The only way to avenge this was to find the guilty partner and prove that guilt—proof that had to be gotten from the land of the ancient Mayans. The obstacles that beset Doc were many, both natural and those put in by design by the villain. Whether these obstacles were two or two hundred depend entirely upon how Les Dent wrote his story. He could stretch a few incidents out, or he could use his fertile imagination to advantage, as he did, and sow obstacles by the hundreds.
>
> 3. OUTCOME.
>
> Doc overcame the obstacles to his goal. He uncovered the evidence that cleared his father's name, and got the heritage that was there for him when this was accomplished.
>
> Neither Les Dent nor any other writer will begin to write a novel on such a skimpy outline of action. This, of course, is not an outline; it's a PLOT. Once you've built your plot, you can dress your outline as you will; either very complete, or just hitting the high spots of your story. What you do with your outline depends upon your method of writing.

Henry W. Ralston

Nanovic was being modest when he wrote those words. Lester Dent had much more to work from than that simple premise. And Nanovic should know. He was involved in the gestation of the Man of Bronze from start to finish. For John Nanovic penned the very first account of Doc Savage's origins, "Doc Savage, Supreme Adventurer."

More than anyone other than Street & Smith general manager Henry W. Ralston, who initially conceived the character, John Nanovic knew the story of how Doc came to be.

Early in 1932 Ralston asked Nanovic to join him in a leisurely lunch at Halloran's, an Irish restaurant on Sixth Avenue. Despite the Depression, *The Shadow Magazine* was selling fabulously. Ralston had an idea to expand on that success.

"We just talked about an adventure character," recalled Nanovic. "We didn't have a name, no. That's why it took a while to develop it. Now the description of the characters was pretty much Ralston. He had lived with these guys. He knew them all, including their fingernails."

Shadow writer Walter B. Gibson recalled that Ralston initially wanted to revive Street & Smith's retired dime-novel heroes, but somehow Doc Savage emerged first.

"We had about six lunches over it," Nanovic asserted. "Do this and do that."

Slowly, the character began to form. From the beginning, Ralston wanted a "science-adventure" hero, one who would roam the globe, righting wrongs and punishing evildoers wherever he found them.

"That was the first time I had heard the term science-adventurer," said Nanovic. "And I think that was one of the secrets of Doc Savage's success. He mentioned that he knew a person named Savage and began to describe him. Of course he could have been describing himself because Ralston was a big powerful man."

Paramount in Ralston's mind was the remarkable Richard Henry Savage, a military hero, engineer, and author who had written for Street & Smith early in Ralston's career. He also borrowed from the company's own immortal Nick Carter.

He would be joined by a group of former Army comrades, all veterans of the First World War, only a dozen years in the past.

"He had all the names, Monk and all," recalled Nanovic. "Monk was described perfectly. I think Renny was added in the fourth meeting.... Most of these people Bill Ralston had known."

Ideas were kicked around for months.

"Naturally, there a lot of different ideas," Nanovic acknowledged. "Most of them I've forgotten. It was all done at lunchtime or in the office. Ralston was a great cigar smoker. And he'd lean back in his chair and wait until he lit up a cigar, blow some smoke and said, 'Let's talk.'

"In fact, we threw out some ideas even before we got to the stage where we gave it to Les. All

"We grabbed him right out of thin air. We made him a surgeon and scientist, because we wanted him to know chemistry, philosophy, and all that stuff. —Henry W. Ralston

these fellows had college degrees. In discussions, we made a point of their college degrees. Because in the '30s, if you had a college degree, you were somebody. As we went along, we decided we didn't want to push the college angle because our readers are not college people."

But they did want Doc to be wealthy, in order finance his globe-spanning crusade.

"Well, his father was," Nanovic noted. "And the point there was we felt we were OK there because Doc was doing good with his money. Riches did not turn people away then. Even Rockefeller, who gave out dimes, and Andrew Carnegie and all the others were well thought of. They were heroes because they were doing good with their money."

Early on, they tapped a 28-year-old ex-telegrapher named Lester Dent to pen the series. Dent, in a rival pulp magazine, had been writing about a scientific detective operating out of a Manhattan office building. Other writers were considered, but Dent was their final choice.

"I might have bought a story or two from Les, short stories," Nanovic said. "And then we had him do a Shadow novel, and then said OK, he's the guy. I know I bought the first one he gave me and we kept in touch. And he sent a couple more. And then when this came up, he had a good reputation. He was a good writer, even before he came to Doc Savage.... So we picked him, and it was a good pick!"

As 1932 lengthened, the Depression worsened. Plans for the newly christened *Doc Savage* were put on hold. Pulp magazine sales picked late in the year, and suddenly it was time to shift into production.

"Then we brought him in and said, 'This is what we have in mind.' And I had a 30-page summary of the first novel, which I gave him. All the characters were described, and we never changed those a bit—well, very slightly. But, this is not taking any credit away from Les Dent. He made those things live."

Here, Nanovic's memory temporarily failed him. The summary had yet to be written. After "Doc Savage, Supreme Adventurer" was unearthed in 1978, Nanovic was given a copy.

"Les must have been in one meeting before I did that outline," Nanovic admitted. "It must have been the meeting where we decided, yes, you will do the stories. We knew he knew how to write. It wasn't a test or anything. I'm sure he must have been in on one meeting because some of the things in there seem to be Les'. But of course, most of it is Ralston's."

One of Dent's main contributions was the Valley of the Vanished, the lost Mayan city which became the source of the new hero's fabulous wealth. Back in 1930, he had plotted a pulp serial in which an American adventurer discovered the Valley of Eternity in Mexico, where descendants of the ancient Mayan culture still thrived in barbaric splendor.

"That whole Mayan thing was Dent's, I'm sure," Nanovic concurred, "because he was an expert on that, and knew all about it. I don't think Ralston mentioned that until Les brought it up. And we went along with that. I think Les deserves full credit for the Mayan thing."

Doc's skyscraper headquarters was also a Dent invention, according to Nanovic. "Les picked the Empire State Building. In discussing it, we had his headquarters somewhere downtown. In fact, our original thinking was to have him at a secret headquarters, meaning that they would be secret. But Les did better than that. He had secret headquarters. I think once we sort of talked about that. The biggest secret you could have is in Times Square. You can murder a guy. Nobody would ever look at you in those days. But that was Les' thinking on that: Put his headquarters in a place where nobody would expect it to be."

Doc's remote Fortress of Solitude was another Dentian contribution. "No, we didn't call it Fortress of Solitude. That was Les'. Les really put in most of those solid details."

Even Doc's famous nom de guerre, which inspired the title of that first novel, *The Man of Bronze,* was a product of the writer's imagination.

"Ralston originally I don't think used the term 'bronze,' Nanovic allowed. "Doc was a well-tanned guy. That was in the 30s and tanning was all a thing, you know. If you weren't tanned by the middle of June, you were a sissy. So that tanning was at that time an expression of vitality and macho—although we didn't know the word then. That was the kind of character he had in mind. I don't recall whether Ralston called him the Man of Bronze. That is Les Dent, I'm sure. I guess Les should get credit for that. I know I didn't throw it in."

Reportedly, Dent didn't care for the name Doc Savage, and wanted to rename the Man of Bronze.

"I don't recall any other name or names," countered Nanovic, "and if there were any they were not at all considered. Doc Savage was completely set when we called Les in to do the job—as far as the

"If you read that 15,000 word outline, all the characters are just figures. The popularity of Doc Savage is 90% Lester Dent and only 10% for Bill Ralston and myself for discussion of plots." —John Nanovic

John L. Nanovic

basics, Les built the characters—the complete set of Doc Savage characters, with the exception of the girl; she came in later. Street & Smith didn't believe in girls, you know. She must have been Les'.

"What we gave Les, Ralston had in mind eight months before," Nanovic added. "It was a complete package Les got. That's not detracting from Les' ability and what he did for Doc Savage. We could have given that set of characters to me or you, and it would have been blah. Les clicked. Les could write that type of character, and he did! Nobody else could describe 'His arm drifted out with lightning speed.' Les is the only guy who could write that and get away with it!"

Lester Dent

But before work could begin on that first novel, Nanovic had to write a blueprint for the story and the series. From the beginning, Ralston referred to his new concept as the "supreme adventurer." So Nanovic told Dent to return in a week, while he wrote "Doc Savage, Supreme Adventurer."

"The only notes I had was the names of the characters and their descriptions," Nanovic later recalled. "You see, this wasn't even written as a story. It was more or less a condensed outline. It's not dramatic. It isn't meant to be dramatic. It's meant to be informative. It's like a newspaper report of something. And the rest I just wrote from the way we discussed it. And some things I think I probably changed slightly from what we were talking about. The character descriptions are Ralston's pretty much word for word, because we talked about it a couple of dozen times before we got to this stage. That was his whole creation. I was too fresh and young to think of that stuff."

The fact that prior to Doc Savage, Lester Dent had written about characters identical to Renny Renwick, and even Monk Mayfair, puzzled Nanovic when he later learned about it.

"Now Les never mentioned to me that he wrote a character like Monk," Nanovic admitted. "He might have. Now that is not an unusual character. Every adventure story has the ape guy and the educated guy and so forth."

On December 10, 1932, Lester Dent was presented with "Doc Savage, Supreme Adventurer" and got right to work on *The Man of Bronze,* fleshing out the outline into a 50,000 word novel. 181 sequels followed. And "Doc Savage, Supreme Adventurer" was filed away forever.

An examination of the historic document shows several other changes made after the fact. Originally, Doc's eyes were as bronze as his skin. Dent transmuted them into a hypnotic flake-gold. And the burned and incomplete letter from Clark Savage, Sr., to his son found in *The Man of Bronze* is intact in "Doc Savage, Supreme Adventurer."

"The pulps were on the way out in the early 30s," Nanovic explained. "The only thing that kept them alive was, in my opinion, the character books. They were the only ones that sold. Even the detective books were hurting."

Looking back on that long process, John Nanovic utimately split the creative credit for Doc Savage between Henry Ralston and Lester Dent.

"Ralston created all those characters. No matter what anybody says, these authors were given them on a silver platter. This I explained with Walter Gibson and Les—yes, well, Gibson's was an accident. But Doc Savage...Les Dent, he was given this thing on a silver platter. But he made it, you know. He wrote them the way he writes. Gibson wrote The Shadow the way he wrote, and so forth. Les built the whole character. What I had in those 30-some pages is really all the solid things we gave him. And everything else in the character he built up himself. As we went along, we did add some thoughts. Basically, it was his work, his creation. After he got that outline, 90 percent of everything done on Doc was his."

As for himself, Doc Savage's first and greatest editor remained characteristically modest about his role as midwife to fiction's first superhero.

"What I added to Doc was trimmings on [Ralston's] original idea," John Nanovic insisted. "I did carry them out. I will take credit for that. That was up to me."

—Will Murray

"They contributed some points ... a trilling sound; he was to make, a patent steal from The Shadow to which I objected at the time, and the fact that he had five associates. All clothing on these skeleteons was my work." " —Lester Dent

DOC SAVAGE,
SUPREME ADVENTURER

by John L. Nanovic

[based upon ideas and characters created by Henry W. Ralston]

THE city of New York was shrouded in the deep gloom of a misty evening. The heaviness of the skies bore down upon the tall buildings, seeming to weigh them down under the oppressive atmosphere. Most of the buildings had been emptied of their daily toilers, but there were occasional shrouded eyes of light gleaming from their sides.

High up under the eaves of one of these chimneys which New Yorkers call buildings, six men were gathered. They were in a beautifully furnished office which overlooked the city through its spacious windows on two sides, but their attention was focused upon one of their number as he talked.

Seated at the massive desk, this man held his five companions by his words as much as by his appearance. He was a large man, yet so well put together that the impression one received was not of size, but of power. And the bulk of his body was forgotten in the smooth symmetry of that powerful build.

With his back toward one of the huge windows that took up the side of the office, his face was not sharply outlined except when he turned to the right or left to speak directly to one of the listeners. Then it struck the watcher as a face of most unusual qualities.

The high strong forehead, the strong but not too-full mouth, the firm-set nose—all denoted character in every line. It was a face that was remarkable from whatever angle it was seen.

The skin was of a healthy bronze color, bespeaking of long years spent beneath tropic suns and northern skies, of an active, exhilarating life of action and adventure. His hair, as if made to match that perfectly-colored skin, was of a deeper bronze, and lay back smoothly. Most striking of his features, though, were the eyes. Set well apart, they were like two powerful magnets that drew everything into their range. Their color, too, was bronze—a deep bronze color with lights playing upon it so that sometimes that bronze was like a heap of flaky gold glistening in the sun. Then their gaze revealed an almost hypnotic quality that would cause the most rash individual to hesitate.

UNDENIABLY this man was the leader of the group, as well as leader of anything he undertook. His very being denoted a knowledge of all things,

To the few who knew him well, he was known as "Doc." To others, he was known as Clark Savage, Jr., son of a man who was known throughout the world for his dominant bearing and his good work. Once wealthy, the elder Savage had lost the bulk of his income in the aftermath of the World War, but though his wealth was gone, his influence remained, and in his son all of his noble characteristics were evident.

The man of bronze was talking now, explaining to his comrades.

"You know why we're here. All of you knew of the death of my father before I did. It was unfortunate that I should be away just at the time—but I didn't expect him to go yet—"

"It was rather sudden—even the doctors were surprised. And we tried to get you every way," spoke one of the man's companions, "but you were as gone as if you had been off the face of the earth."

"I know, Renny," Doc answered sadly. "I have work to do which even you, my best friends, cannot help me accomplish. I must prepare myself for things which even you would not understand. But that is another story entirely; one that someday you may all hear. Now we have something more important.

"We were buddies back in the War, and we all liked the fun. When we came back, the life of ordinary man was not suited to our natures, so we sought something else.

"With the encouragement of my father, we set out upon a plan to further the work of good that he had begun with such success, only to have it all crash with the great conflict. My heart was set upon the completion of that task—upon carrying out the ideal of my father: to go here and there, from one end of the world to the other, looking for excitement and adventure; striving to help those who need help; to punish those who deserve it.

"There were those who criticized my father in that he had sought to amass wealth. He succeeded admirably; he was wealthy beyond measure, and he would have remained so except for the War. But his wealth was not his goal, it was only a requirement, as we know. That wealth, too, we must have for our own if we are to carry out our wishes."

DOC SAVAGE paused. He looked over his companions, one by one, in the soft light of that well-furnished office, the only remaining bit of evidence of the wealth that once belonged to his father.

To one side was an austere, puritanical-looking person, Colonel John Renwick—"Renny," as Doc had called him.

Although the face of the man was as stern as if cut from stone, those who knew him at all were more wont to see his deep, understanding smile. The austerity was on the surface, but beneath it was a kindliness and sympathy that only the greatest of men could have.

Renny was a high-class civil engineer, one whose service to the government in the World War was invaluable. His knowledge of engineering in all its angles was unfathomable, and his ability to apply it on whatever occasion arose made him a man who was never baffled.

He was well over six feet—about six feet four—and weighed close to two hundred and fifty pounds. Yet, with all his size, he was as silent and quick in his movements as a panther.

When only a boy, Renny had been taught the manly art of self-defense by a pugilist who had managed his father's estate. And his development was so marked that, every now and then, merely for the edification of his comrades, he would drive his bare fist through the solid panel of a heavy door.

With all this great strength, the coordination of his muscles and brain was so perfect that he could pick flies on the wing out of the air, so keen were all his senses.

Contrasted to thos powerful engineer was the next man, Major Thomas J. Roberts, or "Long Tom" as the gang called him. Physically, he seemed to be the weakling of the crowd. Undersized, slender, fairrly set up, a none-too-healthy complexion, fair-haired, blue-eyed, he was a perfect Nordic type. He was given to violent fits of passion, occuring rarely but leaving nothing when they did occur.

Nevertheless, Long Tom was a marvel when it came to electricity. Without a doubt he knew more about juice than anyone Doc had ever become acquainted with.

The name "Long Tom" was given him, of course, not because of his size, but because of an incident in their previous experiences. The major was forced to fire one of the old-fashioned cannon used by the privateers in the good old days of the Spanish Main. The similarity in the proportion of the cannon and Long Tom gave him the name permanently.

THE third of Doc's companions was half-seated on the opposite corner of the large desk behind which Doc sat. He seemed very much unlike the type of adventurous being. Rather, he resembled more a studious scientist.

And so he was. For William Harper Littlejohn, "Johnny" for convenience, had previously been with one of our famous universities as a member of the Natural Research Department. His knowledge was sufficient to stamp him as the greatest physicist of the land, and his years in archaeological and geological surveys had given him enough of the touch of adventure to burn it into his soul, even if it did not show on the surface.

He was an even six feet tall, built for endurance, like a marathon runner. And endurance he had, for it was often said of him that he could go three days on a half slice of bread and a canteen of water.

Two more men met the slow gaze of Doc Savage as his eyes scanned the room. One was seated with his chair tilted against the wall, his short legs twined about the top rung. He was a most remarkable character; you could tell that from the very first glimpse.

To his parents he was known as Andrew Blodgett Mayfair, but to his companions he was simply "Monk." He certainly looked like one, for his arms were considerably longer than his legs, and his depth of chest denoted enormous strength.

He was a chemist by profession, and he had attained the rank of Lieutenant Colonel in the United States Army—which he did chiefly because of his ability to bend crowbars over his knee, make playful twists in horseshoes, and do certain other things, such as pull up twenty feet of barbwire entanglements by the roots with a single heave of those mighty arms.

Last of the companions was a tall, thin man, leaning against a letter file in a corner of the room. His black eyes, deep-set, glowed with the light of a born listener whenever others talked.

This was Theodore Marley Brooks, a lawyer Harvard-trained, and well trained. He was the most intellectual man in the group, the quickest and most direct thinker under any conditions. For was it not his quick thinking that made him a Brigadier General in those hurly-burly days of warfare when everyone was taking bad shots at everyone else? It was his rapid-fire thinking that saved regiments, and his reward was the high title.

Still, he himself would tell you that he worked at neither of his professions. And, if you wondered about his nickname, "Ham," which clung to him because he was supposed to know something about some hams disappearing from his kitchen

Doc Savage and his five aides

outfit, he would tell you that he did know something of pigs, for he was forced to associate with five of them most of the time.

THESE were the men who looked upon Doc as their leader. All able men in their own fields, even they were forced to bow to the superior knowledge of the Doc himself.

A surgeon by profession, Doc had ministered to the shattered boys on the other side and repaired, in almost miraculous manner, the effects of shot and shell. Not one of his five companions but owed his very life to the expert skill of Doc.

Everywhere he went, Doc's personality made him friends, and his kindness and sympathy earned him undying devotees. Like his father, he too had sought to serve mankind rather than himself, and thousands of people owed all they had to the aid which he had given them in their moment of need.

In addition to his remarkable ability as a surgeon, Doc knew more about mineralogy and engineering, and how to apply that knowledge practically, than the experts with whom he was associated. In short, there was nothing that a successful specialist could do that Doc Savage could not do.

When asked where he received all his training, Doc would pass the question off with a shrug. But it was very likely, his companions thought, that on these mysterious disappearances of his, when not even his own group knew his whereabouts, he secluded himself somewhere to add to his vast fund of knowledge.

His inspection complete, Doc again returned to his discourse.

"All my life I knew that my future was laid out for me; I was to follow in the footsteps of my father. The work he began, I was to carry on to completion.

"He never took me as an understudy; or as a junior partner. That was not the training I required. I had to go out on my own, and prove myself. Then someday, the burden would fall upon my shoulders, and they would be broad enough.

"The day came sooner than I expected. I am ready for it, though I do miss the words that my father would have spoken before he died. What he could not speak, however, he wrote, and the letter is here.

"For the past week I have considered it. Now I've called you together, deciding that you all shall hear, and give me your decision."

Renny, who irked for action rather than talk, urged on his leader.

"We're ready for it. Anything you say goes with us, you know that, Doc," he said.

Doc picked up the letter. "Here it is," he began, and started to read.

DEAR CLARK,

I have developed you from boyhood into the sort of man you have become, and I have spared no time or expense to make you just what I think you should be. Everything I have done for you has been with the purpose that you should find yourself capable of carrying on the work which I had so hopefully started, and which, in these last few years, has been almost impossible to carry on.

If I do not see you again before this letter is handed to you, I want to assure you that I appreciate the fact that you have lacked nothing in the way of filial devotion. That you have been absent so much of the time has been a secret source of gratification to me, for your absence has, I know, made you self-reliant and able. It was all that I hoped for you.

Now, as to the heritage which I am about to leave you.

Some twenty years ago, in company with Hubert Robertson, I went on an expedition to Hidalgo to investigate the report of a prehistoric mine, from which gold was taken by the Mayans, or by some other race that preceded them.

We were told that if we could placate the fierce tribes who inhabited that particular valley in which the mine was located, it would be feasible to secure a grant to work the mine from the then existing government of the country.

We proceeded almost to the valley itself before we were molested, but one afternoon we were surrounded by thousands of natives, whose language was totally unknown to us. They led us into the valley where, much to our surprise, we found that they had erected a great shrine to the sun.

WE found them, in the most, a very gentle tribe, with apparently no desire to harm us. We lived with them for three months, and while we were carefully watched, we were perfectly free to go anywhere within the confines of the valley. There came a day, however, when Hubert's knowledge of medicine enabled him to prove to this tribe that we were friendly.

In the meantime, I had discovered that the ancient mine was directly under their shrine. Of course, it would have been considered sacrilege by the natives had we made any attempt to explore it. From the material of which the shrine was made, however, I am convinced that it is the richest bit of ground on God's green footstool, for the shrine is literally built of gold.

Realizing the utter futility of attempting anything then, we took our departure when we were permitted to do so. A large party of the natives accompanied us for almost one hundred miles. We had instruments which enabled us to determine the geographical position of the valley. Thereupon we proceeded to use every bit of influence we had to obtain grants from the government.

Things were going along well enough until our plans were laid before the cabinet. Then we met sudden opposition from some unknown source, and it was only with extreme labor that we finally secured the right to mine the gold for ninety-nine years, upon payment to the government of twenty-five per cent of the takings. The papers are all with this letter.

Upon our return to America, I became involved in other big deals and never did quite solve the problem of how to get the gold out of that valley. And, in addition, I experienced some slight difficulty with the government concerning the grants. Since Hubert's death—and now I fear that his end was not entirely natural—attempts have been made to annul the grant, to lessen its duration, or add some other provisions.

The government refused to furnish any help in quelling the natives, or cooperate in any way.

Therefore I am passing this along to you as a doubtful heritage. It may be a heritage of woe; it may even be a heritage of destruction to you if you attempt to capitalize on it. On the other hand, it may enable you to do many things for those who are not so fortunate as you yourself, and will, in that way, be a boon for you in carrying on our work of doing good to all.

All I can say is, 'There is the treasure. It is yours, if you can take it, and may God be with you.

Your affectionate father,
CLARK SAVAGE.

Doc Savage (Ron Ely) stands before a portrait of Clark Savage, Sr., in the 1975 Warner Brothers film.

DOC lifted his head and looked at his companions. "So," he said, "the treasure is there, if we can—"

At that moment, the window behind Doc's chair was shattered and something passed within an inch of the top of his head. A low drone accompanied the missile as it hit the safe on the far side of the room.

Instantly, all six were flat on the floor, transported for the moment to instincts gained in the field of battle.

And then, even as the sound of the projectile was dying, a new sound was heard. It was a low, mellow, trilling sound, like the song of some strange bird of the jungle, or the sound of wind filtering through a jungled forest. It was melodious, though it had no tune; and it was inspiring, though it was not awesome.

It was the sound that was part of Doc—a small, unconscious thing which he did in moments of utter concentration. To his friends it was both the cry of battle and the song of triumph. It would come upon his lips when a plan of action was being arranged, precursing a master stroke which made all things certain.

It would come again in the midst of some struggle, when the odds were all against the companions, when everything seemed lost. And with the sound, new strength would come to all, and the tide would always run.

And again, it might come when some beleaguered member of the group, alone and attacked, had almost given up all hope of survival.

Then that sound would filter through, some way, and the victim knew that help was at hand. For the whistling noise was a sign of Doc, and of safety, of victory.

"Who got it?" asked Johnny.

"No one," said Doc. "Let us crawl, brothers, crawl. Then we shall see."

Suiting the action to the word, Doc crawled on all fours to the doorway of an adjoining room. His friends followed him.

SEATED in the adjoining room, Renny spoke first.

"Well, Doc," he said, "someone seems to like you enough to try a shot at you."

"I cannot imagine who it could be," said Doc. "All my business is finished. I just wonder if we haven't already embarked upon our new venture. I noticed as I dropped that the shot took the whole pane out of the window frame, so it wasn't a gangster bullet. We'll go back and see."

Carefully sneaking back into the first room, Doc Savage turned off the lights, then carefully approached the window and pulled the shade.

With equal stealth he did the same to the second side of the room.

Then the lights came on again, and one after another of the five came back into the room to examine the damage.

An irregular lump of lead, about four ounces in weight, had taken at least six inches off the door of the safe, which it hit.

"By the beard of the prophet," said Long Tom, "that could not have been fired from anything but an elephant gun, and at long range, too."

"The marksman must have had telescopic sights," said Renny, "and if it were during the day, I'd just project a line from the mark to the spot from which it was fired. And next time, Doc, suppose we have bulletproof glass in these windows?"

"Sure," said Doc, "next time. We're on the eighty-sixth floor, and it's quite common to be shot at here."

"Quite uncommon," Long Tom added for emphasis. "Uncommon enough to make me want to know who it is right away. Here, Renny, you get your lines and angles ready, and I'll switch around some lights in here to send a strong beam along those lines. And I'll bet we land the culprits in half an hour!"

With quick sureness, the two men set about their tasks, ordering the others to do little things which were necessary.

Renny picked a slide rule from the drawer of a desk, a compass, and some paper. He made a few rapid calculations, then walked to the spot on the safe-front.

With the help of a chair and a stool, a couple of rulers, he had his angles set.

"All right, Long Tom," he said. "Now get your light along this rule, and we'll see where our shot came from."

Even while Renny was rigging up his little device, Long Tom was busy collecting odds and ends of electrical material. With a few lights, several flashlight lenses, and some other bits of glass which he picked up around the two rooms, he had constructed a powerful beam of light which could pierce well into the darkness. Far enough, at least, to point to the source of the shot.

IT took minutes of careful direction through the one pane which had been broken before a definite point was accepted. Several possible angles were tried, with Renny accurately denying their possibilities.

Finally, the vital spot was reached—blocks away, the gaunt skeleton of a newer skyscraper which had not been fully completed.

From out of the steelwork of this new building, the shot that had entered the room of counsel was fired. The gun had to be a powerful British rifle specially constructed for jungle hunting, in order to throw the bullet such a distance. And the enemy, Doc decided, must be someone who knew of the letter from the dead man—someone who knew of the wealth to which these six now held the key in the form of the government grant and the map.

That someone, no doubt, was the same person who had made it difficult for the elder Savage to go on with his project. It was someone whose purpose was acquisition of the mine, at no matter what great danger, no matter what extent to reach the goal.

It was a challenge to this group of adventurers. Whatever their decision before might have been, now it could be only this: start on the hunt immediately; let everything go and seek a means to gain this immense wealth which lay there for those who were daring enough to wrest it from its resting place.

Challenge enough in that fact alone, but when there was the chance of meeting a foe desirous of the same end, but for evil purpose, there was no hesitation. Unanimously the decision was made—Hidalgo and the lost wealth of the Mayans, and tramp upon the coward who shoots from behind!

So plans were quickly started. The work was

portioned off with the usual efficiency of the group. Johnny was given the task of making a quick survey of the topographical and mineral aspects of the territory, so that the proper equipment could be provided. Ham, in the meantime, was given the papers to check over the legal aspects, ascertaining whether the rights mentioned in the dead man's letter were still inviolate. Doc, carefully overseeing the work of the different members of his little company, saw that everything was fully prepared before the journey began.

HIDALGO was a typical country of the southern republics. Wedged in between two mighty mountains, traversed in its own right by a half dozen smaller ranges, it was a perfect spot for those whose minds ran to revolution. Governments are unstable not so much because of their own lack of ability, but more because of. the opportunities offered others to gather in revolt.

Half of the little valleys in the country were lost to the traveler who followed the usual channels of travel. These were inhabited by various tribes, remnants of once powerful nations, each still a power in its own right, and often engaging in conflict with its neighbors.

It was into such a country, right into its little capital city of Mangato, which Doc Savage and his companions arrived after their journey from the States.

With no little difficulty, Doc finally arranged for a conference with the Department of State, taking Ham's advice to check with the new government on their mining rights.

Armed with the facts as shown by Ham's knowledge of the law, they did not expect the difficulties which became evident. On every hand, the officials of the new government seemed loath to grant any opinion. Still, Ham would not be denied. The contract was renewed with the sanction of the new government, and Doc and Ham headed to their temporary quarters, to give the news to the other boys.

The little, crooked streets of the capital were growing murky with dusk when the two wended their way back. Dark corners were pregnant with danger—danger that might materialize any moment.

And it did—but a moment too late. Before the glistening knife that rose in the air, held by a dark hand, could descend, the strange, trilling whistle came from Doc's lips. His keen eyes had seen the danger as it came, and now, with equally keen body, he avoided the danger by shoving Ham out of the way and letting go with his right fist at the unseen opponent.

The man in the dark went down with one groan, and remained quiet, his body unmoving. The power behind Doc's fist, when landing squarely, was great enough to put any man out for the time.

So, realizing that they had not left danger behind when they left the States, Doc and Ham hurried to their comrades, told them the news, and rushed their trip into the valley of gold.

FOUR days after they left the little capital of Hidalgo, Doc Savage and his group looked down upon the valley of gold. They made it in the early morning, while the sun was still in ascendance. The night before they had camped at the foot of the mountain which separated them from their destination. It was a long trek over that stony range, and it was decided to postpone the climb until morning.

Then, the following day, when they were scarcely half the distance, Monk's eyes noticed a strange cut in the cliffs. A little reconnoitering, and they discovered it to be a deep chasm which cut through the hill, making their day's journey one of but a few hours.

The sight of the invaders did not bring any show of friendship from the natives. Instead, they gathered about them in a sullen, resentful group. The six adventurers were entirely surrounded by the men of the tribe before they had progressed any distance into the group of huts which served as the village of the tribe. There, unable to proceed further, they rested.

It was Doc who took up the burden of confab with the natives. Doc's knowledge of languages and dialects was unique. His adventures had taken him to all parts of the world, and after a few sign words and motions, he established some sort of communication with the natives.

His wishes to see the leader of the tribe were recognized, and the companions were led forth.

With the tribal people following. Doc and his group walked up toward a huge monument of stone, set up much in the manner of the pyramids, but ceasing at halfway to form a flat top upon which a small idol stood.

Even from a distance the stones glistened in the sun, and not only Johnny, the mineralogist, but Doc and the rest of the group immediately realized the truth of the statement in the elder Savage's letter that this monument was made of the precious metal itself. But their thoughts could not remain long on this promise of wealth. Gathered before the monument were the chieftains and priests of the tribe, ready in their full regalia, to meet the strange invaders of their quiet little valley.

To these men Doc was brought, his pals standing behind him silently.

As the leaders made their signs of greeting, Doc recognized the fashion of another tribe with whom he had once had occasion to converse, and answered the greeting in the accustomed manner.

The response worked like a charm. The leaders and natives as well dropped their antagonistic attitude and offered the visitors the signs of friendship. Before the great monument that rose in front of them, offerings were laid upon the altar, and the village gathered in a welcome feast for the friendly strangers.

Encouraging as this ovation was, it brought forcibly to the attention of Doc and his friends another truth of the letter which started them on this journey.

Gold or no gold, it would certainly be next to impossible to reach the hidden treasure through the monument—the altar to the god of these people—without incurring the deadly hatred of the entire tribe. Even the suggestion of such a thing would be dangerous, so Doc decided to bide his time, and in the meanwhile, to investigate the territory thoroughly.

THE investigation proved, beyond a doubt, that the promise of the letter was not far-fetched. The entire region, even to some of the surface cropping, abounded in the valuable mineral. Once Renny could gain entrance to the mine, or even gain knowledge of the exact location of the opening and its direction, it would be but the work of a few days to cut a new lead into it, gaining the tremendous wealth without endangering the monument and its gold.

But the task would not be so easy. The rapid evacuation of the capital by the little band served only to hold danger away for a time. It soon caught up to them, and Doc saw it in the little signs of resentment which were springing up again.

One faction of the tribe, particularly, seemed to be more antagonistic. Doc realized immediately that the influence came from the outside, and traced it back to their original trouble in the capital which in turn, could be traced to the first shot at the reading of the letter.

Little by little these mutterings grew, until they seemed ominous enough to engulf the whole tribe, and cause expulsion of Doc and his friends. Well might have this conclusion been reached, had it not been for an occurrence which took the attention of every one off the question of strangers.

For, like a curse from the gods, there suddenly came upon the natives a strange illness. One by one the natives would falter in their work, go back to their huts, and lie there, sick with a high fever and delirium.

Despite the charms and incantations of their medicine men; despite the offerings to appease their god of the monument, the plague increased.

Now the people who had first caught the dreaded malady were beginning to die. Their huts were marked with the evil sign, and no one was allowed to enter, for fear of causing further anger to the gods.

To Doc, whose knowledge of medicine was complete enough to easily detect the symptoms of the disease, it seemed a foolish fear. From the very first signs of the disease, he attempted to have the natives adopt measures to prevent its spread. But, as before, all his attempts were balked by the enemies which had suddenly sprung up in the tribe.

Only by finally taking things into his own hands did he accomplish his ends.

With the aid of Monk, Doc concocted, from native herbs, a medicine to fight the ailment. And Long Tom, rigging up his compact electrical apparatus, was able to develop a curative ray that helped materially to keep the disease in check and hasten the recovery of those who had seen ill.

Thus, by forceful entry into the huts, by argument with the

chiefs and tribesmen themselves, by staking his own life against that of the natives, Doc finally convinced the tribe leaders and priests that his efforts were sincere.

IT took several months of untiring effort on the part of Doc and his little group, aided by such friends in the tribe as they could muster, to cure the natives of their disease. Then, as one by one the weakened tribesmen regained their hearty color, and the sick arose from the beds on which they had lain to await death—death which their gods had sent upon them—Doc was again the man of honor which he seemed to be from the start.

Peace again seemed to have taken hold of the tribe, and preparations were made for a great testimonial to the god on the monument, as well as to the friendship of Doc and his companions. The tide seemed to have definitely turned toward the visitors, and immense wealth seemed to be within their grasp.

The natives assembled at the gathering in all their splendor. All the different factional chiefs were there, and the people of the entire valley were ready to take part.

The offering to the gods was made; the tribal ritual was performed.

Now remained only the awarding of the great token of friendship to Doc and his friends; the highest honor that the tribe could give; the sign of perpetual love and thanks.

It was then, at the very act of awarding the high honor, that the unexpected happened. From the assembled chieftains of the various groups of the tribe was coming the steady chanting of the prayer of friendship. Their bodies were swaying to the rhythm of their chant.

When, suddenly, out of the praying chieftains, one stopped his even swaying, stepped forward, and cried out for all to stop.

The man was Morning Breeze, leader of the smaller portion of the tribal people, and usually the one to bring about dissension in all tribal gatherings. So it was that after the preliminary shock, the natives were not much surprised, expecting only some foolish objection from the man.

In their expectations they were disappointed, for Morning Breeze made a determined request that tribal custom should not be so easily discarded, and that no strangers should be permitted the honors of their own.

His words had little effect, for the work of Doc and his companions had been so important, and touched so many members of the tribe, that they did not want to deny him anything he wished. Further, it was the plan of the tribal leaders to ask Doc that he make any request that he desire of them, even to their very lives, in return for his kindness in freeing them of the plague of the gods.

But Morning Breeze was obstinate. He called upon the leaders of the tribes to agree with him, to chase these strangers from their midst.

DOC, with his companions around him, was at the head of the ceremonial. The sudden discord in this strange ritual caused some apprehension, for well did Doc understand the purport of this affair. And it was with lighter hearts that the little group of adventurers saw that the protesting chieftain was ordered silent, that his demands were overruled by the others.

Somehow, Doc did not feel that the dissenting member would be so easily overruled. For to Doc it was evident that all the minor irritations that had previously worked against his little group had come from this man's own small group of natives; he had him marked as the disturbing factor in their plan to secure the gold mine.

Doc's suspicions were well founded. Before the ceremonial was ended, members of the dissatisfied cheiftain's faction had secretly trailed away. Now they were returning, and amid the hubbub of the ceremony, their fellow members raced back to them, grasping things from their hands.

It was the attack! Morning Breeze did not mean to let things get by so lightly. He had planned; and, furthermore, it was evident that his plans were backed by other than himself. For the opposing faction's members had gone away to bring up arms and ammunition, and their fellows, now all turned back a distance from the ceremony space, were hastily taking the guns into their hands.

The first few shots disrupted the entire affair. The natives were not unfamiliar with guns, for such modern implements had penetrated even to their mountain fastness. But there were scarcely half a dozen of them in the entire valley—or had been, before this revolt was planned. Now, faced with certain death by the shots of the small dissatisfied group, the tribal members had nothing to do but flee.

To Doc and his friends, the matter of flight seemed hopeless. Faced with the guns in the hands of their enemies, there was nothing to do but surrender and meet the fate that the small faction would impose upon the tribe.

But to the high priests of the natives, other ways of flight were open.

As might be supposed, the immense monument was not erected solely to the glory of their god, nor did their ancient predecessors excavate the mine of gold for the sake of the precious metal. In fact, to them the metal was worth no more than stone; it served no worthier purpose.

WITH a warning cry, the high priests summoned their tribesmen to the escape. The warriors of the group gathered to the front, facing the oncoming enemy, presenting a determined front. For a moment, the oncoming tribesmen were halted. They hesitated to use their arms, thinking that the conquest could be possible without bloodshed It was that moment that gave the beleaguered faction their one opportunity for safety.

Moving aside one of the stones that formed part of the great monument, the high priests whose duty it was to guard the sacred mound made a break which allowed for the safety of all.

As if creaking with the weight of the stone, a huge door swung open in the giant monument. Through this the natives swarmed. Doc and his friends carried in along with the surge. For the inside of the monument was not only hollow, but really did cover the opening of the mine, its glittering shaft visible in the light that reflected through the now-open door.

Before the attacking tribesmen could take much toll from the defenders, the latter had found their way into the immense monument.

Then, while a few of the warriors remained outside to give their lives for the safety of the rest of their followers in the monument, the huge door swung to, safely protecting those outside.

Within the monument, the tribesmen gathered in conclave. Under the leadership of their high priests, they began another ceremonial to their gods, leaving Doc and his companions to look on.

Realizing that his presence near the rites was important, Doc Savage dispatched Johnny and Monk to survey their predicament. That they were safe for the time, Doc knew, but whether this great shelter could provide continued comfort and safety was something else again. And no doubt the forces outside could muster additional help if the beleaguered natives did not do something in a very short time.

Johnny and Monk started off into the mouth of the mine. Their eyes, on every hand, saw immense wealth lying within their grasp. Sometime, back in long years gone by, this mine must have been worked under the most primitive conditions. Chunks of the golden metal were still scattered in spots, chipped clean of all contiguous rock.

DEEPER and deeper into the mine the two went, passing through several types of rock strata, until Monk scuffed his shoe upon a projecting rock. The nails of his heavy-heeled shoes scraped sharply against the stone, with a resulting queer odor.

Both Johnny and Monk stopped instantly as the smell assailed their nostrils. One thought gripped them both, and eagerly they examined the stone more carefully.

"If my guess is right," exclaimed Johnny, "we'll be out of here in less than no time!"

"And it smells that way to me, too—if I'm not mistaken! Say, can we put up a battle!"

"But what'll we use to fire it?"

"Fire it? Well—well, how about the gold? Can't we make shells of gold?"

For when Monk's shoe scuffed the rock and brought forth the strange odor, the brains of both of them jumped to one conclusion. One from his knowledge of chemistry, the other from his knowledge of mineralogy, recognized the smell as coming from an unusual stone, the result of volcanic formations, which had a high explosive content. It was the most primitive gunpowder known to science, and with a little careful grinding, it could be made quite effective. Using the tremendous supply of gold within the mine, they could easily make it into casts, fill it with the ground stone, and, if it could be possible to come upon the enemy unawares, do enough damage to make them take to their heels.

Quickly grabbing enough of the rock to prove their belief, the two went back to the head of the mine, to where the natives were still performing their ceremonial rites. Approaching Doc, the two explained their discovery, told of their plan.

While the natives went on with their prayers and dancing, the six men, entirely unnoticed, set their hands to the task of grinding out some powder. Seizing a small piece of flattened gold which had been a container of some liquid offering to the god, Doc bent it to the shape of a bomb. Then, stuffing the mouth of it with some cloth torn off a shirt, the first bomb was ready.

By that time, the natives had finished their dance, and their leaders and high priests were conferring on their situation. It was then that Doc approached them again, and, by the signs and the few words of their dialect which he could muster, he attempted to show the discovery. Failing to make clear his point, he urged some of them to accompany him into the mouth of the mine, hoping there to demonstrate the bomb to the satisfaction of the chiefs, yet not permitting the attackers outside to gain any knowledge.

IT was a long journey before Doc reached any part of the mine where he could risk an explosion. Then, while Renny carefully considered the chances of a cave-in, Doc took the bomb apart, emptied some of the powder charge so as to lessen its effectiveness, and hurled the missile.

At the impact, the golden shell exploded with powerful force, scattering its fragments about. The reverberations echoed throughout the runnel, but Renny's calculations were accurate enough so that no harm came to any of the watchers.

With the demonstration, the chiefs immediately grasped the idea. With their full vocabulary signs and motions, they showed their approval, and took Doc in charge by way of another shaft of the mine.

What lay at the end of this trail Doc knew not, but he felt certain that it was something which would serve to get them out of this position. After long minutes of traveling, the high priest lifted Doc up a few steps cut into the rock, and parted the top of the shaft with a motion of his hand.

What seemed to be solid rock above was a sliding trapdoor. And above the trapdoor was the sky!

Somewhere in the maze of passages which the ancients had wormed through this storehouse of tremendous wealth they had formed a secret exit, planned for the time when they would have to do exactly what had just occurred. With the monument as their god at one end of the tunnels, and the secret door there as a means of entrance, they could, without difficulty, escape the attacks of any of their enemies. Then, while the opposing forces were vainly endeavoring to storm the great monument, they could escape through this means, come back, and surprise their enemies.

The plan for escape was now complete. Doc did not know exactly where the secret exit had its location, but wherever it was it had to be within easy distance of the entrance, for the walk through the passages was not overly long. And, in the dead of night, it would be easy to make even a long march and surprise the attackers. Feverishly, Doc and his group began the work of perparing enough ammunition for the attack. With all of the natives at their disposal, Renny and Doc directed the flattening of as many vessels as were obtainable within the shrine, hammering the golden metal into shape for bombs. Others were under the direction of Monk and Long Tom, grinding the stone with care so as to have enough powder.

BEFORE nightfall, they had sufficient supply of ammunition to make their attack upon the uprising faction, and the battle lines were formed.

The native chiefs, those who witnessed the demonstration of the bomb by Doc, instructed the warriors in the manner of handling the explosives. Others started the trek toward the secret exit, with Doc and his group among the leaders.

Doc's surmise about the opening was partly correct. It was not far away from the immense monument which hid the mouth of the mine. But it was in a place that was almost impossible of discovery from the outside.

Out of one side of the steep rock that faced away from the small settlement of the natives, the opening led through the thickest jungle brush Doc had ever experienced in all his worldwide traveling. There was no danger of being seen in the exit, that was certain. No care was necessary until the fighting party reached the edge of the undergrowth.

There, not more than several hundred yards to one side, was the monument, with the atacking faction encamped before it, ready for any attack which might come from there.

With great stealth, the invading party organized its attack, and slowly crept upon the unsuspecting insurgents. Then, at the order from their chief, the force of the improvised ammunition was loosed upon the encamped enemy.

Not only was the attack itself surprising—for evidently the secret exit was not known to the leaders of the tribe, but only to the priests of the god to whom it was erected—but the ammunition was especially demoralizing. Even with nothing but their native weapons, such as they might have fashioned in a way from things found inside the monument, the attack would probably have been successful. The insurgent faction was really of small numbers, and had depended upon its arms as well as the surprise of its attack for victory. But with the aid of the powderbombs furnished by the ingenuity of Doc's small group, the victory was complete and unquestioned.

THE subjugation of the enemy disclosed, also, the influence which had caused all the trouble to Doc and his friends. Among the dead who were taken away for burial, Ham and Doc recognized the face of one of the officials who had made a determined effort to hold up their credentials when they paid their visit to the government of Hidalgo.

Now that the trouble had been settled, the natives again held an observance to mark the friendship they held for Doc. This time the sacred ritual was not disturbed by any untoward occurrence, and Doc Savage was vested, together with his five companions, with all the rights and privileges of a member of the tribe. Furthermore, the chieftains offered to grant his little company whatever wish they desired.

Then, with care and much explanation, Doc made clear to the chieftains that they had come as followers of the two men who had first performed equal tasks of mercy for their tribe; that, also, they had come to take along with them some of the gold which was beneath their monument, if they would be permitted to do so.

It was now that the real friendliness of the natives was shown. In their primitive way, they did not value the gold above any other metal. They used it for ordinary purposes, and knew nothing of its possible exploitation. Their only wish was not to incur the wrath of their god by disturbing his monument.

So, with the suggestion that the secret exit be the means of entry into the mine, they granted Doc's request.

It took but a few days, then, to arrange with the natives to do the work of the mine, granting them their goodly share of the proceeds. So, later, was it a simple matter to complete arrangements with the government at the capital, granting the government its proper share of the mined gold, as required by the contracts. The last fight at the monument had brought about the death of the man behind the fight to wrest this wealth from the hands of Doc Savage and his friends, and the interests of the government itself were well served by the gracious portion allotted to them in the original papers.

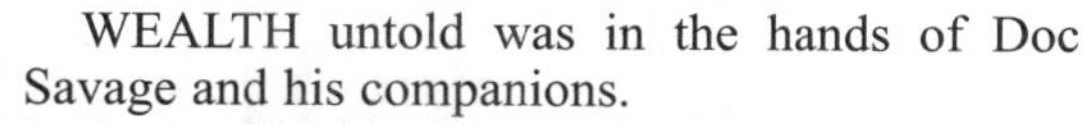

WEALTH untold was in the hands of Doc Savage and his companions.

As much gold as they desired was hidden within that golden valley where they struggled against

death. But their purpose was not alone to gain the gold. Their arrangements were made for a slow, even mining, to furnish only enough capital to carry on the work which was given them in the message from the dead man.

The hopes of the elder Savage would be realized. Doc, true to his father's opinion, had proved himself capable of carrying on the work his father had begun.

From this time on, this tiny group of adventurers had their task set before them. The thought of gold was already out of their minds. The thoughts they now had were only of the road ahead—the battles that they had to face, the experiences they would undergo in doing what the elder Savage wanted them to do—going out to whatever part of the world needed them, answering whatever call was urgent, giving their help and support to causes which needed them. People, tribes and nations would gain their help when sore pressed. Industry would be served by them. Art and science would profit by their daring.

But, most of all, the yearning for adventure, the longing for a life of thrills and excitement, which burned within the heart of each of them, would get its fill in their future experiences together.

THE END

THE ASTOUNDING ART OF EDD CARTIER

Edward Daniel Cartier began selling spot illustrations to Street & Smith while attending Pratt Institute. After graduating in 1936, he was selected to succeed Tom Lovell as the regular interior artist on *The Shadow.*

In 1939, Cartier was recruited by *Astounding Science Fiction's* legendary editor John W. Campbell to illustrate *Unknown,* which quickly became the benchmark for excellence in fantasy fiction. Edd painted five covers and produced more than 200 interior illustrations for *Unknown,* along with nearly 300 illustrations for *Astounding.*

Drafted in 1941, Cartier was severely wounded in Bastogne during the Battle of the Bulge. He returned to Street & Smith after the war, illustrating *The Shadow, Astounding* and *Doc Savage, Science Detective,* and also producing cover and interior art for *Red Dragon Comics.*

If one judges a man by his associates, Edd is in stellar company. Along with his association with The Shadow and Doc Savage, Cartier's bold and whimsical art was regularly requested by the top authors in mystery, fantasy and science fiction

One of the few surviving "living legends" from the Golden Age of Pulps, Edd Cartier celebrated his 93rd birthday on August 1, 2007. —Anthony Tollin

Edd Cartier (above) illustrated the beloved Hoka stories by Poul Anderson and Gordon R. Dickson, including "In Hoka Signo Vinces" (right).

Clockwise from top — Edd Cartier's classic pulp illustrations for:

"Room 1313" by Maxwell Grant (Bruce Elliott)

"The Cold Trail of Death" by John D. MacDonald

"The Devil We Know" by Henry Kuttner

"The Crossroads" by L. Ron Hubbard

Lester Dent

Lester Dent (1904-1959) could be called the father of the superhero. Writing under the house name "Kenneth Robeson," Dent was the principal writer of *Doc Savage,* producing more than 150 of the Man of Bronze's thrilling pulp adventures.

A lonely childhood as a rancher's son paved the way for his future success as a professional storyteller. "I had no playmates," Dent recalled. "I lived a completely distorted youth. My only playmate was my imagination, and that period of intense imaginative creation which kids generally get over at the age of five or six, I carried till I was twelve or thirteen. My imaginary voyages and accomplishments were extremely real."

Dent began his professional writing career while working as an Associated Press telegrapher in Tulsa, Oklahoma. Learning that one of his coworkers had sold a story to the pulps, Dent decided to try his hand at similarly lucrative moonlighting. He pounded out thirteen unsold stories during the slow night shift before making his first sale to Street & Smith's *Top-Notch* in 1929. The following year, he received a telegram from the Dell Publishing Company offering him moving expenses and a $500-a-month drawing account if he'd relocate to New York and write exclusively for the publishing house.

Dent soon left Dell to pursue a freelance career, and in 1932 won the contract to write the lead novels in Street & Smith's new *Doc Savage Magazine.* From 1933-1949, Dent produced Doc Savage thrillers while continuing his busy freelance writing career and eventually adding an aerial photography business.

Dent was also a significant contributor to the legendary *Black Mask* during its golden age, for which he created Miami waterfront detective Oscar Sail. A real-life adventurer, world traveler and member of the Explorers Club, Dent wrote in a variety of genres for magazines ranging from pulps like *Argosy, Adventure* and *Ten Detective Aces* to prestigious slick magazines including *The Saturday Evening Post* and *Collier's.* His mystery novels include *Dead at the Take-off* and *Lady Afraid.* In the pioneering days of radio drama, Dent scripted *Scotland Yard* and the 1934 *Doc Savage* series.

John L. Nanovic (1906-2001) edited Street & Smith's legendary hero pulps for more than a decade, overseeing the adventures of The Shadow, Doc Savage, Nick Carter, The Avenger, Pete Rice, The Whisperer, Cash Corman, The Skipper and the series detectives featured in *Crime Busters.* The Notre Dame graduate was originally hired to edit S&S's *College Stories.* Nanovic worked closely with his writers and S&S circulation manager Henry W. Ralston in plotting the stories for his magazines. "In my opinion, John Nanovic was unequaled as a fiction editor," *The Shadow*'s Walter Gibson observed. "If a story lagged or became too complex, John was prompt to notice it and call for revisions, but his criticisms were always constructive..." In addition to his editorial duties, Nanovic wrote *The Shadow Magazine*'s "Codes" department (under his pseudonym "Henry Lysing"), ghosted nine *Lone Ranger* radio scripts and later worked as an executive at the Kudner Advertising Agency before heading his own New York City public relations company.

Will Murray (1953-) is literary agent for the Dent Estate and the writer of fifty novels including seven Doc Savage paperback originals and forty Remo Williams adventures in the long-running Destroyer series. One of the world's leading pulp fiction historians, Murray unearthed the lost manscripts of "In Hell, Madonna" (a.k.a. *The Red Spider)* and "Doc Savage, Supreme Adventurer," and was responsible for their first publication. Murray scripted the six-part serialization of *The Thousand-Headed Man* for National Public Radio's *Doc Savage* series, and is a contributing editor for *Starlog.*

Will Murray and John Nanovic

Photo by Albert Tonik